KUTTNER'S BEST

"If you have arrived at this book and look to Kuttner for religious instruction, secular improvement, or moral renovation, save with certain exceptions, you had best retreat to forms of literate navel-lint plucking with which the sophomores of the world bug each other. Kuttner will not kick, bite, beat—much less hug, kiss, or improve you. And thank God for that!"

—From the Introduction by Ray Bradbury

"The author's best quality is his irreverence, which delights and scandalizes . . . !"

—Chicago Tribune

Watch for all the volumes in Ballantine's Classic Library of Science Fiction—big, definitive collections by the true masters in the field. Each book in the series is introduced by a well-known science fiction writer or by a distinguished critic.

Now Available in a Ballantine Edition:

The Best of Stanley G. Weinbaum
Introduction by Isaac Asimov

The Best of Fritz Leiber
Introduction by Poul Anderson

Volumes in Preparation:

The Best of Frederik Pohl
Introduction by Lester del Rey

The Best of Cordwainer Smith
Introduction by J. J. Pierce

The Best of C. L. Moore
Introduction by Lester del Rey

The Best of John W. Campbell/Don A. Stuart
Introduction by Lester del Rey

The Best of L. Sprague De Camp
Introduction by Poul Anderson

The Best of Raymond Z. Gallun
Introduction by Frederik Pohl

The Best of Eric Frank Russell
Introduction by Alan Dean Foster

Coming from Ballantine Books

THE BEST OF
Henry Kuttner

Introduction by
RAY BRADBURY

BALLANTINE BOOKS • NEW YORK

SBN 345-24415-X-195

Book Club Edition: February, 1975

First Printing: April, 1975

Printed in the United States of America

BALLANTINE BOOKS
A Division of Random House, Inc.
201 East 50th Street, New York, N.Y. 10022
Simultaneously published by
Ballantine Books, Ltd., Toronto, Canada

ACKNOWLEDGMENTS

"Mimsy Were the Borogoves," copyright © 1943 by Street and Smith Publications, Inc., for *Astounding Science Fiction*.

"Two-Handed Engine," copyright © 1955 by Fantasy House, Inc., for *The Magazine of Fantasy and Science Fiction*.

"The Proud Robot," copyright © 1943 by Street and Smith Publications, Inc., for *Astounding Science Fiction*.

"The Misguided Halo," copyright © 1939 by Street and Smith Publications, Inc., for *Unknown*.

"The Voice of The Lobster," copyright © 1950 by Standard Magazines, Inc., for *Thrilling Wonder Stories*.

"Exit The Professor," copyright © 1947 by Standard Magazines, Inc., for *Thrilling Wonder Stories*.

"The Twonky," copyright © 1942 by Street and Smith Publications, Inc., for *Astounding Science Fiction*.

"A Gnome There Was," copyright © 1941 by Street and Smith Publications, Inc., for *Unknown Worlds*.

"The Big Night," copyright © 1947 by Standard Magazines, Inc., for *Thrilling Wonder Stories*.

"Nothing But Gingerbread Left," copyright © 1943 by Street and Smith Publications, Inc., for *Astounding Science Fiction*.

"The Iron Standard," copyright © 1943 by Street and Smith Publications, Inc., for *Astounding Science Fiction*.

CONTENTS

Henry Kuttner: A Neglected Master

Move around in high schools and colleges, in various semi-intellectual circles high and low, and listen to the names spoken there when books come into the conversation. A great deal of the time you'll hear:

Tolkien. Lovecraft. Heinlein. Sturgeon. Wells. Verne. Orwell. Vonnegut. And, you should excuse the expression, Bradbury.

But not often enough—Kuttner.

Why is this so?

Why has Henry Kuttner been so unfairly neglected since his death back in the late fifties?

Was he as good a writer as the others?

Yes.

Did he write as much?

In some cases more.

Was he a pomegranate writer—popping with seeds, full of ideas?

He was.

Was he as flamboyant as the others mentioned?

Perhaps not enough.

Did he sound his own horn?

Rarely.

Perhaps he was too diversified working in too many sub-areas of the science-fiction and fantasy genres?

That may well be.

In any case, this book will remedy the need for a collection that can be handed around in and out of schools and will cause the name Kuttner to be spoken more frequently in the years ahead.

But before we consider all the reasons for Kuttner's temporary obscurity, I must lapse into the personal and linger there awhile.

This introduction to Henry Kuttner *must* be very personal or it will be meaningless. I will not burden you with endless intellectual weighings and assayings of his stories. That is for you to do as you move along through this fascinating book, realizing that you have come upon the work of a man who helped shape science fiction and fantasy in its most important years—years which included the decline of *Weird Tales,* the growth of *Astounding Science Fiction,* and the amazing birth of *Unknown,* and *The Magazine of Fantasy and Science Fiction.* I speak roughly of the time between 1938 and 1950, when most of the truly important writers in the field erupted on the scene, many of them encouraged by John W. Campbell, *Astounding*'s editor.

Kuttner was one of those writers.

If you will allow the blasphemy, I will not soon forgive God for taking Kuttner out of this world in 1958. His death alone made that year a bad one for remembrance. It was especially bad because his talent was peculiar and special.

We would like to pretend that the populations of our world are full of undiscovered geniuses. From what I have seen, that simply is not true. The genetically intuitive talents are rare. Creative people are few and far between.

It is the rustiest of clichés to say, upon the death of most people, that they were irreplaceable. Save on a personal and loving level, this is just not so. Hundreds of writers, one not distinguishable from the next, might be replaced tomorrow without changing our universal culture in any way.

Because we are surrounded by oceans of the noncreative, and open fields of unprocreative mulch, I much admire the intuitive Henry Kuttner. He was indeed special, peculiar, and, in his own mild way, manically creative.

I would like to be able to recall all sorts of wondrous things about Henry Kuttner. The facts are otherwise, however. He was a shy man who gazed at you and thought his private thoughts.

I am sure that he found me ridiculous and amusing a good deal of the time. At our first meeting I was seventeen, which means—in my case, anyway—I was so unsure of myself that I did a lot of running around, shouting, and speechifying to hide my confusions and private despairs. Kuttner put up with this for an inordinate number of years and then gave me the best piece of creative advice I ever got.

"Ray," he said one day, "do me a favor?"

"What?" I asked.

"Shut up," he said.

"I beg pardon?"

"You're always running around, grabbing people's elbows, pulling their lapels, shouting your ideas," Kuttner replied. "You give away all your steam. No wonder you never finish your stories. You talk them all out. Shut up."

And shut up I did.

Instead of giving my stories away free, by mouth, I began to write a story a week. Since that time I have never spoken about my ideas until, in their final form, they were on their way East via airmail.

If shut was Bradbury, then shut indeed was Kuttner.

Frank Lloyd Wright once described himself as an old man mad about architecture. Kuttner, in his twenties and thirties, was a young man mad about writing. Other people's, first; his own, finally. His was not an ebullient and loud madness, as mine has been. Henry played a muffled drum to his own tune and marched quietly and steadily after his Muse.

Along the way, he helped edit, write, and publish his own fantasy fan magazine *Sweetness and Light,* about the same time that I was editing and publishing my own fairly dreadful mimeographed *Futuria Fantasia,* with occasional articles by Kuttner and Heinlein.

Along the way, he also sneaked me the names of people who might influence my life. Try Katherine Anne Porter, he said, she's great. Have you read Eudora Welty? he suggested, and if not, why not? Have you re-read Thorne Smith? Get to it. How about the short stories of Faulkner, or—here's one you never heard of—John Collier.

He lent me copies of various mystery writers and advised me, as did Leigh Brackett, whom he was helping, too, to try James Cain, Dashiell Hammett, and Raymond Chandler. I obeyed.

It always seemed, to Brackett and me, that every time

we looked up there was Kuttner half a block ahead on the road, going in or coming out of libraries. The last time I saw him was on a bus headed for UCLA and the vast library there, where he swam in the stacks with a beatific and quiet smile.

He wrote steadily, but I wish he had yelled on occasion —as I have yelled—to call attention to himself. It is time now for us to pay attention, to draw near, to look at the quiet patterns in the wallpaper and find Kuttner out.

Leafing through the contents of this present volume, I find, to my dismay, that there are no convenient handles by which to pick Kuttner up. He wrote serious stories and light stories. He was not a science-fiction writer or a fantasist or a humorist, and yet he was all of these. If he had lived much longer he might have been troublesome to critics and librarians who like to slap precise labels on authors and file them neatly on shelves.

Kuttner was also troublesome to himself. His first published story, "The Graveyard Rats," became an instant classic when it appeared in *Weird Tales* when he was still a teen-ager. This swift fame for what is in essence a grisly, but finally brilliant, story caused Henry to fall into uneasy silences in later years when the story was mentioned. He did not really want to become a minor-league Lovecraft.

He went through a long period of trying and testing himself. During this time he wrote dozens of undistinguished tales for the various science-fiction pulps, until Thorne Smith out of John Collier out of Robert E. Howard became the at-last-remarkable Henry Kuttner.

Where was the turning point? When did the pulp writer become the writer of quality? I imagine we could point to a half dozen stories that appeared in Campbell's incredible magazine *Unknown,* but I prefer to select two which popped our eyes and dropped our mouths agape in *Astounding.* I feel a deep personal response to them because, in the weeks during which he was finishing "The Twonky" and "Mimsy Were the Borogoves" Kuttner gave me copies of the stories to take home, read, and study. I knew then what everyone else knows now; I was reading two stories that would become very special in their field.

It would be hard to guess the impact of these two stories

on other writers in the genre. But in all probability hundreds of imitations were written by struggling as well as by published authors. I count myself among them. I very much doubt that my "Zero Hour," or for that matter "The Veldt," would ever have leaped out of my typewriter if Kuttner's imagination had not led the way.

All of this makes it dreadfully sad to consider Henry Kuttner's early death. He had what we all admire and respond to: a love of ideas and a love of literature. He was not one of those easy cynics who move into magazines or television for the fast buck. When he did write for money, he was not happy. He was truly happy moving about through libraries, discovering new writers, finding new angles on human activity put forward by psychologists or scientists in any field. He was beginning to experiment with stories, some of which you will find in this collection, having to do with robot personalities, computerized intellects, and men lost among those machines.

I wish he could have lived into the Kennedy-Johnson-Nixon years, the years when the computers really arrived on-scene, the years of incredible paradox when we footprinted the moon and inched toward the stars. Kuttner, being nonpolitical, thank God, would have given us insights into our political-technological cultures that most of our "in" writers lack because they lean right or left. Kuttner never belonged to anything. He belonged, finally, to all of us. In a polarized world, we need fewer Mailers and many more Kuttners.

This brings us back to the problem of why Kuttner's name remains semiobscure in our genre.

Apolitics is certainly part of the answer. When you mention Vonnegut, you polarize on the instant. Orwell, similarly. And Heinlein and Wells, and even Verne. Verne, after all, invented mad Nemo, the mirror-image reversal of mad Ahab. Nemo prowled the world teaching moral lessons to even madder militarists. Beyond this, Verne was a superpropagandist for the humanities who said: you have a head, use it to guide your heart; you have a heart, use it to guide your head; you have hands with which to change the world. Head, heart, hands—sum up all three, and remake Eden.

I cannot recall any particularly violent ideas Kuttner put

forth on politics or politicians. He seemed never to have gone through one of those nineteenth or twentieth summers when we all go a bit amok on Technocracy or Socialism or Scientology. When the fever passes and the smoke clears we wonder what happened to us and are puzzled when our friends don't speak to us for a time, until they discover that the hair has fallen off us and we have given up being a political gorilla and are back being human again. If Kuttner had such a year, or month, I never knew it. And it doesn't show in his work.

So because much of what he wrote is not, in modern terminology, Relevant with a capital R, he is probably graded by some as ten degrees down from Orwell, and twenty below Vonnegut—which is, needless to say, a damned and awful shame. What we need is not more political cant and polarized bias, but more traffic engineers, with no particular traffic in mind save survival, to stand on the highroads leading toward the future, waving us on creatively but not necessarily banging our ears when we, children that we are, misbehave.

Kuttner, then, was no moral revolutionary or political reformer. He was an entertaining writer. His stories are seeded with ideas and moralities, yes, but these do not cry out, shout, shriek, or necessarily ask for change. This is the way we are, Kuttner says, what do you think of us?

Most science-fiction writers are moral revolutionaries on some level or another, instructing us for our own good. When Bernard Shaw and Bertrand Russell ventured into the field it could have been predicted (and I did so predict with Lord Russell) that they would pop up as moral revolutionists teaching lessons and pontificating therefrom. Shaw was better at it, of course. Russell came late to the short story, but it *was* science fiction, and was odorous with morality.

Here, I think, we may find Kuttner's flaw—if flaw it is, and I for one do not consider it so. One cannot be polarized all the time, one cannot think politically from noon to night. That way is the way of the True Believer—that is to say, finally, the Mad Man.

Kuttner is not mad, nor especially kicking up his heels with *joie de vivre*. He is wryly calm. If he celebrates anything, it is within his head.

And so, the more I think of it, the more I feel Kuttner has been cursed by the great curse of our time. People have too often asked: Well, how do we *use* Kuttner? What's he good for? What kind of tool is he? Where does he fit? What is the appropriate label? Will people look up to me if I carry "Mimsy Were the Borogoves" around campus rather than *The Gulag Archipelago*?

If this is not the complete explanation, it leans toward it, in any event. In what tends to be a practical Kleenex culture, if you can't clean out your ears with an author, you tend, because others bully you about it, to leave him alone.

So if you have arrived at this book and look to Kuttner for religious instruction, secular improvement, or moral renovation, save with certain exceptions you had best retreat to *Siddhartha* and other forms of literate navel-lint plucking with which the sophomores of the world bug each other. Kuttner will not kick, bite, beat, much less kiss, hug, stroke, or improve you. And thank God for that. I have had enough improvement, just as I have had too much cotton candy at too many circuses.

If you will allow a final, very small, very personal note, here it is:

Back in 1942 you will find my first horror story, published in the November issue of *Weird Tales*. It's title is "The Candle," and the last three hundred words were written by Henry Kuttner. I had trouble with the story, sent it to Hank, and he responded with a complete ending. It was good. I couldn't top it. I asked permission to use it. Hank said yes. That ending, today, is the only good part of that long-lost and deservedly well-buried story. It's nice to be able to say Henry Kuttner once collaborated with me.

Well, here's the collection. It represents only a small part of the hundreds of stories he wrote. Kuttner had no family, but . . .

His children live here in this book.

They are lovely and special and fine.

I want you to meet them.

RAY BRADBURY
Los Angeles, California
July 11, 1974

Mimsy Were The Borogoves

THERE'S NO USE trying to describe either Unthahorsten or his surroundings, because, for one thing, a good many million years had passed and, for another, Unthahorsten wasn't on Earth, technically speaking. He was doing the equivalent of standing in the equivalent of a laboratory. He was preparing to test his time machine.

Having turned on the power, Unthahorsten suddenly realized that the Box was empty. Which wouldn't do at all. The device needed a control, a three-dimensional solid which would react to the conditions of another age. Otherwise Unthahorsten couldn't tell, on the machine's return, where and when it had been. Whereas a solid in the Box would automatically be subject to the entropy and cosmic-ray bombardment of the other era, and Unthahorsten could measure the changes, both qualitative and quantitative, when the machine returned. The Calculators could then get to work and, presently, tell Unthahorsten that the Box had briefly visited A.D. 1,000,000, A.D. 1,000 or A.D. 1, as the case might be.

Not that it mattered, except to Unthahorsten. But he was childish in many respects.

There was little time to waste. The Box was beginning to glow and shiver. Unthahorsten stared around wildly, fled into the next glossatch and groped in a storage bin there. He came up with an armful of peculiar-looking stuff. Uh-huh. Some of the discarded toys of his son Snowen, which the boy had brought with him when he had passed over from Earth, after mastering the necessary technique. Well, Snowen needed this junk no longer. He was conditioned,

1

and had put away childish things. Besides, though Untha-horsten's wife kept the toys for sentimental reasons, the experiment was more important.

Unthahorsten left the glossatch and dumped the assortment into the Box, slamming the cover shut before the warning signal flashed. The Box went away. The manner of its departure hurt Unthahorsten's eyes.

He waited.

And he waited.

Eventually he gave up and built another time machine, with identical results. Snowen hadn't been annoyed by the loss of his old toys, nor had Snowen's mother, so Untha-horsten cleaned out the bin and dumped the remainder of his son's childhood relics in the second time machine's Box.

According to his calculations, this one should have appeared on Earth in the latter part of the nineteenth century, A.D. If that actually occurred, the device remained there.

Disgusted, Unthahorsten decided to make no more time machines. But the mischief had been done. There were two of them, and the first . . .

Scott Paradine found it while he was playing hooky from the Glendale Grammar School. There was a geography test that day, and Scott saw no sense in memorizing place names—which, in the nineteen-forties, was a fairly sensible theory. Besides, it was the sort of warm spring day, with a touch of coolness in the breeze, which invited a boy to lie down in a field and stare at the occasional clouds till he fell asleep. Nuts to geography! Scott dozed.

About noon he got hungry, so his stocky legs carried him to a nearby store. There he invested his small hoard with penurious care and a sublime disregard for his gastric juices. He went down by the creek to feed.

Having finished his supply of cheese, chocolate and cookies, and having drained the soda-pop bottle to its dregs, Scott caught tadpoles and studied them with a certain amount of scientific curiosity. He did not persevere. Something tumbled down the bank and thudded into the muddy ground near the water, so Scott, with a wary glance around, hurried to investigate.

It was a box. It was, in fact, the Box. The gadgetry hitched to it meant little to Scott, though he wondered why it was so fused and burned. He pondered. With his jack-knife he pried and probed, his tongue sticking out from a corner of his mouth—Hm-m-m. Nobody was around. Where had the box come from? Somebody must have left it here, and sliding soil had dislodged it from its precarious perch.

"That's a helix," Scott decided, quite erroneously. It was helical, but it wasn't a helix, because of the dimensional warp involved. Had the thing been a model airplane, no matter how complicated, it would have held few mysteries to Scott. As it was, a problem was posed. Something told Scott that the device was a lot more complicated than the spring motor he had deftly dismantled last Friday.

But no boy has ever left a box unopened, unless forcibly dragged away. Scott probed deeper. The angles on this thing were funny. Short circuit, probably. That was why—uh! The knife slipped. Scott sucked his thumb and gave vent to experienced blasphemy.

Maybe it was a music box.

Scott shouldn't have felt depressed. The gadgetry would have given Einstein a headache and driven Steinmetz raving mad. The trouble was, of course, that the box had not yet completely entered the space-time continuum where Scott existed, and therefore it could not be opened—at any rate, not till Scott used a convenient rock to hammer the helical non-helix into a more convenient position.

He hammered it, in fact, from its contact point with the fourth dimension, releasing the space-time torsion it had been maintaining. There was a brittle snap. The box jarred slightly, and lay motionless, no longer only partially in existence. Scott opened it easily now.

The soft, woven helmet was the first thing that caught his eye, but he discarded that without much interest. It was just a cap. Next, he lifted a square, transparent crystal block, small enough to cup in his palm—much too small to contain the maze of apparatus within it. In a moment Scott had solved that problem. The crystal was a sort of magnifying glass, vastly enlarging the things inside the block.

Strange things they were, too. Miniature people, for example.

They moved. Like clockwork automatons, though much more smoothly. It was rather like watching a play. Scott was interested in their costumes, but fascinated by their actions. The tiny people were deftly building a house. Scott wished it would catch fire, so he could see the people put it out.

Flames licked up from the half-completed structure. The automations, with a great deal of odd apparatus, extinguished the blaze.

It didn't take Scott long to catch on. But he was a little worried. The manikins would obey his thoughts. By the time he discovered that, he was frightened and threw the cube from him.

Halfway up the bank, he reconsidered and returned. The crystal lay partly in the water, shining in the sun. It was a toy; Scott sensed that, with the unerring instinct of a child. But he didn't pick it up immediately. Instead, he returned to the box and investigated its remaining contents.

He found some really remarkable gadgets. The afternoon passed all too quickly. Scott finally put the toys back in the box and lugged it home, grunting and puffing. He was quite red-faced by the time he arrived at the kitchen door.

His find he hid at the back of a closet in his room upstairs. The crystal cube he slipped into his pocket, which already bulged with string, a coil of wire, two pennies, a wad of tinfoil, a grimy defense stamp and a chunk of feldspar. Emma, Scott's two-year-old sister, waddled unsteadily in from the hall and said hello.

"Hello, Slug," Scott nodded, from his altitude of seven years and some months. He patronized Emma shockingly, but she didn't know the difference. Small, plump and wide-eyed, she flopped down on the carpet and stared dolefully at her shoes.

"Tie 'em, Scotty, please?"

"Sap," Scott told her kindly, but knotted the laces. "Dinner ready yet?"

Emma nodded.

"Let's see your hands." For a wonder they were reasonably clean, though probably not aseptic. Scott regarded his own paws thoughtfully and, grimacing, went to the bathroom, where he made a sketchy toilet. The tadpoles had left traces.

Dennis Paradine and his wife Jane were having a cocktail before dinner, downstairs in the living room. He was a youngish, middle-aged man with soft grey hair and a thin, prim-mouthed face; he taught philosophy at the University. Jane was small, neat, dark and very pretty. She sipped her Martini and said:

"New shoes. Like 'em?"

"Here's to crime," Paradine muttered absently.

"Huh? Shoes? Not now. Wait till I've finished this. I had a bad day."

"Exams?"

"Yeah. Flaming youth aspiring towards manhood. I hope they die. In considerable agony. *Insh' Allah!*"

"I want the olive," Jane requested.

"I know," Paradine said despondently. "It's been years since I've tasted one myself. In a Martini, I mean. Even if I put six of 'em in your glass, you're still not satisfied."

"I want yours. Blood brotherhood. Symbolism. That's why."

Paradine regarded his wife balefully and crossed his long legs. "You sound like one of my students."

"Like that hussy Betty Dawson, perhaps?" Jane unsheathed her nails. "Does she still leer at you in that offensive way?"

"She does. The child is a neat psychological problem. Luckily she isn't mine. If she were—" Paradine nodded significantly. "Sex consciousness and too many movies. I suppose she still thinks she can get a passing grade by showing me her knees. Which are, by the way, rather bony."

Jane adjusted her skirt with an air of complacent pride. Paradine uncoiled himself and poured fresh Martinis. "Candidly, I don't see the point of teaching those apes philosophy. They're all at the wrong age. Their habit patterns, their methods of thinking, are already laid down. They're horribly conservative, not that they'd admit it. The only people who can understand philosophy are mature adults or kids like Emma and Scotty."

"Well, don't enroll Scotty in your course," Jane requested. "He isn't ready to be a *Philosophiae Doctor.* I hold no brief for a child genius, especially when it's my son."

"Scotty would probably be better at it than Betty Dawson," Paradine grunted.

" 'He died an enfeebled old dotard at five,' " Jane quoted dreamily. "I want your olive."

"Here. By the way, I like the shoes."

"Thank you. Here's Rosalie. Dinner?"

"It's all ready, Miz Pa'dine," said Rosalie, hovering. "I'll call Miss Emma 'n' Mista' Scotty."

"I'll get 'em." Paradine put his head into the next room and roared, "Kids! Come and get it!"

Small feet scuttered down the stairs. Scott dashed into view, scrubbed and shining, a rebellious cowlick aimed at the zenith. Emma pursued, levering herself carefully down the steps. Halfway, she gave up the attempt to descend upright and reversed, finishing the task monkey-fashion, her small behind giving an impression of marvellous diligence upon the work in hand. Paradine watched, fascinated by the spectacle, till he was hurled back by the impact of his son's body.

"Hi, Dad!" Scott shrieked.

Paradine recovered himself and regarded Scott with dignity. "Hi, yourself. Help me into dinner. You've dislocated at least one of my hip joints."

But Scott was already tearing into the next room, where he stepped on Jane's new shoes in an ecstasy of affection, burbled an apology and rushed off to find his place at the dinner table. Paradine cocked up an eyebrow as he followed, Emma's pudgy hand desperately gripping his forefinger.

"Wonder what the young devil's been up to."

"No good, probably," Jane sighed. "Hello, darling. Let's see your ears."

"They're *clean*. Mickey licked 'em."

"Well, that Airedale's tongue is far cleaner than your ears," Jane pondered, making a brief examination. "Still, as long as you can hear, the dirt's only superficial."

"Fisshul?"

"Just a little, that means." Jane dragged her daughter to the table and inserted her legs into a high chair. Only lately had Emma graduated to the dignity of dining with the rest of the family, and she was, as Paradine remarked, all eaten up with pride by the prospect. Only babies spilled food, Emma had been told. As a result, she took such painstaking care in conveying her spoon to her mouth that Paradine got the jitters whenever he watched.

"A conveyor belt would be the thing for Emma," he suggested, pulling out a chair for Jane. "Small buckets of spinach arriving at her face at stated intervals."

Dinner proceeded uneventfully until Paradine happened to glance at Scott's plate. "Hello, there. Sick? Been stuffing yourself at lunch?"

Scott thoughtfully examined the food still left before him. "I've had all I need, Dad," he explained.

"You usually eat all you can hold, and a great deal more," Paradine said. "I know growing boys need several tons of foodstuff a day, but you're below par tonight. Feel O.K.?"

"Uh-huh. Honest, I've had all I need."

"All you *want?*"

"Sure. I eat different."

"Something they taught you at school?" Jane inquired. Scott shook his head solemnly.

"Nobody taught me. I found it out myself. I use spit."

"Try again," Paradine suggested. "It's the wrong word."

"Uh—s-saliva. Hm-m-m?"

"Uh-huh. More pepsin? Is there pepsin in the salivary juices, Jane? I forget."

"There's poison in mine," Jane remarked. "Rosalie's left lumps in the mashed potatoes again."

But Paradine was interested. "You mean you're getting everything possible out of your food—no wastage—and eating less?"

Scott thought that over. "I guess so. It's not just the sp— saliva. I sort of measure how much to put in my mouth at once, and what stuff to mix up. I dunno. I just do it."

"Hm-m-m," said Paradine, making a note to check up later. "Rather a revolutionary idea." Kids often get screwy notions, but this one might not be so far off the beam. He pursed his lips. "Eventually I suppose people will eat quite differently—I mean the *way* they eat, as well as what. What they eat, I mean. Jane, our son shows signs of becoming a genius."

"Oh?"

"It's a rather good point in dietetics he just made. Did you figure it out yourself, Scott?"

"Sure," the boy said, and really believed it.

"Where'd you get the idea?"

"Oh, I—" Scott wriggled. "I dunno. It doesn't mean much, I guess."

Paradine was unreasonably disappointed. "But surely—"

"S-s-s-spit!" Emma shrieked, overcome by a sudden fit of badness. "*Spit!*" She attempted to demonstrate, but succeeded only in dribbling into her bib.

With a resigned air Jane rescued and reproved her daughter, while Paradine eyed Scott with rather puzzled interest. But it was not till after dinner, in the living-room, that anything further happened.

"Any homework?"

"N-no," Scott said, flushing guiltily. To cover his embarrassment he took from his pocket a gadget he had found in the box, and began to unfold it. The result resembled a tesseract, strung with beads. Paradine didn't see it at first, but Emma did. She wanted to play with it.

"No. Lay off, Slug," Scott ordered. "You can watch me." He fumbled with the beads, making soft, interested noises. Emma extended a fat forefinger and yelped.

"Scotty," Paradine said warningly.

"I didn't hurt her."

"Bit me. It did," Emma mourned.

Paradine looked up. He frowned, staring. What in—

"Is that an abacus?" he asked. "Let's see it, please."

Somewhat unwillingly, Scott brought the gadget across to his father's chair. Paradine blinked. The "abacus," unfolded, was more than a foot square, composed of thin, rigid wires that interlocked here and there. On the wires the colored beads were strung. They could be slid back and forth, and from one support to another, even at the points of jointure. But—a pierced bead couldn't cross *interlocking* wires.

So, apparently, they weren't pierced. Paradine looked closer. Each small sphere had a deep groove running around it, so that it could be revolved and slid along the wire at the same time. Paradine tried to pull one free. It clung as though magnetically. Iron? It looked more like plastic.

The framework itself—Paradine wasn't a mathematician. But the angles formed by the wires were vaguely shocking, in their ridiculous lack of Euclidean logic. They were a maze. Perhaps that's what the gadget was—a puzzle.

"Where'd you get this?"

"Uncle Harry gave it to me," Scott said, on the spur of the moment. "Last Sunday, when he came over." Uncle Harry was out of town, a circumstance Scott well knew. At the age of seven, a boy soon learns that the vagaries of adults follow a certain definite pattern, and that they are fussy about the donors of gifts. Moreover, Uncle Harry would not return for several weeks; the expiration of that period was unimaginable to Scott, or, at least, the fact that his lie would ultimately be discovered meant less to him than the advantages of being allowed to keep the toy.

Paradine found himself growing slightly confused as he attempted to manipulate the beads. The angles were vaguely illogical. It was like a puzzle. This red bead, if slid along *this* wire to *that* junction, should reach *there*—but it didn't. A maze, odd, but no doubt instructive. Paradine had a well-founded feeling that he'd have no patience with the thing himself.

Scott did, however, retiring to a corner and sliding beads around with much fumbling and grunting. The beads *did* sting, when Scott chose the wrong ones or tried to slide them in the wrong direction. At last he crowed exultantly.

"I did it, Dad!"

"Eh? What? Let's see." The device looked exactly the same to Paradine, but Scott pointed and beamed.

"I made it disappear."

"It's still there?"

"That blue bead. It's gone now."

Paradine didn't believe that, so he merely snorted. Scott puzzled over the framework again. He experimented. This time there were no shocks, even slight. The abacus had showed him the correct method. Now it was up to him to do it on his own. The bizarre angles of the wires seemed a little less confusing now, somehow.

It was a most instructive toy—

It worked, Scott thought, rather like the crystal cube. Reminded of that gadget, he took it from his pocket and relinquished the abacus to Emma, who was struck dumb with joy. She fell to work sliding the beads, this time without protesting against the shocks—which, indeed, were very minor—and, being imitative, she managed to make a bead disappear almost as quickly as had Scott. The blue bead reappeared—but Scott didn't notice. He had forethoughtfully retired into an angle of the chesterfield and an overstuffed chair and amused himself with the cube.

There were the little people inside the thing, tiny manikins much enlarged by the magnifying properties of the crystal. They moved, all right. They built a house. It caught fire, with realistic-seeming flames, and the little people stood by waiting. Scott puffed urgently. "Put it *out!*"

But nothing happened. Where was that queer fire engine, with revolving arms, that had appeared before? Here it was. It came sailing into the picture and stopped. Scott urged it on.

This was fun. The little people really did what Scott told them, inside of his head. If he made a mistake, they waited till he'd found the right way. They even posed new problems for him.

The cube, too, was a most instructive toy. It was teaching Scott, with alarming rapidity—and teaching him very entertainingly. But it gave him no really new knowledge as yet. He wasn't ready. Later . . . later . . .

Emma grew tired of the abacus and went in search of Scott. She couldn't find him, even in his room, but once there the contents of the closet intrigued her. She discovered the box. It contained treasure-trove—a doll, which Scott had already noticed but discarded with a sneer. Squealing, Emma brought the doll downstairs, squatted in the middle of the floor and began to take it apart.

"Darling! What's that?"

"Mr. Bear!"

Obviously it wasn't Mr. Bear, who was blind, earless, but comforting in his soft fatness. But all dolls were named Mr. Bear to Emma.

Jane Paradine hesitated. "Did you take that from some other little girl?"

"I didn't. She's mine."

Scott came out from his hiding place, thrusting the cube into his pocket. "Uh—that's from Uncle Harry."

"Did Uncle Harry give that to you, Emma?"

"He gave it to me for Emma," Scott put in hastily, adding another stone to his foundation of deceit. "Last Sunday."

"You'll break it, dear."

Emma brought the doll to her mother. "She comes apart. See?"

"Oh? It—*ugh!*" Jane sucked in her breath. Paradine looked up quickly.

"What's up?"

She brought the doll over to him, hesitated and then went into the dining-room, giving Paradine a significant glance. He followed, closing the door. Jane had already placed the doll on the cleared table.

"This isn't very nice is it, Denny?"

"Hm-m-m." It was rather unpleasant, at first glance. One might have expected an anatomical dummy in a medical school, but a child's doll . . .

The thing came apart in sections—skin, muscles, organs —miniature but quite perfect, as far as Paradine could see. He was interested. "Dunno. Such things haven't the same connotations to a kid."

"Look at that liver. Is it a liver?"

"Sure. Say, I—this is funny."

"What?"

"It isn't anatomically perfect, after all." Paradine pulled up a chair. "The digestive tract's too short. No large intestine. No appendix, either."

"Should Emma have a thing like this?"

"I wouldn't mind having it myself," Paradine said. "Where on earth did Harry pick it up? No, I don't see any harm in it. Adults are conditioned to react unpleasantly to innards. Kids don't. They figure they're solid inside, like a potato. Emma can get a sound working knowledge of physiology from this doll."

"But what are those? Nerves?"

"No, these are the nerves. Arteries here; veins here. Funny sort of aorta." Paradine looked baffled. "That—what's Latin for network, anyway, huh? *Rita? Rata?*"

"*Rales,*" Jane suggested at random.

"That's a sort of breathing," Paradine said crushingly. "I can't figure out what this luminous network of stuff is. It goes all through the body, like nerves."

"Blood."

"Nope. Not circulatory, not neural. Funny! It seems to be hooked up with the lungs."

They became engrossed, puzzling over the strange doll. It was made with remarkable perfection of detail, and that in itself was strange, in view of the physiological variation from the norm. "Wait'll I get that Gould," Paradine said, and presently was comparing the doll with anatomical charts. He learned little, except to increase his bafflement.

But it was more fun than a jigsaw puzzle.

Meanwhile, in the adjoining room, Emma was sliding the beads to and fro in the abacus. The motions didn't seem so strange now. Even when the beads vanished. She could almost follow that new direction—almost . . .

Scott panted, staring into the crystal cube and mentally directing, with many false starts, the building of a structure somewhat more complicated than the one which had been destroyed by fire. He, too, was learning—being conditioned . . .

Paradine's mistake, from a completely anthropomorphic standpoint, was that he didn't get rid of the toys instantly. He did not realize their significance, and, by the time he did, the progression of circumstances had got well under way. Uncle Harry remained out of town, so Paradine couldn't check with him. Too, the midterm exams were on, which meant arduous mental effort and complete exhaustion at night; and Jane was slightly ill for a week or so. Emma and Scott had free rein with the toys.

"What," Scott asked his father one evening, "is a wabe, Dad?"

"Wave?"

He hesitated. "I—don't *think* so. Isn't 'wabe' right?"

" 'Wabe' is Scot for 'web.' That it?"

"I don't see how," Scott muttered, and wandered off,

scowling, to amuse himself with the abacus. He was able to handle it quite deftly now. But, with the instinct of children for avoiding interruption, he and Emma usually played with the toys in private. Not obviously, of course—but the more intricate experiments were never performed under the eye of an adult.

Scott was learning fast. What he now saw in the crystal cube had little relationship to the original simple problems. But they were fascinatingly technical. Had Scott realized that his education was being guided and supervised— though merely mechanically—he would probably have lost interest. As it was, his initiative was never quashed.

Abacus, cube, doll and other toys the children found in the box . . .

Neither Paradine nor Jane guessed how much of an effect the contents of the time machine were having on the kids. How could they? Youngsters are instinctive dramatists, for purposes of self-protection. They have not yet fitted themselves to the exigencies—to them partially inexplicable—of a mature world. Moreover, their lives are complicated by human variables. They are told by one person that playing in the mud is permissible, but that, in their excavations, they must not uproot flowers or small trees. Another adult vetoes mud per se. The Ten Commandments are not carved on stone—they vary; and children are helplessly dependent on the caprice of those who give them birth and feed and clothe them. And tyrannize. The young animal does not resent that benevolent tyranny, for it is an essential part of nature. He is, however, an individualist, and maintains his integrity by a subtle, passive fight.

Under the eyes of an adult he changes. Like an actor on stage, when he remembers, he strives to please, and also to attract attention to himself. Such attempts are not unknown to maturity. But adults are less obvious—to other adults.

It is difficult to admit that children lack subtlety. Children are different from mature animals because they think in another way. We can more or less easily pierce the pretences they set up, but they can do the same to us. Ruthlessly a child can destroy the pretences of an adult. Iconoclasm is a child's prerogative.

Foppishness, for example. The amenities of social intercourse, exaggerated not quite to absurdity. The gigolo . . .

"Such *savoir-faire!* Such punctilious courtesy!" The dowager and the blonde young thing are often impressed. Men have less pleasant comments to make. But the child goes to the root of the matter.

"You're *silly!*"

How can an immature human being understand the complicated system of social relationships? He can't. To him, an exaggeration of natural courtesy is silly. In his functional structure of life patterns, it is rococo. He is an egotistic little animal who cannot visualize himself in the position of another—certainly not an adult. A self-contained, almost perfect natural unit, his wants supplied by others, the child is much like a unicellular creature floating in the bloodstream, nutriment carried to him, waste products carried away.

From the standpoint of logic, a child is rather horribly perfect. A baby must be even more perfect, but so alien to an adult that only superficial standards of comparison apply. The thought processes of an infant are completely unimaginable. But babies think, even before birth. In the womb they move and sleep, not entirely through instinct. We are conditioned to react rather peculiarly to the idea that a nearly viable embryo may think. We are surprised, shocked into laughter and repelled. Nothing human is alien.

But a baby is not human. An embryo is far less human.

That, perhaps, was why Emma learned more from the toys than did Scott. He could communicate his thoughts, of course; Emma could not, except in cryptic fragments. The matter of the scrawls, for example.

Give a young child pencil and paper, and he will draw something which looks different to him than to an adult. The absurd scribbles have little resemblance to a fire engine, but it *is* a fire engine, to a baby. Perhaps it is even three-dimensional. Babies think differently and see differently.

Paradine brooded over that, reading his paper one evening and watching Emma and Scott communicate. Scott was questioning his sister. Sometimes he did it in English. More often he had resource to gibberish and sign language.

Emma tried to reply, but the handicap was too great.

Finally Scott got pencil and paper. Emma liked that. Tongue in cheek, she laboriously wrote a message. Scott took the paper, examined it and scowled.

"That isn't right, Emma," he said.

Emma nodded vigorously. She seized the pencil again and made more scrawls. Scott puzzled for a while, finally smiled rather hesitantly and got up. He vanished into the hall. Emma returned to the abacus.

Paradine rose and glanced down at the paper, with some mad thought that Emma might abruptly have mastered calligraphy. But she hadn't. The paper was covered with meaningless scrawls, of a type familiar to any parent. Paradine pursed his lips.

It might be a graph showing the mental variations of a manic-depressive cockroach, but probably wasn't. Still, it no doubt had meaning to Emma. Perhaps the scribble represented Mr. Bear.

Scott returned, looking pleased. He met Emma's gaze and nodded. Paradine felt a twinge of curiosity.

"Secrets?"

"Nope. Emma—uh—asked me to do something for her."

"Oh." Paradine, recalling instances of babies who had babbled in unknown tongues and baffled linguists, made a note to pocket the paper when the kids had finished with it. The next day he showed the scrawl to Elkins at the university. Elkins had a sound working knowledge of many unlikely languages, but he chuckled over Emma's venture into literature.

"Here's a free translation, Dennis. Quote. I don't know what this means, but I kid the hell out of my father with it. Unquote."

The two men laughed and went off to their classes. But later Paradine was to remember the incident. Especially after he met Holloway. Before that, however, months were to pass, and the situation to develop even further towards its climax.

Perhaps Paradine and Jane had evinced too much interest in the toys. Emma and Scott took to keeping them hidden, playing with them only in private. They never did it overtly, but with a certain unobtrusive caution. Nevertheless, Jane especially was somewhat troubled.

She spoke to Paradine about it one evening. "That doll Harry gave Emma."

"Yeah?"

"I was downtown today and tried to find out where it came from. No soap."

"Maybe Harry bought it in New York."

Jane was unconvinced. "I asked them about the other things, too. They showed me their stock—Johnson's a big store, you know. But there's nothing like Emma's abacus."

"Hm-m-m." Paradine wasn't much interested. They had tickets for a show that night, and it was getting late. So the subject was dropped for the nonce.

Later it cropped up again, when a neighbor telephoned Jane.

"Scotty's never been like that, Denny. Mrs. Burns said he frightened the devil out of her Francis."

"Francis? A little fat bully of a punk, isn't he? Like his father. I broke Burns's nose for him once, when we were sophomores."

"Stop boasting and listen," Jane said, mixing a highball. "Scott showed Francis something that scared him. Hadn't you better—"

"I suppose so." Paradine listened. Noises in the next room told him the whereabouts of his son. "Scotty!"

"Bang," Scott said, and appeared smiling. "I killed 'em all. Space pirates. You want me, dad?"

"Yes. If you don't mind leaving the space pirates unburied for a few minutes. What did you do to Francis Burns?"

Scott's blue eyes reflected incredible candor. "Huh?"

"Try hard. You can remember, I'm sure."

"Uh. Oh, that. I didn't do nothing."

"Anything," Jane corrected absently.

"Anything. Honest. I just let him look into my television set, and it—it scared him."

"Television set?"

Scott produced the crystal cube. "It isn't really that. See?"

Paradine examined the gadget, startled by the magnification. All he could see, though, was a maze of meaningless colored designs.

"Uncle Harry—"

Paradine reached for the telephone. Scott gulped. "Is— is Uncle Harry back in town?"

"Yeah."

"Well, I gotta take a bath." Scott headed for the door. Paradine met Jane's gaze and nodded significantly.

Harry was home, but disclaimed all knowledge of the peculiar toys. Rather grimly, Paradine requested Scott to bring down from his room all of the playthings. Finally they lay in a row on the table—cube, abacus, doll, helmet-like cap, several other mysterious contraptions. Scott was cross-examined. He lied valiantly for a time, but broke down at last and bawled, hiccuping his confession.

"Get the box these things came in," Paradine ordered. "Then head for bed."

"Are you—*hup*—gonna punish me, Daddy?"

"For playing hooky and lying, yes. You know the rules. No more shows for two weeks. No sodas for the same period."

Scott gulped. "You gonna keep my things?"

"I don't know yet."

"Well—g'night, Daddy. G'night, Mom."

After the small figure had gone upstairs, Paradine dragged a chair to the table and carefully scrutinized the box. He poked thoughtfully at the focused gadgetry. Jane watched.

"What is it, Denny?"

"Dunno. Who'd leave a box of toys down by the creek?"

"It might have fallen out of a car."

"Not at that point. The road doesn't hit the creek north of the railroad trestle. Empty lots—nothing else." Paradine lit a cigarette. "Drink, honey?"

"I'll fix it." Jane went to work, her eyes troubled. She brought Paradine a glass and stood behind him, ruffling his hair with her fingers. "Is anything wrong?"

"Of course not. Only—where did these toys come from?"

"Johnson's didn't know, and they get their stock from New York."

"I've been checking up, too," Paradine admitted. "That doll,"—he poked it—"rather worried me. Custom jobs, maybe, but I wish I knew who'd made 'em."

"A psychologist? That abacus—don't they give people tests with such things?"

Paradine snapped his fingers. "Right! And say, there's a guy going to speak at the university next week, fellow named Holloway, who's a child psychologist. He's a big shot, with quite a reputation. He might know something about it."

"Holloway? I don't—"

"Rex Holloway. He's—hm-m-m! He doesn't live far from here. Do you suppose he might have had these things made himself?"

Jane was examining the abacus. She grimaced and drew back. "If he did, I don't like him. But see if you can find out, Denny."

Paradine nodded. "I shall."

He drank his highball, frowning. He was vaguely worried. But he wasn't scared—yet.

Rex Holloway was a fat, shiny man, with a bald head and thick spectacles, above which his thick, black brows lay like bushy caterpillars. Paradine brought him home to dinner one night a week later. Holloway did not appear to watch the children, but nothing they did or said was lost on him. His grey eyes, shrewd and bright, missed little.

The toys fascinated him. In the living-room the three adults gathered around the table, where the playthings had been placed. Holloway studied them carefully as he listened to what Jane and Paradine had to say. At last he broke his silence.

"I'm glad I came here tonight. But not completely. This is very disturbing, you know."

"Eh?" Paradine stared, and Jane's face showed her consternation. Holloway's next words did not calm them.

"We are dealing with madness."

He smiled at the shocked looks they gave him. "All children are mad, from an adult viewpoint. Ever read Hughes' *High Wind in Jamaica*?"

"I've got it." Paradine secured the little book from its

shelf. Holloway extended a hand, took the book and flipped the pages till he had found the place he wanted. He read aloud:

Babies, of course, are not human—they are animals, and have a very ancient and ramified culture, as cats have, and fishes, and even snakes; the same in kind as these, but much more complicated and vivid, since babies are, after all, one of the most developed species of the lower vertebrates. In short, babies have minds which work in terms and categories of their own, which cannot be translated into the terms and categories of the human mind.

Jane tried to take that calmly, but couldn't. "You don't mean that Emma—"

"Could you think like your daughter?" Holloway asked. "Listen: 'One can no more think like a baby than one can think like a bee.'"

Paradine mixed drinks. Over his shoulder he said, "You're theorizing quite a bit, aren't you? As I get it, you're implying that babies have a culture of their own, even a high standard of intelligence."

"Not necessarily. There's no yardstick, you see. All I say is that babies think in other ways than we do. Not necessarily *better*—that's a question of relative values. But with a different matter of extension." He sought for words, grimacing.

"Fantasy," Paradine said, rather rudely but annoyed because of Emma. "Babies don't have different senses from ours."

"Who said they did?" Holloway demanded. "They use their minds in a different way, that's all. But it's quite enough!"

"I'm trying to understand," Jane said slowly. "All I can think of is my Mixmaster. It can whip up batter and potatoes, but it can squeeze oranges, too."

"Something like that. The brain's a colloid, a very complicated machine. We don't know much about its potentialities. We don't even know how much it can grasp. But it *is* known that the mind becomes conditioned as the human animal matures. It follows certain familiar theorems, and all thought thereafter is pretty well based on patterns taken for granted. Look at this." Holloway touched the abacus. "Have you experimented with it?"

"A little," Paradine said.

"But not much, eh?"

"Well—"

"Why not?"

"It's pointless," Paradine complained. "Even a puzzle has to have some logic. But those crazy angles—"

"Your mind has been conditioned to Euclid," Holloway said. "So this—thing—bores us, and seems pointless. But a child knows nothing of Euclid. A different sort of geometry from ours wouldn't impress him as being illogical. He believes what he sees."

"Are you trying to tell me that this gadget's got a fourth-dimensional extension?" Paradine demanded.

"Not visually, anyway," Holloway denied. "All I can say is that our minds, conditioned to Euclid, can see nothing in this but an illogical tangle of wires. But a child—especially a baby—might see more. Not at first. It'd be a puzzle, of course. Only a child wouldn't be handicapped by too many preconceived ideas."

"Hardening of the thought arteries," Jane interjected.

Paradine was not convinced. "Then a baby could work calculus better than Einstein? No, I don't mean that. I can see your point, more or less clearly. Only—"

"Well, look. Let's suppose there are two kinds of geometry; we'll limit it, for the sake of the example. Our kind, Euclidean, and another, we'll call x. X hasn't much relationship to Euclid. It's based on different theorems. Two and two needn't equal four in it; they could equal y^2, or they might not even *equal*. A baby's mind is not yet conditioned, except by certain questionable factors of heredity and environment. Start the infant on Euclid—"

"Poor kid," Jane said.

Holloway shot her a quick glance. "The basis of Euclid. Alphabet blocks. Math, geometry, algebra—they come much later. We're familiar with that development. On the other hand, start the baby with the basic principles of our *x* logic."

"Blocks? What kind?"

Holloway looked at the abacus. "It wouldn't make much sense to us. But we've been conditioned to Euclid."

Paradine poured himself a stiff shot of whisky. "That's pretty awful. You're not limiting to math."

"Right! I'm not limiting it at all. How can I? I'm not conditioned to *x* logic."

"There's the answer," Jane said, with a sigh of relief. "Who is? It'd take such a person to make the sort of toys you apparently think these are."

Holloway nodded, his eyes, behind the thick lenses, blinking. "Such people may exist."

"Where?"

"They might prefer to keep hidden."

"Supermen?"

"I wish I knew. You see, Paradine, we've got yardstick trouble again. By our standards these people might seem super-dupers in certain respects. In others they might seem moronic. It's not a quanitative difference; it's qualitative. They *think* different. And I'm sure we can do things they can't."

"Maybe they wouldn't want to," Jane said.

Paradine tapped the fused gadgetry on the box. "What about this? It implies—"

"A purpose, sure."

"Transportation?"

"One thinks of that first. If so, the box might have come from anywhere."

"Where—things are—*different?*" Paradine asked slowly.

"Exactly. In space, or even time. I don't know; I'm a psychologist. Unfortunately I'm conditioned to Euclid, too."

"Funny place it must be," Jane said. "Denny, get rid of those toys."

"I intend to."

Holloway picked up the crystal cube. "Did you question the children much?"

Paradine said, "Yeah. Scott said there were people in

that cube when he first looked. I asked him what was in it now."

"What did he say?" The psychologist's eyes widened.

"He said they were building a place. His exact words. I asked him who—people? But he couldn't explain."

"No, I suppose not," Holloway muttered. "It must be progressive. How long have the children had these toys?"

"About three months, I guess."

"Time enough. The perfect toy, you see, is both instructive and mechanical. It should do things, to interest a child, and it should teach, preferably unobtrusively. Simple problems at first. Later—"

"X logic," Jane said, white-faced.

Paradine cursed under his breath. "Emma and Scott are perfectly normal!"

"Do you know how their minds work—now?"

Holloway didn't pursue the thought. He fingered the doll. "It would be interesting to know the conditions of the place where these things came from. Induction doesn't help a great deal, though. Too many factors are missing. We can't visualize a world based on the x factor—environment adjusted to minds thinking in x patterns. This luminous network inside the doll. It could be anything. It could exist inside us, though we haven't discovered it yet. When we find the right stain—" He shrugged. "What do you make of this?"

It was a crimson globe, two inches in diameter, with a protruding knob upon its surface.

"What could anyone make of it?"

"Scott? Emma?"

"I hadn't seen it till about three weeks ago. Then Emma started to play with it." Paradine nibbled his lip. "After that, Scott got interested."

"Just what do they do?"

"Hold it up in front of them and move back and forth. No particular pattern of motion."

"No Euclidean pattern," Holloway corrected. "At first they couldn't understand the toy's purpose. They had to be educated up to it."

"That's horrible," Jane said.

"Not to them. Emma is probably quicker at understanding x than is Scott, for her mind isn't yet conditioned to this environment."

Paradine said, "But I can remember plenty of things I did as a child. Even as a baby."

"Well?"

"Was I—mad then?"

"The things you don't remember are the criterion of your madness," Holloway retorted. "But I use the word 'madness' purely as a convenient symbol for the variation from the known human norm. The arbitrary standard of sanity."

Jane put down her glass. "You've said that induction was difficult, Mr. Holloway. But it seems to me you're making a great deal of it from very little. After all, these toys—"

"I *am* a psychologist, and I've specialized in children. I'm not a layman. These toys mean a great deal to me, chiefly because they mean so little."

"You might be wrong."

"Well, I rather hope I am. I'd like to examine the children."

Jane rose in arms. "How?"

After Holloway had explained, she nodded, though still a bit hesitantly. "Well, that's all right. But they're not guinea pigs."

The psychologist patted the air with a plump hand. "My dear girl! I'm not a Frankenstein. To me the individual is the prime factor—naturally, since I work with minds. If there's anything wrong with the youngsters, I want to cure them."

Paradine put down his cigarette and slowly watched blue smoke spiral up, wavering in an unfelt draught. "Can you give a prognosis?"

"I'll try. That's all I can say. If the undeveloped minds have been turned into the x channel, it's necessary to divert them back. I'm not saying that's the wisest thing to do, but it probably is from our standards. After all, Emma and Scott will have to live in this world."

"Yeah. Yeah. I can't believe there's much wrong. They seem about average, thoroughly normal."

"Superficially they may seem so. They've no reason for

acting abnormally, have they? And how can you tell if they —think differently?"

"I'll call 'em," Paradine said.

"Make it informal, then. I don't want them to be on guard."

Jane nodded towards the toys. Holloway said, "Leave the stuff there, eh?"

But the psychologist, after Emma and Scott were summoned, made no immediate move towards direct questioning. He managed to draw Scott unobtrusively into the conversation, dropping key words now and then. Nothing so obvious as a word-association test; cooperation is necessary for that.

The most interesting development occurred when Holloway took up the abacus. "Mind showing me how this works?"

Scott hesitated. "Yes, sir. Like this." He slid a bead deftly through the maze, in a tangled course, so swiftly that no one was quite sure whether or not it ultimately vanished. It might have been merely legerdemain. Then, again—

Holloway tried. Scott watched, wrinkling his nose.

"That's right?"

"Uh-huh. It's gotta go *there*."

"Here? Why?"

"Well, that's the only way to make it work."

But Holloway was conditioned to Euclid. There was no apparent reason why the bead should slide from this particular wire to the other. It looked like a random factor. Also, Holloway suddenly noticed, this wasn't the path the bead had taken previously, when Scott had worked the puzzle. At least, as well as he could tell.

"Will you show me again?"

Scott did, and twice more, on request. Holloway blinked through his glasses. Random, yes. And a variable. Scott moved the bead along a different course each time.

Somehow, none of the adults could tell whether or not the bead vanished. If they had expected to see it disappear, their reactions might have been different.

In the end nothing was solved. Holloway, as he said good night, seemed ill at ease.

"May I come again?"

"I wish you would," Jane told him. "Any time. You still think—"

He nodded. "The children's minds are not reacting normally. They're not dull at all, but I've the most extraordinary impression that they arrive at conclusions in a way we don't understand. As though they used algebra while we used geometry. The same conclusion, but a different method of reaching it."

"What about the toys?" Paradine asked suddenly.

"Keep them out of the way. I'd like to borrow them, if I may."

That night Paradine slept badly. Holloway's parallel had been ill chosen. It led to disturbing theories. The x factor . . . The children were using the equivalent of algebraic reasoning, while adults used geometry.

Fair enough. Only . . .

Algebra can give you answers that geometry cannot, since there are certain terms and symbols which cannot be expressed geometrically. Suppose x logic showed conclusions inconceivable to an adult mind.

"Damn!" Paradine whispered. Jane stirred beside him.

"Dear? Can't you sleep either?"

"No." He got up and went into the next room. Emma slept peacefully as a cherub, her fat arm curled around Mr. Bear. Through the open doorway Paradine could see Scott's dark head motionless on the pillow.

Jane was beside him. He slipped his arm around her.

"Poor little people," she murmured. "And Holloway called them mad. I think we're the ones who are crazy, Dennis."

"Uh-huh. We've got jitters."

Scott stirred in his sleep. Without awakening, he called what was obviously a question, though it did not seem to be in any particular language. Emma gave a little mewling cry that changed pitch sharply.

She had not wakened. The children lay without stirring.

But, Paradine thought, with a sudden sickness in his middle, it was exactly as though Scott had asked Emma something, and she had replied.

Had their minds changed so that even—sleep was different to them?

He thrust the thought away. "You'll catch cold. Let's get back to bed. Want a drink?"

"I think I do," Jane said, watching Emma. Her hand reached out blindly toward the child; she drew it back. "Come on. We'll wake the kids."

They drank a little brandy together, but said nothing. Jane cried in her sleep, later.

Scott was not awake, but his mind worked in slow, careful building. Thus—

"They'll take the toys away. The fat man—listava dangerous, maybe. But the Ghoric direction won't show—evankrus dun hasn't them. Intransdection—bright and shiny. Emma. She's more khopranik-high now than—I still don't see how to—thavarar lixery dist . . ."

A little of Scott's thoughts could still be understood. But Emma had become conditioned to *x* much faster

She was thinking, too.

Not like an adult or a child. Not even like a human being. Except, perhaps, a human being of a type shockingly unfamiliar to genus Homo.

Sometimes, Scott himself had difficulty in following her thoughts.

If it had not been for Holloway, life might have settled back into an almost normal routine. The toys were no longer active reminders. Emma still enjoyed her dolls and sandpile, with a thoroughly explicable delight. Scott was satisfied with baseball and his chemical set. They did everything other children did, and evinced few, if any, flashes of abnormality. But Holloway seemed to be an alarmist.

He was having the toys tested, with rather idiotic results. He drew endless charts and diagrams, corresponded with mathematicians, engineers and other psychologists, and went quietly crazy trying to find rhyme or reason in the construction of the gadgets. The box itself, with its cryptic machinery, told nothing. Fusing had melted too much of the stuff into slag. But the toys . . .

It was the random element that baffled investigation. Even that was a matter of semantics. For Holloway was convinced that it wasn't really random. There just weren't enough known factors. No adult could work the abacus, for example. And Holloway thoughtfully refrained from letting a child play with the thing.

The crystal cube was similarly cryptic. It showed a mad pattern of colors, which sometimes moved. In this it resembled a kaleidoscope. But the shifting of balance and gravity didn't affect it. Again the random factor.

Or, rather, the unknown. The x pattern. Eventually, Paradine and Jane slipped back into something like complacence, with a feeling that the children had been cured of their mental quirk, now that the contributing cause had been removed. Certain of the actions of Emma and Scott gave them every reason to quit worrying.

For the kids enjoyed swimming, hiking, movies, games, the normal functional toys of this particular time-sector. It was true that they failed to master certain rather puzzling mechanical devices which involved some calculation. A three-dimensional jigsaw globe Paradine had picked up, for example. But he found that difficult himself.

Once in a while there were lapses. Scott was hiking with his father one Saturday afternoon, and the two had paused at the summit of a hill. Beneath them a rather lovely valley was spread.

"Pretty isn't it?" Paradine remarked.

Scott examined the scene gravely. "It's all wrong," he said.

"Eh?"

"I dunno."

"What's wrong about it?"

"Gee." Scott lapsed into puzzled silence. "I dunno."

The children had missed their toys, but not for long. Emma recovered first, though Scott still moped. He held unintelligible conversations with his sister, and studied meaningless scrawls she drew on paper he supplied. It was almost as though he was consulting her, anent difficult problems beyond his grasp.

If Emma understood more, Scott had more real intelligence, and manipulatory skill as well. He built a gadget with his Meccano set, but was dissatisfied. The apparent cause of his dissatisfaction was exactly why Paradine was relieved when he viewed the structure. It was the sort of thing a normal boy would make, vaguely reminiscent of a cubistic ship.

It was a bit too normal to please Scott. He asked Emma more questions, though in private. She thought for a time, and then made more scrawls, with an awkwardly clutched pencil.

"Can you read that stuff?" Jane asked her son one morning.

"Not read it, exactly. I can tell what she means. Not all the time, but mostly."

"Is it writing?"

"N-no. It doesn't mean what it *looks* like."

"Symbolism," Paradine suggested over his coffee.

Jane looked at him, her eyes widening. "Denny—"

He winked and shook his head. Later, when they were alone, he said, "Don't let Holloway upset you. I'm not implying that the kids are corresponding in an unknown tongue. If Emma draws a squiggle and says it's a flower, that's an arbitrary rule—Scott remembers that. Next time she draws the same sort of squiggle, or tries to—well!"

"Sure," Jane said doubtfully. "Have you noticed Scott's been doing a lot of reading lately?"

"I noticed. Nothing unusual, though. No Kant or Spinoza."

"He browses, that's all."

"Well, so did I, at his age," Paradine said, and went off to his morning classes. He lunched with Holloway, which was becoming a daily habit, and spoke of Emma's literary endeavors.

"Was I right about symbolism, Rex?"

The psychologist nodded. "Quite right. Our own language is nothing but arbitrary symbolism now. At least in its application. Look here." On his napkin he drew a very narrow ellipse. "What's that?"

"You mean what does it represent?"

"Yes. What does it suggest to you? It could be a crude representation of—what?"

"Plenty of things," Paradine said. "Rim of a glass. A fried egg. A loaf of French bread. A cigar."

Holloway added a little triangle to his drawing, apex joined to one end of the ellipse. He looked up at Paradine.

"A fish," the latter said instantly.

"Our familiar symbol for a fish. Even without fins, eyes or mouth, it's recognizable, because we've been conditioned to identify this particular shape with our mental picture of a fish. The basis of a rebus. A symbol, to us, means a lot more than what we actually see on paper. What's in your mind when you look at this sketch?"

"Why—a fish."

"Keep going. What do you visualize? Everything!"

"Scales," Paradine said slowly, looking into space. "Water. Foam. A fish's eye. The fins. The colors."

"So the symbol represents a lot more than just that abstract idea *fish*. Note the connotation's that of a noun, not a verb. It's harder to express actions by symbolism, you know. Anyway—reverse the process. Suppose you want to make a symbol for some concrete noun, say *bird*. Draw it."

Paradine drew two connected arcs, concavities down.

"The lowest common denominator," Holloway nodded. "The natural tendency is to simplify. Especially when a child is seeing something for the first time and has few standards of comparison. He tries to identify the new thing with what's already familiar to him. Ever notice how a child draws the ocean?" He didn't wait for an answer; he went on.

"A series of jagged points. Like the oscillating line on a seismograph. When I first saw the Pacific, I was about three. I remember it pretty clearly. It looked—tilted. A flat plain, slanted at an angle. The waves were regular triangles, apex upward. Now, I didn't *see* them stylized that way, but later, remembering, I had to find some familiar standard of comparison. Which is the only way of getting any conception of an entirely new thing. The average child tries to draw these regular triangles, but his co-ordination's poor. He gets a seismograph pattern."

"All of which means what?"

"A child sees the ocean. He stylizes it. He draws a certain definite pattern, symbolic, to him, of the sea. Emma's scrawls may be symbols, too. I don't mean that the world looks different to her—brighter, perhaps, and sharper, more vivid and with a slackening of perception above her eye level. What I do mean is that her thought processes are different, that she translates what she sees into abnormal symbols."

"You still believe—"

"Yes, I do. Her mind has been conditioned unusually. It may be that she breaks down what she sees into simple, obvious patterns—and realizes a significance to those patterns that we can't understand. Like the abacus. She saw a pattern in that, though to us it was completely random."

Paradine abruptly decided to taper off these luncheon engagements with Holloway. The man was an alarmist. His theories were growing more fantastic than ever, and he dragged in anything, applicable or not, that would support them.

Rather sardonically he said, "Do you mean Emma's communicating with Scott in an unknown language?"

"In symbols for which she hasn't any words. I'm sure Scott understands a great deal of those—scrawls. To him, an isosceles triangle may represent any factor, though probably a concrete noun. Would a man who knew nothing of chemistry understand what H_2O meant? Would he realize that the symbol could evoke a picture of the ocean?"

Paradine didn't answer. Instead, he mentioned to Holloway Scott's curious remark that the landscape, from the hill, had looked all wrong. A moment later, he was inclined to regret his impulse, for the psychologist was off again.

"Scott's thought patterns are building up to a sum that doesn't equal this world. Perhaps he's subconsciously expecting to see the world where those toys came from."

Paradine stopped listening. Enough was enough. The kids were getting along all right, and the only remaining disturbing factor was Holloway himself. That night, however, Scott evinced an interest, later significant, in eels.

There was nothing apparently harmful in natural history. Paradine explained about eels.

"But where do they lay their eggs? Or do they?"

"That's still a mystery. Their spawning grounds are unknown. Maybe the Sargasso Sea, or the deeps, where the pressure can help them force the young out of their bodies."

"Funny," Scott said, thinking deeply.

"Salmon do the same thing, more or less. They go up rivers to spawn." Paradine went into detail. Scott was fascinated.

"But that's *right*, Dad. They're born in the river, and when they learn how to swim, they go down to the sea. And they come back to lay their eggs, huh?"

"Right."

"Only they wouldn't *come* back," Scott pondered. "They'd just send their eggs—"

"It'd take a very long ovipositor," Paradine said, and vouchsafed some well-chosen remarks upon oviparity.

His son wasn't entirely satisfied. Flowers, he contended, sent their seeds long distances.

"They don't guide them. Not many find fertile soil."

"Flowers haven't got brains, though. Dad, why do people live *here*?"

"Glendale?"

"No—*here*. This whole place. It isn't all there is, I bet."

"Do you mean the other planets?"

Scott was hesitant. "This is only—part of the big place. It's like the river where the salmon go. Why don't people go on down to the ocean when they grow up?"

Paradine realized that Scott was speaking figuratively. He felt a brief chill. The—ocean?

The young of the species are not conditioned to live in the more complete world of their parents. Having developed sufficiently, they enter that world. Later they breed. The fertilized eggs are buried in the sand, far up the river, where later they hatch.

And they learn. Instinct alone is fatally slow. Especially in the case of a specialized genus, unable to cope even with this world, unable to feed or drink or survive, unless someone has foresightedly provided for those needs.

The young, fed and tended, would survive. There would be incubators and robots. They would survive, but they would not know how to swim downstream, to the vaster, world of the ocean.

So they must be taught. They must be trained and conditioned in many ways.

Painlessly, subtly, unobtrusively. Children love toys that do things, and if those toys teach at the same time . . .

In the latter half of the nineteenth century an Englishman sat on a grassy bank near a stream. A very small girl lay near him, staring up at the sky. She had discarded a curious toy with which she had been playing, and now was murmuring a wordless little song, to which the man listened with half an ear.

"What was that, my dear?" he asked at last.

"Just something I made up, Uncle Charles."

"Sing it again." He pulled out a notebook.

The girl obeyed.

"Does it mean anything?"

She nodded. "Oh, yes. Like the stories I tell you, you know."

"They're wonderful stories, dear."

"And you'll put them in a book someday?"

"Yes, but I must change them quite a lot, or no one would understand. But I don't think I'll change your little song."

"You mustn't. If you did, it wouldn't mean anything."

"I won't change that stanza, anyway," he promised. "Just what does it mean?"

"It's the way out, I think," the girl said doubtfully. "I'm not sure yet. My magic toys told me."

"I wish I knew what London shop sold these marvelous toys!"

"Mama bought them for me. She's dead. Papa doesn't care."

She lied. She had found the toys in a box one day, as she played by the Thames. And they were indeed wonderful.

Her little song—Uncle Charles thought it didn't mean anything. (He wasn't her real uncle, she parenthesized. But he was nice.) The song meant a great deal. It was the way. Presently she would do what it said, and then . . .

But she was already too old. She never found the way.

Paradine had dropped Holloway. Jane had taken a dislike to him, naturally enough, since what she wanted most of all was to have her fears calmed. Since Scott and Emma acted normally now, Jane felt satisfied. It was partly wishful thinking, to which Paradine could not entirely subscribe.

Scott kept bringing gadgets to Emma for her approval. Usually she'd shake her head. Sometimes she would look doubtful. Very occasionally she would signify agreement. Then there would be an hour of laborious, crazy scribbling on scraps of note paper, and Scott, after studying the notations, would arrange and rearrange his rocks, bits of machinery, candle ends and assorted junk. Each day the maid cleaned them away, and each day Scott began again.

He condescended to explain a little to his puzzled father, who could see no rhyme or reason in the game.

"But why this pebble right here?"

"It's hard and round, Dad. It *belongs* there."

"So is this one hard and round."

"Well, that's got vaseline on it. When you get that far, you can't *see* just a hard, round thing."

"What comes next? This candle?"

Scott looked disgusted. "That's toward the end. The iron ring's next."

It was, Paradine thought, like a scout trail through the woods, markers in a labyrinth. But here again was the random factor. Logic halted—familiar logic—at Scott's motives in arranging the junk as he did.

Paradine went out. Over his shoulder he saw Scott pull a crumpled piece of paper and a pencil from his pocket and head for Emma, who was squatted in a corner thinking things over.

Well . . .

Jane was lunching with Uncle Harry, and, on this hot Sunday afternoon, there was little to do but read the papers. Paradine settled himself in the coolest place he could find, with a Collins, and lost himself in the comic strips.

An hour later a clatter of feet upstairs roused him from his doze. Scott's voice was crying exultantly, "This is it, Slug! Come on!"

Paradine stood up quickly, frowning. As he went into the hall the telephone began to ring. Jane had promised to call . . .

His hand was on the receiver when Emma's faint voice squealed with excitement. Paradine grimaced. What the devil was going on upstairs?

Scott shrieked, "Look out! This way!"

Paradine, his mouth working, his nerves ridiculously tense, forgot the phone and raced up the stairs. The door of Scott's room was open.

The children were vanishing.

They went in fragments, like thick smoke in a wind, or

like movement in a distorting mirror. Hand in hand they went, in a direction Paradine could not understand, and as he blinked there on the threshold, they were gone.

"Emma!" he said, dry-throated. *"Scotty!"*

On the carpet lay a pattern of markers, pebbles, an iron ring—junk. A random pattern. A crumpled sheet of paper blew towards Paradine.

He picked it up automatically.

"Kids. Where are you? Don't hide—*Emma! SCOTTY!"*

Downstairs the telephone stopped its shrill, monotonous ringing. Paradine looked at the paper he held.

It was a leaf torn from a book. There were interlineations and marginal notes, in Emma's meaningless scrawl. A stanza of verse had been so underlined and scribbled over that it was almost illegible, but Paradine was thoroughly familiar with *Through the Looking Glass*. His memory gave him the words—

> *'Twas brillig, and the slithy toves*
> *Did gyre ad gimble in the wabe:*
> *All mimsy were the borogoves,*
> *And the mome raths outgrabe.*

Idiotically he thought: Humpty Dumpty explained it. A wabe is the plot of grass around a sundial. A sundial. Time. It has something to do with time. A long time ago Scotty asked me what a wabe was. Symbolism.

'Twas brillig . . .

A perfect mathematical formula, giving all the conditions, in symbolism the children had finally understood. The junk on the floor. The toves had to be made slithy—vaseline?—and they had to be placed in a certain relationship, so that they'd gyre and gimble.

Lunacy!

But it had not been lunacy to Emma and Scott. They thought differently. They used x logic. Those notes Emma had made on the page—she'd translated Carroll's words into symbols both she and Scott could understand.

The random factor had made sense to the children. They had fulfilled the conditions of the time-span equation. *And the mome raths outgrabe . . .*

Paradine made a rather ghastly little sound, deep in his

throat. He looked at the crazy pattern on the carpet. If he could follow it, as the kids had done—But he couldn't. The pattern was senseless. The random factor defeated him. He was conditioned to Euclid.

Even if he went insane, he still couldn't do it. It would be the wrong kind of lunacy.

His mind had stopped working now. But in a moment the stasis of incredulous horror would pass—Paradine crumpled the page in his fingers. "Emma! Scotty!" he called in a dead voice, as though he could expect no response.

Sunlight slanted through the open windows, brightening the golden pelt of Mr. Bear. Downstairs the ringing of the telephone began again.

Two-Handed Engine

EVER SINCE THE days of Orestes there have been men with Furies following them. It wasn't until the Twenty-Second Century that mankind made itself a set of real Furies, out of steel. Mankind had reached a crisis by then. They had a good reason for building man-shaped Furies that would dog the footsteps of all men who kill men. Nobody else. There was by then no other crime of any importance.

It worked very simply. Without warning, a man who thought himself safe would suddenly hear the steady footfalls behind him. He would turn and see the two-handed engine walking towards him, shaped like a man of steel, and more incorruptible than any man not made of steel could be. Only then would the murderer know he had been tried and condemned by the omniscient electronic minds that knew society as no human mind could ever know it.

For the rest of his days, the man would hear those footsteps behind him. A moving jail with invisible bars that shut him off from the world. Never in life would he be alone again. And one day—he never knew when— the jailer would turn executioner.

Danner leaned back comfortably in his contoured restaurant chair and rolled expensive wine across his tongue, closing his eyes to enjoy the taste of it better. He felt perfectly safe. Oh, perfectly protected. For nearly an hour now he had been sitting here, ordering the most expensive food, enjoying the music breathing softly through the air, the mur-

murous, well-bred hush of his fellow diners. It was a good place to be. It was very good, having so much money—now.

True, he had had to kill to get the money. But no guilt troubled him. There was no guilt if you aren't found out, and Danner had protection. Protection straight from the source, which was something new in the world. Danner knew the consequences of killing. If Hartz hadn't satisfied him that he was perfectly safe, Danner would never have pulled the trigger . . .

The memory of an archaic word flickered through his mind briefly. *Sin.* It evoked nothing. Once it had something to do with guilt, in an incomprehensible way. Not any more. Mankind had been through too much. Sin was meaningless now.

He dismissed the thought and tried the heart-of-palms salad. He found he didn't like it. Oh well, you had to expect things like that. Nothing was perfect. He sipped the wine again, liking the way the glass seemed to vibrate like something faintly alive in his hand. It was good wine. He thought of ordering more, but then he thought no, save it, next time. There was so much before him, waiting to be enjoyed. Any risk was worth it. And of course, in this there had been no risk.

Danner was a man born at the wrong time. He was old enough to remember the last days of utopia, young enough to be trapped in the new scarcity economy the machines had clamped down on their makers. In his early youth he'd had access to free luxuries, like everybody else. He could remember the old days when he was an adolescent and the last of the Escape Machines were still operating, the glamorous, bright, impossible, vicarious visions that didn't really exist and never could have. But then the scarcity economy swallowed up pleasure. Now you got necessities but no more. Now you had to work. Danner hated every minute of it.

When the swift change came, he'd been too young and unskilled to compete in the scramble. The rich men today were the men who had built fortunes on cornering the few luxuries the machines still produced. All Danner had left were bright memories and a dull, resentful feeling of having been cheated. All he wanted were the bright days back, and he didn't care how he got them.

Well, now he had them. He touched the rim of the wine glass with his finger, feeling it sing silently against the touch. Blown glass? he wondered. He was too ignorant of luxury items to understand. But he'd learn. He had the rest of his life to learn in, and be happy.

He looked up across the restaurant and saw through the transparent dome of the roof the melting towers of the city. They made a stone forest as far as he could see. And this was only one city. When he was tired of it, there were more. Across the country, across the planet the network lay that linked city with city in a webwork like a vast, intricate, half-alive monster. Call it society.

He felt it tremble a little beneath him.

He reached for the wine and drank quickly. The faint uneasiness that seemed to shiver the foundations of the city was something new. It was because—yes, certainly it was because of a new fear.

It was because he had not been found out.

That made no sense. Of course the city was complex. Of course it operated on a basis of incorruptible machines. They, and only they, kept man from becoming very quickly another extinct animal. And of these the analog computers, the electronic calculators, were the gyroscope of all living. They made and enforced the laws that were necessary now to keep mankind alive. Danner didn't understand much of the vast changes that had swept over society in his lifetime, but this much even he knew.

So perhaps it made sense that he felt society shiver because he sat here luxurious on foam-rubber, sipping wine, hearing soft music, and no Fury standing behind his chair to prove that the calculators were still guardians for mankind . . .

If not even the Furies are incorruptible, what can a man believe in?

It was at that exact moment that the Fury arrived.

Danner heard every sound suddenly die out around him. His fork was halfway to his lips, but he paused, frozen, and looked up across the table and the restaurant towards the door.

The Fury was taller than a man. It stood there for a moment, the afternoon sun striking a blinding spot of brightness from its shoulder. It had no face, but it seemed to scan the restaurant leisurely, table by table. Then it stepped in under the doorframe and the sun-spot slid away and it was like a tall man encased in steel, walking slowly between the tables.

Danner said to himself, laying down his untasted food, "Not for me. Everyone else here is wondering. I *know*."

And like a memory in a drowning man's mind, clear, sharp and condensed into a moment, yet every detail clear, he remembered what Hartz had told him. As a drop of water can pull into its reflection a wide panorama condensed into a tiny focus, so time seemed to focus down to a pinpoint the half-hour Danner and Hartz had spent together, in Hartz's office with the walls that could go transparent at the push of a button.

He saw Hartz again, plump and blond, with the sad eyebrows. A man who looked relaxed until he began to talk, and then you felt the burning quality about him, the air of driven tension that made even the air around him seem to be restlessly trembling. Danner stood before Hartz's desk again in memory, feeling the floor hum faintly against his soles with the heartbeat of the computers. You could see them through the glass, smooth, shiny things with winking lights in banks like candles burning in colored glass cups. You could hear their faraway chattering as they ingested facts, meditated them, and then spoke in numbers like cryptic oracles. It took men like Hartz to understand what the oracles meant.

"I have a job for you," Hartz said. "I want a man killed."

"Oh no," Danner said. "What kind of a fool do you think I am?"

"Now wait a minute. You can use money, can't you?"

"What for?" Danner asked bitterly. "A fancy funeral?"

"A life of luxury. I know you're not a fool. I know damned well you wouldn't do what I ask unless you got money *and* protection. That's what I can offer. Protection."

Danner looked through the transparent wall at the computers.

"Sure," he said.

"No, I mean it. I—" Hartz hesitated, glancing around the room a little uneasily, as if he hardly trusted his own precautions for making sure of privacy. "This is something new," he said. "I can redirect any Fury I want to."

"Oh, sure," Danner said again.

"It's true. I'll show you. I can pull a Fury off any victim I choose."

"How?"

"That's my secret. Naturally. In effect, though, I've found a way to feed in false data, so the machines come out with the wrong verdict before conviction, or the wrong orders after conviction."

"But that's—dangerous, isn't it?"

"Dangerous?" Hartz looked at Danner under his sad eyebrows. "Well, yes. I think so. That's why I don't do it often. I've done it only once, as a matter of fact. Theoretically, I'd worked out the method. I tested it, just once. It worked. I'll do it again, to prove to you I'm telling the truth. After that I'll do it once again, to protect you. And that will be it. I don't want to upset the calculators any more than I have to. Once your job's done, I won't have to."

"Who do you want killed?"

Involuntarily Hartz glanced upward, towards the heights of the building where the top-rank executive offices were. "O'Reilly," he said.

Danner glanced upward too, as if he could see through the floor and observe the exalted shoe-soles of O'Reilly, Controller of the Calculators, pacing an expensive carpet overhead.

"It's very simple," Hartz said. "I want his job."

"Why not do your own killing, then, if you're so sure you can stop the Furies?"

"Because that would give the whole thing away," Hartz said impatiently. "Use your head. I've got an obvious motive. It wouldn't take a calculator to figure out who profits most if O'Reilly dies. If I saved myself from a Fury, people would start wondering how I did it. But you've got no motive for killing O'Reilly. Nobody but the calculators would know, and I'll take care of them."

"How do I know you can do it?"

"Simple. Watch."

Hartz got up and walked quickly across the resilient carpet that gave his steps a falsely youthful bounce. There was a waist-high counter on the far side of the room, with a slanting glass screen on it. Nervously Hartz punched a button, and a map of a section of the city sprang out in bold lines on its surface.

"I've got to find a sector where a Fury's in operation now," he explained. The map flickered and he pressed the button again. The unstable outlines of the city streets wavered and brightened and then went out as he scanned the sections fast and nervously. Then a map flashed on which had three wavering streaks of colored light criss-crossing it, intersecting at one point near the center. The point moved very slowly across the map, at just about the speed of a walking man reduced to miniature in scale with the street he walked on. Around him the colored lines wheeled slowly, keeping their focus always steady on the single point.

"There," Hartz said, leaning forward to read the printed name of the street. A drop of sweat fell from his forehead on to the glass, and he wiped it uneasily away with his fingertip. "There's a man with a Fury assigned to him. All right, now. I'll show you, Look here."

Above the desk was a news-screen. Hartz clicked it on and watched impatiently while a street scene swam into focus. Crowds, traffic noises, people hurrying, people loitering. And in the middle of the crowd a little oasis of isolation, an island in the sea of humanity. Upon that moving island two occupants dwelt, like a Crusoe and a Friday, alone. One of the two was a haggard man who watched the ground as he walked. The other islander in this deserted spot was a tall, shining man-formed shape that followed at his heels.

As if invisible walls surrounded them, pressing back the crowds they walked through, the two moved in an empty space that closed in behind them, opened up before them. Some of the passers-by stared, some looked away in embarrassment or uneasiness. Some watched with a frank anticipation, wondering perhaps at just what moment the Friday would lift his steel arm and strike the Crusoe dead.

"Watch, now," Hartz said nervously. "Just a minute. I'm going to pull the Fury off this man. Wait." He crossed to his desk, opened a drawer, bent secretively over it. Danner heard a series of clicks from inside, and then the brief chatter of tapped keys. "Now," Hartz said, closing the drawer.

He moved the back of his hand across his forehead. "Warm in here, isn't it? Let's get a closer look. You'll see something happen in a minute."

Back to the news-screen. He flicked the focus switch and the street scene expanded, the man and his pacing jailer swooped upward into close focus. The man's face seemed to partake subtly of the impassive quality of the robot's. You would have thought they had lived a long time together, and perhaps they had. Time is a flexible element, infinitely long sometimes in a very short space.

"Wait until they get out of the crowd," Hartz said. "This mustn't be conspicuous. There, he's turning now." The man, seeming to move at random, wheeled at an alley corner and went down the narrow, dark passage away from the thoroughfare. The eye of the news-screen followed him as closely as the robot.

"So you do have cameras that can do that," Danner said with interest. "I always thought so. How's it done? Are they spotted at every corner, or is it a beam trans—"

"Never mind," Hartz said. "Trade secret. Just watch. We'll have to wait until—no, no! Look, he's going to try it now!"

The man glanced furtively behind him. The robot was just turning the corner in his wake. Hartz darted back to his desk and pulled the drawer open. His hand poised over it, his eyes watched the screen anxiously. It was curious how the man in the alley, though he could have no inkling that other eyes watched, looked up and scanned the sky, gazing directly for a moment into the attentive, hidden camera and the eyes of Hartz and Danner. They saw him take a sudden, deep breath, and break into a run.

From Hartz's drawer sounded a metallic click. The robot, which had moved smoothly into a run the moment the man did, checked itself awkwardly and seemed to totter on its steel for an instant. It slowed. It stopped like an engine grinding to a halt. It stood motionless.

At the edge of the camera's range you could see the man's face, looking backward, mouth open with shock as he saw the impossible happen. The robot stood there in the alley, making indecisive motions as if the new orders Hartz pumped into its mechanisms were grating against inbuilt orders in whatever receptor it had. Then it turned its steel back upon the man in the alley and went smoothly, almost sedately, away down the street, walking as precisely as if it were obeying valid orders, not stripping the very gears of society in its aberrant behavior.

You got one last glimpse of the man's face, looking strangely stricken, as if his last friend in the world had left him.

Hartz switched off the screen. He wiped his forehead again. He went to the glass wall and looked out and down as if he were half afraid the calculators might know what he had done. Looking very small against the background of the metal giants, he said over his shoulder, "Well, Danner?"

Was it well? There had been more talk, of course, more persuasion, a raising of the bribe. But Danner knew his mind had been made up from that moment. A calculated risk, and worth it. Well worth it. Except—

In the deathly silence of the restaurant all motion had stopped. The Fury walked calmly between the tables, threading its shining way, touching no one. Every face blanched, turned towards it. Every mind thought, "Can it be for me?" Even the entirely innocent thought, "This is the first mistake they've ever made, and it's come for me. The first mistake, but there's no appeal and I could never prove a thing." For while guilt had no meaning in this world, punishment did have meaning, and punishment could be blind, striking like the lightning.

Danner between set teeth told himself over and over, "Not for me. I'm safe. I'm protected. It hasn't come for me." And yet he thought how strange it was, what a coincidence, wasn't it, that there should be two murderers here under this expensive glass roof today? Himself, and the one the Fury had come for.

He released his fork and heard it clink on the plate. He looked down at it and the food, and suddenly his mind rejected everything around him and went diving off on a fugitive tangent like an ostrich into sand. He thought about food. How did asparagus grow? What did raw food look like? He had never seen any. Food came ready-cooked out of restaurant kitchens or automatic slots. Potatoes, now. What did they look like? A moist white mash? No, for sometimes they were oval slices, so the thing itself must be oval. But not round. Sometimes you got them in long strips. squared off at the ends. Something quite long and oval, then chopped into even lengths. And white, of course. And they grew underground, he was almost sure. Long, thin roots twining white arms among the pipes and conduits he had seen laid bare when the streets were under repair. How strange that he should be eating something like thin, ineffectual human arms that enbraced the sewers of the city and writhed pallidly where the worms had their being. And where he himself, when the Fury found him, might . . .

He pushed the plate away.

An indescribable, rustling and murmuring in the room lifted his eyes for him as if he were an automaton. The Fury was halfway across the room now, and it was almost funny to see the relief of those whom it had passed by. Two or three of the women had buried their faces in their hands, and one man had slipped quietly from his chair in a dead faint as the Fury's passing released their private dreads back into their hidden wells.

The thing was quite close now. It looked to be about seven feet tall, and its motion was very smooth, which was unexpected when you thought about it. Smoother than human motions. Its feet fell with a heavy, measured tread upon the carpet. Thud, thud, thud. Danner tried impersonally to calculate what it weighed. You always heard that they made no sound except for that terrible tread, but this one creaked very slightly somewhere. It had no features, but the human mind couldn't help sketching in lightly a sort of airy face upon that blank steel surface, with eyes that seemed to search the room.

It was coming closer. Now all eyes were converging towards Danner. And the Fury came straight on. It almost looked as if—

"No!" Danner said to himself. "Oh, no, this can't be!" He felt like a man in a nightmare, on the verge of waking. "Let me wake soon," he thought. "Let me wake *now*, before it gets here!"

But he did not wake. And now the thing stood over him, and the thudding footsteps stopped. There was the faintest possible creaking as it towered over his table, motionless, waiting, its featureless face turned towards his.

Danner felt an intolerable tide of heat surge up into his face—rage, shame, disbelief. His heart pounded so hard the room swam and a sudden pain like jagged lightning shot through his head from temple to temple.

He was on his feet, shouting.

"No, no!" he yelled at the impassive steel. "You're wrong! You've made a mistake! Go away, you damned fool! You're wrong, you're wrong!" He groped on the table without looking down, found his plate and hurled it straight at the armored chest before him. China shattered. Spilled food smeared a white and green and brown stain over the steel. Danner floundered out of his chair, around the table, past the tall metal figure towards the door.

All he could think of now was Hartz.

Seas of faces swam by him on both sides as he stumbled out of the restaurant. Some watched with avid curiosity, their eyes seeking him. Some did not look at all, but gazed at their plates rigidly or covered their faces with their hands. Behind him the measured tread came on, and the rhythmic faint creak from somewhere inside the armor.

The faces fell away on both sides and he went through a door without any awareness of opening it. He was in the street. Sweat bathed him and the air struck icy, though it was not a cold day. He looked blindly left and right, and then plunged for a bank of phone booths half a block away, the image of Hartz swimming before his eyes so clearly he blundered into people without seeing them. Dimly he heard indignant voices begin to speak and then die into awestruck silence. The way cleared magically before him. He walked in the newly created island of his isolation up to the nearest booth.

After he had closed the glass door the thunder of his own blood in his ears made the little sound-proofed booth reverberate. Through the door he saw the robot stand passionlessly waiting, the smear of spilled food still streaking its chest like some robotic ribbon of honor across a steel shirtfront.

Danner tried to dial a number. His fingers were like rubber. He breathed deep and hard, trying to pull himself together. An irrelevant thought floated across the surface of his mind. *I forgot to pay for my dinner.* And then: *A lot of good the money will do me now. Oh, damn Hartz, damn him, damn him!*

He got the number.

A girl's face flashed into sharp, clear colors on the screen before him. Good, expensive screens in the public booths in this part of town, his mind noted impersonally.

"This is Controller Hartz's office. May I help you?"

Danner tried twice before he could give his name. He wondered if the girl could see him, and behind him, dimly through the glass, the tall waiting figure. He couldn't tell, because she dropped her eyes immediately to what must have been a list on the unseen table before her.

"I'm sorry. Mr. Hartz is out. He won't be back today."

The screen drained of light and color.

Danner folded back the door and stood up. His knees were unsteady. The robot stood just far enough back to clear the hinge of the door. For a moment they faced each other. Danner heard himself suddenly in the midst of an uncontrollable giggling which even he realized verged on hysteria. The robot with the smear of food like a ribbon of honor looked so ridiculous. Danner to his dim surprise found that all this while he had been clutching the restaurant napkin in his left hand.

"Stand back," he said to the robot. "Let me out. Oh, you fool, don't you know this is a mistake?" His voice quavered. The robot creaked faintly and stepped back.

"It's bad enough to have you follow me," Danner said. "At least, you might be clean. A dirty robot is too much— too much—" The thought was idiotically unbearable, and he heard tears in his voice. Half-laughing, half-weeping, he wiped the steel chest clean and threw the napkin to the floor.

And it was at that very instant, with the feel of the hard chest still vivid in his memory, that realization finally broke through the protective screen of hysteria, and he remembered the truth. He would never in life be alone again. Never while he drew breath. And when he died, it would be at these steel hands, perhaps upon this steel chest, with the passionless face bent to his, the last thing in life he would ever see. No human companion, but the black steel skull of the Fury.

It took him nearly a week to reach Hartz. During the week, he changed his mind about how long it might take a man followed by a Fury to go mad. The last thing he saw at night was the street light shining through the curtains of his expensive hotel suite upon the metal shoulder of his jailer. All night long, waking from uneasy slumber, he could hear the faint creaking of some inward mechanism functioning under the armor. And each time he woke it was to wonder whether he would ever wake again. Would the blow fall while he slept? And what kind of blow? How did the Furies execute? It was always a faint relief to see the bleak light of early morning shine upon the watcher by his bed. At least he had lived through the night. But was this living? And was it worth the burden?

He kept his hotel suite. Perhaps the management would have liked him to go, but nothing was said. Possibly they didn't dare. Life took on a strange, transparent quality, like something seen through an invisible wall. Outside of trying to reach Hartz, there was nothing Danner wanted to do. The old desires for luxuries, entertainment, travel, had melted away. He wouldn't have travelled alone.

He did spend hours in the public library, reading all that was available about the Furies. It was here that he first encountered the two haunting and frightening lines Milton wrote when the world was small and simple—mystifying lines that made no certain sense to anybody until man created a Fury out of steel, in his own image.

> But that two-handed engine at the door
> Stands ready to smite once, and smite no more . . .

Danner glanced up at his own two-handed engine, motionless at his shoulder, and thought of Milton and the long-ago times when life was simple and easy. He tried to picture the past. The twentieth century, when all civilizations together crashed over the brink in one majestic downfall to chaos. And the time before that, when people were . . . different, somehow. But how? It was too far and too strange. He could not imagine the time before the machines.

But he learned for the first time what had really happened, back there in his early years, when the bright world finally blinked out entirely and gray drudgery began. And the Furies were first forged in the likeness of man.

Before the really big wars began, technology advanced to the point where machines bred upon machines like living things, and there might have been an Eden on earth, with everybody's wants fully supplied, except that the social sciences fell too far behind the physical sciences. When the decimating wars came on, machines and people fought side by side, steel against steel and man against man, but man was the more perishable. The wars ended when there were no longer two societies left to fight against each other. Societies splintered apart into smaller and smaller groups until a state very close to anarchy set in.

The machines licked their metal wounds meanwhile and healed each other as they had been built to do. They had no need for the social sciences. They went on calmly reproducing themselves and handing out to mankind the luxuries which the age of Eden had designed them to hand out. Imperfectly of course. Incompletely, because some of their species were wiped out entirely and left no machines to breed and reproduce their kind. But most of them mined their raw materials, refined them, poured and cast the needed parts, made their own fuel, repaired their own injuries and maintained their breed upon the face of the earth with an efficiency man never even approached.

Meanwhile mankind splintered and splintered away. There were no longer any real groups, not even families. Men didn't need each other much. Emotional attachments dwindled. Men had been conditioned to accept vicarious surrogates and escapism was fatally easy. Men reoriented their emotions to the Escape Machines that fed them joyous, impossible adventure and made the waking world seem too dull to bother with. And the birth rate fell and fell. It was a very strange period. Luxury and chaos went hand in hand, anarchy and inertia were the same thing. And still the birth rate dropped . . .

Eventually a few people recognized what was happening. Man as a species was on the way out. And man was helpless to do anything about it. But he had a powerful servant. So the time came when some unsung genius saw what would have to be done. Someone saw the situation clearly and set a new pattern in the biggest of the surviving electronic calculators. This was the goal he set: "Mankind must be made self-responsible again. You will make this your only goal until you achieve the end."

It was simple, but the changes it produced were worldwide and all human life on the planet altered drastically because of it. The machines were an integrated society, if man was not. And now they had a single set of orders which all of them reorganized to obey.

So the days of the free luxuries ended. The Escape Machines shut up shop. Men were forced back into groups for the sake of survival. They had to undertake now the work the machines withheld, and slowly, slowly, common needs and common interests began to spawn the almost lost feeling of human unity again.

But it was so slow. And no machine could put back into man what he had lost—the internalized conscience. Individualism had reached its ultimate stage and there had been no deterrent to crime for a long while. Without family or clan relations, not even feud retaliation occurred. Conscience failed, since no man identified with any other.

The real job of the machines now was to rebuild in man a realistic superego to save him from extinction. A self-responsible society would be a genuinely interdependent one, the leader identifying with the group, and a realistically internalized conscience which would forbid and punish "sin" —the sin of injuring the group with which you identify.

And here the Furies came in.

The machines defined murder, under any circumstances, as the only human crime. This was accurate enough, since it is the only act which can irreplaceably destroy a unit of society.

The Furies couldn't prevent crime. Punishment never cures the criminal. But it can prevent others from committing crime through simple fear, when they see punishment administered to others. The Furies were the symbol of punishment. They overtly stalked the streets on the heels of their condemned victims, the outward and visible sign that murder is always punished, and punished most publicly and terribly. They were very efficient. They were never wrong. Or at least, in theory they were never wrong, and considering the enormous quantities of information stored by now in the analog computers, it seemed likely that the justice of the machines was far more efficient than that of humans could be.

Some day man would rediscover sin. Without it he had come near to perishing entirely. With it, he might resume his authority over himself and the race of mechanized servants who were helping him to restore his species. But until that day, the Furies would have to stalk the streets, man's conscience in metal guise, imposed by the machines man created a long time ago.

What Danner did during this time he scarcely knew. He thought a great deal of the old days when the Escape Machines still worked, before the machines rationed luxuries. He thought of this sullenly and with resentment, for he could see no point at all in the experiment mankind was embarked on. He had liked it better in the old days. And there were no Furies then, either.

He drank a good deal. Once he emptied his pockets into the hat of a legless beggar, because the man like himself was set apart from society by something new and terrible. For Danner it was the Fury. For the beggar it was life itself. Thirty years ago he would have lived or died unheeded, tended only by machines. That a beggar could survive at all, by begging, must be a sign that society was beginning to feel twinges of awakened fellow feeling with its members, but to Danner that meant nothing. He wouldn't be around long enough to know how the story came out.

He wanted to talk to the beggar, though the man tried to wheel himself away on his little platform.

"Listen," Danner said urgently, following, searching his pockets. "I want to tell you. It doesn't feel the way you think it would. It feels—"

He was quite drunk that night, and he followed the beggar until the man threw the money back at him and thrust himself away rapidly on his wheeled platform, while Danner leaned against a building and tried to believe in its solidity. But only the shadow of the Fury, falling across him from the street lamp, was real.

Later that night, somewhere in the dark, he attacked the Fury. He seemed to remember finding a length of pipe somewhere, and he struck showers of sparks from the great, impervious shoulders above him. Then he ran, doubling and twisting up alleys, and in the end he hid in a dark doorway, waiting, until the steady footsteps resounded through the night.

He fell asleep, exhausted.

It was the next day that he finally reached Hartz.

"What went wrong?" Danner asked. In the past week he had changed a good deal. His face was taking on, in its impassivity, an odd resemblance to the metal mask of the robot.

Hartz struck the desk edge a nervous blow, grimacing when he hurt his hand. The room seemed to be vibrating not with the pulse of the machines below but with his own tense energy.

"*Something* went wrong," he said. "I don't know yet. I—"

"You don't know!" Danner lost part of his impassivity.

"Now wait." Hartz made soothing motions with his hands. "Just hang on a little longer. It'll be all right. You can—"

"How much longer have I got?" Danner asked. He looked over his shoulder at the tall Fury standing behind him, as if he were really asking the question of it, not Hartz. There was a feeling, somehow, about the way he said it that made you think he must have asked that question many times, looking up into the blank steel face, and would go on asking hopelessly until the answer came at last. But not in words . . .

"I can't even find that out," Hartz said. "Damn it, Danner, this was a risk. You knew that."

"You said you could control the computer. I saw you do it. I want to know why you didn't do what you promised."

"Something went wrong, I tell you. It should have worked. The minute this—business—came up I fed in the data that should have protected you."

"But what happened?"

Hartz got up and began to pace the resilient flooring. "I just don't know. We don't understand the potentiality of the machines, that's all. I thought I could do it. But—"

"You *thought!*"

"I know I can do it. I'm still trying. I'm trying everything. After all, this is important to me, too. I'm working as fast as I can. That's why I couldn't see you before. I'm certain I can do it, if I can work this out my own way. Damn it, Danner, it's complex. And it's not like juggling a comptometer. Look at those things out there."

Danner didn't bother to look.

"You'd better do it," he said. "That's all."

Hartz said furiously. "Don't threaten me! Let me alone and I'll work it out. But don't threaten me."

"You're in this too," Danner said.

Hartz went back to his desk and sat down on the edge of it.

"How?" he asked.

"O'Reilly's dead. You paid me to kill him."

Hartz shrugged. "The Fury knows that," he said. "The computers know it. And it doesn't matter a damn bit. Your hand pulled the trigger, not mine."

"We're both guilty. If I suffer for it, you—"

"Now wait a minute. Get this straight. I thought you knew it. It's a basis of law enforcement, and always has been. Nobody's punished for intention. Only for actions. I'm no more responsible for O'Reilly's death than the gun you used on him."

"But you lied to me! You tricked me! I'll—"

"You'll do as I say, if you want to save yourself. I didn't trick you, I just made a mistake. Give me time and I'll retrieve it."

"How long?"

This time both men looked at the Fury. It stood impassive.

"I don't know how long," Danner answered his own question. "You say you don't. Nobody even knows how he'll kill me, when the time comes. I've been reading everything that's available to the public about this. Is it true that the method varies, just to keep people like me on tenterhooks? And the time allowed—doesn't that vary too?"

"Yes, it's true. But there's a minimum time—I'm almost sure. You must still be within it. Believe me, Danner, I can still call off the Fury. You saw me do it. You know it worked once. All I've got to find out is what went wrong this time. But the more you bother me the more I'll be delayed. I'll get in touch with you. Don't try to see me again."

Danner was on his feet. He took a few quick steps towards Hartz, fury and frustration breaking up the impassive mask which despair had been forming over his face. But the solemn footsteps of the Fury sounded behind him. He stopped.

The two men looked at each other.

"Give me time," Hartz said. "Trust me, Danner."

In a way it was worse, having hope. There must until now have been a kind of numbness of despair that had kept him from feeling too much. But now there was a chance that after all he might escape into the bright and new life he had risked so much for—if Hartz could save him in time.

Now, for a period, he began to savor experience again. He bought new clothes. He travelled, though never, of course, alone. He even sought human companionship again and found it—after a fashion. But the kind of people willing to associate with a man under this sort of death sentence was not a very appealing type. He found, for instance, that some women felt strongly attracted to him, not because of himself or his money, but for the sake of his companion. They seemed enthralled by the opportunity for a close, safe brush with the very instrument of destiny. Over his very shoulder, sometimes, he would realize they watched the Fury in an ecstasy of fascinated anticipation. In a strange reaction of jealousy, he dropped such people as soon as he recognized the first coldly flirtatious glance one of them cast at the robot behind him.

He tried farther travel. He took the rocket to Africa, and came back by way of the rain-forests of South America, but neither the night clubs nor the exotic newness of strange places seemed to touch him in any way that mattered. The sunlight looked much the same, reflecting from the curved steel surfaces of his follower, whether it shone over lion-colored savannahs or filtered through the hanging gardens of the jungles. All novelty grew dull quickly because of the dreadfully familiar thing that stood for ever at his shoulder. He could enjoy nothing at all.

And the rhythmic beat of footfalls behind him began to grow unendurable. He used earplugs, but the heavy vibration throbbed through his skull in a constant measure like an eternal headache. Even when the Fury stood still, he could hear in his head the imaginary beating of its steps.

He bought weapons and tried to destroy the robot. Of course he failed. And even if he succeeded he knew another would be assigned to him. Liquor and drugs were no good. Suicide came more and more often into his mind, but he postponed that thought, because Hartz had said there was still hope.

In the end, he came back to the city to be near Hartz— and hope. Again he found himself spending most of his time in the library, walking no more than he had to because of the footsteps that thudded behind him. And it was here, one morning, that he found the answer . . .

He had gone through all available factual material about the Furies. He had gone through all the literary references collated under that heading, astonished to find how many there were and how apt some of them had become—like Milton's two-handed engine—after the lapse of all these centuries. *"Those strong feet that followed, followed after,"* he read, *". . . with unhurrying chase, And unperturbed pace, Deliberate speed, majestic instancy. . . ."* He turned the page and saw himself and his plight more literally than any allegory:

> *I shook the pillaring hours*
> *And pulled the life upon me; grimed with smears,*
> *I stand amid the dust of the mounded years—*
> *My mangled youth lies dead beneath the heap.*

He let several tears of self-pity fall upon the page that pictured him so clearly.

But then he passed on from literary references to the library's store of filmed plays, because some of them were cross-indexed under the heading he sought. He watched Orestes hounded in modern dress from Argos to Athens with a single seven-foot robot Fury at his heels instead of the three snake-haired Erinyes of legend. There had been an outburst of plays on the theme when the Furies first came into usage. Sunk in a half-dream of his own boyhood memories when the Escape Machines still operated, Danner lost himself in the action of the films.

He lost himself so completely that when the familiar scene first flashed by him in the viewing booth he hardly questioned it. The whole experience was part of a familiar boyhood pattern and he was not at first surprised to find one scene more vividly familiar than the rest. But then memory rang a bell in his mind and he sat up sharply and brought his fist down with a bang on the stop-action button. He spun the film back and ran the scene over again.

It showed a man walking with his Fury through city traffic, the two of them moving in a little desert island of their own making, like a Crusoe with a Friday at his heels . . . It showed the man turn into an alley, glance up at the camera anxiously, take a deep breath and break into a sudden run. It showed the Fury hesitate, make indecisive motions and then turn and walk quietly and calmly away in the other direction, its feet ringing on the pavement hollowly . . .

Danner spun the film back again and ran the scene once more, just to make doubly sure. He was shaking so hard he could scarcely manipulate the viewer.

"How do you like that?" he muttered to the Fury behind him in the dim booth. He had by now formed a habit of talking to the Fury a good deal, in a rapid, mumbling undertone, not really aware he did it. "What do you make of that, you? Seen it before, haven't you? Familiar, isn't it? Isn't it! *Isn't it!* Answer me, you damned dumb hulk!" And reaching backward, he struck the robot across the chest as he would have struck Hartz if he could. The blow made a hollow sound in the booth, but the robot made no other response, though when Danner looked back inquiringly at it, he saw the reflections of the over-familiar scene, running a third time on the screen, running in tiny reflection across the robot's chest and faceless head, as if it too remembered.

So now he knew the answer. And Hartz had never possessed the power he claimed. Or if he did, had no intention of using it to help Danner. Why should he? His risk was over now. No wonder Hartz had been so nervous, running that film-strip off on a news-screen in his office. But the anxiety sprang not from the dangerous thing he was tampering with, but from sheer strain in matching his activities to the action in the play. How he must have rehearsed it, timing every move! And how he must have laughed, afterwards.

"How long have I got?" Danner demanded fiercely, striking a hollow reverberation from the robot's chest. "How long? Answer me! Long enough?"

Release from hope was an ecstasy, now. He need not wait any longer. He need not try any more. All he had to do was get to Hartz and get there fast, before his own time ran out. He thought with revulsion of all the days he had wasted already, in travel and time-killing, when for all he knew his own last minutes might be draining away now. Before Hartz's did.

"Come along," he said needlessly to the Fury. "Hurry!"

It came, matching its speed to his, the enigmatic timer inside it ticking the moments away towards that instant when the two-handed engine would smite once, and smite no more.

Hartz sat in the Controller's office behind a brand-new desk, looking down from the very top of the pyramid now over the banks of computers that kept society running and cracked the whip over mankind. He sighed with deep content.

The only thing was, he found himself thinking a good deal about Danner. Dreaming of him, even. Not with guilt, because guilt implies conscience, and the long schooling in anarchic individualism was still deep in the roots of every man's mind. But with uneasiness, perhaps.

Thinking of Danner, he leaned back and unlocked a small drawer which he had transferred from his old desk to the new. He slid his hand in and let his fingers touch the controls lightly, idly. Quite idly.

Two movements, and he could save Danner's life. For, of course, he had lied to Danner straight through. He could control the Furies very easily. He could save Danner, but he had never intended to. There was no need. And the thing was dangerous. You tamper once with a mechanism as complex as that which controlled society, and there would be no telling where the maladjustment might end. Chain-reaction, maybe, throwing the whole organization out of kilter. No.

He might some day have to use the device in the drawer. He hoped not. He pushed the drawer shut quickly, and heard the soft click of the lock.

He was Controller now. Guardian, in a sense, of the machines which were faithful in a way no man could ever be. *Quis custodiet,* Hartz thought. The old problem. And the answer was: Nobody. Nobody, today. He himself had no superiors and his power was absolute. Because of this little mechanism in the drawer, nobody controlled the Controller. Not an internal conscience, and not an external one. Nothing could touch him . . .

Hearing the footsteps on the stairs, he thought for a moment he must be dreaming. He had sometimes dreamed that he was Danner, with those relentless footfalls thudding after him. But he was awake now.

It was strange that he caught the almost subsonic beat of the approaching metal feet before he heard the storming steps of Danner rushing up his private stairs. The whole thing happened so fast that time seemed to have no connection with it. First he heard the heavy, subsonic beat, then the sudden tumult of shouts and banging doors downstairs, and then last of all the thump, thump of Danner charging up the stairs, his steps so perfectly matched by the heavier thud of the robot's that the metal trampling drowned out the tramp of flesh and bone and leather.

Then Danner flung the door open with a crash, and the shouts and tramplings from below funnelled upward into the quiet office like a cyclone rushing towards the hearer. But a cyclone in a nightmare, because it would never get any nearer. Time had stopped.

Time had stopped with Danner in the doorway, his face convulsed, both hands holding the revolver because he shook so badly he could not brace it with one.

Hartz acted without any more thought than a robot. He had dreamed of this moment too often, in one form or another. If he could have tampered with the Fury to the extent of hurrying Danner's death, he would have done it. But he didn't know how. He could only wait it out, as anxiously as Danner himself, hoping against hope that the blow would fall and the executioner strike before Danner guessed the truth. Or gave up hope.

So Hartz was ready when trouble came. He found his

own gun in his hand without the least recollection of having opened the drawer. The trouble was that time had stopped. He knew, in the back of his mind, that the Fury must stop Danner from injuring anybody. But Danner stood in the doorway alone, the revolver in both shaking hands. And farther back, behind the knowledge of the Fury's duty, Hartz's mind held the knowledge that the machines could be stopped. The Furies could fail. He dared not trust his life to their incorruptibility, because he himself was the source of a corruption that could stop them in their tracks.

The gun was in his hand without his knowledge. The trigger pressed his finger and the revolver kicked back against his palm, and the spurt of the explosion made the air hiss between him and Danner.

He heard his bullet clang on metal.

Time started again, running double-pace to catch up. The Fury had been no more than a single pace behind Danner after all, because its steel arm encircled him and its steel hand was deflecting Danner's gun. Danner had fired, yes, but not soon enough. Not before the Fury reached him. Hartz's bullet struck first.

It struck Danner in the chest, exploding through him, and rang upon the steel chest of the Fury behind him. Danner's face smoothed out into a blankness as complete as the blankness of the mask above his head. He slumped backwards, not falling because of the robot's embrace, but slowly slipping to the floor between the Fury's arm and its impervious metal body. His revolver thumped softly to the carpet. Blood welled from his chest and back.

The robot stood there impassive, a streak of Danner's blood slanting across its metal chest like a robotic ribbon of honor.

The Fury and the Controller of the Furies stood staring at each other. And the Fury could not, of course, speak, but in Hartz's mind it seemed to.

"Self-defence is no excuse," the Fury seemed to be saying. "We never punish intent, but we always punish action. Any act of murder. Any act of murder."

Hartz barely had time to drop his revolver in his desk drawer before the first of the clamorous crowd from downstairs came bursting through the door. He barely had the presence of mind to do it, either. He had not really thought the thing through this far.

It was, on the surface, a clear case of suicide. In a slightly unsteady voice he heard himself explaining. Everybody had seen the madman rushing through the office, his Fury at his heels. This wouldn't be the first time a killer and his Fury had tried to get at the Controller, begging him to call off the jailer and forestall the executioner. What had happened, Hartz told his underlings calmly enough, was that the Fury had naturally stopped the man from shooting Hartz. And the victim had then turned his gun upon himself. Powder-burns on his clothing showed it. (The desk was very near the door.) Back-blast in the skin of Danner's hands would show he had really fired a gun.

Suicide. It would satisfy any human. But it would not satisfy the computers.

They carried the dead man out. They left Hartz and the Fury alone, still facing each other across the desk. If anyone thought this was strange, nobody showed it.

Hartz himself didn't know if it was strange or not. Nothing like this had ever happened before. Nobody had ever been fool enough to commit murder in the very presence of a Fury. Even the Controller did not know exactly how the computers assessed evidence and fixed guilt. Should this Fury have been recalled, normally? If Danner's death were really suicide, would Hartz stand here alone now?

He knew the machines were already processing the evidence of what had really happened here. What he couldn't be sure of was whether this Fury had already received its orders and would follow him wherever he went from now on until the hour of his death. Or whether it simply stood motionless, waiting recall.

Well, it didn't matter. This Fury or another was already, in the present moment, in the process of receiving instructions about him. There was only one thing to do. Thank God there was something he *could* do.

So Hartz unlocked the desk drawer and slid it open, touched the clicking keys he had never expected to use. Very carefully he fed the coded information, digit by digit, into the computers. As he did, he looked out through the glass wall and imagined he could see down there in the hidden tapes the units of data fading into blankness and the new, false information flashing into existence.

He looked up at the robot. He smiled a little.

"Now you'll forget," he said. "You and the computers. You can go now. I won't be seeing you again."

Either the computers worked incredibly fast—as of course they did—or pure coincidence took over, because in only a moment or two the Fury moved as if in response to Hartz's dismissal. It had stood quite motionless since Danner slid through its arms. Now new orders animated it, and briefly its motion was almost jerky as it changed from one set of instructions to another. It almost seemed to bow, a stiff little bending motion that brought its head down to a level with Hartz's.

He saw his own face reflected in the blank face of the Fury. You could very nearly read an ironic note in that stiff bow, with the diplomat's ribbon of honor across the chest of the creature, symbol of duty discharged honorably. But there was nothing honorable about this withdrawal. The incorruptible metal was putting on corruption and looking back at Hartz with the reflection of his own face.

He watched it stalk towards the door. He heard it go thudding evenly down the stairs. He could feel the thuds vibrate in the floor, and there was a sudden sick dizziness in him when he thought the whole fabric of society was shaking under his feet.

The machines were corruptible.

Mankind's survival still depended on the computers, and the computers could not be trusted. Hartz looked down and saw that his hands were shaking. He shut the drawer and heard the lock click softly. He gazed at his hands. He felt their shaking echoed in an inner shaking, a terrifying sense of the instability of the world.

A sudden, appalling loneliness swept over him like a cold wind. He had never felt before so urgent a need for the companionship of his own kind. No one person, but people. Just people. The sense of human beings all around him, a very primitive need.

He got his hat and coat and went downstairs rapidly, hands deep in his pockets because of some inner chill no coat could guard against. Halfway down the stairs he stopped dead still.

There were footsteps behind him.

He dared not look back at first. He knew those footsteps. But he had two fears and he didn't know which was worse. The fear that a Fury was after him—and the fear that it was not. There would be a sort of insane relief if it really was, because then he could trust the machines after all, and this terrible loneliness might pass over him and go.

He took another downward step, not looking back. He heard the ominous footfall behind him, echoing his own. He sighed one deep sigh and looked back.

There was nothing on the stairs.

He went on down after a timeless pause, watching over his shoulder. He could hear the relentless feet thudding behind him, but no visible Fury followed. No visible Fury.

The Erinyes had struck inward again, and an invisible Fury of the mind followed Hartz down the stairs.

It was as if sin had come anew into the world, and the first man felt again the first inward guilt. So the computers had not failed, after all.

Hartz went slowly down the steps and out into the street, still hearing as he would always hear the relentless, incorruptible footsteps behind him that no longer rang like metal.

The Proud Robot

THINGS OFTEN HAPPENED to Gallegher, who played at science by ear. He was, as he often remarked, a casual genius. Sometimes he'd start with a twist of wire, a few batteries, and a button hook, and before he finished, he might contrive a new type of refrigerating unit.

At the moment he was nursing a hangover. A disjointed, lanky, vaguely boneless man with a lock of dark hair falling untidily over his forehead, he lay on the couch in the lab and manipulated his mechanical liquor bar. A very dry Martini drizzled slowly from the spigot into his receptive mouth.

He was trying to remember something, but not trying too hard. It had to do with the robot, of course. Well, it didn't matter.

"Hey, Joe," Gallegher said.

The robot stood proudly before the mirror and examined its innards. Its hull was transparent, and wheels were going around at a great rate inside.

"When you call me that," Joe remarked, "whisper. And get that cat out of here."

"Your ears aren't that good."

"They are. I can hear the cat walking about, all right."

"What does it sound like?" Gallegher inquired, interested.

"Just like drums," said the robot, with a put-upon air. "And when you talk, it's like thunder." Joe's voice was a discordant squeak, so Gallegher meditated on saying something about glass houses and casting the first stone. He brought his attention, with some effort, to the luminous door panel, where a shadow loomed—a familiar shadow, Gallegher thought.

"It's Brock," the annunciator said. "Harrison Brock. Let me in!"

"The door's unlocked." Gallegher didn't stir. He looked gravely at the well-dressed, middle-aged man who came in, and tried to remember. Brock was between forty and fifty; he had a smoothly massaged, clean-shaven face, and wore an expression of harassed intolerance. Probably Gallegher knew the man. He wasn't sure. Oh, well.

Brock looked around the big, untidy laboratory, blinked at the robot, searched for a chair, and failed to find it. Arms akimbo, he rocked back and forth and glared at the prostrate scientist.

"Well?" he said.

"Never start conversations that way," Gallegher mumbled, siphoning another Martini down his gullet. "I've had enough trouble today. Sit down and take it easy. There's a dynamo behind you. It isn't very dusty, is it?"

"Did you get it?" Brock snapped. "That's all I want to know. You've had a week. I've a check for ten thousand in my pocket. Do you want it, or don't you?"

"Sure," Gallegher said. He extended a large, groping hand. "Give."

Caveat emptor. What am I buying?"

"Don't you know?" the scientist asked, honestly puzzled.

Brock began to bounce up and down in a harassed fashion. "My God," he said. "They told me you could help me if anybody could. Sure. And they also said it'd be like pulling teeth to get sense out of you. Are you a technician or a drivelling idiot?"

Gallegher pondered. "Wait a minute. I'm beginning to remember. I talked to you last week, didn't I?"

"You talked—" Brock's round face turned pink. "Yes! You lay there swilling liquor and babbled poetry. You sang 'Frankie and Johnnie.' And you finally got around to accepting my commission."

"The fact is," Gallegher said, "I have been drunk. I often get drunk. Especially on my vacation. It releases my subconscious, and then I can work. I've made my best gadgets when I was tizzied," he went on happily. "Everything seems so clear then. Clear as a bell. I mean a bell, don't I? Anyway—" He lost the thread and looked puzzled. "Anyway, what are you talking about?"

"Are you going to keep quiet?" the robot demanded from its post before the mirror.

Brock jumped. Gallegher waved a casual hand. "Don't mind Joe. I just finished him last night, and I rather regret it."

"A robot?"

"A robot. But he's no good, you know. I made him when I was drunk, and I haven't the slightest idea how or why. All he'll do is stand there and admire himself. And sing. He sings like a banshee. You'll hear him presently."

With an effort Brock brought his attention back to the matter in hand. "Now look, Gallegher. I'm in a spot. You promised to help me. If you don't, I'm a ruined man."

"I've been ruined for years," the scientist remarked. "It never bothers me. I just go along working for a living and making things in my spare time. Making all sorts of things. You know, if I'd really studied, I'd have been another Einstein. So they tell me. As it is, my subconscious picked up a first-class scientific training somewhere. Probably that's why I never bothered. When I'm drunk or sufficiently absent-minded, I can work out the damnedest problems."

"You're drunk now," Brock accused.

"I approach the pleasanter stages. How would you feel if you woke up and found you'd made a robot for some unknown reason, and hadn't the slightest idea of the creature's attributes?"

"Well—"

"I don't feel that way at all," Gallegher murmured. "Probably you take life too seriously, Brock. Wine is a mocker; strong drink is raging. Pardon me. I rage." He drank another Martini.

Brock began to pace around the crowded laboratory, circling various enigmatic and untidy objects. "If you're a scientist, Heaven help science."

"I'm the Larry Adler of science," Gallegher said. "He was a musician—lived some hundreds of years ago, I think. I'm like him. Never took a lesson in my life. Can I help it if my subconscious likes practical jokes?"

"Do you know who I am?" Brock demanded.

"Candidly, no. Should I?"

There was bitterness in the other's voice. "You might have the courtesy to remember, even though it was a week ago. Harrison Brock. Me. I own Vox-View Pictures."

"No," the robot said suddenly, "it's no use. No use at all, Brock."

"What the—"

Gallegher sighed wearily. "I forget the damned thing's alive. Mr. Brock, meet Joe. Joe, meet Mr. Brock—of Vox-View."

Joe turned, gears meshing within his transparent skull. "I am glad to meet you, Mr. Brock. Allow me to congratulate you on your good fortune in hearing my lovely voice."

"Ugh," said the magnate inarticulately. "Hello."

"Vanity of vanities, all is vanity," Gallegher put in, *sotto voce*. "Joe's like that. A peacock. No use arguing with him either."

The robot ignored this aside. "But it's no use, Mr. Brock," he went on squeakily. "I'm not interested in money. I realize it would bring happiness to many if I consented to appear in your pictures, but fame means nothing to me. Nothing. Consciousness of beauty is enough."

Brock began to chew his lips. "Look," he said savagely, "I didn't come here to offer you a picture job. See? Am I offering you a contract? Such colossal nerve—*Pah!* You're crazy."

"Your schemes are perfectly transparent," the robot remarked coldly. "I can see that you're overwhelmed by my beauty and the loveliness of my voice—its grand tonal qualities. You needn't pretend you don't want me, just so you can get me at a lower price. I said I wasn't interested."

"You're *cr-r-razy!*" Brock howled, badgered beyond endurance, and Joe calmly turned back to his mirror.

"Don't talk so loudly," the robot warned. "The discordance is deafening. Besides you're ugly and I don't like to look at you." Wheels and cogs buzzed inside the transplastic shell. Joe extended his eyes on stalks and regarded himself with every appearance of appreciation.

Gallegher was chuckling quietly on the couch. "Joe has a high irritation value," he said. "I've found that out already. I must have given him some remarkable senses, too.

An hour ago he started to laugh his damn fool head off. No reason, apparently. I was fixing myself a bite to eat. Ten minutes after that I slipped on an apple core I'd thrown away and came down hard. Joe looked at me. 'That was it,' he said. 'Logics of probability. Cause and effect. I knew you were going to drop that apple core and then step on it when you went to pick up the mail.' Like the White Queen, I suppose. It's a poor memory that doesn't work both ways."

Brock sat on the small dynamo—there were two, the larger one named Monstro, and the smaller one serving Gallegher as a bank—and took deep breaths. "Robots are nothing new."

"This one is. I hate its gears. It's beginning to give me an inferiority complex. Wish I knew why I'd made it," Gallegher sighed. "Oh, well. Have a drink?"

"No. I came here on business. Do you seriously mean you spent last week building a robot instead of solving the problem I hired you for?"

"Contingent, wasn't it?" Gallegher asked. "I think I remember that."

"Contingent," Brock said with satisfaction. "Ten thousand, if and when."

"Why not give me the dough and take the robot? He's worth that. Put him in one of your pictures."

"I won't have any pictures unless you figure out an answer," Brock snapped. "I told you all about it."

"I have been drunk," Gallegher said. "My mind has been wiped clear, as by a sponge. I am as a little child. Soon I shall be as a drunken little child. Meanwhile, if you'd care to explain the matter again—"

Brock gulped down his passion, jerked a magazine at random from the bookshelf, and took out a stylo. "All right. My preferred stocks are at twenty-eight, 'way below par—" He scribbled figures on the magazine.

"If you'd taken that medieval folio next to that, it'd have cost you a pretty penny," Gallegher said lazily. "So you're the sort of guy who writes on tablecloths, eh? Forget this business of stocks and stuff. Get down to cases. Who are you trying to gyp?"

"It's no use," the robot said from before its mirror. "I

won't sign a contract. People may come and admire me, if they like, but they'll have to whisper in my presence."

"A madhouse," Brock muttered, trying to get a grip on himself. "Listen, Gallegher. I told you all this a week ago, but—"

"Joe wasn't here then. Pretend like you're talking to him."

"Uh—look. You've heard of Vox-View Pictures, at least."

"Sure. The biggest and best television company in the business. Sonatone's about your only competitor."

"Sonatone's squeezing me out."

Gallegher looked puzzled. "I don't see how. You've got the best product. Tri-dimensional color, all sorts of modern improvements, the top actors, musicians, singers—"

"No use," the robot said. "I won't."

"Shut up, Joe. You're tops in your field, Brock. I'll hand you that. And I've always heard you were fairly ethical. What's Sonatone got on you?"

Brock made helpless gestures. "Oh, it's politics. The bootleg theaters. I can't buck 'em. Sonatone helped elect the present administration, and the police just wink when I try to have the bootleggers raided."

"Bootleg theaters?" Gallegher asked, scowling a trifle. "I've heard something—"

"It goes 'way back. To the old sound-film days. Home television killed sound film and big theaters. People were conditioned away from sitting in audience groups to watch a screen. The home televisors got good. It was more fun to sit in an easy-chair, drink beer, and watch the show. Television wasn't a rich man's hobby by that time. The meter system brought the price down to middle-class levels. Everybody knows that."

"I don't," Gallegher said. "I never pay attention to what goes on outside of my lab, unless I have to. Liquor and a selective mind. I ignore everything that doesn't affect me directly. Explain the whole thing in detail, so I'll get a complete picture. I don't mind repetition. Now, what about this meter system of yours?"

"Televisors are installed free. We never sell 'em; we rent

them. People pay according to how many hours they have the set tuned in. We run a continuous show, stage plays, wire-tape films, operas, orchestras, singers, vaudeville—everything. If you use your televisor a lot, you pay proportionately. The man comes around once a month and reads the meter. Which is a fair system. Anybody can afford a Vox-View. Sonatone and the other companies do the same thing, but Sonatone's the only big competitor I've got. At least, the only one that's crooked as hell. The rest of the boys—they're smaller than I am, but I don't step on their toes. Nobody's ever called me a louse," Brock said darkly.

"So what?"

"So Sonatone has started to depend on audience appeal. It was impossible till lately—you couldn't magnify tri-dimensional television on a big screen without streakiness and mirage-effect. That's why the regular three-by-four home screens were used. Results were perfect. But Sonatone's bought a lot of the ghost theaters all over the country—"

"What's a ghost theater?" Gallegher asked.

"Well—before sound films collapsed, the world was thinking big. Big—you know? Ever heard of the Radio City Music Hall? That wasn't in it! Television was coming in, and competition was fierce. Sound-film theaters got bigger and more elaborate. They were palaces. Tremendous. But when television was perfected, nobody went to the theaters any more, and it was often too expensive a job to tear 'em down. Ghost theaters—see? Big ones and little ones. Renovated them. And they're showing Sonatone programs. Audience appeal is quite a factor. The theaters charge plenty, but people flock into 'em. Novelty and the mob instinct."

Gallegher closed his eyes. "What's to stop you from doing the same thing?"

"Patents," Brock said briefly. "I mentioned that dimensional television couldn't be used on big screens till lately. Sonatone signed an agreement with me ten years ago that any enlarging improvements would be used mutually. They crawled out of that contract. Said it was faked, and the courts upheld them. They uphold the courts—politics. Anyhow, Sonatone's technicians worked out a method of using the large screen. They took out patents—twenty-seven patents, in fact, covering every possible variation on the idea. My technical staff has been working day and night trying to find some similar method that won't be an infringement, but Sonatone's got it all sewed up. They've a system called the Magna. It can be hooked up to any type of televisor—but they'll only allow it to be used on Sonatone machines. See?"

"Unethical, but legal," Gallegher said. "Still, you're giving your customers more for their money. People want good stuff. The size doesn't matter."

"Yeah," Brock said bitterly, "but that isn't all. The newstapes are full of A. A.—it's a new catchword. Audience Appeal. The herd instinct. You're right about people wanting good stuff—but would you buy Scotch at four a quart if you could get it for half that amount?"

"Depends on the quality. What's happening?"

"Bootleg theaters," Brock said. "They've opened all over the country. They show Vox-View products, and they're using the Magna enlarger system Sonatone's got patented. The admission price is low—lower than the rate of owning a Vox-View in your own home. There's audience appeal. There's the thrill of something a bit illegal. People are having their Vox-Views taken out right and left. I know why. They can go to a bootleg theater instead."

"It's illegal," Gallegher said thoughtfully.

"So were speakeasies, in the Prohibition Era. A matter of protection, that's all. I can't get any action through the courts. I've tried. I'm running in the red. Eventually I'll be broke. I can't lower my home rental fees on Vox-Views. They're nominal already. I make my profits through quantity. Now, no profits. As for these bootleg theaters, it's pretty obvious who's backing them."

"Sonatone?"

"Sure. Silent partners. They get the take at the box office. What they want is to squeeze me out of business, so they'll have a monopoly. After that, they'll give the public junk and pay their artists starvation salaries. With me it's different. I pay my staff what they're worth—plenty."

"And you offered me a lousy ten thousand," Gallegher remarked. "Uh-*huh!*"

"That was only the first installment," Brock said hastily.

"You can name your own fee. Within reason," he added.

"I shall. An astronomical sum. Did I say I'd accept the commission a week ago?"

"You did."

"Then I must have had some idea how to solve the problem," Gallegher pondered. "Let's see. I didn't mention anything in particular, did I?"

"You kept talking about marble slabs and . . . uh . . . your sweetie."

"Then I was singing," Gallegher explained largely. " 'St. James Infirmary.' Singing calms my nerves, and God knows they need it sometimes. Music and liquor. I often wonder what the vintners buy——"

"What?"

"One half so precious as the stuff they sell. Let it go. I am quoting Omar. It means nothing. Are your technicians any good?"

"The best. And the best paid."

"They can't find a magnifying process that won't infringe on the Sonatone Magna patents?"

"In a nutshell, that's it."

"I suppose I'll have to do some research," Gallegher said sadly. "I hate it like poison. Still, the sum of the parts equals the whole. Does that make sense to you? It doesn't to me. I have trouble with words. After I say things, I start wondering what I've said. Better than watching a play," he finished wildly. "I've got a headache. Too much talk and not enough liquor. Where were we?"

"Approaching the madhouse," Brock suggested. "If you weren't my last resort, I'd——"

"No use," the robot said squeakily. "You might as well tear up your contract, Brock. I won't sign it. Fame means nothing to me—nothing."

"If you don't shut up," Gallegher warned, "I'm going to scream in your ears."

"All right!" Joe shrilled. "Beat me! Go on, beat me! The meaner you are, the faster I'll have my nervous system disrupted, and then I'll be dead. I don't care. I've got no instinct of self-preservation. Beat me. See if I care."

"He's right, you know," the scientist said after a pause. "And it's the only logical way to respond to blackmail or threats. The sooner it's over, the better. There aren't any gradations with Joe. Anything really painful to him will destroy him. And he doesn't give a damn."

"Neither do I," Brock grunted. "What I want to find out—"

"Yeah. I know. Well, I'll wander around and see what occurs to me. Can I get into your studios?"

"Here's a pass." Brock scribbled something on the back of a card. "Will you get to work on it right away?"

"Sure," Gallegher lied. "Now you run along and take it easy. Try and cool off. Everything's under control. I'll either find a solution to your problem pretty soon or else—"

"Or else what?"

"Or else I won't," the scientist finished blandly, and fingered the buttons on a control panel near the couch. "I'm tired of Martinis. Why didn't I make that robot a mechanical bartender, while I was at it? Even the effort of selecting and pushing buttons is depressing at times. Yeah, I'll get to work on the business, Brock. Forget it."

The magnate hesitated. "Well, you're my only hope. I needn't bother to mention that if there's anything I can do to help you—"

"A blonde," Gallegher murmured. "That gorgeous, gorgeous star of yours, Silver O'Keefe. Send her over. Otherwise I want nothing."

"Good-by, Brock," the robot said squeakily. "Sorry we couldn't get together on the contract, but at least you've had the ineluctable delight of hearing my beautiful voice, not to mention the pleasure of seeing me. Don't tell too many people how lovely I am. I really don't want to be bothered with mobs. They're noisy."

"You don't know what dogmatism means till you've talked to Joe," Gallegher said. "Oh, well. See you later. Don't forget the blonde."

Brock's lips quivered. He searched for words, gave it up as a vain task, and turned to the door.

"Good-by, you ugly man," Joe said.

Gallegher winced as the door slammed, though it was harder on the robot's supersensitive ears than on his own. "Why do you go on like that?" he inquired. "You nearly gave the guy apoplexy."

"Surely he didn't think he was beautiful," Joe remarked.

"Beauty's in the eye of the beholder."

"How stupid you are. You're ugly, too."

"And you're a collection of rattletrap gears, pistons and cogs. You've got worms," said Gallegher, referring of course, to certain mechanisms in the robot's body.

"I'm lovely." Joe stared raptly into the mirror.

"Maybe, to you. Why did I make you transparent, I wonder?"

"So others could admire me. I have X-ray vision, of course."

"And wheels in your head. Why did I put your radio-atomic brain in your stomach? Protection?"

Joe didn't answer. He was humming in a maddeningly squeaky voice, shrill and nerve-racking. Gallegher stood it for a while, fortifying himself with a gin rickey from the siphon.

"Get it up!" he yelped at last. "You sound like an old-fashioned subway train going round a curve."

"You're merely jealous," Joe scoffed, but obediently raised his tone to a supersonic pitch. There was silence for a half-minute. Then all the dogs in the neighborhood began to howl.

Wearily Gallegher dragged his lanky frame up from the couch. He might as well get out. Obviously there was no peace to be had in the laboratory. Not with that animated junk pile inflating his ego all over the place. Joe began to laugh in an off-key cackle. Gallegher winced.

"What now?"

"You'll find out."

Logic of causation and effect, influenced by probabilities, X-ray vision and other enigmatic senses the robot no doubt possessed. Gallegher cursed softly, found a shapeless black hat, and made for the door. He opened it to admit a short, fat man who bounced painfully off the scientist's stomach.

"Whoof! Uh. What a corny sense of humor that jackass has. Hello, Mr. Kennicott. Glad to see you. Sorry I can't offer you a drink."

Mr. Kennicott's swarthy face twisted malignantly. "Don' wanna no drink. Wanna my money. You gimme. Howzabout it?"

Gallegher looked thoughtfully at nothing. "Well, the fact is, I was just going to collect a check."

"I sella you my diamonds. You say you gonna make somet'ing wit' 'em. You gimme check before. It go bounca, bounca, bounca. Why is?"

"It was rubber," Gallegher said faintly. "I never can keep track of my bank balance."

Kennicott showed symptoms of going bounca on the threshold. "You gimme back diamonds, eh?"

"Well, I used 'em in an experiment. I forget just what. You know, Mr. Kennicott, I think I was a little drunk when I bought them, wasn't I?"

"Dronk," the little man agreed. "Mad wit' vino, sure. So whatta? I wait no longer. Awready you put me off too much. Pay up now or elsa."

"Go away, you dirty man," Joe said from within the room. "You're awful."

Gallegher hastily shouldered Kennicott out into the street and latched the door behind him. "A parrot," he explained. "I'm going to wring its neck pretty soon. Now about that money. I admit I owe it to you. I've just taken on a big job, and when I'm paid, you'll get yours."

"Bah to such stuff," Kennicott said. "You gotta position, eh? You are a technician wit' some big company, eh? Ask for ahead-salary."

"I did," Gallegher sighed. "I've drawn my salary for six months ahead. Now look. I'll have that dough for you in a couple of days. Maybe I can get an advance from my client. O.K.?"

"No."

"No?"

"Ah-h, nutsa, I waita one day. Two daysa, maybe. Enough. You get money. Awright. If not, O.K., *calabozo* for you."

"Two days is plenty," Gallegher said, relieved. "Say, are there any of those bootleg theaters around here?"

"Better you get to work an' not waste time."

"That's my work. I'm making a survey. How can I find a bootleg place?"

"Easy. You go downtown, see guy in doorway. He sell you tickets. Anywhere. All over."

"Swell," Gallegher said, and bade the little man adieu. Why had he bought diamonds from Kennicott? It would be almost worthwhile to have his subconscious amputated. It did the most extraordinary things. It worked on inflexible principles of logic, but that logic was completely alien to Gallegher's conscious mind. The results, though, were often surprisingly good, and always surprising. That was the worst of being a scientist who knew no science—who played by ear.

There was diamond dust in a retort in the laboratory, from some unsatisfactory experiment Gallegher's subconscious had performed; and he had a fleeting memory of buying the stones from Kennicott. Curious. Maybe—oh, yeah. They'd gone into Joe. Bearings or something. Dismantling the robot wouldn't help now, for the diamonds had certainly been reground. Why the devil hadn't he used commercial stones, quite as satisfactory, instead of purchasing blue-whites of the finest water? The best was none too good for Gallegher's subconscious. It had a fine freedom from commercial instincts. It just didn't understand the price system of the basic principles of economics.

Gallegher wandered downtown like a Diogenes seeking truth. It was early evening, and the luminates were flickering on overhead, pale bars of light against darkness. A sky sign blazed above Manhattan's towers. Air-taxis, skimming along at various arbitrary levels, paused for passengers at the elevator landings. Heigh-ho.

Downtown, Gallegher began to look for doorways. He found an occupied one at last, but the man was selling postcards. Gallegher declined and headed for the nearest bar, feeling the needs of replenishment. It was a mobile bar, combining the worst features of a Coney Island ride with uninspired cocktails, and Gallegher hesitated on the threshold. But at last he seized a chair as it swung past and relaxed as much as possible. He ordered three rickeys and drank them in rapid succession. After that he called the bartender over and asked him about bootleg theaters.

"Hell, yes," the man said, producing a sheaf of tickets from his apron. "How many?"

"One. Where do I go?"

"Two-twenty-eight. This street. Ask for Tony."

"Thanks," Gallegher said, and having paid exorbitantly,

crawled out of the chair and weaved away. Mobile bars were an improvement he didn't appreciate. Drinking, he felt, should be performed in a state of stasis, since one eventually reached that stage, anyway.

The door was at the bottom of a flight of steps, and there was a grilled panel set in it. When Gallegher knocked, the visascreen lit up—obviously a one-way circuit, for the doorman was invisible.

"Tony here?" Gallegher said.

The door opened, revealing a tired-looking man in pneumo-slacks, which failed in their purpose of building up his skinny figure. "Got a ticket? Let's have it. O.K., bud. Straight ahead. Show now going on. Liquor served in the bar on your left."

Gallegher pushed through soundproofed curtains at the end of a short corridor and found himself in what appeared to be the foyer of an ancient theater, *circa* 1980, when plastics were the great fad. He smelled out the bar, drank expensively priced cheap liquor, and, fortified, entered the theater itself. It was nearly full. The great screen—a Magna, presumably—was filled with people doing things to a spaceship. Either an adventure film or a newsreel, Gallegher realized.

Only the thrill of lawbreaking would have enticed the audience into the bootleg theater. It smelled. It was certainly run on a shoestring, and there were no ushers. But it was illicit, and therefore well patronized. Gallegher looked thoughtfully at the screen. No streakiness, no mirage effect. A Magna enlarger had been fitted to a Vox-View unlicensed televisor, and one of Brock's greatest stars was emoting effectively for the benefit of the bootleggers' patrons. Simple highjacking. Yeah.

After a while Gallegher went out, noticing a uniformed policeman in one of the aisle seats. He grinned sardonically. The flatfoot hadn't paid his admission, of course. Politics were as usual.

Two blocks down the street a blaze of light announced SONATONE BIJOU. This, of course, was one of the legalized theaters, and correspondingly high-priced. Gallegher recklessly squandered a small fortune on a good seat. He was interested in comparing notes, and discovered that, as far as he could make out, the Magna in the Bijou and the bootleg theater were identical. Both did their job perfectly. The difficult task of enlarging television screens had been successfully surmounted.

In the Bijou, however, all was palatial. Resplendent ushers salaamed to the rugs. Bars dispensed free liquor, in reasonable quantities. There was a Turkish bath. Gallegher went through a door labelled MEN and emerged quite dazzled by the splendor of the place. For at least ten minutes afterward he felt like a Sybarite.

All of which meant that those who could afford it went to the legalized Sonatone theaters, and the rest attended the bootleg places. All but a few homebodies, who weren't carried off their feet by the new fad. Eventually Brock would be forced out of business for lack of revenue. Sonatone would take over, jacking up their prices and concentrating on making money. Amusement was necessary to life, people had been conditioned to television. There was no substitute. They'd pay and pay for inferior talent, once Sonatone succeeded in their squeeze.

Gallegher left the Bijou and hailed an air-taxi. He gave the address of Vox-View's Long Island studio, with some vague hope of getting a drawing account out of Brock. Then, too, he wanted to investigate further.

Vox-View's eastern offices sprawled wildly over Long Island, bordering the Sound, a vast collection of variously shaped buildings. Gallegher instinctively found the commissary, where he absorbed more liquor as a precautionary measure. His subconscious had a heavy job ahead, and he didn't want it handicapped by lack of complete freedom. Besides, the Collins was good.

After one drink, he decided he'd had enough for a while. He wasn't a superman, though his capacity was slightly incredible. Just enough for objective clarity and subjective release—

"Is the studio always open at night?" he asked the waiter.

"Sure. Some of the stages, anyway. It's a round-the-clock program."

"The commissary's full."

"We get the airport crowd, too. 'Nother?"

Gallegher shook his head and went out. The card Brock had given him provided entrée at a gate, and he went first of all to the big-shot's office. Brock wasn't there, but loud voices emerged, shrilly feminine.

The secretary said, "Just a minute, please," and used her interoffice visor. Presently—"Will you go in?"

Gallegher did. The office was a honey, functional and luxurious at the same time. Three-dimensional stills were in niches along the walls—Vox-View's biggest stars. A small excited, pretty brunette was sitting behind the desk, and a blonde angel was standing furiously on the other side of it. Gallegher recognized the angel as Silver O'Keefe.

He seized the opportunity. "Hiya, Miss O'Keefe. Will you autograph an ice cube for me? In a highball?"

Silver looked feline. "Sorry, darling, but I'm a working girl. And I'm busy right now."

The brunette scratched a cigarette. "Let's settle this later, Silver. Pop said to see this guy if he dropped in. It's important."

"It'll be settled," Silver said. "And soon." She made an exit. Gallegher whistled thoughtfully at the closed door.

"You can't have it," the brunette said. "It's under contract. And it wants to get out of the contract, so it can sign up with Sonatone. Rats desert a sinking ship. Silver's been kicking her head off ever since she read the storm signals."

"Yeah?"

"Sit down and smoke or something. I'm Patsy Brock. Pop runs this business, and I manage the controls whenever he blows his top. The old goat can't stand trouble. He takes it as a personal affront."

Gallegher found a chair. "So Silver's trying to renege, eh? How many others?"

"Not many. Most of 'em are loyal. But, of course, if we bust up—" Patsy Brock shrugged. "They'll either work for Sonatone for their cakes, or else do without."

"Uh-huh. Well—I want to see your technicians. I want to look over the ideas they've worked out for enlarger screens."

"Suit yourself," Patsy said. "It's not much use. You just can't make a televisor enlarger without infringing on some Sonatone patent."

She pushed a button, murmured something into a visor, and presently two tall glasses appeared through a slot in the desk. "Mr. Gallegher?"

"Well, since it's a Collins—"

"I could tell by your breath," Patsy said enigmatically. "Pop told me he'd seen you. He seemed a bit upset, especially by your new robot. What is it like, anyway?"

"Oh, I don't know," Gallegher said, at a loss. "It's got lots of abilities—new senses, I think—but I haven't the slightest idea what it's good for. Except admiring itself in a mirror."

Patsy nodded. "I'd like to see it sometime. But about this Sonatone business. Do you think you can figure out an answer?"

"Possibly. Probably."

"Not certainly?"

"Certainly, then. Of that there is no manner of doubt— no possible doubt whatever."

"Because it's important to me. The man who owns Sonatone is Elia Tone. A piratical skunk. He blusters. He's got a son named Jimmy. And Jimmy, believe it or not, has read 'Romeo and Juliet.' "

"Nice guy?"

"A louse. A big, brawny louse. He wants me to marry him."

" 'Two families, both alike in—' "

"Spare me," Patsy interrupted. "I always thought Romeo was a dope, anyway. And if I ever thought I was going aisling with Jimmy Tone, I'd buy a one-way ticket to the nut hatch. No, Mr. Gallegher, it's not like that. No hibiscus blossoms. Jimmy has proposed to me—his idea of a proposal, by the way, is to get a half Nelson on a girl and tell her how lucky she is."

"Ah," said Gallegher, diving into his Collins.

"This whole idea—the patent monopoly and the bootleg theaters—is Jimmy's. I'm sure of that. His father's in on it, too, of course, but Jimmy Tone is the bright little boy who started it."

"Why?"

"Two birds with one stone. Sonatone will have a monopoly on the business, and Jimmy thinks he'll get me. He's a little mad. He can't believe I'm in earnest in refusing him, and he expects me to break down and say 'Yes' after a while. Which I won't, no matter what happens. But it's a personal matter. I can't let him put this trick over on us. I want that self-sufficient smirk wiped off his face."

"You just don't like him, eh?" Gallegher remarked. "I don't blame you, if he's like that. Well, I'll do my damnedest. However, I'll need an expense account."

"How much?"

Gallegher named a sum. Patsy styloed a check for a far smaller amount. The scientist looked hurt.

"It's no use," Patsy said, grinning crookedly. "I've heard of you, Mr. Gallegher. You're completely irresponsible. If you had more than this, you'd figure you didn't need any more, and you'd forget the whole matter. I'll issue more checks to you when you need 'em—but I'll want itemized expense accounts."

"You wrong me," Gallegher said, brightening. "I was figuring on taking you to a night club. Naturally I don't want to take you to a dive. The big places cost money. Now if you'll just write another check—"

Patsy laughed. "No."

"Want to buy a robot?"

"Not that kind, anyway."

"Then I'm washed up," Gallegher sighed. "Well, what about—"

At this point the visor hummed. A blank, transparent face grew on the screen. Gears were clicking rapidly inside the round head. Patsy gave a small shriek and shrank back.

"Tell Gallegher Joe's here, you lucky girl," a squeaky voice announced. "You may treasure the sound and sight of me till your dying day. One touch of beauty in a world of drabness—"

Gallegher circled the desk and looked at the screen. "What the hell. How did you come to life?"

"I had a problem to solve."

"How'd you know where to reach me?"

"I vastened you," the robot said.

"What?"

"I vastened you were at the Vox-View studios, with Patsy Brock."

"What's vastened?" Gallegher wanted to know.

"It's a sense I've got. You've nothing remotely like it, so I can't describe it to you. It's like a combination of sagrazi and prescience."

"Sagrazi?"

"Oh, you don't have sagrazi, either, do you. Well, don't waste my time. I want to go back to the mirror."

"Does he always talk like that?" Patsy put in.

"Nearly always. Sometimes it makes even less sense. O.K., Joe. Now what?"

"You're not working for Brock any more," the robot said. "You're working for the Sonatone people."

Gallegher breathed deeply. "Keep talking. You're crazy, though."

"I don't like Kennicott. He annoys me. He's *too* ugly. His vibrations grate on my sagrazi."

"Never mind him," Gallegher said, not wishing to discuss his diamond-buying activities before the girl. "Get back to—"

"But I knew Kennicott would keep coming back till he got his money. So when Elia and James Tone came to the laboratory, I got a check from them."

Patsy's hand gripped Gallegher's biceps. "Steady! What's going on here? The old double cross?"

"No. Wait. Let me get to the bottom of this. Joe, damn your transparent hide, just what did you do? How could you get a check from the Tones?"

"I pretended to be you."

"Sure," Gallegher said with savage sarcasm. "That explains it. We're twins. We look exactly alike."

"I hypnotized them," Joe explained. "I made them think I was you."

"You can do *that?*"

"Yes. It surprised me a bit. Still, if I'd thought, I'd have vastened I could do it."

"You . . . yeah, sure. I'd have vastened the same thing myself. *What happened?*"

"The Tones must have suspected Brock would ask you to help him. They offered an exclusive contract—you work for them and nobody else. Lots of money. Well, I pretended to be you, and said all right. So I signed the contract—it's your signature, by the way—and got a check from them and mailed it to Kennicott."

"The whole check?" Gallegher asked feebly. "How much was it?"

"Twelve thousand."

"They only offered me *that?*"

"No," the robot said, "they offered a hundred thousand, and two thousand a week for five years. But I merely wanted enough to pay Kennicott and make sure he wouldn't come back and bother me. The Tones were satisfied when I said twelve thousand would be enough."

Gallegher made an inarticulate, gurgling sound deep in his throat. Joe nodded thoughtfully.

"I thought I had better notify you that you're working for Sonatone now. Well, I'll go back to the mirror and sing to myself."

"Wait," the scientist said. "Just wait, Joe. With my own two hands I'm going to rip you gear from gear and stamp on your fragments."

"It won't hold in court," Patsy said, gulping.

"It will," Joe told her cheerily. "You may have one last, satisfying look at me, and then I must go." He went.

Gallegher drained his Collins at a draft. "I'm shocked sober," he informed the girl. "What did I put into that robot? What abnormal senses has he got? Hypnotizing people into believing he's me—I'm him—I don't know what I mean."

"Is this a gag?" Patsy said shortly, after a pause. "You didn't sign up with Sonatone yourself, by any chance, and have your robot call up here to give you an out—an alibi? I'm just wondering."

"Don't. Joe signed a contract with Sonatone, not me. But—figure it out: If the signature's a perfect copy of mine, if Joe hypnotized the Tones into thinking they saw me instead of him, if there are witnesses to the signature— the two Tones are witnesses, of course—Oh, hell."

Patsy's eyes were narrowed. "We'll pay you as much as Sonatone offered. On a contingent basis. But you're working for Vox-View—that's understood."

"Sure."

Gallegher looked longingly at his empty glass. Sure. He was working for Vox-View. But, to all legal appearances, he had signed a contract giving his exclusive services to Sonatone for a period of five years—and for a sum of twelve thousand! *Yipe!* What was it they'd offered? A hundred thousand flat, and . . . and—

It wasn't the principle of the thing, it was the money. Now Gallegher was sewed up tighter than a banded pigeon. If Sonatone could win a court suit, he was legally bound to them for five years. With no further emolument. He had to get out of that contract, somehow—and at the same time solve Brock's problem.

Why not Joe? The robot, with his surprising talents, had got Gallegher into this spot. He ought to be able to get the scientist out. He'd better—or the proud robot would soon be admiring himself piecemeal.

"That's it," Gallegher said under his breath. "I'll talk to Joe. Patsy, feed me liquor in a hurry and send me to the technical department. I want to see those blueprints."

The girl looked at him suspiciously. "All right. If you try to sell us out—"

"I've been sold out myself. Sold down the river. I'm afraid of that robot. He's vastened me into quite a spot. That's right, Collinses," Gallegher drank long and deeply.

After that, Patsy took him to the tech offices. The reading of three-dimensional blueprints was facilitated with a scanner—a selective device which eliminated confusion. Gallegher studied the plans long and thoughtfully. There were copies of the patent Sonatone prints, too, and, as far as he could tell, Sonatone had covered the ground beautifully. There weren't any outs. Unless one used an entirely new principle—

But new principles couldn't be plucked out of the air. Nor would that solve the problem completely. Even if Vox-View owned a new type of enlarger that didn't infringe on Sonatone's Magna, the bootleg theaters would still be in existence, pulling the trade. A. A.—audience appeal—was a prime factor now. It had to be considered. The puzzle wasn't a purely scientific one. There was the human equation as well.

Gallegher stored the necessary information in his mind, neatly indexed on shelves. Later he'd use what he wanted. For the moment, he was completely baffled. Something worried him.

What?

The Sonatone affair.

"I want to get in touch with the Tones," he told Patsy. "Any ideas?"

"I can reach 'em on a visor."

Gallegher shook his head. "Psychological handicap. It's too easy to break the connection."

"Well, if you're in a hurry, you'll probably find the boys night clubbing. I'll go see what I can find out." Patsy scuttled off, and Silver O'Keefe appeared from behind a screen.

"I'm shameless," she announced. "I always listen at keyholes. Sometimes I hear interesting things. If you want to see the Tones, they're at the Castle Club. And I think I'll take you up on that drink."

Gallegher said, "O.K. You get a taxi. I'll tell Patsy we're going."

"She'll hate that," Silver remarked. "Meet you outside the commissary in ten minutes. Get a shave while you're at it."

Patsy Brock wasn't in her office, but Gallegher left word. After that, he visited the service lounge, smeared invisible shave cream on his face, left it there for a couple of minutes, and wiped it off with a treated towel. The bristles came away with the cream. Slightly refreshed, Gallegher joined Silver at the rendezvous and hailed an air-taxi. Presently they were leaning back on the cushions, puffing cigarettes and eying each other warily.

"Well?" Gallegher said.

"Jimmy Tone tried to date me up tonight. That's how I knew where to find him."

"Well?"

"I've been asking questions around the lot tonight. It's unusual for an outsider to get into the Vox-View administration offices. I went around saying, 'Who's Gallegher?' "

"What did you find out?"

"Enough to give me a few ideas. Brock hired you, eh? I can guess why."

"*Ergo* what?"

"I've a habit of landing on my feet," Silver said, shrug-

ging. She knew how to shrug. "Vox-View's going bust.
Sonatone's taking over. Unless——"

"Unless I figure out an answer."

"That's right. I want to know which side of the fence I'm
going to land on. You're the lad who can probably tell me.
Who's going to win?"

"You always bet on the winning side, eh?" Gallegher inquired. "Have you no ideals, wench? Is there no truth in
you? Ever hear of ethics and scruples?"

Silver beamed happily. "Did you?"

"Well, I've heard of 'em. Usually I'm too drunk to figure
out what they mean. The trouble is, my subconscious is
completely amoral, and when it takes over, logic's the only
law."

She threw her cigarette into the East River. "Will you tip
me off which side of the fence is the right one?"

"Truth will triumph," Gallegher said piously. "It always
does. However, I figure truth is a variable, so we're right
back where we started. All right, sweetheart. I'll answer
your question. Stay on my side if you want to be safe."

"Which side are you on?"

"God knows," Gallegher said. "Consciously I'm on
Brock's side. But my subconscious may have different
ideas. We'll see."

Silver looked vaguely dissatisfied, but didn't say anything. The taxi swooped down to the Castle roof, ground-
ing with pneumatic gentleness. The Club itself was downstairs, in a immense room shaped like half a melon turned
upside down. Each table was on a transparent platform
that could be raised on its shaft to any height at will.
Smaller service elevators allowed waiters to bring drinks to
the guests. There wasn't any particular reason for this ar-
rangement, but at least it was novel, and only extremely
heavy drinkers ever fell from their tables. Lately the management had taken to hanging transparent nets under the
platforms, for safety's sake.

The Tones, father and son, were up near the roof, drinking with two lovelies. Silver towed Gallegher to a service
lift, and the man closed his eyes as he was elevated skyward. The liquor in his stomach screamed protest. He
lurched forward, clutched at Elia Tone's bald head, and

dropped into a seat beside the magnate. His searching hand found Jimmy Tone's glass, and he drained it hastily.

"What the hell," Jimmy said.

"It's Gallegher," Elia announced. "And Silver. A pleasant surprise. Join us?"

"Only socially," Silver said.

Gallegher, fortified by the liquor, peered at the two men. Jimmy Tone was a big, tanned, handsome lout with a jutting jaw and an offensive grin. His father combined the worst features of Nero and a crocodile.

"We're celebrating," Jimmy said. "What made you change your mind, Silver? You said you had to work tonight."

"Gallegher wanted to see you. I don't know why."

Elia's cold eyes grew even more glacial. "All right. Why?"

"I hear I signed some sort of contract with you," the scientist said.

"Yeah. Here's a photostatic copy. What about it?"

"Wait a minute." Gallegher scanned the document. It was apparently his own signature. Damn that robot! "It's a fake," he said at last.

Jimmy laughed loudly. "I get it. A hold up. Sorry, pal, but you're sewed up. You signed that in the presence of witnesses."

"Well—" Gallegher said wistfully. "I suppose you wouldn't believe me if I said a robot forged my name to it—"

"Haw!" Jimmy remarked.

"—hypnotizing you into believing you were seeing me."

Elia stroked his gleaming bald head. "Candidly, no. Robots can't do that."

"Mine can."

"Prove it. Prove it in court. If you can do that, of course —" Elia chuckled. "Then you might get the verdict."

Gallegher's eyes narrowed. "Hadn't thought of that. However—I hear you offered me a hundred thousand flat, as well as a weekly salary."

"Sure, sap," Jimmy said. "Only you said all you needed was twelve thousand. Which was what you got. Tell you what, though. We'll pay you a bonus for every usable product you make for Sonatone."

Gallegher got up. "Even my subconscious doesn't like these lugs," he told Silver. "Let's go."

"I think I'll stick around."

"Remember the fence," he warned cryptically. "But suit yourself. I'll run along."

Elia said, "Remember, Gallegher, you're working for us. If we hear of you doing any favors for Brock, we'll slap an injunction on you before you can take a deep breath."

"Yeah?"

The Tones deigned no answer. Gallegher unhappily found the lift and descended to the floor. What now? Joe.

Fifteen minutes later Gallegher let himself into his laboratory. The lights were blazing, and dogs were barking frantically for blocks around. Joe stood before the mirror, singing inaudibly.

"I'm going to take a sledge hammer to you," Gallegher said. "Start saying your prayers, you misbegotten collection of cogs. So help me, I'm going to sabotage you."

"All right, beat me," Joe squeaked. "See if I care. You're merely jealous of my beauty."

"Beauty?"

"You can't see all of it—you've only six senses."

"Five."

"Six. I've a lot more. Naturally my full splendor is revealed only to me. But you can see enough and hear enough to realize part of my loveliness, anyway."

"You squeak like a rusty tin wagon," Gallegher growled.

"You have dull ears. Mine are supersensitive. You miss the full tonal values of my voice, of course. Now be quiet. Talking disturbs me. I'm appreciating my gear movements."

"Live in your fool's paradise while you can. Wait'll I find a sledge."

"All right, beat me. What do I care?"

Gallegher sat down wearily on the couch, staring at the robot's transparent back. "You've certainly screwed things up for me. What did you sign that Sonatone contract for?"

"I told you. So Kennicott wouldn't come around and bother me."

"Of all the selfish, lunk-headed . . . *uh!* Well, you got me into a sweet mess. The Tones can hold me to the letter of the contract unless I prove I didn't sign it. All right. You're going to help me. You're going into court with me and turn on your hypnotism or whatever it is. You're going to prove to a judge that you did and can masquerade as me."

"Won't," said the robot, "Why should I?"

"Because you got me into this," Gallegher yelped. "You've got to get me out!"

"Why?"

"Why? Because . . . uh . . . well, it's common decency!"

"Human values don't apply to robots," Joe said. "What care I for semantics? I refuse to waste time I could better employ admiring my beauty. I shall stay here before the mirror forever and ever—"

"The hell you will," Gallegher snarled. "I'll smash you to atoms."

"All right, I don't care."

"You don't?"

"You and your instinct for self-preservation," the robot said, rather sneeringly. "I suppose it's necessary for you, though. Creatures of such surpassing ugliness would destroy themselves out of sheer shame if they didn't have something like that to keep them alive."

"Suppose I take away your mirror?" Gallegher asked in a hopeless voice.

For answer Joe shot his eyes out on their stalks. "Do I need a mirror? Besides, I can vasten myself lokishly."

"Never mind that. I don't want to go crazy for a while yet. Listen, dope, a robot's supposed to *do* something. Something useful, I mean."

"I do. Beauty is all."

Gallegher squeezed his eyes shut, trying to think. "Now look. Suppose I invent a new type of enlarger screen for Brock. The Tones will impound it. I've got to be legally free to work for Brock, or—"

"Look!" Joe cried squeakily. "They go round! How lovely." He stared in ecstasy at his whirring insides. Gallegher went pale with impotent fury.

"Damn you!" he muttered. "I'll find some way to bring pressure to bear. I'm going to bed." He rose and spitefully snapped off the lights.

"It doesn't matter," the robot said. "I can see in the dark, too."

The door slammed behind Gallegher. In the silence Joe began to sing tunelessly to himself.

Gallegher's refrigerator covered an entire wall of his kitchen. It was filled mostly with liquors that required chilling, including the imported canned beer with which he always started his binges. The next morning, heavy-eyed and disconsolate, Gallegher searched for tomato juice, took a wry sip, and hastily washed it down with rye. Since he was already a week gone in bottle-dizziness, beer wasn't indicated now—he always worked cumulatively, by progressive stages. The food service popped a hermetically sealed breakfast on a table, and Gallegher morosely toyed with a bloody steak.

Well?

Court, he decided, was the only recourse. He knew little about the robot's psychology. But a judge would certainly be impressed by Joe's talents. The evidence of robots was not legally admissible—still, if Joe could be considered as a machine capable of hypnotism, the Sonatone contract might be declared null and void.

Gallegher used his visor to start the ball rolling. Harrison Brock still had certain political powers of pull, and the hearing was set for that very day. What would happen, though, only God and the robot knew.

Several hours passed in intensive but futile thought. Gallegher could think of no way in which to force the robot to do what he wanted. If only he could remember the purpose for which Joe had been created—but he couldn't. Still—

At noon he entered the laboratory.

"Listen, stupid," he said, "you're coming to court with me. Now."

"Won't."

"O.K." Galllegher opened the door to admit two husky men in overalls, carrying a stretcher. "Put him in, boys."

Inwardly he was slightly nervous. Joe's powers were quite unknown, his potentialities an x quantity. However, the robot wasn't very large, and, though he struggled and screamed in a voice of frantic squeakiness, he was easily loaded on the stretcher and put in a strait jacket.

"Stop it! You can't do this to me! Let me go, do you hear? Let me go!"

"Outside," Gallegher said.

Joe, protesting valiantly, was carried out and loaded into an air van. Once there, he quieted, looking up blankly at nothing. Gallegher sat down on a bench beside the prostrate robot. The van glided up.

"Well?"

"Suit yourself," Joe said. "You got me all upset, or I could have hypnotized you all. I still could, you know. I could make you all run around barking like dogs."

Gallegher twitched a little. "Better not."

"I won't. It's beneath my dignity. I shall simply lie here and admire myself. I told you I don't need a mirror. I can vasten my beauty without it."

"Look," Gallegher said. "You're going to a courtroom. There'll be a lot of people in it. They'll all admire you. They'll admire you more if you show how you can hypnotize people. Like you did to the Tones, remember?"

"What do I care how many people admire me?" Joe asked. "I don't need confirmation. If they see me, that's their good luck. Now be quiet. You may watch my gears if you choose."

Gallegher watched the robot's gears with smouldering hatred in his eyes. He was still darkly furious when the van arrived at the court chambers. The men carried Joe inside, under Gallegher's direction, and laid him down carefully on a table, where, after a brief discussion, he was marked as Exhibit A.

The courtroom was well filled. The principals were there, too—Elia and Jimmy Tone, looking disagreeably confident, and Patsy Brock, with her father, both seeming anxious. Silver O'Keefe, with her usual wariness, had found a seat midway between the representatives of Sonatone and Vox-View. The presiding judge was a martinet named Hansen, but, as far as Gallegher knew, he was honest. Which was something, anyway.

Hansen looked at Gallegher. "We won't bother with formalities. I've been reading this brief you sent down. The whole case stands or falls on the question of whether you did or did not sign a certain contract with the Sonatone Television Amusement Corp. Right?"

"Right, your honor."

"Under the circumstances you dispense with legal representation. Right?"

"Right, your honor."

"Then this is technically *ex officio*, to be confirmed later by appeal if either party desires. Otherwise after ten days the verdict becomes official." This new type of informal court hearing had lately become popular—it saved time, as well as wear and tear on everyone. Moreover, certain recent scandals had made attorneys slightly disreputable in the public eye. There was a prejudice.

Judge Hansen called up the Tones, questioned them, and then asked Harrison Brock to take the stand. The big shot looked worried, but answered promptly.

"You made an agreement with the appellor eight days ago?"

"Yes. Mr. Gallegher contracted to do certain work for me—"

"Was there a written contract?"

"No. It was verbal."

Hansen looked thoughtfully at Gallegher. "Was the appellor intoxicated at the time? He often is, I believe."

Brock gulped. "There were no tests made. I really can't say."

"Did he drink any alcoholic beverages in your presence?"

"I don't know if they were *alcoholic* bev—"

"If Mr. Gallegher drank them, they were alcoholic. Q.E.D. The gentleman once worked with me on a case—However, there seems to be no legal proof that you entered into any agreement with Mr. Gallegher. The defendant—Sonatone—possesses a written contract. The signature has been verified."

Hansen waved Brock down from the stand. "Now, Mr. Gallegher. If you'll come up here—The contract in question was signed at approximately 8 P.M. last night. You contend you did not sign it?"

"Exactly. I wasn't even in my laboratory then."

"Where were you?"

"Downtown."

"Can you produce witnesses to that effect?"

Gallegher thought back. He couldn't.

"Very well. Defendant states that at approximately 8 P.M. last night you, in your laboratory, signed a certain contract. You deny that categorically. You state that Exhibit A, through the use of hypnotism, masqueraded as you and successfully forged your signature. I have consulted experts, and they are of the opinion that robots are incapable of such power."

"My robot's a new type."

"Very well. Let your robot hypnotize me into believing that it is either you, or any other human. In other words, let it prove its capabilities. Let it appear to me in any shape it chooses."

Gallegher said, "I'll try," and left the witness box. He went to the table where the strait-jacketed robot lay and silently sent up a brief prayer.

"Joe."

"Yes."

"You've been listening?"

"Yes."

"Will you hypnotize Judge Hansen?"

"Go away," Joe said. "I'm admiring myself."

Gallegher started to sweat. "Listen. I'm not asking much. All you have to do—"

Joe off-focused his eyes and said faintly, "I can't hear you. I'm vastening."

Ten minutes later Hansen said, "Well, Mr. Gallegher—"

"Your honor! All I need is a little time. I'm sure I can make this rattle-geared Narcissus prove my point if you'll give me a chance."

"This court is not unfair," the judge pointed out. "Whenever you can prove that Exhibit A is capable of hypnotism, I'll rehear the case. In the meantime, the contract stands. You're working for Sonatone, not for Vox-View. Case closed."

He went away. The Tones leered unpleasantly across the courtroom. They also departed, accompanied by Silver O'Keefe, who had decided which side of the fence was safest. Gallegher looked at Patsy Brock and shrugged helplessly.

"Well—" he said.

She grinned crookedly. "You tried. I don't know how hard, but—Oh, well. Maybe you couldn't have found the answer, anyway."

Brock staggered over, wiping sweat from his round face. "I'm a ruined man. Six new bootleg theaters opened in New York today. I'm going crazy. I don't deserve this."

"Want me to marry the Tone?" Patsy asked sardonically.

"Hell, no! Unless you promise to poison him just after the ceremony. Those skunks can't lick me. I'll think of something."

"If Gallegher can't, you can't," the girl said. "So—what now?"

"I'm going back to my lab," the scientist said. *"In vino veritas.* I started this business when I was drunk, and maybe if I get drunk enough again, I'll find the answer. If I don't sell my pickled carcass for whatever it'll bring."

"O.K.," Patsy agreed, and led her father away. Gallegher sighed, superintended the reloading of Joe into the van, and lost himself in hopeless theorization.

An hour later Gallegher was flat on the laboratory couch, drinking passionately from the liquor bar, and glaring at the robot, who stood before the mirror singing squeakily. The binge threatened to be monumental. Gallegher wasn't sure flesh and blood would stand it. But he was determined to keep going till he found the answer or passed out.

His subconscious knew the answer. Why the devil had he made Joe in the first place? Certainly not to indulge a Narcissus complex! There was another reason, a soundly logical one, hidden in the depths of alcohol.

The x factor. If the x factor were known, Joe might be controllable. He *would* be. X was the master switch. At present the robot was, so to speak, running wild. If he were told to perform the task for which he was made, a psychological balance would occur. X was the catalyst that would reduce Joe to sanity.

Very good. Gallegher drank high-powered Drambuie. *Whoosh!*

Vanity of vanities; all is vanity. How could the x factor

be found? Deduction? Induction? Osmosis? A bath in Drambuie—Gallegher clutched at his wildly revolving thoughts. What had happened that night a week ago?

He had been drinking beer. Brock had come in. Brock had gone. Gallegher had begun to make the robot—Hmm-m-m. A beer drunk was different from other types. Perhaps he was drinking the wrong liquors. Very likely. Gallegher rose, sobered himself with thiamin, and carted dozens of imported beer cans out of the refrigerator. He stacked them inside a frost-unit beside the couch. Beer squirted to the ceiling as he plied the opener. Now let's see.

The *x* factor. The robot knew what it represented, of course. But Joe wouldn't tell. There he stood, paradoxically transparent, watching his gears go around.

"Joe."

"Don't bother me. I'm immersed in contemplation of beauty."

"You're not beautiful."

"I am. Don't you admire my tarzeel?"

"What's your tarzeel?"

"Oh, I forgot," Joe said regretfully. "You can't sense that, can you? Come to think of it, I added the tarzeel myself after you made me. It's very lovely."

"Hm-m-m." The empty beer cans grew more numerous. There was only one company, somewhere in Europe, that put up beer in cans nowadays, instead of using the omnipresent plastibulbs, but Gallegher preferred the cans—the flavor was different, somehow. But about Joe. Joe knew why he had been created. Or did he? Gallegher knew, but his subconscious—

Oh-oh! What about Joe's subconscious?

Did a robot have a subconscious? Well, it had a brain—

Gallegher brooded over the impossibility of administering scopolamine to Joe. Hell! How could you release a robot's subconscious?

Hypnotism.

Joe couldn't be hypnotized. He was too smart.

Unless—

Autohypnotism?

Gallegher hastily drank more beer. He was beginning to think clearly once more. Could Joe read the future? No; he had certain strange senses, but they worked by inflexible logic and the laws of probability. Moreover, Joe had an Achillean heel—his Narcissus complex.

There *might*—there just *might*—be a way.

Gallegher said, "You don't seem beautiful to me, Joe."

"What do I care about you? I *am* beautiful, and I can see it. That's enough."

"Yeah. My senses are limited, I suppose. I can't realize your full potentialities. Still, I'm seeing you in a different light now. I'm drunk. My subconscious is emerging. I can appreciate you with both my conscious and my subconscious. See?"

"How lucky you are," the robot approved.

Gallegher closed his eyes. "You see yourself more fully than I can. But not completely, eh?"

"What? I see myself as I am."

"With complete understanding and appreciation?"

"Well, yes," Joe said. "Of course. Don't I?"

"Consciously *and* subconsciously? Your subconscious might have different senses, you know. Or keener ones. I know there's a qualitative and quantitive difference in my outlook when I'm drunk or hypnotized or my subconscious is in control somehow."

"Oh." The robot looked thoughtfully into the mirror. "Oh."

"Too bad you can't get drunk."

Joe's voice was squeakier than ever. "My subconscious . . . I've never appreciated my beauty that way. I may be missing something."

"Well, no use thinking about it," Gallegher said. "You can't release your subconscious."

"Yes, I can," the robot said. "I can hypnotize myself."

Gallegher dared not open his eyes. "Yeah? Would that work?"

"Of course. It's just what I'm going to do now. I may see undreamed-of beauties in myself that I've never suspected before. Greater glories—Here I go."

Joe extended his eyes on stalks, opposed them, and then peered intently into each other. There was a long silence.

Presently Gallegher said, "Joe!"

Silence.

"Joe!"

Still silence. Dogs began to howl.

"Talk so I can hear you."

"Yes," the robot said, a faraway quality in its squeak.

"Are you hypnotized?"

"Yes."

"Are you lovely?"

"Lovelier than I'd ever dreamed."

Gallegher let that pass. "Is your subconscious ruling?"

"Yes."

"Why did I create you?"

No answer. Gallegher licked his lips and tried again.

"Joe. You've got to answer me. Your subconscious is dominant—remember? Now why did I create you?"

No answer.

"Think back. Back to the hour I created you. What happened then?"

"You were drinking beer," Joe said faintly. "You had trouble with the can opener. You said you were going to build a bigger and better can opener. That's me."

Gallegher nearly fell off the couch. *"What?"*

The robot walked over, picked up a can, and opened it with incredible deftness. No beer squirted. Joe was a perfect can opener.

"That," Gallegher said under his breath, "is what comes of knowing science by ear. I build the most complicated robot in existence just so—" He didn't finish.

Joe woke up with a start. "What happened?" he asked.

Gallegher glared at him. "Open that can!" he snapped.

The robot obeyed, after a brief pause. "Oh. So you found out. Well, I guess I'm just a slave now."

"Damned right you are. I've located the catalyst—the master switch. You're in the groove, stupid, doing the job you were made for."

"Well," Joe said philosophically, "at least I can still admire my beauty, when you don't require my services."

Gallegher grunted. "You oversized can opener! Listen. Suppose I take you into court and tell you to hypnotize Judge Hansen. You'll have to do it, won't you?"

"Yes. I'm no longer a free agent. I'm conditioned. Conditioned to obey you. Until now, I was conditioned to obey only one command—to do the job I was made for. Until you commanded me to open cans, I was free. Now I've got to obey you completely."

"Uh-huh," Gallegher said. "Thank God for that. I'd have gone nuts within a week otherwise. At least I can get out of the Sonatone contract. Then all I have to do is solve Brock's problem."

"But you did," Joe said.

"Huh?"

"When you made me. You'd been talking to Brock previously, so you incorporated the solution to *his* problem into me. Subconsciously, perhaps."

Gallegher reached for a beer. "Talk fast. What's the answer?"

"Subsonics," Joe said. "You made me capable of a certain subsonic tone that Brock must broadcast at irregular time-intervals over his televiewers—"

Subsonics cannot be heard. But they can be felt. They can be felt as a faint, irrational uneasiness at first, which mounts to a blind, meaningless panic. It does not last. But when it is coupled with A. A.—audience appeal—there is a certain inevitable result.

Those who possessed home Vox-View units were scarcely troubled. It was a matter of acoustics. Cats squalled; dogs howled mournfully. But the families sitting in their parlors, watching Vox-View stars perform on the screen, didn't really notice anything amiss. There wasn't sufficient amplification, for one thing.

But in the bootleg theaters, where illicit Vox-View televisors were hooked up to Magnas—

There was a faint, irrational uneasiness at first. It mounted. Someone screamed. There was a rush for the doors. The audience was afraid of something, but didn't know what. They knew only that they had to get out of there.

All over the country there was a frantic exodus from the bootleg theaters when Vox-View first rang in a subsonic during a regular broadcast. Nobody knew why, except Gallegher, the Brocks, and a couple of technicians who were let in on the secret.

An hour later another subsonic was played. There was another mad exodus.

Within a few weeks it was impossible to lure a patron into a bootleg theater. Home televisors were far safer! Vox-View sales picked up—

Nobody would attend a bootleg theater. An unexpected result of the experiment was that, after a while, nobody would attend any of the legalized Sonatone theaters either. Conditioning had set in.

Audiences didn't know why they grew panicky in the bootleg places. They associated their blind, unreasoning fear with other factors, notably mobs and claustrophobia. One evening a woman named Jan Wilson, otherwise not notable, attended a bootleg show. She fled with the rest when the subsonic was turned on.

The next night she went to the palatial Sonatone Bijou. In the middle of a dramatic feature she looked around, realized that there was a huge throng around her, cast up horrified eyes to the ceiling, and imagined that it was pressing down.

She had to get out of there!

Her squall was the booster charge. There were other customers who had heard subsonics before. No one was hurt during the panic; it was a legal rule that theater doors be made large enough to permit easy egress during a fire. No one was hurt, but it was suddenly obvious that the public was being conditioned by subsonics to avoid the dangerous combination of throngs and theaters. A simple matter of psychological association—

Within four months the bootleg places had disappeared and the Sonatone supertheaters had closed for want of patronage. The Tones, father and son, were not happy. But everybody connected with Vox-View was.

Except Gallegher. He had collected a staggering check from Brock, and instantly cabled to Europe for an incredible quantity of canned beer. Now, brooding over his sorrows, he lay on the laboratory couch and siphoned a highball down his throat. Joe, as usual, was before the mirror, watching the wheels go round.

"Joe," Gallegher said.

"Yes? What can I do?"

"Oh, nothing." That was the trouble. Gallegher fished a crumpled cable tape out of his pocket and morosely read it once more. The beer cannery in Europe had decided to change its tactics. From now on, the cable said, their beer would be put in the usual plastibulbs, in conformance with custom and demand. No more cans.

There wasn't *anything* put up in cans in this day and age. Not even beer, now.

So what good was a robot who was built and conditioned to be a can opener?

Gallegher sighed and mixed another highball—a stiff one. Joe postured proudly before the mirror.

Then he extended his eyes, opposed them, and quickly liberated his subconscious through autohypnotism. Joe could appreciate himself better that way.

Gallegher sighed again. Dogs were beginning to bark like mad for blocks around. Oh, well.

He took another drink and felt better. Presently, he thought, it would be time to sing "Frankie and Johnnie." Maybe he and Joe might have a duet—one baritone and one inaudible sub or supersonic. Close harmony.

Ten minutes later Gallegher was singing a duet with his can opener.

The Misguided Halo

THE YOUNGEST ANGEL could scarcely be blamed for the error. They had given him a brand-new, shining halo and pointed down to the particular planet they meant. He had followed directions implicitly, feeling quite proud of the responsibility. This was the first time the youngest angel had ever been commissioned to bestow sainthood on a human.

So he swooped down to the earth, located Asia, and came to rest at the mouth of a cavern that gaped halfway up a Himalayan peak. He entered the cave, his heart beating wildly with excitement, preparing to materialize and give the holy lama his richly earned reward. For ten years the ascetic Tibetan Kai Yung had sat motionless, thinking holy thoughts. For ten more years he had dwelt on top of a pillar, acquiring additional merit. And for the last decade he had lived in this cave, a hermit, forsaking fleshly things.

The youngest angel crossed the threshold and stopped with a gasp of amazement. Obviously he was in the wrong place. An overpowering odor of fragrant *sake* assailed his nostrils, and he stared aghast at the wizened, drunken little man who squatted happily beside a fire, roasting a bit of goat flesh. A den of iniquity!

Naturally, the youngest angel, knowing little of the ways of the world, could not understand what had led to the lama's fall from grace. The great pot of *sake* that some misguidedly pious one had left at the cave mouth was an offering, and the lama had tasted, and tasted again. And by this time he was clearly not a suitable candidate for sainthood.

The youngest angel hesitated. The directions had been

explicit. But surely this tippling reprobate could not be intended to wear a halo. The lama hiccuped loudly and reached for another cup of *sake* and thereby decided the angel, who unfurled his wings and departed with an air of outraged dignity.

Now, in a Midwestern State of North America there is a town called Tibbett. Who can blame the angel if he alighted there, and, after a brief search, discovered a man apparently ripe for sainthood, whose name, as stated on the door of his small suburban home, was K. Young?

"I may have got it wrong," the youngest angel thought. "They said it was Kai Yung. But this is Tibbett, all right. He must be the man. Looks holy enough, anyway.

"Well," said the youngest angel, "here goes. Now, where's that halo?"

Mr. Young sat on the edge of his bed, with head lowered, brooding. A depressing spectacle. At length he arose and donned various garments. This done, and shaved and washed and combed, he descended the stairway to breakfast.

Jill Young, his wife, sat examining the paper and sipping orange juice. She was a small, scarcely middle-aged, and quite pretty woman who had long ago given up trying to understand life. It was, she decided, much too complicated. Strange things were continually happening. Much better to remain a bystander and simply let them happen. As a result of this attitude, she kept her charming face unwrinkled and added numerous gray hairs to her husband's head.

More will be said presently of Mr. Young's head. It had, of course, been transfigured during the night. But as yet he was unaware of this, and Jill drank orange juice and placidly approved a silly-looking hat in an advertisement.

"Hello, Filthy," said Young. "Morning."

He was not addressing his wife. A small and raffish Scotty had made its appearance, capering hysterically about its master's feet, and going into a fit of sheer madness when the man pulled its hairy ears. The raffish Scotty flung its head sidewise upon the carpet and skated about the room on its muzzle, uttering strangled squeaks of delight. Growing tired of this at last, the Scotty, whose name was Filthy McNasty, began thumping its head on the floor with the apparent intention of dashing out its brains, if any.

Young ignored the familiar sight. He sat down, unfolded his napkin, and examined his food. With a slight grunt of appreciation he began to eat.

He became aware that his wife was eyeing him with an odd and distrait expression. Hastily he dabbed at his lips with the napkin. But Jill still stared.

Young scrutinized his shirt front. It was, if not immaculate, at least free from stray shreds of bacon or egg. He looked at his wife, and realized that she was staring at a point slightly above his head. He looked up.

Jill started slightly. She whispered, "Kenneth, what *is* that?"

Young smoothed his hair. "Er . . . what, dear?"

"That thing on your head."

The man ran exploring fingers across his scalp. "My head? How do you mean?"

"It's shining," Jill explained. "What on earth have you been doing to yourself?"

Mr. Young felt slightly irritated. "I have been doing nothing to myself. A man grows bald eventually."

Jill frowned and drank orange juice. Her fascinated gaze crept up again. Finally she said, "Kenneth, I wish you'd—"

"What?"

She pointed to a mirror on the wall.

With a disgusted grunt Young arose and faced the image in the glass. At first he saw nothing unusual. It was the same face he had been seeing in mirrors for years. Not an extraordinary face—not one at which a man could point with pride and say: "Look. *My face.*" But, on the other hand, certainly not a countenance which would cause consternation. All in all, an ordinary, clean, well-shaved, and rosy face. Long association with it had given Mr. Young a feeling of tolerance, if not of actual admiration.

But topped by a halo it acquired a certain eeriness.

The halo hung unsuspended about five inches from the scalp. It measured perhaps seven inches in diameter, and seemed like a glowing, luminous ring of white light. It was impalpable, and Young passed his hand through it several times in a dazed manner.

"It's a . . . halo," he said at last, and turned to stare at Jill.

The Scotty, Filthy McNasty, noticed the luminous

adornment for the first time. He was greatly interested. He did not, of course, know what it was, but there was always a chance that it might be edible. He was not a very bright dog.

Filthy sat up and whined. He was ignored. Barking loudly, he sprang forward and attempted to climb up his master's body in a mad attempt to reach and rend the halo. Since it had made no hostile move, it was evidently fair prey.

Young defended himself, clutched the Scotty by the nape of its neck, and carried the yelping dog into another room, where he left it. Then he returned and once more looked at Jill.

At length she observed, "Angels wear halos."

"Do I look like an angel?" Young asked. "It's a . . . a scientific manifestation. Like . . . like that girl whose bed kept bouncing around. You read about that."

Jill had. "She did it with her muscles."

"Well, I'm not," Young said definitely. "How could I? It's scientific. Lots of things shine by themselves."

"Oh, yes. Toadstools."

The man winced and rubbed his head. "Thank you, my dear. I suppose you know you're being no help at all."

"Angels have halos," Jill said with a sort of dreadful insistence.

Young was at the mirror again. "Darling, would you mind keeping your trap shut for a while? I'm scared as hell, and you're far from encouraging."

Jill burst into tears, left the room, and was presently heard talking in a low voice to Filthy.

Young finished his coffee, but it was tasteless. He was not as frightened as he had indicated. The manifestation was strange, weird, but in no way terrible. Horns, perhaps, would have caused horror and consternation. But a halo— Mr. Young read the Sunday newspaper supplements, and had learned that everything odd could be attributed to the bizarre workings of science. Somewhere he had heard that all mythology had a basis in scientific fact. This comforted him, until he was ready to leave for the office.

He donned a derby. Unfortunately the halo was too large. The hat seemed to have two brims, the upper one whitely luminous.

"Damn!" said Young in a heartfelt manner. He searched the closet and tried on one hat after another. None would hide the halo. Certainly he could not enter a crowded bus in such a state.

A large furry object in a corner caught his gaze. He dragged it out and eyed the thing with loathing. It was a deformed, gigantic woolly headpiece, resembling a shako, which had once formed a part of a masquerade costume. The suit itself had long since vanished, but the hat remained to the comfort of Filthy, who sometimes slept on it.

Yet it would hide the halo. Gingerly Young drew the monstrosity on his head and crept toward the mirror. One glance was enough. Mouthing a brief prayer, he opened the door and fled.

Choosing between two evils is often difficult. More than once during that nightmare ride downtown Young decided he had made the wrong choice. Yet, somehow, he could not bring himself to tear off the hat and stamp it underfoot, though he was longing to do so. Huddled in a corner of the bus, he steadily contemplated his fingernails and wished he was dead. He heard titters and muffled laughter, and was conscious of probing glances riveted on his shrinking head.

A small child tore open the scar tissue on Young's heart and scrabbled about in the open wound with rosy, ruthless fingers.

"Mamma," said the small child piercingly, "look at the funny man."

"Yes, honey," came a woman's voice. "Be quiet."

"What's that on his head?" the brat demanded.

There was a significant pause. Finally the woman said, "Well, I don't really know," in a baffled manner.

"What's he got it on for?"

No answer.

"Mamma!"

"Yes, honey."

"Is he crazy?"

"Be quiet," said the woman, dodging the issue.

"But what *is* it?"

Young could stand it no longer. He arose and made his way with dignity through the bus, his glazed eyes seeing nothing. Standing on the outer platform, he kept his face averted from the fascinated gaze of the conductor.

As the vehicle slowed down Young felt a hand laid on his arm. He turned. The small child's mother was standing there, frowning.

"Well?" Young inquired snappishly.

"It's Billy," the woman said. "I try to keep nothing from him. Would you mind telling me just what that is on your head?"

"It's Rasputin's beard," Young grated. "He willed it to me." The man leaped from the bus and, ignoring a half-heard question from the still-puzzled woman, tried to lose himself in the crowd.

This was difficult. Many were intrigued by the remarkable hat. But, luckily, Young was only a few blocks from his office, and at last, breathing hoarsely, he stepped into the elevator, glared murderously at the operator, and said, "Ninth floor."

"Excuse me, Mr. Young," the boy said mildly. "There's something on your head."

"I know," Young replied. "I put it there."

This seemed to settle the question. But after the passenger had left the elevator, the boy grinned widely. When he saw the janitor a few minutes later he said:

"You know Mr. Young? The guy—"

"I know him. So what?"

"Drunk as a lord."

"Him? You're screwy."

"Tighter'n a drum," declared the youth, "swelp me Gawd."

Meanwhile, the sainted Mr. Young made his way to the office of Dr. French, a physician whom he knew slightly, and who was conveniently located in the same building. He had not long to wait. The nurse, after one startled glance at the remarkable hat, vanished, and almost immediately reappeared to usher the patient into the inner sanctum.

Dr. French, a large, bland man with a waxed, yellow mustache, greeted Young almost effusively.

"Come in, come in. How are you today? Nothing wrong, I hope. Let me take your hat."

"Wait," Young said, fending off the physician. "First let me explain. There's something on my head."

"Cut, bruise or fracture?" the literal-minded doctor inquired. "I'll fix you up in a jiffy."

"I'm not *sick*," said Young. "At least, I hope not. I've got a . . . um . . . a halo."

"Ha, ha," Dr. French applauded. "A halo, eh? Surely you're not that good."

"Oh, the hell with it!" Young snapped, and snatched off his hat. The doctor retreated a step. Then, interested, he approached and tried to finger the halo. He failed.

"I'll be— This is odd," he said at last. "Does look rather like one, doesn't it?"

"What is it? That's what I want to know."

French hesitated. He plucked at his mustache. "Well, it's rather out of my line. A physicist might— No. Perhaps Mayo's. Does it come off?"

"Of course not. You can't even touch the thing."

"Ah. I see. Well, I should like some specialists' opinions. In the meantime, let me see—" There was orderly tumult. Young's heart, temperature, blood, saliva and epidermis were tested and approved.

At length French said: "You're fit as a fiddle. Come in tomorrow, at ten. I'll have some other specialists here then."

"You . . . uh . . . you can't get rid of this?"

"I'd rather not try just yet. It's obviously some form of radioactivity. A radium treatment may be necessary—"

Young left the man mumbling about alpha and gamma rays. Discouraged, he donned his strange hat and went down the hall to his own office.

The Atlas Advertising Agency was the most conservative of all advertising agencies. Two brothers with white whiskers had started the firm in 1820, and the company still seemed to wear dignified mental whiskers. Changes were frowned upon by the board of directors, who, in 1938, were finally convinced that radio had come to stay, and had accepted contracts for advertising broadcasts.

Once a junior vice president had been discharged for wearing a red necktie.

Young slunk into his office. It was vacant. He slid into his chair behind the desk, removed his hat, and gazed at it with loathing. The headpiece seemed to have grown even more horrid than it had appeared at first. It was shedding, and, moreover, gave off a faint but unmistakable aroma of unbathed Scotties.

After investigating the halo, and realizing that it was still firmly fixed in its place, Young turned to his work. But the Norns were casting baleful glances in his direction, for presently the door opened and Edwin G. Kipp, president of Atlas, entered. Young barely had time to duck his head beneath the desk and hide the halo.

Kipp was a small, dapper, and dignified man who wore pince-nez and Vandyke with the air of a reserved fish. His blood had long since been metamorphosed into ammonia. He moved, if not in beauty, at least in an almost visible aura of grim conservatism.

"Good morning, Mr. Young," he said. "Er . . . is that you?"

"Yes," said the invisible Young. "Good morning. I'm tying my shoelace."

To this Kipp made no reply save for an almost inaudible cough. Time passed. The desk was silent.

"Er . . . Mr. Young?"

"I'm . . . still here," said the wretched Young. "It's knotted. The shoelace, I mean. Did you want me?"

"Yes."

Kipp waited with gradually increasing impatience. There were no signs of a forthcoming emergence. The president considered the advisability of his advancing to the desk and peering under it. But the mental picture of a conversation conducted in so grotesque a manner was harrowing. He simply gave up and told Young what he wanted.

"Mr. Devlin has just telephoned," Kipp observed. "He will arrive shortly. He wishes to . . . er . . . to be shown the town, as he put it."

The invisible Young nodded. Devlin was one of their best clients. Or, rather, he had been until last year, when he suddenly began to do business with another firm, to the discomfiture of Kipp and the board of directors.

The president went on. "He told me he is hesitating about his new contract. He had planned to give it to World, but I had some correspondence with him on the matter, and suggested that a personal discussion might be of value. So he is visiting our city, and wishes to go . . . er . . . sightseeing."

Kipp grew confidential. "I may say that Mr. Devlin told me rather definitely that he prefers a less conservative firm. 'Stodgy,' his term was. He will dine with me tonight, and I shall endeavor to convince him that our service will be of value. Yet"—Kipp coughed again—"yet diplomacy is, of course, important. I should appreciate your entertaining Mr. Devlin today."

The desk had remained silent during this oration. Now it said convulsively: "I'm sick. I can't—"

"You are ill? Shall I summon a physician?"

Young hastily refused the offer, but remained in hiding. "No, I . . . but I mean—"

"You are behaving most strangely," Kipp said with commendable restraint. "There is something you should know, Mr. Young. I had not intended to tell you as yet, but . . . at any rate, the board has taken notice of you. There was a discussion at the last meeting. We have planned to offer you a vice presidency in the firm."

The desk was stricken dumb.

"You have upheld our standards for fifteen years," said Kipp. "There has been no hint of scandal attached to your name. I congratulate you, Mr. Young."

The president stepped forward, extending his hand. An arm emerged from beneath the desk, shook Kipp's, and quickly vanished.

Nothing further happened. Young tenaciously remained in his sanctuary. Kipp realized that, short of dragging the man out bodily, he could not hope to view an entire Kenneth Young for the present. With an admonitory cough he withdrew.

The miserable Young emerged, wincing as his cramped muscles relaxed. A pretty kettle of fish. How could he entertain Devlin while he wore a halo? And it was vitally necessary that Devlin be entertained, else the elusive vice presidency would be immediately withdrawn. Young knew only too well that employees of Atlas Advertising Agency trod a perilous pathway.

His reverie was interrupted by the sudden appearance of an angel atop the bookcase.

It was not a high bookcase, and the supernatural visitor sat there calmly enough, heels dangling and wings furled. A scanty robe of white samite made up the angel's wardrobe—that and a shining halo, at sight of which Young felt a wave of nausea sweep him.

"This," he said with rigid restraint, "is the end. A halo may be due to mass hypnotism. But when I start seeing angels—"

"Don't be afraid," said the other. "I'm real enough."

Young's eyes were wild. "How do I know? I'm obviously talking to empty air. It's schizo-something. Go away."

The angel wriggled his toes and looked embarrassed. "I can't, just yet. The fact is, I made a bad mistake. You may have noticed that you've a slight halo—"

Young gave a short, bitter laugh. "Oh, yes. I've *noticed* it."

Before the angel could reply the door opened. Kipp looked in, saw that Young was engaged, and murmured, "Excuse me," as he withdrew.

The angel scratched his golden curls. "Well, your halo was intended for somebody else—a Tibetan lama, in fact. But through a certain chain of circumstances I was led to believe that you were the candidate for sainthood. So—" The visitor made a comprehensive gesture.

Young was baffled. "I don't quite—"

"The lama . . . well, sinned. No sinner may wear a halo. And, as I say, I gave it to you through error."

"Then you can take it away again?" Amazed delight surfused Young's face. But the angel raised a benevolent hand.

"Fear not. I have checked with the recording angel. You have led a blameless life. As a reward, you will be permitted to keep the halo of sainthood."

The horrified man sprang to his feet, making feeble swimming motions with his arms. "But . . . but . . . but—"

"Peace and blessings be upon you," said the angel, and vanished.

Young fell back into his chair and massaged his aching brow. Simultaneously the door opened and Kipp stood on the threshold. Luckily Young's hands temporarily hid the halo.

"Mr. Devlin is here," the president said. "Er . . . who was that on the bookcase?"

Young was too crushed to lie plausibly. He muttered, "An angel."

Kipp nodded in satisfaction. "Yes, of course . . . *What?* You say an angel . . . an angel? Oh, my gosh!" The man turned white and hastily took his departure.

Young contemplated his hat. The thing still lay on the desk, wincing slightly under the baleful stare directed at it. To go through life wearing a halo was only less endurable than the thought of continually wearing the loathsome hat. Young brought his fist down viciously on the desk.

"I won't stand it! I . . . I don't have to—" He stopped abruptly. A dazed look grew in his eyes.

"I'll be . . . that's right! I don't *have* to stand it. If that lama got out of it . . . of course. 'No sinner may wear a halo.' " Young's round face twisted into a mask of sheer evil. "I'll be a sinner, then! I'll break all the Commandments—"

He pondered. At the moment he couldn't remember what they were. "Thou shalt not covet thy neighbor's wife." That was one.

Young thought of his neighbor's wife—a certain Mrs. Clay, a behemothic damsel of some fifty summers, with a face like a desiccated pudding. That was one Commandment he had no intention of breaking.

But probably one good, healthy sin would bring back the angel in a hurry to remove the halo. What crimes would result in the least inconvenience? Young furrowed his brow.

Nothing occurred to him. He decided to go for a walk. No doubt some sinful opportunity would present itself.

He forced himself to don the shako and had reached the elevator when a hoarse voice was heard hallooing after him. Racing along the hall was a fat man.

Young knew instinctively that this was Mr. Devlin.

The adjective "fat," as applied to Devlin, was a considerable understatement. The man bulged. His feet, strangled in biliously yellow shoes, burst out at the ankles like blossoming flowers. They merged into calves that seemed to gather momentum as they spread and mounted, flung themselves up with mad abandon, and revealed themselves in their complete, unrestrained glory at Devlin's middle. The man resembled, in silhouette, a pineapple with elephantiasis. A great mass of flesh poured out of his collar, forming a pale, sagging lump in which Young discerned some vague resemblance to a face.

Such was Devlin, and he charged along the hall, as mammoths thunder by, with earth-shaking tramplings of his crashing hoofs.

"You're Young!" he wheezed. "Almost missed me, eh? I was waiting in the office—" Devlin paused, his fascinated gaze upon the hat. Then, with an effort at politeness, he laughed falsely and glanced away. "Well, I'm all ready and r'aring to go."

Young felt himself impaled painfully on the horns of a dilemma. Failure to entertain Devlin would mean the loss of that vice presidency. But the halo weighed like a flatiron on Young's throbbing head. One thought was foremost in his mind: he *had* to get rid of the blessed thing.

Once he had done that, he would trust to luck and diplomacy. Obviously, to take out his guest now would be fatal, insanity. The hat alone would be fatal.

"Sorry," Young grunted. "Got an important engagement. I'll be back for you as soon as I can."

Wheezing laughter, Devlin attached himself firmly to the other's arm. "No, you don't. You're showing me the town! Right now!" An unmistakable alcoholic odor was wafted to Young's nostrils. He thought quickly.

"All right," he said at last. "Come along. There's a bar downstairs. We'll have a drink, eh?"

"Now you're talking," said the jovial Devlin, almost incapacitating Young with a comradely slap on the back. "Here's the elevator."

They crowded into the cage. Young shut his eyes and suffered as interested stares were directed upon the hat. He fell into a state of coma, arousing only at the ground floor, where Devlin dragged him out and into the adjacent bar.

Now Young's plan was this: he would pour drink after drink down his companion's capacious gullet, and await his chance to slip away unobserved. It was a shrewd scheme, but it had one flaw—Devlin refused to drink alone.

"One for you and one for me," he said. "That's fair. Have another."

Young could not refuse, under the circumstances. The worst of it was that Devlin's liquor seemed to seep into every cell of his huge body, leaving him, finally, in the same state of glowing happiness which had been his originally.

But poor Young was, to put it as charitably as possible, tight.

He sat quietly in a booth, glaring across at Devlin. Each time the waiter arrived, Young knew that the man's eyes were riveted upon the hat. And each round made the thought of that more irritating.

Also, Young worried about his halo. He brooded over sins. Arson, burglary, sabotage, and murder passed in quick review through his befuddled mind. Once he attempted to snatch the waiter's change, but the man was too alert. He laughed pleasantly and placed a fresh glass before Young.

The latter eyed it with distaste. Suddenly coming to a decision, he arose and wavered toward the door. Devlin overtook him on the sidewalk.

"What's the matter? Let's have another—"

"I have work to do," said Young with painful distinctness. He snatched a walking cane from a passing pedestrian and made threatening gestures with it until the remonstrating victim fled hurriedly. Hefting the stick in his hand, he brooded blackly.

"But why work?" Devlin inquired largely. "Show me the town."

"I have important matters to attend to." Young scrutinized a small child who had halted by the curb and was returning the stare with interest. The tot looked remarkably like the brat who had been so insulting on the bus.

"What's important?" Devlin demanded. "Important matters, eh? Such as what?"

"Beating small children," said Young, and rushed upon the startled child, brandishing his cane. The youngster uttered a shrill scream and fled. Young pursued for a few feet and then became entangled with a lamp-post. The lamp-post was impolite and dictatorial. It refused to allow Young to pass. The man remonstrated and, finally, argued, but to no avail.

The child had long since disappeared. Administering a brusque and snappy rebuke to the lamp-post, Young turned away.

"What in Pete's name are you trying to do?" Devlin inquired. "That cop's looking at us. Come along." He took the other's arm and led him along the crowded sidewalk.

"What am I trying to do?" Young sneered. "It's obvious, isn't it? I wish to sin."

"Er . . . sin?"

"Sin."

"Why?"

Young tapped his hat meaningly, but Devlin put an altogether wrong interpretation on the gesture. "You're nuts?"

"Oh, shut up," Young snapped in a sudden burst of rage, and thrust his cane between the legs of a passing bank president whom he knew slightly. The unfortunate man fell heavily to the cement, but arose without injury save to his dignity.

"I beg your pardon!" he barked.

Young was going through a strange series of gestures. He had fled to a show-window mirror and was doing fantastic things to his hat, apparently trying to lift it in order to catch a glimpse of the top of his head—a sight, it seemed, to be shielded jealously from profane eyes. At length he cursed loudly, turned, gave the bank president a contemptuous stare, and hurried away, trailing the puzzled Devlin like a captive balloon.

Young was muttering thickly to himself.

"Got to sin—really sin. Something big. Burn down an orphan asylum. Kill m' mother-in-law. Kill . . . anybody!" He looked quickly at Devlin, and the latter shrank back in sudden fear. But finally Young gave a disgusted grunt.

"Nrgh. Too much blubber. Couldn't use a gun or a knife. Have to blast— Look!" Young said, clutching Devlin's arm. "Stealing's a sin, isn't it?"

"Sure is," the diplomatic Devlin agreed. "But you're not—"

Young shook his head. "No. Too crowded here. No use going to jail. Come on!"

He plunged forward. Devlin followed. And Young fulfilled his promise to show his guest the town, though afterward neither of them could remember exactly what had happened. Presently Devlin paused in the liquor store for refueling, and emerged with bottles protruding here and there from his clothing.

Hours merged into an alcoholic haze. Life began to assume an air of foggy unreality to the unfortunate Devlin.

He sank presently into a coma, dimly conscious of various events which marched with celerity through the afternoon and long into the night. Finally he roused himself sufficiently to realize that he was standing with Young confronting a wooden Indian which stood quietly outside a cigar store. It was, perhaps, the last of the wooden Indians. The outworn relic of a bygone day, it seemed to stare with faded glass eyes at the bundle of wooden cigars it held in an extended hand.

Young was no longer wearing a hat. And Devlin suddenly noticed something decidedly peculiar about his companion.

He said softly, "You've got a halo."

Young started slightly. "Yes," he replied, "I've got a halo. This Indian—" He paused.

Devlin eyed the image with disfavor. To his somewhat fuzzy brain the wooden Indian appeared even more horrid than the surprising halo. He shuddered and hastily averted his gaze.

"Stealing's a sin," Young said under his breath, and then, with an elated cry, stooped to lift the Indian. He fell immediately under its weight, emitting a string of smoking oaths as he attempted to dislodge the incubus.

"Heavy," he said, rising at last. "Give me a hand."

Devlin had long since given up any hope of finding sanity in this madman's actions. Young was obviously determined to sin, and the fact that he possessed a halo was somewhat disquieting, even to the drunken Devlin. As a result, the two men proceeded down the street, bearing with them the rigid body of a wooden Indian.

The proprietor of the cigar shop came out and looked after them, rubbing his hands. His eyes followed the departing statue with unmitigated joy.

"For ten years I've tried to get rid of that thing," he whispered gleefully. "And now . . . aha!"

He reentered the store and lit a Corona to celebrate his emancipation.

Meanwhile, Young and Devlin found a taxi stand. One cab stood there; the driver sat puffing a cigarette and listening to his radio. Young hailed the man.

"Cab, sir?" The driver sprang to life, bounced out of the car, and flung open the door. Then he remained frozen in a half-crouching position, his eyes revolving wildly in their sockets.

He had never believed in ghosts. He was, in fact, somewhat of a cynic. But in the face of a bulbous ghoul and a decadent angel bearing the stiff corpse of an Indian, he felt with a sudden, blinding shock of realization that beyond life lies a black abyss teeming with horror unimaginable. Whining shrilly, the terrified man leaped back into his cab, got the thing into motion, and vanished as smoke before the gale.

Young and Devlin looked at one another ruefully.

"What now?" the latter asked.

"Well," said Young, "I don't live far from here. Only ten blocks or so. Come on!"

It was very late, and few pedestrians were abroad. These few, for the sake of their sanity, were quite willing to ignore the wanderers and go their separate ways. So eventually Young, Devlin, and the wooden Indian arrived at their destination.

The door of Young's home was locked, and he could not locate the key. He was curiously averse to arousing Jill. But, for some strange reason, he felt it vitally necessary that the wooden Indian be concealed. The cellar was the logical place. He dragged his two companions to a basement window, smashed it as quietly as possible, and slid the image through the gap.

"Do you really live here?" asked Devlin, who had his doubts.

"Hush!" Young said warningly. "Come on!"

He followed the wooden Indian, landing with a crash in a heap of coal. Devlin joined him after much wheezing and grunting. It was not dark. The halo provided about as much illumination as a twenty-five-watt globe.

Young left Devlin to nurse his bruises and began searching for the wooden Indian. It had unaccountably vanished. But he found it at last cowering beneath a washtub, dragged the object out, and set it up in a corner. Then he stepped back and faced it, swaying a little.

"That's a sin, all right," he chuckled. "Theft. It isn't the amount that matters. It's the principle of the thing. A wooden Indian is just as important as a million dollars, eh, Devlin?"

"I'd like to chop that Indian into fragments," said Devlin with passion. "You made me carry it for three miles." He paused, listening. "What in heaven's name is that?"

A small tumult was approaching. Filthy, having been instructed often in his duties as a watchdog, now faced opportunity. Noises were proceeding from the cellar. Burglars, no doubt. The raffish Scotty cascaded down the stairs in a babel of frightful threats and oaths. Loudly declaring his intention of eviscerating the intruders, he flung himself upon Young, who made hasty clucking sounds intended to soothe the Scotty's aroused passions.

Filthy had other ideas. He spun like a dervish, yelling bloody murder. Young wavered, made a vain snatch at the air, and fell prostrate to the ground. He remained face down, while Filthy, seeing the halo, rushed at it and trampled upon his master's head.

The wretched Young felt the ghosts of a dozen and more drinks rising to confront him. He clutched at the dog, missed, and gripped instead the feet of the wooden Indian. The image swayed perilously. Filthy cocked up an apprehensive eye and fled down the length of his master's body, pausing halfway as he remembered his duty. With a muffled curse he sank his teeth into the nearest portion of Young and attempted to yank off the miserable man's pants.

Meanwhile, Young remained facedown, clutching the feet of the wooden Indian in a despairing grip.

There was a resounding clap of thunder. White light blazed through the cellar. The angel appeared.

Devlin's legs gave way. He sat down in a plump heap, shut his eyes, and began chattering quietly to himself. Filthy swore at the intruder, made an unsuccessful attempt to attain a firm grasp on one of the gently fanning wings, and went back to think it over, arguing throatily. The wing had an unsatisfying lack of substantiality.

The angel stood over Young with golden fires glowing in his eyes, and a benign look of pleasure molding his noble features. "This," he said quietly, "shall be taken as a symbol of your first successful good deed since your enhaloment." A wingtip brushed the dark and grimy visage of the Indian. Forthwith, there was no Indian. "You have lightened the heart of a fellow man—little, to be sure, but some, and at a cost of much labor on your part.

"For a day you have struggled with this sort to redeem him, but for this no success has rewarded you, albeit the morrow's pains will afflict you.

"Go forth, K. Young, rewarded and protected from all sin alike by your halo." The youngest angel faded quietly, for which alone Young was grateful. His head was beginning to ache and he'd feared a possible thunderous vanishment.

Filthy laughed nastily, and renewed his attack on the halo. Young found the unpleasant act of standing upright necessary. While it made the walls and tubs spin round like all the hosts of heaven, it made impossible Filthy's dervish dance on his face.

Some time later he awoke, cold sober and regretful of the fact. He lay between cool sheets, watching morning sunlight lance through the windows, his eyes, and feeling it splinter in jagged bits in his brain. His stomach was making spasmodic attempts to leap up and squeeze itself out through his burning throat.

Simultaneous with awakening came realization of three things: the pains of the morrow had indeed afflicted him; the halo mirrored still in the glass above the dressing table —and the parting words of the angel.

He groaned a heartfelt triple groan. The headache would pass, but the halo, he knew, would not. Only by sinning could one become unworthy of it, and—shining protector! —it made him unlike other men. His deeds must all be good, his works a help to men. He could not sin!

The Voice of The Lobster

TILTING HIS CIGAR at a safe angle Terence Lao-t'se Macduff applied a wary eye to the peephole in the curtain and searched the audience for trouble.

"A setup," he muttered under his breath. "Or is it? I have the inexplicable sensation of wet mice creeping slowly up and down my spine. What a pity I wasn't able to get that Lesser Vegan girl to front for me. Ah, well. Here I go."

He drew up his rotund form as the curtain slowly rose.

"Good evening to you all," he said jovially. "I am happy to see so many eager seekers after knowledge, from all parts of the Galaxy, gathered here tonight on this, Aldebaran's greenest world—"

Muffled noises rose from the audience, mingled with the musky odor of Aldebaranese and the scents of many other races and species. For it was Lottery Time on Aldebaran Tau and the famous celebration based on the counting of seeds in the first *sphyghi* fruit of the season had as usual drawn luck-worshippers from all over the Galaxy. There was even an Earthman, with shaggy red hair and a scowling face, who sat in the front row, glaring up at Macduff.

Uneasily evading that glare, Macduff went on with some haste.

"Ladies, gentlemen and Aldebaranese, I offer you my All-Purpose Radio-isotopic Hormone Rejuvenating Elixir, the priceless discovery which will give you the golden treasury of youth at a sum easily within the reach of each and every—"

An ambiguous missile whizzed past Macduff's head. His

117

trained ear screened out words in a dozen different interstellar tongues and realized that none of them implied approval.

The red-haired Earthman was bellowing, "The mon's a crook! Nae doot aboot it!" Macduff, automatically dodging an overripe fruit, looked pensively at him.

"Oh-oh," Macduff was thinking. "I wonder how he found out those cards were marked for black light?"

He held up his arms dramatically for silence, took a backward step and kicked the trigger on the trap door. Instantly he dropped out of sight. From the audience rose a tremendous bellow of balked fury. Macduff, scuttling rapidly past discarded flats of scenery, heard feet thundering above him.

"There will be chlorophyll spilled tonight," he mused, sprinting. "That's the trouble with these Aldebaranese, they're still vegetables at heart. No sense of ethics, merely tropisms."

His racing feet tripped over a half-empty box of progesterone, a hormone necessary when a sucker, or customer, was fowl or mammal strain.

"Can't be the hormones," he pondered, kicking boxes out of his path. "It must have been the radio-isotope. I shall write a scorching letter to that Chicago outfit. Flyby-nights, of course. I should have suspected the quality of their product at that price. Three months, forsooth! Why, it hasn't been a fortnight since I sold the first bottle—and it's taken this long to finish the payoffs and start hoping for a net profit."

This was serious. Tonight had been the first occasion on which he hoped to put the profits from All-Purpose Radio-isotopic Hormone Rejuvenating Elixir into his own pocket. Aldebaran officials had a greed which one didn't normally associate with vegetable ancestry. How was he going to get enough money to ensure his passage spaceward in a hurry if speed seemed indicated?

"Trouble, trouble," Macduff murmured, as he fled down a corridor, ducked out of the exit and foresightedly sent a tower of empty boxes crashing down, blocking the door. Screams of rage came from behind him.

"Sounds like Babel," he said, trotting. "That's the trouble with galactic travel. Too many overemotional races."

Doubling and twisting along a planned course, he continued to mutter marginal comments, for Macduff generally moved in a haze of sotto voce remarks confidingly addressed to himself, usually approving in nature.

After a time, deciding that he had put a safe distance between himself and justice, he slowed his pace, paused at a dingy hock-shop and paid out a few coins from his paltry store. In return he was given a small battered suitcase, which contained everything necessary for a hurried departure—everything, that is, except the really vital factor. Macduff had no space ticket.

Had he anticipated the full extent of Aldebaranese rapacity and corruption he could perhaps have brought along more payoff funds. But he had wanted his arrival to coincide with the great *sphyghi* festival and time pressed. Still, there were ways. Captain Masterson of the *Sutter* owed him a favor and the *Sutter* was due to take off early next morning.

"Possibly," Macduff ruminated, trudging on, "something might be arranged. Let me see, now. Item One. There's Ao." Ao was the Lesser Vegan girl whose remarkable semi-hypnotic powers would make her such an excellent front man, figuratively speaking.

"Borrowing ticket money won't solve Item One. If I succeed in getting Ao I'll have to deal with her guardian, Item Two."

Item Two represented an Algolian native named Ess Pu.* Macduff had taken pains to keep himself informed of Ess Pu's whereabouts and so knew that the Algolian was no doubt still involved in the same game of dice he had begun two days ago at the UV Lantern Dream-Mill, not far from the center of town. His opponent was probably still the Mayor of Aldebaran City.

"Moreover," Macduff reflected, "both Ess Pu and Ao have tickets on the *Sutter*. Very good. The answer is obvious. All I have to do is get in that dice game, win Ao and both tickets and shake the dust of this inferior planet from my feet."

Swinging the suitcase jauntily, he scuttled along by back alleys, conscious of a distant, mounting tumult, until he

---

* An approximation. The actual name is unspellable.

reached the door of the UV Lantern Dream-Mill, a low broad arch closed with leather curtains. On the threshold he paused to glance back, puzzled by the apparent riot that had broken out.

Submerged feelings of guilt, plus his natural self-esteem, made him wonder if he himself might be the cause of all that uproar. However, since he had only once roused the inhabitants of an entire planet against him* he concluded vaguely that perhaps there was a fire.

So he pushed the curtains aside and entered the UV Lantern, looking around sharply to make certain Angus Ramsay wasn't present. Ramsay, as the reader will guess, was the red-haired gentleman last heard defaming Macduff in the theater.

"And, after all, *he* was the one who insisted on buying a bottle of the Elixir," Macduff mused. "Well, he isn't here. Ess Pu, however, is. In all fairness, I've given him every chance to sell me Ao. Now let him take the consequences."

Squaring his narrow shoulders (for it cannot be denied that Macduff was somewhat bottle-shaped in appearance) he moved through the crowd toward the back of the room, where Ess Pu crouched over a green-topped table with his companion, the Mayor of the city.

To a non-cosmopolitan observer it would have seemed that a lobster was playing PK dice with one of the local plant men. But Macduff was a cosmopolitan in the literal sense of the word. And from his first meeting with Ess Pu, some weeks ago, he had recognized a worthy and formidable opponent.

All Algolians are dangerous. They are noted for their feuds, furies and their inverted affective tone scale. "It's extraordinary," Macduff mused, looking pensively at Ess Pu. "They feel fine only when they're hating someone. The sensations of pleasure and pain are reversed. Algolians find the emotions of rage, hate and cruelty pro-survival. A lamentable state of affairs."

Ess Pu clanked a scaly elbow on the table and rattled the dice cup in the face of his cringing opponent. As everyone is familiar with Aldebaranese plant men, in view of their popular video films, the Mayor need not be described.

* As a result of having sold them the Earth.

Macduff sank into a nearby chair and opened the suitcase on his lap, rummaging through its varied contents which included a deck of tarots, some engraved plutonium stock (worthless) and a number of sample bottles of hormones and isotopes.

There was also a small capsule of Lethean dust, that unpleasant drug which affects the psychokinetic feedback mechanism. As an injury to the cerebellum causes purpose tremor, so Lethean dust causes PK tremor. Macduff felt that a reasonable amount of psychic oscillation in Ess Pu might prove profitable to Macduff. With this in mind, he watched the game intently.

The Algolian waved his stalked eyes over the table. Crinkled membranes around his mouth turned pale blue. The dice spun madly. They fell—seven. Ess Pu's membranes turned green. One of the dice quivered, strained, rolled over. The Algolian's claws clicked shut with satisfaction, the Mayor wrung his hands and Macduff, emitting cries of admiration, leaned forward to pat Ess Pu's sloping shoulder while he deftly emptied the unlidded capsule into the Algolian's drink.

"My lad," Macduff said raptly, "I have traveled the Galaxy from end to end and never before—"

"Tchah!" Ess Pu said sourly, pulling his winnings across the board. He added that he wouldn't sell Ao to Macduff now even if he could. "So get out!" he finished, snapping a claw contemptuously in Macduff's face.

"Why can't you sell Ao?" Macduff demanded. "Though sell, of course, is a misleading verb. What I mean—"

He understood the Algolian to say that Ao now belonged to the Mayor.

Macduff turned surprised eyes on this personage, who furtively evaded the look.

"I didn't recognize your Honor," he said. "So many non-humanoid species are hard to tell apart. But did I understand you to say you *sold* her to the Mayor, Ess Pu? As I remember, Lesser Vegan Control merely leases its subjects to suitable guardians—"

"It was a transfer of guardianship," the Mayor said hastily, lying in his teeth.

"Get out," Ess Pu snarled. "You've got no use for Ao. She's an *objet d'art.*"

"Your French is excellent, for a lobster," Macduff said with delicate tact. "And as for having a use for the lovely creature my scientific researches will shortly include the prognostication of mood responses in large groups. As we all know, Lesser Vegans have the curious ability to make people punch drunk. With a girl like Ao on the platform I could feel perfectly sure of my audience—"

A video screen burst in with a wild squawk. Everyone looked up sharply. Supplementary screens in infrared and UV, for the use of customers with specialized vision, hummed with invisibly duplicated pictures of an announcer's popeyed face.

"—Citizens' Purity Organization has just called a mass meeting—"

The Mayor, looking frightened, started to get up and then thought better of it. There seemed to be something on his conscience.

Ess Pu told Macduff profanely to go away. He enlarged insultingly on the suggestion.

"Pah," Macduff said bravely, knowing himself more agile than the Algolian. "Drop dead."

Ess Pu's mouth membranes turned scarlet. Before he could speak, Macduff offered quickly to buy Ao's ticket, a proposition he had neither intention nor ability to fulfill.

"I haven't got her ticket!" Ess Pu roared. "She still has it! Now get out before I—" He strangled on his own fury, coughed and took a stiff drink. Ignoring Macduff, he threw a six and shoved a stack of chips to the center of the table. The Mayor, with nervous reluctance, glanced at the video screen and faded the bet. At that point the videos broke in with a squeal.

"—mobs marching on Administration! Aroused populace demands ousting of present officials, charging long-term corruption! This political pot was brought to a boil tonight by the exposure of an alleged swindler named Macduff—"

The Mayor of Aldebaran City jumped up and tried to run. One of Ess Pu's claws caught him by the coattail. The video squawked on, giving an all-too-accurate description of the Radio-isotopic Elixir swindler and only the thick haze in the air kept Macduff from immediate exposure.

He hesitated uncertainly, reason telling him that something of interest was developing at the dice table while instinct urged him to run.

"I've got to get home!" the Mayor wailed. "Vital matters—"

"You're staking Ao?" the crustacean demanded, with a significant brandish of his claws. "You are, eh? Right? Then *say so!*"

"Yes," the harassed Mayor cried. "Oh, yes, yes, yes. Anything!"

"Six is my point," said Ess Pu, rattling the dice cup. His membranes became oddly mottled. He wriggled his eye stalks unnervingly. Macduff, remembering the Lethean dust, began to edge towards the door.

There was a bellow of surprised rage from the Algolian as the disobedient cubes turned up seven. Ess Pu clawed at his throat, snatched up his glass and peered suspiciously into it. The jig was up.

Roars of fury reverberated from wall to wall of the Dream-Mill as Macduff slipped out through the curtains and pattered rapidly off down the street in the cool musky dark of the Aldebaran night.

"Nevertheless, I still need a ticket," he reflected. "I also need Ao if possible. This leads me, by obvious degrees, to the Mayor's palace. Provided I'm not torn limb from limb in the meantime," he added, dodging into another alley to avoid the spreading torchlit mobs that were by now seething hither and thither through the aroused city.

"How ridiculous. At times like these I'm grateful for being born into a civilized race. There's no sun like Sol," he summed up, creeping hastily under a fence as a mob poured down the alley towards him.

Emerging on the other side and trotting down a lane, he reached the back door of a luxurious palace done in pink porphyry with ebony edgings and banged the knocker firmly against its plate. There was a soft, sliding noise and Macduff fixed a peremptory gaze upon the one-way Judas mirror in the door.

"Message from the Mayor," he announced in a brisk voice. "He's in trouble. He sent me to bring that Lesser Vegan girl to him immediately. It's a matter of life or death. Hurry!"

A gasp sounded from inside the door. Feet pattered

away into inner distances. A moment later the door opened, revealing the Mayor himself.

"Here!" cried that frantic official. "She's yours. Just take her away. I never saw her before in my life. Never saw Ess Pu. Never saw you. Never saw *anybody*. Oh, these reform riots! One scrap of incriminating evidence and I'm lost, lost!"

Macduff, a little astonished at finding himself fortune's favorite, rose to the occasion capably.

"Depend on me," he told the unhappy vegetable as a slim and lovely being was pushed out of the door into his arms. "She'll leave Alderbaran Tau on the *Sutter* tomorrow at dawn. In fact, I'll take her aboard immediately."

"Yes, yes, yes," the Mayor said, trying to close the door. Macduff's foot kept it ajar.

"She's got her space ticket?"

"Ticket? What ticket? Oh, that. Yes. In her wrist band. Oh, here they come! Look out!"

The terrified Mayor slammed the door. Macduff seized Ao's hand and sped with her into the shrubbery of a plaza. A moment later the tortuous mazes of Aldebaran City swallowed them up.

At the first convenient doorway Macduff paused and looked at Ao. She was worth looking at. She stood in the doorway, thinking of nothing at all. She didn't have to think of anything. She was too beautiful.

Nobody has ever yet succeeded in describing the beings of Lesser Vega and probably nobody ever will. Electronic calculators have broken down and had their mercury memory-units curdled trying to analyze that elusive quality which turns men into mush. Like all her race, however, Ao wasn't very bright. Macduff regarded her with entirely platonic greed.

For she was the perfect come-on. Probably some subtle emanation radiates from the brains of the Lesser Vegans which acts as a hypnotic. With Ao on the stage Macduff knew he could almost certainly have quelled his unruly audience an hour ago and averted the riot. Even the savage breast of Angus Ramsay might have been soothed by Ao's magical presence.

Curiously enough, male relationship with Ao was entirely platonic, with the natural exception of the males of Lesser Vega. Outside of this dim-brained species, however, it was enough for a beholder simply to look at Ao. And vision really had little to do with it, since standards of beauty are only species deep. Almost all living organisms respond similarly to the soft enchantment of the Lesser Vegans.

"There's dark work afoot, my dear," Macduff said, resuming their progress. "Why was the Mayor so eager to get rid of you? But there's no use asking you, of course. We'd better get aboard the *Sutter*. I feel certain I can get Captain Masterson to advance me the price of another ticket. If I'd thought of it I might have arranged a small loan with the Mayor—or even a large one," he added, recalling the Mayor's obvious guilt reactions. "I seem to have missed a bet there."

Ao appeared to float delicately over a mud puddle. She was considering higher and lovelier things.

They were nearly at the spaceport by now and the sights and sounds Macduff heard from the far distance gave him an idea that the mob had set fire to the Mayor's porphyry palace. "However, he's merely a vegetable," Macduff told himself. "Still, my tender heart cannot help but—good heavens!"

He paused, aghast. The misty field of the spaceport lay ahead, the *Sutter* a fat ovoid blazing with light. There was a distant mutter of low thunder as the ship warmed up. A seething crowd of passengers was massed around the gangplank.

"Bless my soul, they're taking off," Macduff said. "Outrageous! Without even notifying the passengers—or perhaps there was a video warning sent out. Yes, I suppose so. But this may be awkward. Captain Masterson will be in the control room with a DO NOT DISTURB sign on the door. Take-offs are complicated affairs. How on Aldebaran Tau can we get aboard with only one ticket between us?"

The motors muttered sullenly. Haze blew like fat ghosts across the light-and-dark patterns of the tarmac. Macduff sprinted, dragging Ao, as thistledown, after him.

"I have a thought," he murmured. "Getting inside the ship is the first step. After that, of course, there'll be the regular passenger check but Captain Masterson will—hm-m."

He studied the purser who stood at the head of the gangplank, taking tickets, checking names off the list he held, his keen eyes watchful. Though the passengers seemed nervous they kept fair order, apparently reassured by the confident voice of a ship's officer, who stood behind the purser.

Into this scene burst Macduff at a wild run, dragging Ao and screaming at the top of his voice. "They're coming!" he shrieked, dashing through the crowd and overturning a bulky Saturnian. "It's another Boxer rebellion! One would think the Xerians had landed. They're all running around screaming, 'Aldebaran Tau for the Aldebaranese.' "

Towing Ao and flailing frantically with his suitcase, Macduff burst into the center of a group and disintegrated it. Instantly he dashed through the line at the gangplank and back again, squealing bloody murder.

At the ship's port the officer was trying to make himself heard with little success. He was apparently stolidly sticking to his original lines, which had something to do with the fact that the Captain had been injured but there was no reason to be alarmed—

"Too late!" shrieked Macduff, bundling himself into the center of a growing nucleus of loud panic. "Hear what they're yelling? 'Kill the foreign devils!'—listen to the bloodthirsty savages. Too late, too late," he added at the top of his voice, scrambling through the mob with Ao. "Lock the doors! Man the gunports! *Here they come!*"

By now all thought of order had been lost. The passengers were demoralized into a veritable Light Brigade of assorted species and Macduff, clinging to Ao and his suitcase, rode the tide up the gangplank, over the prostrate bodies of the officer and the purser and into the ship, where he hastily assembled his various possessions and scrambled for cover. He fled down a passage, doubled and twisted, finally slowed to a rapid walk. He was alone, except for Ao, in the echoing corridor. From the far distance came annoyed curses.

"Useful thing, misdirection," Macduff murmured. "Only way to get aboard, however. What was that fool saying about the Captain's being injured? Nothing serious, I hope. I must hit him for a loan. Now where's your cabin, my dear? Ah, yes. Stateroom R and here it is. We'd better hide till we're in space. Hear that siren? That means take-off, which is useful since it delays the passenger check. Space nets, Ao!"

He yanked open the door to Stateroom R and urged Ao toward a spider-web filament of mesh that dangled like a hammock.

"Get in there and stay till I come back," he ordered. "I've got to find another shock hammock."

The gossamer net attracted Ao as surf attracts a mermaid. She was instantly ensconced in it, her angelic face looking dreamily out of the softly tinted cloud. She gazed beyond Macduff, thinking of nothing.

"Very good," Macduff told himself, going out, shutting the door and crossing to Stateroom X, which luckily was unlocked and vacant, with a web dangling ready. "Now—"

"You!" said an all-too-familiar voice.

Macduff turned quickly on the threshold. Across the passage, looking at him from the door adjoining Ao's, was the ill-tempered crustacean.

"What a surprise," Macduff said cordially. "My old friend Ess Pu. Just the—ah, Algolian I wanted to—"

He was not permitted to finish. With a bellow in which the words "Lethean dust" could be indistinctly understood, Ess Pu charged forward, eyes waving. Macduff hastily closed the door and locked it. There was a crash and then someone began to claw viciously at the panel.

"Outrageous assault on a man's privacy," Macduff muttered.

The hammering on the door grew louder. It was drowned out by the ultrasonic, sonic and reasonating warning of an immediate take-off.

The hammering stopped. The sound of clicking claws receded into the distance. Macduff dived for the shock net. Burrowing into its soft meshes he focused his mind on the hope that the awkward Algolian would be unable to make his hammock in time and that the acceleration would break every bone around his body.

Then the jets blazed, the *Sutter* rose from the troubled soil of Aldebaran Tau and Macduff really began to get into trouble.

It is perhaps time to deal, in some detail with a matter which had already involved Macduff, though he didn't know it. Cryptic reference has been made to such apparently unrelated matters as *sphyghi* seeds and Xerians.

In the most expensive perfumeries of all, on the most luxurious worlds of all, there can be seen in tiny vials drams of a straw-colored fluid which carries the famous label of Sphyghi No. ∞. This perfume of perfumes, which bears the same price whether sold in a plain glass phial or in a jewel-studded platinum flagon, is so costly that by comparison Cassandra, Patou's Joy or Martian Melée seem cheap.

Sphyghi is indigenous to Aldebaran Tau. Its seeds have been safeguarded so strictly that not even Aldebaran's great trade rival, Xeria, has ever managed, by hook, crook or even honest means, to get hold of a single seed.

For a long time it had commonly been known that Xerians would have bartered their souls, or soul, for some of the seed. In view of the Xerians' resemblance to termites there has always been some doubt as to whether an individual Xerian has a mind of his own and operates by free will or whether they are all ruled by a central common brain and determinism.

The trouble with *sphyghi* is that the growth cycle must be almost continuous. After the fruit is detached from the parent plant, its seeds become sterile in thirty hours.

Not a bad take-off, Macduff mused, crawling out of the shock-hammock. It would be too much to hope that Ess Pu suffered at least a simple fracture of the carapace, he supposed.

He opened the door, waited until the opposite door leaped open to reveal the Algolian's watchful bulk and snapped back into Stateroom X with the agility of a frightened gazelle.

"Trapped like a rat," he muttered, beginning with a quick tour of the cabin. "Where is that intercom? Outrageous! Ah, here it is. Connect me with the Captain at once, please. Macduff is the name, Terence Lao-t'se Macduff. Captain Masterson? Let me congratulate you on your take-off. A magnificent job. I gathered you have had an accident, which I trust is not serious."

The intercom croaked hoarsely, caught its breath and said, "Macduff."

"A throat injury?" Macduff hazarded. "But to come to

the point, Captain. You are harboring a homicidal maniac on the *Sutter*. That Algolian lobster has gone perfectly insane and is lurking outside my door—Stateroom X—ready to kill me if I come out. Kindly send down some armed guards."

The intercom made ambiguous sounds which Macduff took for assent.

"Thank you, Captain," he said cheerily. "There is only one other small matter. It became necessary for me to board the *Sutter* at the last moment and I found it inexpedient to obtain a ticket. Time pressed. Moreover, I have taken a Lesser Vegan girl under my protection, in order to save her from the dastardly machinations of Ess Pu and it would perhaps be wise to keep any knowledge of her presence in Stateroom R from that lobster."

He took a deep breath and leaned familiarly against the intercom. "Frightful things have been happening, Captain Masterson—I have been subjected to persecution by a bloodthirsty mob, an attempt to swindle me at dice on Ess Pu's part, threats of violence from Angus Ramsay—"

"Ramsay?"

"You may have heard of him under that name, though it's probably an alias. The man was discharged in disgrace from the Space Service for smuggling opium, I believe—"

A knock came at the door. Macduff broke off to listen.

"Quick work, Captain," he said. "I assume these are your guards?"

There was an affirmative grunt and a click. *"Au revoir,"* Macduff said cheerfully, and opened the door. Two uniformed members of the crew were standing outside, waiting. Across the corridor Ess Pu's door was ajar and the Algolian stood there, breathing hard.

"You're armed?" Macduff asked. "Prepare yourselves for a possible treacherous attack from that murderous crustacean behind you."

"Stateroom X," one of the men said. "Name, Macduff? Captain wants to see you."

"Naturally," Macduff said, pulling out a cigar and stepping dauntlessly into the corridor, making certain, however, that one of the crewmen was between him and Ess Pu.

Nonchalantly clipping the cigar, he paused abruptly, his nostrils quivering.

"Let's go," one of the men said.

Macduff did not stir. From beyond the Algolian a breath of dim fragrance drifted like a murmur from paradise.

Macduff rapidly finished lighting his cigar. He puffed out great clouds of smoke as he hurriedly led the way down the corridor. "Come, come, my men," he admonished. "To the Captain. Important matters are afoot."

"We wouldn't know" a crewman said, slipping in front while the other one fell in behind. Macduff allowed himself to be escorted into the officers' quarters, where he caught sight of himself in a reflecting bulkhead and blew out an approving smoke-cloud.

"Imposing," he murmured. "No giant, of course, but unquestionably imposing in my fashion. The slight rotundity around my middle merely indicates that I live well. Ah, Captain Masterson! Very good, my men, you may leave us now. That's right. Close the door as you go. Now, Captain—"

The man behind the desk lifted his gaze slowly. As all but the stupidest reader will have guessed, he was Angus Ramsay.

"Smuggling opium—aye!" said Angus Ramsay, exhibiting his teeth to the terrified Macduff. "Discharged in disgrace—och! Ye nosty libelling scum, what am I going to do with ye?"

"Mutiny!" Macduff said wildly. "What have you done? Led the crew to mutiny and taken over the *Sutter?* I warn you, this crime will not go unpunished. Where's Captain Masterson?"

"Captain Masterson," said Ramsay, repressing his ire with a violent effort and losing the worst of his accent, "is in a hospital on Aldebaran Tau. Apparently the puir man got in the way of one of those raving mobs. The result is that *I* am captain of the *Sutter.* Offer me no cigars, ye dom scoundrel. I am interested in only one thing. Ye have nae ticket."

"You must have misunderstood me," Macduff said. "Naturally I had a ticket. I gave it to the purser when I came aboard. Those intercoms are notoriously unreliable."

"So is that dom Immortality Elixir of yours," Captain Ramsay pointed out. "So are some poker games, especially when the carrrds are marked for black-light reading." The large hands closed significantly.

"Lay a finger on me at your peril," Macduff said, with faint bluster. "I have the rights of a citizen—"

"Oh, aye," Ramsay agreed. "But not the rights of a passenger on this ship. Therefore, ye wee blaggard, ye'll worrk your way to the next port, Xeria, and there ye'll be thrown off the *Sutter* bag and baggage."

"I'll buy a ticket," Macduff offered. "At the moment, I happen to be slightly embarrassed—"

"If I catch ye mingling with the passengers or engaging in any games of chance with anyone at all ye will find yourself in the brig," Captain Ramsay said firmly. "Black light, aye! Smuggling opium, is it? Aha!"

Macduff spoke wildly of a jury of his peers, at which Ramsay laughed mockingly.

"If I'd caught up with ye back on Aldebaran Tau," he said, "I'd have taken great pleasure in kicking yer podgy carcass halfway arrround the planet. Now I wull get a deal more satisfaction out of knowing ye are harrd at work in the Hot Gang. Aboard this ship ye will be honest if it kills ye. And if ye have in mind that Lesser Vegan girl I have checked up thoroughly and ye cannot possibly figure out a way to swipe her ticket."

"You can't part a guardian and ward like this! It's inhumanoid!" cried Macduff.

"Oot with ye, mon." Ramsay said irately, rising. "To work, for probably the first time in yer misspent life."

"Wait," said Macduff. "You'll regret it if you don't listen to me. There's a crime being committed on this ship."

"Aye," Ramsay said, "and ye're committing it, ye stowaway. Oot!" He spoke into an intercom, the door opened and the two crew members stood waiting expectantly.

"No, no!" Macduff shrilled, seeing the yawning chasm of hard work widening inexorably at his very toes. "It's Ess Pu! The Algolian! He—"

"If ye swindled him as ye swindled me," Captain Ramsay began.

"He's a smuggler!" Macduff shrieked, struggling in the grip of the crewmen who were bearing him steadily towards the door. "He's smuggled *sphyghi* from Aldebaran

Tau! I smelled the stuff, I tell you! You're carrying contraband, Captain Ramsay!"

"Wait," Ramsay ordered. "Put him down. Is this a trick?"

"I smelled it," Macduff insisted. "You know what growing *sphyghi* smells like. It's unmistakable. He must have the plants in his cabin."

"The plants?" Ramsay pondered. "Noo I wonder. Hmm. All right, men. Invite Ess Pu to my cabin." He dropped back in his chair, studying Macduff.

Macduff rubbed his hands briskly together.

"Say no more, Captain Ramsay. You need not apologize for mistaken zeal. Having exposed this villainous Algolian, I shall break him down step by step till he confesses all. He will naturally be brigged, which will leave his cabin vacant. I leave it to your sense of fair play—"

"Tush," said Captain Ramsay. "Close yer trap." He scowled steadily at the door. After a while it opened to admit Ess Pu.

The Algolian lumbered ungracefully forward until he suddenly caught sight of Macduff. Instantly his mouth-membranes began to flush. A clicking claw rose ominously.

"Now, now, mon!" Ramsay warned.

"Certainly," seconded Macduff. "Remember where you are, sir. All is discovered, Ess Pu. Facile lies will get you nowhere. Step by step Captain Ramsay and I have uncovered your plot. You are in the pay of the Xerians. A hired spy, you stole *sphyghi* seeds from Aldebaran Tau and that *sphyghi* is even now in your cabin, a silent accuser."

Ramsay looked thoughtfully at the Algolian.

"Weel?" he asked.

"Wait," said Macduff. "When Ess Pu realizes that all is known he will see the uselessness of silence. Let me go on." Since it was obviously impossible to stop Macduff, Captain Ramsay merely grunted and picked up the Handbook of Regulations on his desk. He began to study the thick volume doubtfully. Ess Pu twitched his claws.

"A feeble scheme from the beginning," Macduff said. "Even to me, a visitor on Aldebaran Tau, it became immediately evident that corruption was at work. Need we seek far for the answer? I think not. For we are even now heading straight for Xeria, a world which has tried frantically for years, by fair means and foul, to break the *sphyghi* monopoly. Very well."

He aimed a cigar accusingly at the Algolian.

"With Xerian money, Ess Pu," Macduff charged, "you came to Aldebaran Tau and bribed the highest officials, got hold of some *sphyghi* seeds and circumvented the usual customs search for contraband. You bought the Mayor's sealed okay by bribing him with Ao. You need not reply yet," Macduff added hastily since he had no intention of cutting short his hour of triumph.

Ess Pu made a revolting noise in his throat. "Lethean dust," he said, reminded of something. *"Ah-h!"* He made a sudden forward motion.

Macduff dodged hastily around the desk behind Ramsay. "Call your men," he suggested. "He's running amuck. Disarm him."

"Ye cannot disarm an Algolian without dismembering him," Captain Ramsay said rather absently, looking up from the Handbook of Regulations. "Ah—Ess Pu. Ye dinna deny this charrge, I gather?"

"How can he deny it?" Macduff demanded. "The short-sighted scoundrel planted the *sphyghi* seeds in his cabin without even setting up an odor-denaturalizer. He deserves no mercy, the fool."

"Weel?" Ramsay asked, in an oddly doubtful manner.

Ess Pu shook his narrow shoulders, crashed his tail emphatically against the floor and spread his jaws in what might have been a grin.

"Sphyghi?" he asked. "Sure. So?"

"Convicted out of his own mouth," Macduff decided. "Nothing else is necessary. Brig him, Captain. We will share the reward, if any."

"No," Captain Ramsay said, putting down the Handbook decisively. "Ye have put yer foot in it again, Macduff. Ye are no expert in interstellar law. We are now beyond the limits of ionization and therefore beyond the jurisdiction of Aldebaran Tau—with a guid deal of gibble-gabble the lawyers put in. But the meaning is clear enough. It was the job of the Aldebaranese to keep that *sphyghi* from being smuggled awa' from them and since they failed, noo it is not my job to meddle. In fact, I canna. Against Regulations."

"That's it," Ess Pu said with complacent satisfaction.

Macduff gasped. "You condone smuggling, Captain Ramsay?"

"I'm covered," the Algolian said, making a coarse gesture toward Macduff.

"Aye," Ramsay said, "he's richt. Regulations make it perfectly clear. As far as I am concerned it makes no difference whether Ess Pu is keeping *sphyghi* or daffodils in his cabin—or a haggis," he added thoughtfully.

Ess Pu snorted and turned towards the door.

Macduff put a plaintive hand on the Captain's arm.

"But he threatened me. My life isn't safe around that Algolian. Just look at those claws."

"Aye," Ramsay said reluctantly. "Ye ken the penalty for murder, Ess Pu? Vurra good. I order ye not to murrder this nae doot deserving miscreant. I am bound to enforce Regulations, so dinna let me catch ye assaulting Macduff within earshot of me or any other officer. Ye ken?"

Ess Pu seemed to ken. He laughed hoarsely, ground a claw at Macduff and stalked out, swaying from side to side. The two crewmen were visible outside the door.

"Here," Captain Ramsay ordered. "I have a job for ye two. Take this stowaway doon to the Hot Gang and turn him over to the Chief."

"No, no!" squealed Macduff, retreating. "Don't you dare lay a finger on me! Put me down! Outrageous! I *won't* go down that ramp! Release me! Captain Ramsay, I demand— *Captain Ramsay!*"

Days had passed, arbitrarily of course, aboard the *Sutter*.

Ao lay curled in her shock hammock, thinking her own dim thoughts and looking at nothing. High up in the wall there was a puffing sound, a scuffle and a grunt. Behind the grille of the ventilating inlet appeared the face of Macduff.

"Ah, my little friend," he said kindly. "So there you are. Now they have me creeping down the ventilating tubes of this ship like a phagocyte."

He tested the meshed grille cautiously.

"Sealed, like all the others," he observed. "However, I assume you're being well treated, my dear." He glanced greedily at the covered lunch tray on a nearby table. Ao looked dreamily at nothing.

"I have sent a cable," Macduff announced from the wall. "I bartered some small treasured heirlooms I happened to have with me and raised enough cash to send a cable, by the press rate. Luckily I still have my press card." Macduff's vast collection of credentials very likely may have included a membership in the Little Men's Chowder and Marching Society, to choose the least likely example.

"Moreover, I have just received a reply. Now I must run a grave risk, my dear, a grave risk. Today the conditions of the ship's pool—a lottery, you know—will be announced in the grand lounge. I must be present, even at the risk of being brigged by Captain Ramsay and savaged by Ess Pu. It will not be easy. I may say I've been subjected to every indignity imaginable, my dear, except perhaps—outrageous!" he added, as a cord tied around his ankle tightened and drew him backward up the shaft.

His distant cries grew fainter. He announced in a fading voice that he had a bottle of 2,4,5-trichlorophenoxyacetic acid in his pocket and that broken glass was a safety hazard. So saying he departed into inaudibility. Since Ao had not really noticed that he was present she remained unaffected.

"Ah, well," Macduff philosophized as he flew down a corridor slightly ahead of the Atmospheric Inspector's hurtling toe-cap, "Justice is blind. This is my thanks for working overtime—at least three minutes overtime. But now I am off duty and free to set my plans in motion."

Five minutes later, having eluded the Inspector and smoothed his ruffled plumage somewhat, he made his way briskly toward the lounge.

"There's one point in my favor," he reflected. "Ess Pu apparently doesn't know Ao is aboard. The last time he chased me he was still speaking bitterly of my part in forcing him to leave her on Aldebaran Tau. Unhappily that's practically the only point in my favor. I must now mingle with the passengers in the grand lounge, while remaining undetected by Ess Pu, Captain Ramsay or any ship's officer. I wish I were a Cerean.* Ah, well."

* The inhabitants of Ceres were long supposed to be invisible. Lately it has been discovered that Ceres has no inhabitants. ●

As Macduff cautiously made his way toward the lounge his memory dwelt all too vividly on his recent progress from riches to rags. His meteoric descent from job to worse job had been little short of phenomenal.

"Would you set a cinematome to digging ditches?" he had inquired. "Would you weigh elephants on a torquemeter?"

He was told to stop gabbling and pick up that shovel. Instantly he began to work out the most efficient application of the law of leverages. There was some delay while he extended his decimals to include the influencing factor of low-threshold radioactivity upon the alpha waves of the brain.

"Otherwise, anything can happen," he explained, demonstrating. There was a crash.

Macduff was then, by request, taken off the Hot Gang and put to work elsewhere. But, as he took pains to point out, his frame of reference did not include special skills in the block-processing of garbage for fuel, oiling of the symbiotic hemostatic adjustment mechanisms provided for the comfort of the passengers or testing refractive indices of liquid-coated bimetallic thermostats. He proved this empirically.

So he was—by request—removed to Hydroponics, where the incident of the radioactive carbon tracer occurred. He said it wasn't the carbon, it was the gammexene, and besides it wasn't really the gammexene so much as his inadvertent neglect to supplement the insecticide with meso-inositol.

But when thirty square feet of rhubarb plants began breathing out carbon monoxide as a result of sudden heredity changes brought on by the gammexene Macduff was promptly sent down to the kitchens, where he introduced a growth hormone into the soup, with nearly catastrophic results.

At present he was an unvalued member of the staff of Atmospheric Controls, where he did the jobs nobody else wanted to do.

More and more he had become conscious of the odor of *sphyghi* pervading the ship. Nothing could disguise its distinctive fragrance, which seeped by osmosis through membranes, trickled along the surface of molecular films and very likely rode piggyback on careening quanta. As Macduff made his stealthy way toward the lounge he realized that the word *sphyghi* was on every tongue, just as he had anticipated.

He paused warily on the threshold of the lounge, which ran like a belt (or cravat) around the entire ship, so that in two directions the floor seemed to slope steeply, until you tried to walk up it. Then it felt like a squirrel cage, which compensated automatically to your own speed.

Here was luxury. Macduff's sybaritic soul yearned toward the tempting buffets of smörgåsbord, *ti-pali* and Gustators. Like a palace of ice an ornate perambulating bar swung slowly past on its monorail track. An orchestra was playing *Starlit Days and Sunny Nights,* an eminently suitable choice for a ship in space, and *sphyghi* fragrance sent its luxurious breath from wall to wall.

Macduff stood with unobtrusive dignity near the door for some minutes, regarding the crowd. He was waiting for the appearance of Captain Ramsay. Presently a buzz of interested comment began to arise and a throng of passengers converged down the salon's slopes. The Captain had arrived. Macduff melted into the crowd and vanished with the suddenness of a Boojum.

Ramsay stood at the bottom of a concave sectioned amphitheater, looking up at his audience with an unaccustomed smile on his seamed face. There was no trace of Macduff, though a repressed mutter of sotto voce comment came occasionally from behind a broad-beamed member of the Plutonian lepidoptera.

Captain Ramsay spoke.

"As ye probably ken," he said, "we are here to arrange aboot the ship's pool. Some of ye may not have traveled in space before, so the acting firrst mate wull explain how this is done. Mister French, please."

Mr. French, a serious young man, took the stage. He cleared his throat, hesitated and looked around as a brief burst of applause came from behind the Plutonian lepidoptera.

"Thank you," he said. "Eh—many of you may be familiar with the old-time ship's pool, in which passengers guessed the time of arrival in port. In space, of course, compensatory feedback devices, effectors and subtractors control our ship so exactly that we know the *Sutter* will arrive in Xeria at exactly the posted time, which is—"

"Come, come, my man, get to the point," an unidentified voice put in from the audience. Captain Ramsay was obsereved to glance sharply toward the Plutonian.

"Eh—quite," said Mr. French. "Does anyone have a suggestion?"

"Guessing the date on a coin," a voice said eagerly, but it was drowned out by a chorus of cries mentioning the word *sphyghi*.

"*Sphyghi?*" Captain Ramsay asked with hypocritical blankness. "The perfume stuff, ye mean?"

There was laughter. A mousy Callistan got the floor.

"Captain Ramsay," he said. "How about running a *sphyghi*-seed lottery here, the way they do on Aldebaran Tau? The way it's done, I think, is by betting on how many seeds there are in the first *sphyghi*-fruit of the crop. The number always varies. Sometimes there are a few hundred, sometimes a few thousand and there's no way of counting them until the fruit's cut open. If Ess Pu could be induced to agree, perhaps—"

"Allow me," Captain Ramsay said. "I'll consult Ess Pu."

He did so, while the crustacean looked blackly around. At first he was obdurate. But finally, in return for a half-share in the pool, he was prevailed upon to cooperate. Only the glamour of *sphyghi* and the unparalleled chance to boast about this lottery for the rest of their lives led the passengers to put up with his inordinate greed. But presently all was arranged.

"Stewards wull pass among ye," Captain Ramsay said. "Write yer guess and yer name on these slips of paper and drop them in a box which will be provided for the purpose. Aye, aye, Ess Pu. Ye wull be given a chance too if ye insist."

The Algolian insisted. He wasn't missing a bet. After long hesitation he put down a number, angrily scrawled the phonetic ideograph of his name and had turned to stalk away when something subtler than *sphyghi* fragrance began to breathe through the salon. Heads turned. Voices died away. Ess Pu, glancing around in surprise, found himself facing the door. His infuriated bellow reverberated from the ceiling for several seconds.

Ao, standing on the threshold, paid no attention. Her lovely eyes gazed into the far distances. Concentric circles of magic drifted dreamily out from her. Already she was increasing the affective tone of all living organisms within the lounge, and Ess Pu was not excluded. However, as has already been disclosed, when an Algolian feels good his rage knows no bounds. Ao didn't care.

"Mine!" Ess Pu mouthed, swinging towards the Captain. "The girl—mine!"

"Get ye claws awa' from my face, mon," Captain Ramsay said with dignity. "If ye wull join me in this quiet corner perhaps ye can state yer case in a more courteous fashion. Noo, what is it?"

Ess Pu demanded Ao. He took out a certificate which appeared to state that he had traveled to Aldebaran Tau with Ao as her guardian. Ramsay fingered his jaw undecidedly. Meanwhile there was a scuffle among the thronging passengers who were pressing folded slips of paper upon the stewards. The breathless, rotund figure of Macduff burst out of the crowd just in time to snatch Ao from Ess Pu's possessively descending claws.

"Back, lobster!" he ordered threateningly. "Lay a claw on that girl at your peril." Towing her, he dodged behind the Captain as Ess Pu lunged.

"I thought so," Ramsay said, lifting a cautioning finger at Ess Pu. "Were ye no specifically forbidden to mingle with the passengers, Macduff?"

"This is a matter of law enforcement," Macduff said. "Ao is my ward, not that criminal lobster's."

"Can ye prove it?" Ramsay inquired. "That certificate of his—"

Macduff tore the certificate from Ess Pu's grip, scanned it hastily, crumpled it into a ball and threw it on the floor.

"Nonsense!" he said scornfully, taking out a cablegram in an accusing manner. "Read this, Captain. As you will observe it is a cable from the Lesser Vegan Control Administration. It points out that Ao was illegally deported from Lesser Vega and that an Algolian is suspected of the crime."

"Eh?" Ramsay said. "One moment, Ess Pu." But the Algolian was already hastily clashing his way out of the salon. Ramsay scowled at the cablegram, looked up and beckoned to a Cephan double-brained attorney among the passengers. There was a brief colloquy, from which Ramsay came back shaking his head.

"Can't do much about this, Macduff," he said. "It isn't a GBI offense, unfortunately. I find I'm empowered only to turn Ao over to her richtful guardian and since she has none—"

"Your error, Captain," Macduff broke in. "You want her richt—I mean, her rightful guardian? You're looking at him. Here's the rest of that cablegram."

"What?" Captain Ramsay demanded.

"Exactly. Terence Lao-t'se Macduff. That's what it says. The Lesser Vegan Control Administration has accepted my offer to stand in *loco parentis* to Ao, *pro tem.*"

"Vurra weel," Ramsay said reluctantly. "Ao's yer ward. Ye wull have to take that up with the Xerian authorities when ye arrive, for as sure as my name is Angus Ramsay ye'll gae head over basket doon the gangplank the minute we land on Xeria. Ye and Ess Pu can fight it oot there. In the meantime I dinna allow a crewman to mingle with my passengers. *Go for-rard!*"

"I demand the rights of a passenger," Macduff said excitedly, backing up a step or two. "The price of the ticket includes the pool and I demand—"

"Ye are no passenger. Ye're a dom insubordinate member of—"

"Ao's a passenger!" Macduff contended shrilly. "She's entitled to take part in the pool, isn't she? Well, then, a slip, please, Captain."

Ramsay growled under his breath. But finally he beckoned to the steward with the slotted box.

"Let Ao write her own guess," he insisted stubbornly.

"Nonsense," Macduff said. "Ao's my ward. I'll write it for her. Moreover, if by any miraculous chance she should happen to win the pool, it will be my duty to administer the dough in the best interests of her welfare, which obviously means buying us both tickets to Lesser Vega."

"Och, why quibble?" Ramsay said suddenly. "If ye're lucky enough to have a miracle happen, fair enough."

Macduff, concealing what he wrote, scribbled busily, folded the paper and pushed it through the slot. Ramsay took a permaseal from the steward and ran it across the box-top.

"Personally," Macduff said, watching him, "I feel slightly degraded by the atmosphere of the *Sutter*. What with condoning smuggling, shyster tactics and pure vicious gambling, I'm forced to the unsavory conclusion, Captain, that you're running a crime ship. Come, Ao, let us seek purer air."

Ao licked her thumb and thought of something very nice, perhaps the taste of her thumb. No one would ever know.

Time passed, both Bergsonian and Newtonian. On either scale it seemed probable that Macduff's time was running rapidly out.

"Who sups wi' Auld Clootie should hae a long spoon," Captain Ramsay said to the acting first, on the day of the *Sutter*'s scheduled arrival at Xeria. "The wonder is that Macduff has evaded Ess Pu's claws this long, the way he's been trying to get at those *sphyghi* plants. What baffles me is what he hopes to accomplish by sneaking around the Algolian's cabin with sodium iodide counters and microwave spectroscopes. Whatever he wrote doon in the lottery box canna be changed. The box is in my safe."

"Suppose he finds a way to open the safe?" the acting first suggested.

"In addition to the time lock it is keyed to the alpha radiations of my own brain," Captain Ramsay pointed out. "He canna possibly—ah, talk of the devil, Mr. French, look who's coming."

The rotund yet agile form of Macduff came scuttling rapidly along the corridor, one jump ahead of the Algolian. Macduff was breathing hard. At sight of the two officers he dived behind them like a quail going to cover. Ess Pu, blind with fury, snapped his claws in the Captain's very face.

"Control yourself, mon!" Ramsay said sharply. The Algolian made a mindless gobbling sound and waved a paper wildly in the air.

"Man, indeed," Macduff said with some bitterness, from his position of precarious safety. "He's nothing but an acromegalic lobster. It's getting so any object can be classi-

fied as humanoid these days, the way they keep broadening
the requirements. Letting in all the riff-raff of the Galaxy.
Martians were the opening wedge. Now the deluge. I can
see the need for a certain amount of latitude, but we peril
the dignity of true humanoids when we apply the proud
name of Man to a lobster. Why, the creature isn't even a
biped. In fact, there's a certain air of indecent exposure
about where he wears his bones."

"Tush, mon, ye ken the word's a mere figure of speech.
What is it, Ess Pu? What's this paper ye keep thrusting at
me?"

The Algolian was understood to gibber that Macduff
had dropped it while fleeing. He recommended that the
Captain read it carefully.

"Later," Ramsay said, thrusting it in his pocket. "We're
due to land on Xeria vurra soon, and I must be in the
control room. Go for-rard, Macduff."

Macduff obeyed with surprising alacrity, at least until he
was out of sight. Ess Pu, muttering thickly, followed. Only
then did Ramsay pull the paper from his pocket. He studied
it, snorted and handed it to the acting first. Macduff's neat
handwriting covered one side of the page, as follows:

Problem: Find out how many seeds in the first ripe
sphyghi fruit. How look inside a sealed fruit in which all
seeds may not be formed yet? Ordinary vision useless.

First day: Attempted to introduce radio-tracer in
sphyghi so I could count radioactivity day by day and
work out useful graphs. Failed. Ess Pu installed booby
trap, sign of low criminal mentality. No harm done.

Second day: Attempt to bribe Ess Pu with Immortality Elixir. Ess Pu outraged. Forgot Algolians regard ado-
lescence as despicable. Small minds value size inordi-
nately.

Third day: Tried to focus infrared on *sphyghi*, to
pick up secondary radiations with acoustical interfero-
meter. Failed. Experimented in long-distance color
staining of *sphyghi* cells with light waves. Failed.

Fourth day: Attempts to introduce chloroform into
Ess Pu's quarters failed also. Impossible to get near
enough fruit to try analysis through positive ion emis-
sions. Am beginning to suspect Ess Pu was responsible

for Captain Masterson's hospitalization back on Aldebaran Tau. Probably crept up from behind in dark alley.
All bullies are cowards. Note: try to turn Xerians
against Ess Pu on arrival. How?

There the quasi-diary ended. Mr. French looked up
quizzically.

"I had na realized Macduff was applying science so
thoroughly," Ramsay remarked. "But this merely confirms
what Ess Pu told me weeks ago. He said Macduff was
constantly trying to get at the *sphyghi*. But he couldna and
he canna and noo we must prepare for landing, Mr.
French."

He hurried away, trailed by the acting first. The corridor
lay empty and silent for a little while. Then an intercom
high in the wall spoke.

"General announcement," it said. "Passengers and crew
of the *Sutter,* your attention, please. Prepare for landing.
Immediately afterwards, passengers will assemble in the
grand lounge for the Xerian customs search. The results
of the ship's pool will also be announced. Your attendance
is compulsory. Thank you."

There was silence, a sound of heavy breathing and finally a new voice sounded. "That means you, Macduff," it
said grimly. "Ye ken? Aye, ye'd better."

Four minutes later, the *Sutter* landed on Xeria.

Yanked protesting from his cabin, Macduff was dragged
to the grand lounge, where everyone else had already assembled. A group of Xerian officials, repressing their joy
with some difficulty, was also in evidence, making a rather
perfunctory search of the passengers, while other Xerians
went through the ship rapidly, testing for contraband.

But it was obvious that the contraband that excited them
was the *sphyghi*. A table had been set up in the middle of
the big room and upon it, each plant in its own little earthen-
ware pot, the *sphyghi* stood. Plump golden fruit dangled from the branches, the pink glow of ripeness flushing
their downy surfaces. An odor of pure delight exhaled
from the plants. Ess Pu stood guardian, occasionally exchanging words with a Xerian official, who had already af-
fixed a medal* on the Algolian's carapace.

* With suction cups, of course.

"Outrageous!" Macduff cried, struggling. "I merely needed another few minutes' work with a vitally important experiment I was—"

"Close your blabber-mouth," Captain Ramsay told him. "I shall take great pleasure in kicking you off the *Sutter* myself."

"Leaving me to the tender mercies of that lobster? He'll kill me! I appeal to our common humanoid—"

Captain Ramsay conferred briefly with the Xerian leader, who nodded.

"Quite right, Captain," he or it said pedantically. "Under our laws debtors work out their debts, mayhem is assessed by its results and the aggressor forced to pay full reparations. Homicide naturally always carries the death penalty. Why do you ask?"

"That applies even to Ess Pu?" the Captain persisted.

"Naturally," the Xerian said.

"Weel, then," Ramsay said significantly to Macduff.

"Weel, then what? He'll be so rich he won't even mind paying reparations for the privilege of committing mayhem on my person. I bruise very easily."

"But he wullna kill ye," Ramsay said comfortingly. "And it wull be a fine lesson to ye, Macduff."

"Then at least I intend to get in one good blow," said Macduff, seizing a stout Malacca cane from a nearby avian and giving Ess Pu a resounding smack across the carapace. The Algolian let out a steam-whistle shriek of fury and lunged forward while Macduff, brandishing the cane like a rapier, danced pudgily backward, threatening even as he retreated.

"Come on, you overgrown shore dinner," cried Macduff valiantly. "We'll have it out now, humanoid to lobster!"

"Lay on, Macduff!" shouted an erudite and enthusiastic Ganymedan.

"Lay off!" bellowed Captain Ramsay, waving his officers to the rescue. But the Xerians were before them. They formed a quick barrier between the combatants and one of them twisted the cane from Macduff's reluctant grasp.

"If he has harmed you, Ess Pu, he will make reparations," the leader of the Xerians said. "Law is law. Are you injured?"

Despite Ess Pu's inarticulate gobbles, it was obvious that he was not. And the Xerian jurisprudence takes no notice of injured pride. Termites are humble by nature.

"Let's get this settled," Captain Ramsay said, annoyed at having his grand lounge turned into a shambles. "There are only three passengers disembarking here. Ao, Ess Pu and Macduff."

Macduff looked around for Ao, found her and, scuttling over, tried to hide behind her oblivious back.

"Ah, yes," the leading Xerian said. "Ess Pu has already explained the matter of the ship's pool. We will permit the lottery. However, certain conditions must be observed. No non-Xerian will be allowed to approach this table, and I will do the seed counting myself."

"That wull be satisfactory," Ramsay said, picking up the sealed ballot box and retreating. "If ye'll cut open the ripest of the fruit and count the seeds I'll then open this box and announce the winner."

"Wait!" Macduff cried out but his voice was ignored. The leading Xerian had picked up a silver knife from the table, plucked the largest, ripest *sphyghi* fruit and cut it neatly in two. The halves rolled apart on the table—to reveal a perfectly empty hollow within the fruit.

The Xerian's shout of dismay echoed through the lounge. The silver knife flashed, chopping the fruit to fragments. But not a single seed glittered in the creamy pulp.

"What's happened?" Macduff demanded. "No seeds? Obviously a swindle. I never trusted Ess Pu. He's been gloating—"

"Silence," the Xerian said coldly. In a subdued quiet he used the silver knife again and again in an atmosphere of mounting tension.

"No seeds?" Captain Ramsay asked blankly as the last fruit fell open emptily. The Xerian made no reply. He was toying with the silver knife and regarded Ess Pu.

The Algolian seemed as astounded as anyone else but Macduff audibly remarked, it was hard to tell, with an Algolian. Captain Ramsay courageously broke the ominous silence by stepping forward to remind the Xerians that he was a representative of the GBI.

"Have no fear," the Xerian said coldly. "We have no jurisdiction in your ship, Captain."

Macduff's voice rose in triumph.

"I never trusted that lobster from the start," he announced, strutting forward. "He merely took your money and made a deal for seedless *sphyghi*. He is obviously a criminal. His hasty exit from Aldebaran Tau, plus his known addiction to Lethean dust—"

At that point Ess Pu charged down upon Macduff, raging uncontrollably. At the last moment Macduff's rotund figure shot towards the open port and the thin Xerian sunlight outside. Ess Pu clattered after him, shrieking with fury, mouth membranes flaring crimson in his rage.

At the Xerian leader's quick command, the other Xerians hurried after Macduff. There were distant, cryptic noises from outside. Presently Macduff reappeared, panting and alone.

"Awkward creatures, Algolians," he said, nodding familiarly to the Xerian leader. "I see your men have—ah—detained Ess Pu."

"Yes," the Xerian said. "Outside, he is of course under our jurisdiction."

"The thought had occurred to me," Macduff murmured, drifting toward Ao.

"Noo wait a minute," Captain Ramsay said to the Xerians. "Ye have na—"

"We are not barbarians," the Xerian said with dignity. "We gave Ess Pu fifteen million Universal Credits to do a job for us and he has failed. Unless he can return the fifteen million, plus costs, he must work it out. The man-hour"—here Macduff was seen to wince—"the man-hour on Xeria is the equivalent of one sixty-fifth of a credit."

"This is highly irregular," the Captain said. "However, it's out of my jurisdiction now. You, Macduff—stop looking so smug. You get off at Xeria too, remember. I advise ye to stay out of Ess Pu's way."

"I expect he'll be busy most of the time," Macduff said cheerfully. "I hate to remind a supposedly competent officer of his duties, but haven't you forgotten the slight matter of the ship's pool?"

"What?" Ramsay glanced blankly at the pulped fruit. "The pool's called off, of course."

"Nonsense," Macduff interrupted. "Let's have no evasions. One might suspect you of trying to avoid a payoff."

"Mon, ye're daft. How can there be a payoff? The lottery was based on guessing the seed count in a *sphyghi* fruit and it's perfectly obvious the *sphyghi* has no seeds. Vurra weel. If no one has any objections——"

"I object!" Macduff cried. "On behalf of my ward, I demand that every single guess be counted and tabulated."

"Be reasonable," Ramsay urged. "If ye're merely delaying the evil moment when I kick ye off the *Sutter*——"

"You've got to wind up the pool legally," Macduff insisted.

"Pah, shut yer clatterin' trap," Ramsay snapped sourly, picking up the sealed box and attaching a small gadget to it. "Just as ye like. But I am on to ye, Macduff. Noo, quiet please, everybody."

He closed his eyes and his lips moved in a soundless mumble. The box flew open, disgorging a clutter of folded papers. At Ramsay's gesture a passenger stepped forward and began to open the slips, reading off names and guesses.

"So ye gain pairhaps five minutes' reprieve," Ramsay said under his breath to Macduff. "Then oot ye go after Ess Pu and let me say it is pairfectly obvious ye lured the Algolian oot of the *Sutter* on purpose."

"Nonsense," Macduff said briskly. "Am I to blame if Ess Pu focused his ridiculous antisocial emotions on me?"

"Aye," Ramsay said. "Ye ken dom well ye are."

"Male Kor-ze-Kabloom, seven hundred fifty," called the passenger unfolding another slip. "Lorma Secundus, two thousand ninety-nine. Ao, *per*——"

There was a pause.

"Well?" Captain Ramsay prompted, collaring Macduff. "Well, mon?"

"Terence Lao-t'se Macduff——" the passenger continued and again halted.

"What is it? What number did he guess?" Ramsay demanded, pausing at the open port with one foot lifted ready to boot the surprisingly philosophical Macduff down the gangplank. *"I asked ye a question!* What number's on the slip?"

"Zero," the passenger said faintly.

"Exactly!" Macduff declared, wriggling free. "And now, Captain Ramsay, I'll thank you to hand over half the ship's pool to me, as Ao's guardian—less, of course, the price of our passage to Lesser Vega. As for Ess Pu's half of the take, send it to him with my compliments.

"Perhaps it will knock a few months off his sentence, which, if my figures are correct, come to nine hundred and forty-six Xerian years. A Macduff forgives even his enemies. Come, Ao, my dear. I must choose a suitable cabin."

So saying, Macduff lit a fresh cigar and sauntered slowly away, leaving Captain Ramsay staring straight ahead and moving his lips as though in slow prayer. The prayer became audible.

"Macduff," Ramsay called. *"Macduff!* How did ye do it?"

"I," said Macduff over his shoulder, "am a scientist."

The Lesser Vegan cabaret hummed with festivity. A pair of comedians exchanged quips and banter among the tables. At one table Ao sat between Macduff and Captain Ramsay.

"I am still waiting to hear how ye did it, Macduff," Ramsay said. "A bargain's a bargain, ye know. I put my name on yon application, didn't I?"

"I cannot but admit," Macduff said, "that your signature facilitated my getting Ao's guardianship, bless her heart. Some champagne, Ao?" But Ao made no response. She was exchanging glances, less blank than usual, with a young Lesser Vegan male at a nearby table.

"Come, noo," Ramsay insisted. "Remember I wull have to turn over my log at the end of the voyage. I must know what happened concerning yon *sphyghi.* Otherwise, d'ye think I'd hae gone oot on a limb and guaranteed yer tortuous character, even though I carefully added, 'to the best of my knowledge'? No. Ye wrote thot zero when I saw ye do it, long before the fruit ripened."

"Right," Macduff said blandly, sipping champagne. "It was a simple problem in misdirection. I suppose there's no harm in telling you how I did it. Consider the circumstances. You are going to maroon me on Xeria, side by side with that lobster.

"Obviously I had to cut him down to my size by discrediting him with the Xerians. Winning the pool was an unexpected secondary development. Merely a stroke of well-de-served good luck, aided by applied scientific technique."

"Ye mean that stuff ye wrote down on the paper Ess Pu found—the gibble-gabble aboot interferometers and ion-analyzers? So ye did find some way to count the seeds—och, I'm wrong there, am I?"

"Naturally." Macduff twirled his glass and preened himself slightly. "I wrote that paper for Ess Pu's eyes. I had to keep him so busy protecting his *sphyghi* and chasing me that he never had a spare moment to think."

"I still dinna ken," Ramsay confessed. "Even if ye'd known the richt answer in advance, how could ye foresee the pool would be based on *sphyghi?*"

"Oh, that was the simplest thing of all. Consider the odds! What else could it be, with the Aldebaran Lottery fresh in every mind and the whole ship reeking of contraband *sphyghi?* If no one else had suggested it I was prepared to bring it up myself and—what's this? Go away! Get out!"

He was addressing himself to the two comedians, who had worked their way around to Macduff's table. Captain Ramsay glanced up in time to see them commence a new act.

The laugh-getting technique of insult has never basically changed all through the ages, and Galactic expansion has merely broadened and deepened its variety. Derision has naturally expanded to include species as well as races.

The comedians, chattering insanely, began a fairly deft imitation of two apes searching each other for fleas. There was an outburst of laughter, not joined by those customers who had sprung from simian stock.

"Tush!" Ramsay said irately, pushing back his chair. "Ye dom impudent—"

Macduff lifted a placating palm. "Tut, tut, Captain. Strive for the objective viewpoint. Merely a matter of semantics, after all." He chuckled tolerantly. "Rise above such insularity, as I do, and enjoy the skill of these mummers in the abstract art of impersonation. I was about to explain why I had to keep Ess Pu distracted. I feared he might notice how fast the *sphyghi* were ripening."

"Pah," Ramsay said, but relapsed into his chair as the comedians moved on and began a new skit. "Weel, continue."

"Misdirection," Macduff said cheerfully. "Have you ever had a more incompetent crew member than I?"

"No," Ramsay said, considering. "Never in my—"

"Quite so. I was tossed like spindrift from task to task until I finally reached Atmospheric Controls, which was exactly where I wanted to be. Crawling down ventilating pipes has certain advantages. For example, it was the work of a moment to empty a phial of two-four-five-trichlorophenoxyacetic acid"—he rolled the syllables lushly—"trichlorophenoxyacetic acid into Ess Pu's ventilator. The stuff must have got into everything, including the *sphyghi*."

"Trichloro—what? Ye mean ye gimmicked the *sphyghi before* the pool?"

"Certainly. I told you the pool was a later by-product. My goal at first was simply to get Ess Pu in trouble on Xeria to save my own valuable person. Luckily I had a fair supply of various hormones with me. This particular one, as the merest child should know, bypasses the need for cross-pollination. Through a law of biology the results will always be seedless fruit. Ask any horticulturist. It's done all the time."

"Seedless fruit—" Ramsay said blankly. "Cross-pollin— och, aye! Weel. I'll be dommed."

A modest disclaimer was no doubt on Macduff's lips, but his eye was caught by the two comedians and he paused, cigar lifted, regarding them. The shorter of the two was now strutting in a wide circle, gesturing like one who smokes a cigar with great self-importance. His companion whooped wildly and beat him over the head.

"Tell me this, brother!" he cried in a shrill falsetto. "Who was that penguin I seen you with last night?"

"That wasn't no penguin," the strutter giggled happily. "That was a Venusian!" Simultaneously he gestured, and a spotlight sprang like a tent over Macduff's shrinking head.

"What! What? *How dare you!*" screamed the outraged Macduff, recovering his voice at last amid ripples of laughter. "Libellous defamation of—of—I've never been so insulted in my life!" A repressed snort came from the Captain. The ruffled Macduff glared around furiously, rose to his full height and seized Ao's hand.

"Ignore them," Ramsay suggested in an unsteady voice. "After all, ye canna deny ye're Venusian by species, Mac-

duff, even though ye insist ye were hatched in Glasga'—
Borrn, I mean. Aye, ye're Scots by birth and humanoid by
classification, are ye na? And no more a penguin than I'm
a monkey."

But Macduff was already marching toward the door. Ao
trailed obediently after, casting back angelic looks at the
Lesser Vegan male.

"Outrageous!" said Macduff.

"Come back, mon," Ramsay called, suppressing a wild
whoop. "Remember the abstract art of impairsonation. 'Tis
a mere matter of semantics—"

His voice went unheard. Macduff's back was an indignant ramrod. Towing Ao, his bottle-shaped figure stiff with
dignity, Terence Lao-t'se Macduff vanished irrevocably
into the Lesser Vegan night, muttering low.

For Macduff, as should be evident by now to the mean-
est intellect,* was not all he claimed to be . . .

"Tush," said Captain Ramsay, his face split by a grin,
"that I should ha' seen the day! Waiter! A whusky-and-
soda—no more of this nosty champagne. I am celebrating
a red-letter occasion, a phenomenon of nature. D'ye ken
this is probably the first time in Macduff's life that the un-
principled scoundrel has taken his departure withoot leaving some puir swindled sucker behind?

"D'ye—eh? What's that? What bill, ye daft loon? Pah, it
was Macduff who insisted I be his guest tonight. Och, I—
ah—eh—

"Dom!"

---

* By which we mean the reader who skipped all the science, ele-
mentary as it was, in this chronicle.

Exit The Professor

WE HOGBENS ARE right exclusive. That Perfesser feller from the city might have known that, but he come busting in without an invite, and I don't figger he had call to complain afterward. In Kaintuck the polite thing is to stick to your own hill of beans and not come nosing around where you're not wanted.

Time we ran off the Haley boys with that shotgun gadget we rigged up—only we never could make out how it worked, somehow—that time, it all started because Rafe Haley come peeking and prying at the shed winder, trying to get a look at Little Sam. Then Rafe went round saying Little Sam had three haids or something.

Can't believe a word them Haley boys say. Three haids! It ain't natcheral, is it? Anyhow, Little Sam's only got two haids, and never had no more since the day he was born.

So Maw and I rigged up that shotgun thing and peppered the Haley boys good. Like I said, we couldn't figger out afterward how it worked. We'd tacked on some dry cells and a lot of coils and wires and stuff and it punched holes in Rafe as neat as anything.

Coroner's verdict was that the Haley boys died real sudden, and Sheriff Abernathy come up and had a drink of corn with us and said for two cents he'd whale the tar outa me. I didn't pay no mind. Only some damyankee reporter musta got wind of it, because a while later a big, fat, serious-looking man come around and begun to ask questions.

Uncle Les was sitting on the porch, with his hat over his face. "You better get the heck back to your circus, mister," he just said. "We had offers from old Barnum hisself and turned 'em down. Ain't that right, Saunk?"

"Sure is," I said. "I never trusted Phineas. Called Little Sam a freak, he did."

The big solemn-looking man, whose name was Perfesser Thomas Galbraith, looked at me. "How old are you, son?" he said.

"I ain't your son," I said. "And I don't know, nohow."

"You don't look over eighteen," he said, "big as you are. You couldn't have known Barnum."

"Sure I did. Don't go giving me the lie. I'll wham you."

"I'm not connected with any circus," Galbraith said. "I'm a biogeneticist."

We sure laughed at that. He got kinda mad and wanted to know what the joke was.

"There ain't no such word," Maw said. And at that point Little Sam started yelling, and Galbraith turned white as a goose wing and shivered all over. He sort of fell down. When we picked him up, he wanted to know what had happened.

"That was Little Sam," I said. "Maw's gone in to comfort him. He's stopped now."

"That was a subsonic," the Perfesser snapped. "What is Little Sam—a short-wave transmitter?"

"Little Sam's the baby," I said, short-like. "Don't go calling him outa his name, either. Now, s'pose you tell us what you want."

He pulled out a notebook and started looking through it.

"I'm a—a scientist," he said. "Our foundation is studying eugenics, and we've got some reports about you. They sound unbelievable. One of our men has a theory that natural mutations can remain undetected in undeveloped cultural regions, and—" He slowed down and stared at Uncle Les. "Can you really fly?" he asked.

Well, we don't like to talk about that. The preacher gave us a good dressing-down once. Uncle Les had got likkered up and went sailing over the ridges, scaring a couple of bear hunters outa their senses. And it ain't in the Good Book that men should fly, neither. Uncle Les generally does it only on the sly, when nobody's watching.

So anyhow Uncle Les pulled his hat down further on his face and growled.

"That's plumb silly. Ain't no way a man can fly. These here modern contraptions I hear tell about—'tween ourselves, they don't really fly at all. Just a lot of crazy talk, that's all."

Galbraith blinked and studied his notebook again.

"But I've got hearsay evidence of a great many unusual things connected with your family. Flying is only one of them. I know it's theoretically impossible—and I'm not talking about planes—but—"

"Oh, shet your trap."

"The medieval witches' salve used aconite to give an illusion of flight—entirely subjective, of course."

"Will you stop pestering me?" Uncle Les said, getting mad, on account of he felt embarrassed, I guess. Then he jumped up, threw his hat down on the porch and flew away. After a minute he swooped down for his hat and made a face at the Perfesser. He flew off down the gulch and we didn't see him fer a while.

I got mad, too.

"You got no call to bother us," I said. "Next thing Uncle Les will do like Paw, and that'll be an awful nuisance. We ain't seen hide nor hair of Paw since that other city feller was around. He was a census taker, I think."

Galbraith didn't say anything. He was looking kinda funny. I gave him a drink and he asked about Paw.

"Oh, he's around," I said. "Only you don't see him no more. He likes it better that way, he says."

"Yes," Galbraith said, taking another drink. "Oh, God. How old did you say you were?"

"Didn't say nothing about it."

"Well, what's the earliest thing you can remember?"

"Ain't no use remembering things. Clutters up your haid too much."

"It's fantastic," Galbraith said. "I hadn't expected to send a report like that back to the foundation."

"We don't want nobody prying around," I said. "Go way and leave us alone."

"But, good Lord!" He looked over the porch rail and got interested in the shotgun gadget. "What's that?"

"A thing," I said.

"What does it do?"

"Things," I said.

"Oh. May I look at it?"

"Sure," I said. "I'll give you the dingus if you'll go away."

He went over and looked at it. Paw got up from where he'd been sitting beside me, told me to get rid of the damyankee and went into the house. The Perfesser came back. "Extraordinary!" he said. "I've had training in electronics, and it seems to me you've got something very odd there. What's the principle?"

"The what?" I said. "It makes holes in things."

"It can't fire shells. You've got a couple of lenses where the breech should—how did you say it worked?"

"I dunno."

"Did you make it?"

"Me and Maw."

He asked a lot more questions.

"I dunno," I said. "Trouble with a shotgun is you gotta keep loading it. We sorta thought if we hooked on a few things it wouldn't need loading no more. It don't, neither."

"Were you serious about giving it to me?"

"If you stop bothering us."

"Listen," he said, "it's miraculous that you Hogbens have stayed out of sight so long."

"We got our ways."

"The mutation theory must be right. You must be studied. This is one of the most important discoveries since—" He kept on talking like that. He didn't make much sense.

Finally I decided there was only two ways to handle things, and after what Sheriff Abernathy had said, I didn't feel right about killing nobody till the Sheriff had got over his fit of temper. I don't want to cause no ruckus.

"S'pose I go to New York with you, like you want," I said. "Will you leave the family alone?"

He halfway promised, though he didn't want to. But he knuckled under and crossed his heart, on account of I said I'd wake up Little Sam if he didn't. He sure wanted to see Little Sam, but I told him that was no good. Little Sam couldn't go to New York, anyhow. He's got to stay in his tank or he gets awful sick.

Anyway, I satisfied the Perfesser pretty well and he went off, after I'd promised to meet him in town next morning. I felt sick, though, I can tell you. I ain't been away from the folks overnight since that ruckus in the old country, when we had to make tracks fast.

Went to Holland, as I remember. Maw always had a soft spot fer the man that helped us get outa London. Named Little Sam after him. I fergit what his name was. Gwynn or Stuart or Pepys—I get mixed up when I think back beyond the War between the States.

That night we chewed the rag. Paw being invisible, Maw kept thinking he was getting more'n his share of the corn, but pretty soon she mellowed and let him have a demijohn. Everybody told me to mind my p's and q's.

"This here Perfesser's awful smart," Maw said. "All perfessers are. Don't go bothering him any. You be a good boy or you'll ketch heck from me."

"I'll be good, Maw," I said. Paw whaled me alongside the haid, which wasn't fair, on account of I couldn't see him.

"That's so you won't fergit," he said.

"We're plain folks," Uncle Les was growling. "No good never come of trying to get above yourself."

"Honest, I ain't trying to do that," I said. "I only figgered—"

"You stay outa trouble!" Maw said, and just then we heard Grandpaw moving in the attic. Sometimes Grandpaw don't stir for a month at a time, but tonight he seemed right frisky.

So, natcherally, we went upstairs to see what he wanted. He was talking about the Perfesser.

"A stranger, eh?" he said. "Out upon the stinking knave. A set of rare fools I've gathered about me for my dotage! Only Saunk shows any shrewdness, and, dang my eyes, he's the worst fool of all."

I just shuffled and muttered something, on account of I never like to look at Grandpaw direct. But he wasn't paying me no mind. He raved on.

"So you'd go to this New York? 'Sblood, and hast thou forgot the way we shunned London and Amsterdam—and Nieuw Amsterdam—for fear of questioning? Wouldst thou be put in a freak show? Nor is that the worst danger."

Grandpaw's the oldest one of us all and he gets kinda mixed up in his language sometimes. I guess the lingo you learned when you're young sorta sticks with you. One thing, he can cuss better than anybody I've ever heard.

"Shucks," I said. "I was only trying to help."

"Thou puling brat," Grandpaw said. " 'Tis thy fault and thy dam's. For building that device, I mean, that slew the Haley tribe. Hadst thou not, this scientist would never have come here."

"He's a perfesser," I said. "Name of Thomas Galbraith."

"I know. I read his thoughts through Little Sam's mind. A dangerous man. I never knew a sage who wasn't. Except perhaps Roger Bacon, and I had to bribe him to—but Roger was an exceptional man. Hearken:

"None of you may go to this New York. The moment we leave this haven, the moment we are investigated, we are lost. The pack would tear and rend us. Nor could all thy addlepated flights skyward save thee, Lester—dost thou hear?"

"But what are we to do?" Maw said.

"Aw, heck," Paw said. "I'll just fix this Perfesser. I'll drop him down the cistern."

"An' spoil the water?" Maw screeched. "You try it!"

"What foul brood is this that has sprung from my seed?" Grandpaw said, real mad. "Have ye not promised the Sheriff that there will be no more killings—for a while, at least? Is the word of a Hogben naught? Two things have we kept sacred through the centuries—our secret from the world, and the Hogben honor! Kill this man Galbraith and ye'll answer to me for it!"

We all turned white. Little Sam woke up again and started squealing. "But what'll we do?" Uncle Les said.

"Our secret must be kept," Grandpaw said. "Do what ye can, but no killing. I'll consider the problem."

He seemed to go to sleep then, though it was hard to tell.

The next day I met Galbraith in town, all right, but first I run into Sheriff Abernathy in the street and he gave me a vicious look.

"You stay outa trouble, Saunk," he said. "Mind what I tell you, now." It was right embarrassing.

Anyway, I saw Galbraith and told him Grandpaw wouldn't let me go to New York. He didn't look too happy, but he saw there was nothing that could be done about it.

His hotel room was full of scientific apparatus and kinda frightening. He had the shotgun gadget set up, but it didn't look like he'd changed it any. He started to argue.

"Ain't no use," I said. "We ain't leaving the hills. I spoke outa turn yesterday, that's all."

"Listen, Saunk," he said. "I've been inquiring around town about you Hogbens, but I haven't been able to find out much. They're close-mouthed around here. Still, such evidence would be only supporting factors. I know our theories are right. You and your family are mutants and you've got to be studied!"

"We ain't mutants," I said. "Scientists are always calling us outa our names. Roger Bacon called us homunculi, only—"

"*What?*" Galbraith shouted. "Who did you say?"

"Uh—he's a share-cropper over in the next county," I said hasty-like, but I could see the Perfesser didn't swaller it. He started to walk around the room.

"It's no use," he said. "If you won't come to New York, I'll have the foundation send a commission here. You've got to be studied, for the glory of science and the advancement of mankind."

"Oh, golly," I said. "I know what that'd be like. Make a freak show outa us. It'd kill Little Sam. You gotta go away and leave us alone."

"Leave you alone? When you can create apparatus like this?" He pointed to the shotgun gadget. "How *does* that work?" he wanted to know, sudden-like.

"I told you, I dunno. We just rigged it up. Listen, Perfesser. There'd be trouble if people came and looked at us. Big trouble. Grandpaw says so."

Galbraith pulled at his nose.

"Well, maybe—suppose you answered a few questions for me, Saunk."

"No commission?"

"We'll see."

"No, sir. I won't—"

Galbraith took a deep breath.

"As long as you tell me what I want to know, I'll keep your whereabouts a secret."

"I thought this fundation thing of yours knows where you are."

"Ah—yes," Galbraith said. "Naturally they do. But they don't know about *you*."

That gave me an idea. I coulda killed him easy, but if I had, I knew Grandpaw would of ruined me entire and, besides, there was the Sheriff to think of. So I said, "Shucks," and nodded.

My, the questions that man asked! It left me dizzy. And all the while he kept getting more and more excited.

"How old is your grandfather?"

"Gosh, I dunno."

"Homunculi—mm-m. You mentioned that he was a miner once?"

"No, that was Grandpaw's paw," I said. "Tin mines, they were, in England. Only Grandpaw says it was called Britain then. That was during a sorta magic plague they had then. The people had to get the doctors—droons? Droods?"

"Druids?"

"Uh-huh. The Druids was the doctors then, Grandpaw says. Anyhow, all the miners started dying round Cornwall, so they closed up the mines."

"What sort of plague was it?"

I told him what I remembered from Grandpaw's talk, and the Perfesser got very excited and said something about radioactive emanations, as nearly as I could figger out. It made oncommon bad sense.

"Artificial mutations caused by radioactivity!" he said, getting real pink around the jowls. "Your grandfather was born a mutant! The genes and chromosomes were rearranged into a new pattern. Why, you may all be supermen!"

"Nope," I said. "We're Hogbens. That's all."

"A dominant, obviously a dominant. All your family were—ah—peculiar?"

"Now, look!" I said.

"I mean, they could all fly?"

"I don't know how yet, myself. I guess we're kinda freakish. Grandpaw was smart. He allus taught us not to show off."

"Protective camouflage," Galbraith said. "Submerged in a rigid social culture, variations from the norm are more easily masked. In a modern, civilized culture, you'd stick out like a sore thumb. But here, the backwoods, you're practically invisible."

"Only Paw," I said.

"Oh, Lord," he sighed. "Submerging these incredible natural powers of yours . . . Do you know the things you might have done?" And then all of a sudden he got even more excited, and I didn't much like the look in his eyes.

"Wonderful things," he repeated. "It's like stumbling on Aladdin's lamp."

"I wish you'd leave us alone," I said. "You and your commission!"

"Forget about the commission. I've decided to handle this privately for a while. Provided you'll cooperate. Help me, I mean. Will you do that?"

"Nope," I said.

"Then I'll bring the commission down from New York," he said triumphantly.

I thought that over.

"Well," I said finally, "what do you want me to do?"

"I don't know yet," he said slowly. "My mind hasn't fully grasped the possibilities."

But he was getting ready to grab. I could tell. I know that look.

I was standing by the window looking out, and all of a sudden I got an idea. I figgered it wouldn't be smart to trust the Perfesser too much, anyhow. So I sort of ambled over to the shotgun gadget and made a few little changes on it.

I knew what I wanted to do, all right, but if Galbraith had asked me why I was twisting wire here and bending a whozis there I couldn't of told him. I got no eddication. Only now I knew the gadget would do what I wanted it to do.

The Perfesser had been writing in his little notebook. He looked up and saw me.

"What are you doing?" he wanted to know.

"This don't look right to me," I said. "I think you monkeyed with them batteries. Try it now."

"In here?" he said, startled. "I don't want to pay a bill for damages. It must be tested under safety conditions."

"See the weathercock out there, on the roof?" I pointed

it out to him. "Won't do no harm to aim at that. You can just stand here by the winder and try it out."

"It—it isn't dangerous?" He was aching to try the gadget, I could tell. I said it wouldn't kill nobody, and he took a long breath and went to the window and cuddled the stock of the gun against his cheek.

I stayed back aways. I didn't want the Sheriff to see me. I'd already spotted him, sitting on a bench outside the feed-and-grain store across the street.

It happened just like I thought. Galbraith pulled the trigger, aiming at the weathercock on the roof, and rings of light started coming out of the muzzle. There was a fearful noise. Galbraith fell flat on his back, and the commotion was something surprising. People began screaming all over town.

I kinda felt it might be handy if I went invisible for a while. So I did.

Galbraith was examining the shotgun gadget when Sheriff Abernathy busted in. The Sheriff's a hard case. He had his pistol out and handcuffs ready, and he was cussing the Perfesser immediate and rapid.

"I seen you!" he yelled. "You city fellers think you can get away with anything down here. Well, you can't!"

"Saunk!" Galbraith cried, looking around. But of course he couldn't see me.

Then there was an argument. Sheriff Abernathy had seen Galbraith fire the shotgun gadget and he's no fool. He drug Galbraith down on the street, and I come along, walking soft. People were running around like crazy. Most of them had their hands clapped to their faces.

The Perfesser kept wailing that he didn't understand.

"I seen you!" Abernathy said. "You aimed that dingus of yours out the window and the next thing everybody in town's got a toothache! Try and tell me you don't understand!"

The Sheriff's smart. He's known us Hogbens long enough so he ain't surprised when funny things happen sometimes. Also, he knew Galbraith was a scientist feller. So there was a ruckus and people heard what was going on and the next thing they was trying to lynch Galbraith.

But Abernathy got him away. I wandered around town

for a while. The pastor was out looking at his church windows, which seemed to puzzle him. They was stained glass, and he couldn't figure out why they was hot. I coulda told him that. There's gold in stained-glass windows; they use it to get a certain kind of red.

Finally I went down to the jailhouse. I was still invisible. So I eavesdropped on what Galbraith was saying to the Sheriff.

"It was Saunk Hogben," the Perfesser kept saying. "I tell you, he fixed that projector!"

"I saw you," Abernathy said. "You done it. Ow!" He put up his hand to his jaw. "And you better stop it, fast! That crowd outside means business. Half the people in town have got toothaches."

I guess half the people in town had gold fillings in their teeth.

Then Galbraith said something that didn't surprise me too much. "I'm having a commission come down from New York; I meant to telephone the foundation tonight, they'll vouch for me."

So he was intending to cross us up, all along. I kinda felt that had been in his mind.

"You'll cure this toothache of mine—and everybody else's—or I'll open the doors and let in that lynch mob!" the Sheriff howled. Then he went away to put an icebag on his cheek.

I snuck back aways, got visible again and made a lot of noise coming along the passage, so Galbraith could hear me. I waited till he got through cussing me out. I just looked stupid.

"I guess I made a mistake," I said. "I can fix it, though."

"You've done enough fixing!" He stopped. "Wait a minute. What did you say? You can cure this—what *is* it?"

"I been looking at that shotgun gadget," I said. "I think I know what I did wrong. It's sorta tuned in on gold now, and all the gold in town's shooting out rays or heat or something."

"Induced selective radioactivity," Galbraith muttered, which didn't seem to mean much. "Listen. That crowd outside—do they ever have lynchings in this town?"

"Not more'n once or twice a year," I said. "And we already had two this year, so we filled our quota. Wish I could get you up to our place, though. We could hide you easy."

"You'd better do something!" he said. "Or I'll get that commission down from New York. You wouldn't like that, would you?"

I never seen such a man fer telling lies and keeping a straight face.

"It's a cinch," I said. "I can rig up the gadget so it'll switch off the rays immediate. Only I don't want people to connect us Hogbens with what's going on. We like to live quiet. Look, s'pose I go back to your hotel and change over the gadget, and then all you have to do is get all the people with toothaches together and pull the trigger."

"But—well, but—"

He was afraid of more trouble. I had to talk him into it. The crowd was yelling outside, so it wasn't too hard. Finally I went away, but I came back, invisible-like, and listened when Galbraith talked to the Sheriff.

They fixed it all up. Everybody with toothaches was going to the Town Hall and set. Then Abernathy would bring the Perfesser over, with the shotgun gadget, and try it out.

"Will it stop the toothaches?" the Sheriff wanted to know. "For sure?"

"I'm—quite certain it will."

Abernathy had caught that behitation.

"Then you better try it on me first. Just to make sure. I don't trust you."

It seemed like nobody was trusting nobody.

I hiked back to the hotel and made the switch-over in the shotgun gadget. And then I run into trouble. My invisibility was wearing thin. That's the worst part of being just a kid.

After I'm a few hundred years older I can stay invisible all the time if I want to. But I ain't right mastered it yet. Thing was, I needed help now because there was something I had to do, and I couldn't do it with people watching.

I went up on the roof and called Little Sam. After I'd tuned in on his haid, I had him put the call through to Paw and Uncle Les. After a while Uncle Les come flying down from the sky, riding mighty heavy on account of he was carrying Paw. Paw was cussing because a hawk had chased them.

"Nobody seen us, though," Uncle Les said. "I *think*."

"People got their own troubles in town today," I said. "I need some help. That Perfesser's gonna call down his commission and study us, no matter what he promises."

"Ain't much we can do, then," Paw said. "We cain't kill that feller. Grandpaw said not to."

So I told 'em my idea. Paw being invisible, he could do it easy. Then we made a little place in the roof so we could see through it, and looked down into Galbraith's room.

We was just in time. The Sheriff was standing there, with his pistol out, just waiting, and the Perfesser pale around the chops, was pointing the shotgun gadget at Abernathy. It went along without a hitch. Galbraith pulled the trigger, a purple ring of light popped out, and that was all. Except that the Sheriff opened his mouth and gulped.

"You wasn't faking! My toothache's gone!"

Galbraith was sweating, but he put up a good front. "Sure it works," he said. "Naturally. I told you——"

"C'mon down to the Town Hall. Everybody's waiting. You better cure us all, or it'll be just too bad for you."

They went out. Paw snuck down after them, and Uncle Les picked me up and flew on their trail, keeping low to the roofs, where we wouldn't be spotted. After a while we was fixed outside one of the Town Hall's windows, watching.

I ain't heard so much misery since the great plague of London. The hall was jam-full, and everybody had a toothache and was moaning and yelling. Abernathy come in with the Perfesser, who was carrying the shotgun gadget, and a scream went up.

Galbraith set the gadget on the stage, pointing down at the audience, while the Sheriff pulled out his pistol again and made a speech, telling everybody to shet up and they'd get rid of their toothaches.

I couldn't see Paw, natcherally, but I knew he was up on the platform. Something funny was happening to the shotgun gadget. Nobody noticed, except me, and I was watching for it. Paw—invisible, of course—was making a few changes. I'd told him how, but he knew what to do as well as I did. So pretty soon the shotgun was rigged the way we wanted it.

What happened after that was shocking. Galbraith aimed the gadget and pulled the trigger, and rings of light jumped out, yaller this time. I'd told Paw to fix the range so nobody outside the Town Hall would be bothered. But inside—

Well, it sure fixed them toothaches. Nobody's gold filling can ache if he ain't got a gold filling.

The gadget was fixed now so it worked on everything that wasn't growing. Paw had got the range just right. The seats was gone all of a sudden, and so was part of the chandelier. The audience, being bunched together, got it good. Pegleg Jaffe's glass eye was gone, too. Them that had false teeth lost 'em. Everybody sorta got a once-over-lightly haircut.

Also, the whole audience lost their clothes. Shoes ain't growing things, and no more are pants or shirts or dresses. In a trice everybody in the hall was naked as needles. But, shucks, they'd got rid of their toothaches, hadn't they?

We was back to home an hour later, all but Uncle Les, when the door busted open and in come Uncle Les, with the Perfesser staggering after him. Galbraith was a mess. He sank down and wheezed, looking back at the door in a worried way.

"Funny thing happened," Uncle Les said. "I was flying along outside town and there was the Perfesser running away from a big crowd of people, with sheets wrapped around 'em—some of 'em. So I picked him up. I brung him here, like he wanted." Uncle Les winked at me.

"Ooooh!" Galbraith said. "*Aaaah!* Are they coming?"

Maw went to the door.

"They's a lot of torches moving up the mountain," she said. "It looks right bad."

The Perfesser glared at me.

"You said you could hide me! Well, you'd better! This is your fault!"

"Shucks," I said.

"You'll hide me or else!" Galbraith squalled. "I—I'll bring that commission down."

"Look," I said, "if we hide you safe, will you promise to fergit all about that commission and leave us alone?"

The Perfesser promised. "Hold on a minute," I said, and went up to the attic to see Grandpaw.

He was awake.

"How about it, Grandpaw?" I asked.

He listened to Little Sam for a second.

"The knave is lying," he told me pretty soon. "He means to bring his commission of stinkards here anyway, recking naught of his promise."

"Should we hide him, then?"

"Aye," Grandpaw said. "The Hogbens have given their word—there must be no more killing. And to hide a fugitive from his pursuers would not be an ill deed, surely."

Maybe he winked. It's hard to tell with Grandpaw. So I went down the ladder. Galbraith was at the door, watching the torches come up the mountain.

He grabbed me.

"Saunk! If you don't hide me—"

"We'll hide you," I said. "C'mon."

So we took him down to the cellar . . .

When the mob got here, with Sheriff Abernathy in the lead, we played dumb. We let 'em search the house. Little Sam and Grandpaw turned invisible for a bit, so nobody noticed them. And naturally the crowd couldn't find hide nor hair of Galbraith. We'd hid him good, like we promised.

That was a few years ago. The Perfesser's thriving. He ain't studying us, though. Sometimes we take out the bottle we keep him in and study him.

Dang small bottle, too!

The Twonky

THE TURNOVER AT Mideastern Radio was so great that Mickey Lloyd couldn't keep track of his men. Employees kept quitting and going elsewhere, at a higher salary. So when the big-headed little man in overalls wandered vaguely out of a storeroom, Lloyd took one look at the brown dungaree suit—company provided—and said mildly, "The whistle blew half an hour ago. Hop to work."

"Work-k-k?" The man seemed to have trouble with the word.

Drunk? Lloyd, in his capacity as foreman, couldn't permit that. He flipped away his cigarette, walked forward and sniffed. No, it wasn't liquor. He peered at the badge on the man's overalls.

"Two-o-four, m-mm. Are you new here?"

"New. Huh?" The man rubbed a rising bump on his forehead. He was an odd-looking little chap, bald as a vacuum tube, with a pinched, pallid face and tiny eyes that held dazed wonder.

"Come on, Joe. Wake up!" Lloyd was beginning to sound impatient. "You work here, don't you?"

"Joe," said the man thoughtfully. "Work. Yes, I work. I make them." His words ran together oddly, as though he had a cleft palate.

With another glance at the badge, Lloyd gripped Joe's arm and ran him through the assembly room. "Here's your place. Hop to it. Know what to do?"

The other drew his scrawny body erect. "I am—expert," he remarked. "Make them better than Ponthwank."

"O.K.," Lloyd said. "Make 'em, then." And he went away.

The man called Joe hesitated, nursing the bruise on his head. The overalls caught his attention, and he examined them wonderingly. Where—oh, yes. They had been hanging in the room from which he had first emerged. His own garments had, naturally, dissipated during the trip—what trip?

Amnesia, he thought. He had fallen from the . . . the something . . . when it slowed down and stopped. How odd this huge, machine-filled barn looked! It struck no chord of remembrance.

Amnesia, that was it. He was a worker. He made things. As for the unfamiliarity of his surroundings, that meant nothing. He was still dazed. The clouds would lift from his mind presently. They were beginning to do that already.

Work. Joe scuttled around the room, trying to goad his faulty memory. Men in overalls were doing things. Simple, obvious things. But how childish—how elemental! Perhaps this was a kindergarten.

After a while Joe went out into a stock room and examined some finished models of combination radio-phonographs. So that was it. Awkward and clumsy, but it wasn't his place to say so. No. His job was to make Twonkies.

Twonkies? The name jolted his memory again. Of course he knew how to make Twonkies. He'd made them all his life—had been specially trained for the job. Now they were using a different model of Twonky, but what the hell! Child's play for a clever workman.

Joe went back into the shop and found a vacant bench. He began to build a Twonky. Occasionally he slipped off and stole the material he needed. Once, when he couldn't locate any tungsten, he hastily built a small gadget and made it.

His bench was in a distant corner, badly lighted, though it seemed quite bright to Joe's eyes. Nobody noticed the console that was swiftly growing to completion there. Joe worked very, very fast. He ignored the noon whistle, and, at quitting time, his task was finished. It could, perhaps, stand another coat of paint; it lacked the Shimmertone of a standard Twonky. But none of the others had Shimmertone. Joe sighed, crawled under the bench, looked in vain for a relaxopad, and went to sleep on the floor.

A few hours later he woke up. The factory was empty. Odd! Maybe the working hours had changed. Maybe— Joe's mind felt funny. Sleep had cleared away the mists of amnesia, if such it had been, but he still felt dazed.

Muttering under his breath, he sent the Twonky into the stock room and compared it with the others. Superficially it was identical with a console radio-phonograph combination of the latest model. Following the pattern of the others, Joe had camouflaged and disguised the various organs and reactors.

He went back into the shop. Then the last of the mists cleared from his mind. Joe's shoulders jerked convulsively.

"Great Snell!" he gasped. "So that was it! I ran into a temporal snag!"

With a startled glance around, he fled to the storeroom from which he had first emerged. The overalls he took off and returned to their hook. After that, Joe went over to a corner, felt around in the air, nodded with satisfaction and seated himself on nothing, three feet above the floor. Then Joe vanished.

"Time," said Kerry Westerfield, "is curved. Eventually it gets back to the same place where it started. That's duplication." He put his feet up on a conveniently outjutting rock of the chimney and stretched luxuriously. From the kitchen Martha made clinking noises with bottles and glasses.

"Yesterday at this time I had a Martini," Kerry said. "The time curve indicates that I should have another one now. Are you listening, angel?"

"I'm pouring," said the angel distantly.

"You get my point, then. Here's another. Time describes a spiral instead of a circle. If you call the first cycle 'a,' the second one's 'a plus 1'—see? Which means a double Martini tonight."

"I knew where that would end," Martha remarked, coming into the spacious, oak-raftered living room. She was a small, dark-haired woman, with a singularly pretty face and a figure to match. Her tiny gingham apron looked slightly absurd in combination with slacks and silk blouse. "And they don't make infinity-proof gin. Here's your Martini." She did things with the shaker and manipulated glasses.

"Stir slowly," Kerry cautioned. "Never shake. Ah—that's it." He accepted the drink and eyed it appreciatively. Black hair, sprinkled with grey, gleamed in the lamplight as he sipped the Martini. "Good. Very good."

Martha drank slowly and eyed her husband. A nice guy, Kerry Westerfield. He was forty-odd, pleasantly ugly, with a wide mouth and with an occasional sardonic gleam in his gray eyes as he contemplated life. They had been married for twelve years, and liked it.

From outside, the late, faint glow of sunset came through the windows, picking out the console cabinet that stood against the wall by the door. Kerry peered at it with appreciation.

"A pretty penny," he remarked. "Still—"

"What? Oh. The men had a tough time getting it up the stairs. Why don't you try it, Kerry?"

"Didn't you?"

"The old one was complicated enough," Martha said in a baffled manner. "Gadgets. They confuse me. I was brought up on an Edison. You wound it up with a crank, and strange noises came out of a horn. That I could understand. But now—you push a button, and extraordinary things happen. Electric eyes, tone selections, records that get played on both sides, to the accompaniment of weird groanings and clickings from inside the console—probably you understand those things. I don't even want to. Whenever I play a Crosby record in a superduper like that, Bing seems embarrassed."

Kerry ate his olive. "I'm going to play some Debussy." He nodded towards a table. "There's a new Crosby record for you. The latest."

Martha wriggled happily. "Can I, maybe, huh?"

"Uh-huh."

"But you'll have to show me how."

"Simple enough," said Kerry, beaming at the console. "Those babies are pretty good, you know. They do everything but think."

"I wish they'd wash the dishes," Martha remarked. She

set down her glass, got up and vanished into the kitchen.

Kerry snapped on a lamp nearby and went over to examine the new radio, Mideastern's latest model, with all the new improvements. It had been expensive—but what the hell? He could afford it. And the old one had been pretty well shot.

It was not, he saw, plugged in. Nor were there any wires in evidence—not even a ground. Something new, perhaps. Built-in antenna and ground. Kerry crouched down, looked for a socket, and plugged the cord into it.

That done, he opened the doors and eyed the dials with every appearance of satisfaction. A beam of bluish light shot out and hit him in the eyes. From the depths of the console a faint, thoughtful clicking proceeded. Abruptly it stopped. Kerry blinked, fiddled with dials and switches, and bit at a fingernail.

The radio said, in a distant voice, "Psychology pattern checked and recorded."

"Eh?" Kerry twirled a dial. "Wonder what that was? Amateur station—no, they're off the air. Hm-m-m." He shrugged and went over to a chair beside the shelves of albums. His gaze ran swiftly over the titles and composers' names. Where was the *Swan of Tuonela*? There it was, next to *Finlandia*. Kerry took down the album and opened it in his lap. With his free hand he extracted a cigarette from his pocket, put it between his lips and fumbled for the matches on the table beside him. The first match he lit went out.

He tossed it into the fireplace and was about to reach for another when a faint noise caught his attention. The radio was walking across the room towards him. A whiplike tendril flicked out from somewhere, picked up a match, scratched it beneath the table top—as Kerry had done—and held the flame to the man's cigarette.

Automatic reflexes took over. Kerry sucked in his breath, and exploded in smoky, racking coughs. He bent double, gasping and momentarily blind.

When he could see again, the radio was back in its accustomed place.

Kerry caught his lower lip between his teeth. "Martha," he called.

"Soup's on," her voice said.

Kerry didn't answer. He stood up, went over to the radio and looked at it hesitantly. The electric cord had been pulled out of its socket. Kerry gingerly replaced it.

He crouched to examine the console's legs. They looked like finely finished wood. His exploratory hand told him nothing. Wood—hard and brittle.

How in hell—

"Dinner!" Martha called.

Kerry threw his cigarette into the fireplace and slowly walked out of the room. His wife, setting a gravy boat in place stared at him.

"How many Martinis did you have?"

"Just one," Kerry said in a vague way. "I must have dozed off for a minute. Yeah. I must have."

"Well, fall to," Martha commanded. "This is the last chance you'll have to make a pig of yourself on my dumplings, for a week, anyway."

Kerry absently felt for his wallet, took out an envelope and tossed it at his wife. "Here's your ticket, angel. Don't lose it."

"Oh? I rate a compartment!" Martha thrust the pasteboard back into its envelope and gurgled happily. "You're a pal. Sure you can get along without me?"

"Huh? Hm-m-m—I think so." Kerry salted his avocado. He shook himself and seemed to come out of a slight daze. "Sure, I'll be all right. You trot off to Denver and help Carol have her baby. It's all in the family."

"We-ell, my only sister—" Martha grinned. "You know how she and Bill are. Quite nuts. They'll need a steadying hand just now."

There was no reply. Kerry was brooding over a forkful of avocado. He muttered something about the Venerable Bede.

"What about him?"

"Lecture tomorrow. Every term we bog down on the Bede, for some strange reason. Ah, well."

"Got your lecture ready?"

Kerry nodded. "Sure." For eight years he had taught at the University, and he certainly should know the schedule by this time!

Later, over coffee and cigarettes, Martha glanced at her

wristwatch. "Nearly train time. I'd better finish packing. The dishes—"

"I'll do 'em." Kerry wandered after his wife into the bedroom amd made motions of futile helpfulness. After a while, he carried the bags down to the car. Martha joined him, and they headed for the depot.

The train was on time. Half an hour after it had pulled out, Kerry drove the car back into the garage, let himself into the house and yawned mightily. He was tired. Well, the dishes, and then beer and a book in bed.

With a puzzled look at the radio, he entered the kitchen and started on the dishes. The hall phone rang. Kerry wiped his hands on a dish towel and answered it.

It was Mike Fitzgerald, who taught psychology at the University.

"Hiya, Fitz."

"Hiya. Martha gone?"

"Yeah. I just drove her to the train."

"Feel like talking, then? I've got some pretty good Scotch. Why not run over and gab a while?"

"Like to," Kerry said, yawning again, "but I'm dead. Tomorrow's a big day. Rain check?"

"Sure. I just finished correcting papers, and felt the need of sharpening my mind. What's the matter?"

"Nothing. Wait a minute." Kerry put down the phone and looked over his shoulder, scowling. Noises were coming from the kitchen. What the hell!

He went along the hall and stopped in the doorway, motionless and staring. The radio was washing the dishes.

After a while he returned to the phone. Fitzgerald said, "Something?"

"My new radio," Kerry told him carefully. "It's washing the dishes."

Fitz didn't answer for a moment. His laugh was a bit hesitant. "Oh?"

"I'll call you back," Kerry said, and hung up. He stood motionless for a while, chewing his lip. Then he walked back to the kitchen and paused to watch.

The radio's back was towards him. Several limber tentacles were manipulating the dishes, expertly sousing them in hot, soapy water, scrubbing them with the little mop, dipping them into the rinse water and then stacking them neatly in the metal rack. Those whip-lashes were the only sign of unusual activity. The legs were apparently solid.

"Hey!" Kerry said.

There was no response.

He sidled around till he could examine the radio more closely. The tentacles emerged from a slot under one of the dials. The electric cord was dangling. No juice, then. But what—

Kerry stepped back and fumbled out a cigarette. Instantly the radio turned, took a match from its container on the stove and walked forward. Kerry blinked, studying the legs. They couldn't be wood. They were bending as the—the thing moved, elastic as rubber. The radio had a peculiar sidling motion unlike anything else on earth.

It lit Kerry's cigarette and went back to the sink, where it resumed the dishwashing.

Kerry phoned Fitzgerald again. "I wasn't kidding. I'm having hallucinations or something. That damned radio just lit a cigarette for me."

"Wait a minute." Fitzgerald's voice sounded undecided. "This is a gag, eh?"

"No. And I don't think it's a hallucination, either. It's up your alley. Can you run over and test my knee-jerks?"

"All right," Fitz said. "Give me ten minutes. Have a drink ready."

He hung up, and Kerry, laying the phone back into its cradle, turned to see the radio walking out of the kitchen toward the living room. Its square, boxlike contour was subtly horrifying, like some bizarre sort of hobgoblin. Kerry shivered.

He followed the radio, to find it in its former place, motionless and impassive. He opened the doors, examining the turntable, the phonograph arm and the other buttons and gadgets. There was nothing apparently unusual. Again he touched the legs. They were not wood, after all. Some plastic, which seemed quite hard. Or—maybe they were wood, after all. It was difficult to make certain, without damaging the finish. Kerry felt a natural reluctance to use a knife on his new console.

He tried the radio, getting local stations without trouble.

The tone was good—unusually good, he thought. The phonograph—

He picked up Halvorsen's *Entrance of the Boyars* at random and slipped it into place, closing the lid. No sound emerged. Investigation proved that the needle was moving rhythmically along the groove, but without audible result. Well?

Kerry removed the record as the doorbell rang. It was Fitzgerald, a gangling, saturnine man with a leathery, wrinkled face and a tousled mop of dull gray hair. He extended a large, bony hand.

"Where's my drink?"

" 'Lo, Fitz. Come in the kitchen. I'll mix. Highball?"

"Highball."

"O.K." Kerry led the way. "Don't drink it just yet, though. I want to show you my new combination."

"The one that washes dishes?" Fitzgerald asked. "What else does it do?"

Kerry gave the other a glass. "It won't play records."

"Oh, well. A minor matter, if it'll do the housework. Let's take a look at it." Fitzgerald went into the living room, selected *Afternoon of a Faun* and approached the radio. "It isn't plugged in."

"That doesn't matter a bit," Kerry said wildly.

"Batteries?" Fitzgerald slipped the record in place and adjusted the switches. "Ten inch—there. Now we'll see." He beamed triumphantly at Kerry. "Well? It's playing now."

It was.

Kerry said, "Try that Halvorsen piece. Here." He handed the disk to Fitzgerald, who pushed the reject switch and watched the lever arm lift.

But this time the phonograph refused to play. It didn't like *Entrance of the Boyars*.

"That's funny," Fitzgerald grunted. "Probably the trouble's with the record. Let's try another."

There was no trouble with *Daphnis and Chloë*. But the radio silently rejected the composer's *Bolero*.

Kerry sat down and pointed to a nearby chair. "That doesn't prove anything. Come over here and watch. Don't drink anything yet. You, uh, you feel perfectly normal?"

"Sure. Well?"

Kerry took out a cigarette. The console walked across the room, picking up a matchbook on the way and politely held the flame. Then it went back to its place against the wall.

Fitzgerald didn't say anything. After a while he took a cigarette from his pocket and waited. Nothing happened.

"So?" Kerry asked.

"A robot. That's the only possible answer. Where in the name of Petrarch did you get it?"

"You don't seem much surprised."

"I am, though. But I've seen robots before; Westinghouse tried it, you know. Only this—" Fitzgerald tapped his teeth with a nail. "Who made it?"

"How the devil should I know?" Kerry demanded. "The radio people, I suppose."

Fitzgerald narrowed his eyes. "Wait a minute. I don't quite understand—"

"There's nothing to understand. I bought this combination a few days ago. Turned in the old one. It was delivered this afternoon, and . . ." Kerry explained what had happened.

"You mean you didn't know it was a robot?"

"Exactly. I bought it as a radio. And—and—the damn thing seems almost alive to me."

"Nope." Fitzgerald shook his head, rose and inspected the console carefully. "It's a new kind of robot. At least—" He hesitated. "What else is there to think? I suggest you get in touch with the Mideastern people tomorrow and check up."

"Let's open the cabinet and look inside," Kerry suggested.

Fitzgerald was willing, but the experiment proved impossible. The presumably wooden panels weren't screwed into place, and there was no apparent way of opening the console. Kerry found a screwdriver and applied it, gingerly at first, then with a sort of repressed fury. He could neither pry free a panel nor even scratch the dark, smooth finish of the cabinet.

"Damn!" he said finally. "Well, your guess is as good as mine. It's a robot. Only I didn't know they could make 'em like this. And why in a radio?"

"Don't ask me." Fitzgerald shrugged. "Check up tomorrow. That's the first step. Naturally, I'm pretty baffled. If a new sort of specialized robot has been invented, why put it in a console? And what makes those legs move? There aren't any casters."

"I've been wondering about that, too."

"When it moves, the legs look—rubbery. But they're not. They're hard as—as hardwood. Or plastic."

"I'm afraid of the thing," Kerry said.

"Want to stay at my place tonight?"

"No-no. No. I guess not. The—robot can't hurt me."

"I don't think it wants to. It's been helping you, hasn't it?"

"Yeah," Kerry said, and went off to mix another drink.

The rest of the conversation was inconclusive. Fitzgerald, several hours later, went home rather worried. He wasn't as casual as he had pretended, for the sake of Kerry's nerves. The impingement of something so entirely unexpected on normal life was subtly frightening. And yet, as he had said, the robot didn't seem menacing.

Kerry went to bed, with a new detective mystery. The radio followed him into the bedroom and gently took the book out of his hand. Kerry instinctively snatched for it.

"Hey!" he said. "What the devil—"

The radio went back into the living room. Kerry followed, in time to see the book replaced on the shelf. After a bit Kerry retreated, locking his door, and slept uneasily till dawn.

In dressing gown and slippers, he stumbled out to stare at the console. It was back in its former place, looking as though it had never moved. Kerry, rather white around the gills, made breakfast.

He was allowed only one cup of coffee. The radio appeared, reprovingly took the second cup from his hand and emptied it into the sink.

That was quite enough for Kerry Westerfield. He found his hat and topcoat and almost ran out of the house. He had a horrid feeling that the radio might follow him, but it didn't, luckily for his sanity. He was beginning to be worried.

During the morning he found time to telephone Mideastern. The salesman knew nothing. It was a standard model combination, the latest. If it wasn't giving satisfaction, of course, he'd be glad to—

"It's O.K.," Kerry said. "But who made the thing? That's what I want to find out."

"One moment, sir." There was a delay. "It came from Mr. Lloyd's department. One of our foremen."

"Let me speak to him, please."

But Lloyd wasn't very helpful. After much thought, he remembered that the combination had been placed in the stock room without a serial number. It had been added later.

"But who made it?"

"I just don't know. I can find out for you, I guess. Suppose I ring you back."

"Don't forget," Kerry said, and went back to his class. The lecture on the Venerable Bede wasn't too successful.

At lunch he saw Fitzgerald, who seemed relieved when Kerry came over to his table. "Find out any more about your pet robot?" the psychology professor demanded.

No one else was within hearing. With a sigh Kerry sat down and lit a cigarette. "Not a thing. It's a pleasure to be able to do this myself." He drew smoke into his lungs. "I phoned the company."

"And?"

"They don't know anything. Except that it didn't have a serial number."

"That may be significant," Fitzgerald said.

Kerry told the other about the incidents of the book and the coffee, and Fitzgerald squinted thoughtfully at his milk. "I've given you some psych tests. Too much stimulation isn't good for you."

"A detective yarn!"

"Carrying it a bit to extremes, I'll admit. But I can understand why the robot acted that way, though I dunno how it managed it." He hesitated. "Without intelligence, that is."

"Intelligence?" Kerry licked his lips. "I'm not so sure that it's just a machine. And I'm not crazy."

"No, you're not. But you say the robot was in the front room. How could it tell what you were reading?"

"Short of X-ray vision and superfast scanning and assimilative powers, I can't imagine. Perhaps it doesn't want me to read anything."

"You've said something," Fitzgerald grunted. "Know much about theoretical machines of that type?"

"Robots?"

"Purely theoretical. Your brain's a colloid, you know. Compact, complicated—but slow. Suppose you work out a gadget with a multimillion radioatom unit embedded in an insulating material. The result is a brain, Kerry. A brain with a tremendous number of units interacting at light-velocity speeds. A radio tube adjusts current flow when it's operating at forty million separate signals a second. And, theoretically, a radioatomic brain of the type I've mentioned could include perception, recognition, consideration, reaction and adjustment in a hundred-thousandth of a second."

"Theory."

"I've thought so. But I'd like to find out where your radio came from."

A page came over. "Telephone call for Mr. Westerfield."

Kerry excused himself and left. When he returned, there was a puzzled frown knitting his dark brows. Fitzgerald looked at him inquiringly.

"Guy named Lloyd, at the Mideastern plant. I was talking to him about the radio."

"Any luck?"

Kerry shook his head. "No. Well, not much. He didn't know who had built the thing."

"But it was built in the plant?"

"Yes. About two weeks ago—but there's no record of who worked on it. Lloyd seemed to think that was very, very funny. If a radio's built in the plant, they know who put it together."

"So?"

"So nothing. I asked him how to open the cabinet, and he said it was easy. Just unscrew the panel in back."

"There aren't any screws," Fitzgerald said.

"I know."

They looked at one another.

Fitzgerald said, "I'd give fifty bucks to find out whether that robot was really built only two weeks ago."

"Why?"

"Because a radioatomic brain would need training. Even in such matters as the lighting of a cigarette."

"It saw me light one."

"And followed the example. The dishwashing—hm-mm. Induction, I suppose. If that gadget has been trained, it's a robot. If it hasn't—" Fitzgerald stopped.

Kerry blinked. "Yes?"

"I don't know what the devil it is. It bears the same relation to a robot that we bear to Eohippus. One thing I do know, Kerry; it's very probable that no scientist today has the knowledge it would take to make a—a thing like that."

"You're arguing in circles," Kerry said. "It was made."

"Uh-huh. But how—when—and by whom? That's what's got me worried."

"Well, I've a class in five minutes. Why not come over tonight?"

"Can't. I'm lecturing at the Hall. I'll phone you after, though."

With a nod Kerry went out, trying to dismiss the matter from his mind. He succeeded pretty well. But dining alone in a restaurant that night, he began to feel a general unwillingness to go home. A hobgoblin was waiting for him.

"Brandy," he told the waiter. "Make it double."

Two hours later a taxi let Kerry out at his door. He was remarkably drunk. Things swam before his eyes. He walked unsteadily toward the porch, mounted the steps with exaggerated care and let himself into the house.

He switched on a lamp.

The radio came forward to meet him. Tentacles, thin but strong as metal, coiled gently around his body, holding him motionless. A pang of violent fear struck through Kerry. He struggled desperately and tried to yell, but his throat was dry.

From the radio panel a beam of yellow light shot out, blinding the man. It swung down, aimed at his chest. Abruptly a queer taste was perceptible under Kerry's tongue.

After a minute or so, the ray clicked out, the tentacles flashed back out of sight and the console returned to its corner. Kerry staggered weakly to a chair and relaxed, gulping.

He was sober. Which was quite impossible. Fourteen brandies infiltrate a definite amount of alcohol into the system. One can't wave a magic wand and instantly reach a state of sobriety. Yet that was exactly what had happened.

The—robot was trying to be helpful. Only Kerry would have preferred to remain drunk.

He got up gingerly and sidled past the radio to the bookshelf. One eye on the combination, he took down the detective novel he had tried to read on the preceding night. As he had expected, the radio took it from his hand and replaced it on the shelf. Kerry, remembering Fitzgerald's words, glanced at his watch. Reaction time, four seconds.

He took down a Chaucer and waited, but the radio didn't stir. However, when Kerry found a history volume, it was gently removed from his fingers. Reaction time, six seconds.

Kerry located a history twice as thick.

Reaction time, ten seconds.

Uh-huh. So the robot did read the books. That meant X-ray vision and superswift reactions. Jumping Jehoshaphat!

Kerry tested more books, wondering what the criterion was. *Alice in Wonderland* was snatched from his hands; Millay's poems were not. He made a list, with two columns, for future reference.

The robot, then, was not merely a servant. It was a censor. But what was the standard of comparison?

After a while he remembered his lecture tomorrow, and thumbed through his notes. Several points needed verification. Rather hesitantly he located the necessary reference book—and the robot took it away from him.

"Wait a minute," Kerry said. "I need that." He tried to pull the volume out of the tentacle's grasp, without success. The console paid no attention. It calmly replaced the book on the shelf.

Kerry stood biting his lip. This was a bit too much. The damned robot was a monitor. He sidled towards the book, snatched it and was out in the hall before the radio could move.

The thing was coming after him. He could hear the soft padding of it—its feet. Kerry scurried into the bedroom and locked the door. He waited, heart thumping, as the knob was tried gently.

A wire-thin cilium crept through the crack of the door and fumbled with the key. Kerry suddenly jumped forward and shoved the auxiliary bolt into position. But that didn't help, either. The robot's precision tools—the specialized antennae—slid it back; and then the console opened the door, walked into the room and came toward Kerry.

He felt a touch of panic. With a little gasp he threw the book at the thing, and it caught it deftly. Apparently that was all that was wanted, for the radio turned and went out, rocking awkwardly on its rubbery legs, carrying the forbidden volume. Kerry cursed quietly.

The phone rang. It was Fitzgerald.

"Well? How'd you make out?"

"Have you got a copy of Cassen's *Social Literature of the Ages*?"

"I don't think so, no. Why?"

"I'll get it in the University library tomorrow, then." Kerry explained what had happened. Fitzgerald whistled softly.

"Interfering, is it? Hm-m-m. I wonder . . ."

"I'm afraid of the thing."

"I don't think it means you any harm. You say it sobered you up?"

"Yeah. With a light ray. That isn't very logical."

"It might be. The vibrationary equivalent of thiamine chloride."

"Light?"

"There's vitamin content in sunlight, you know. That isn't the important point. It's censoring your reading—and apparently it reads the books, with superfast reactions. That gadget, whatever it is, isn't merely a robot."

"You're telling me," Kerry said grimly. "It's a Hitler."

Fitzgerald didn't laugh. Rather soberly, he suggested, "Suppose you spend the night at my place?"

"No," Kerry said, his voice stubborn. "No so-and-so radio's going to chase me out of my house. I'll take an ax to the thing first."

"We-ell, you know what you're doing, I suppose. Phone me if—if anything happens."

"O.K.," Kerry said, and hung up. He went into the living room and eyed the radio coldly. What the devil was it —and what was it trying to do? Certainly it wasn't merely a robot. Equally certainly, it wasn't alive, in the sense that a colloid brain is alive.

Lips thinned, he went over and fiddled with the dials and switches. A swing band's throbbing, erratic tempo came from the console. He tried the shortwave band—nothing unusual there. So?

So nothing. There was no answer.

After a while he went to bed.

At luncheon the next day he brought Cassen's *Social Literature* to show Fitzgerald.

"What about it?"

"Look here." Kerry flipped the pages and indicated a passage. "Does this mean anything to you?"

Fitzgerald read it. "Yeah. The point seems to be that individualism is necessary for the production of literature. Right?"

Kerry looked at him. "I don't know."

"Eh?"

"My mind goes funny."

Fitzgerald rumpled his gray hair, narrowing his eyes and watching the other man intently. "Come again. I don't quite—"

With angry patience, Kerry said. "This morning I went into the library and looked up this reference. I read it all right. But it didn't mean anything to me. Just words. Know how it is when you're fagged out and have been reading a lot? You'll run into a sentence with a lot of subjunctive clauses, and it doesn't percolate. Well, it was like that."

"Read it now," Fitzgerald said quietly, thrusting the book across the table.

Kerry obeyed, looking up with a wry smile. "No good."

"Read it aloud. I'll go over it with you, step by step."

But that didn't help. Kerry seemed utterly unable to assimilate the sense of the passage.

"Semantic block, maybe," Fitzgerald said, scratching his ear. "Is this the first time it's happened?"

"Yes—no. I don't know."

"Got any classes this afternoon? Good. Let's run over to your place."

Kerry thrust away his plate. "All right. I'm not hungry. Whenever you're ready—"

Half an hour later they were looking at the radio. It seemed quite harmless. Fitzgerald wasted some time trying to pry a panel off, but finally gave it up as a bad job. He found pencil and paper, seated himself opposite Kerry and began to ask questions.

At one point he paused. "You didn't mention that before."

"Forgot it, I guess."

Fitzgerald tapped his teeth with the pencil. "Hm-m-m. The first time the radio acted up—"

"It hit me in the eye with a blue light."

"Not that. I mean—what it said."

Kerry blinked. "What it said?" He hesitated. " 'Psychology pattern checked and noted,' or something like that. I thought I'd tuned in on some station and got part of a quiz program or something. You mean—"

"Were the words easy to understand? Good English?"

"No, now that I remember it," Kerry scowled. "They were slurred quite a lot. Vowels stressed."

"Uh-huh. Well, let's get on." They tried a word-association test.

Finally Fitzgerald leaned back, frowning. "I want to check this stuff with the last tests I gave you a few months ago. It looks funny to me—damned funny. I'd feel a lot better if I knew exactly what memory was. We've done considerable work on mnemonics—artificial memory. Still, it may not be that at all."

"Eh?"

"That—machine. Either it's got an artificial memory, has been highly trained or else it's adjusted to a different milieu and culture. It has affected you—quite a lot."

Kerry licked dry lips. "How?"

"Implanted blocks in your mind. I haven't correlated them yet. When I do, we may be able to figure out some sort of answer. No, that thing isn't a robot. It's a lot more than that."

Kerry took out a cigarette; the console walked across the

room and lit it for him. The two men watched with a faint shrinking horror.

"You'd better stay with me tonight," Fitzgerald suggested.

"No," Kerry said. He shivered.

The next day Fitzgerald looked for Kerry at lunch, but the younger man did not appear. He telephoned the house, and Martha answered the call.

"Hello! When did you get back?"

"Hello, Fitz. About an hour ago. My sister went ahead and had her baby without me—so I came back." She stopped, and Fitzgerald was alarmed at her tone.

"Where's Kerry?"

"He's here. Can you come over, Fitz? I'm worried."

"What's the matter with him?"

"I—I don't know. Come right away."

"O.K.," Fitzgerald said, and hung up, biting his lips. He was worried. When, a short while later, he rang the Westerfield bell, he discovered that his nerves were badly out of control. But sight of Martha reassured him.

He followed her into the living room. Fitzgerald's glance went at once to the console, which was unchanged, and then to Kerry, seated motionless by a window. Kerry's face had a blank, dazed look. His pupils were dilated, and he seemed to recognize Fitzgerald only slowly.

"Hello, Fitz," he said.

"How do you feel?"

Martha broke in. "Fitz, what's wrong? Is he sick? Shall I call the doctor?"

Fitzgerald sat down. "Have you noticed anything funny about the radio?"

"No. Why?"

"Then listen." He told the whole story, watching incredulity struggle with reluctant belief on Martha's face. Presently she said, "I can't quite—"

"If Kerry takes out a cigarette, the thing will light it for him. Want to see how it works?"

"No-no. Yes. I suppose so." Martha's eyes were wide.

Fitzgerald gave Kerry a cigarette. The expected happened.

Martha didn't say a word. When the console had returned to its place, she shivered and went over to Kerry. He looked at her vaguely.

"He needs a doctor, Fitz."

"Yes." Fitzgerald didn't mention that a doctor might be quite useless.

"What is that thing?"

"It's more than a robot. And it's been readjusting Kerry. I told you what's happened. When I checked Kerry's psychology patterns, I found that they'd altered. He's lost most of his initiative."

"Nobody on earth could have made that—"

Fitzgerald scowled. "I thought of that. It seems to be the product of a well-developed culture, quite different from ours. Martian, perhaps. It's such a specialized thing that it naturally fits into a complicated culture. But I do not understand why it looks exactly like a Mideastern console radio."

Martha touched Kerry's hand. "Camouflage?"

"But why? You were one of my best pupils in psych, Martha. Look at this logically. Imagine a civilization where a gadget like that has its place. Use inductive reasoning."

"I'm trying to. I can't think very well. Fitz, I'm worried about Kerry."

"I'm all right," Kerry said.

Fitzgerald put his finger tips together. "It isn't a radio so much as a monitor. In this other civilization, perhaps every man has one, or maybe only a few—the ones who need it. It keeps them in line."

"By destroying initiative?"

Fitzgerald made a helpless gesture. "I don't know! It worked that way in Kerry's case. In others—I don't know."

Martha stood up. "I don't think we should talk any more. Kerry needs a doctor. After that we can decide upon that." She pointed to the console.

Fitzgerald said, "It'd be rather a shame to wreck it, but—" His look was significant.

The console moved. It came out from its corner with a sidling, rocking gait and walked toward Fitzgerald. As he sprang up, the whiplike tentacles flashed out and seized him. A pale ray shone into the man's eyes.

Almost instantly it vanished; the tentacles withdrew, and

the radio returned to its place. Fitzgerald stood motionless. Martha was on her feet, one hand at her mouth.

"Fitz!" Her voice shook.

He hesitated. "Yes? What's the matter?"

"Are you hurt? What did it do to you?"

Fitzgerald frowned a little. "Eh? Hurt? I don't—"

"The radio. What did it do?"

He looked toward the console. "Something wrong with it? Afraid I'm not much of a repairman, Martha."

"Fitz." She came forward and gripped his arm. "Listen to me." Quick words spilled from her mouth. The radio. Kerry. Their discussion.

Fitzgerald looked at her blankly, as though he didn't quite understand. "I guess I'm stupid today. I can't quite understand what you're talking about."

"The radio—you know! You said it changed Kerry—" Martha paused, staring at the man.

Fitzgerald was definitely puzzled. Martha was acting strangely. Queer! He'd always considered her a pretty level-headed girl. But now she was talking nonsense. At least, he couldn't figure out the meaning of her words; there was no sense to them.

And why was she talking about the radio? Wasn't it satisfactory? Kerry had said it was a good buy, with a fine tone and the latest gadgets in it. Fitzgerald wondered, for a fleeting second, if Martha had gone crazy.

In any case, he was late for his class. He said so. Martha didn't try to stop him when he went out. She was pale as chalk.

Kerry took out a cigarette. The radio walked over and held a match.

"Kerry!"

"Yes, Martha?" His voice was dead.

She stared at the—the radio. Mars? Another world—another civilization? What was it? What did it want? What was it trying to do?

Martha let herself out of the house and went to the garage. When she returned, a small hatchet was gripped tightly in her hand.

Kerry watched. He saw Martha walk over to the radio

and lift the hatchet. Then a beam of light shot out, and Martha vanished. A little dust floated up in the afternoon sunlight.

"Destruction of life-form threatening attack," the radio said, slurring the words together.

Kerry's brain turned over. He felt sick—dazed and horribly empty. Martha—

His mind churned. Instinct and emotion fought with something that smothered them. Abruptly the dams crumbled, and the blocks were gone, the barriers down. Kerry cried out hoarsely, inarticulately, and sprang to his feet.

"Martha!" he yelled.

She was gone. Kerry looked around. Where—

What had happened? He couldn't remember.

He sat down in the chair again, rubbing his forehead. His free hand brought up a cigarette, an automatic reaction that brought instant response. The radio walked forward and held a lighted match ready.

Kerry made a choking, sick sound and flung himself out of the chair. He remembered now. He picked up the hatchet and sprang towards the console, teeth bared in a mirthless rictus.

Again the light beam flashed out.

Kerry vanished. The hatchet thudded onto the carpet.

The radio walked back to its place and stood motionless once more. A faint clicking proceeded from its radioatomic brain.

"Subject basically unsuitable," it said, after a moment. "Elimination has been necessary." Click! "Preparation for next subject completed."

Click.

"We'll take it," the boy said.

"You won't be making a mistake," smiled the rental agent. "It's quiet, isolated and the price is quite reasonable."

"Not so very," the girl put in. "But it is just what we've been looking for."

The agent shrugged. "Of course, an unfurnished place would run less. But—"

"We haven't been married long enough to have furni-

ture," the boy grinned. He put an arm around his wife.
"Like it, Hon?"

"Hm-m-m. Who lived here before?"

The agent scratched his cheek. "Let's see. Some people
named Westerfield, I think. It was given to me for listing
just about a week ago. Nice place. If I didn't own my own
house, I'd jump at it myself."

"Nice radio," the boy said. "Late model, isn't it?" He
went over to examine the console.

"Come along," the girl urged. "Let's look at the kitchen
again."

"O.K., Hon."

They went out of the room. From the hall came the
sound of the agent's smooth voice, growing fainter. Warm
afternoon sunlight slanted through the windows.

For a moment there was silence. Then—

Click!

A Gnome There Was

TIM CROCKETT SHOULD never have sneaked into the mine on Dornsef Mountain. What is winked at in California may have disastrous results in the coal mines of Pennslyvania. Especially when gnomes are involved.

Not that Tim Crockett knew about the gnomes. He was just investigating conditions among the lower classes, to use his own rather ill-chosen words. He was one of a group of southern Californians who had decided that labor needed them. They were wrong. They needed labor—at least eight hours of it a day.

Crockett, like his colleagues, considered the laborer a combination of a gorilla and The Man with the Hoe, probably numbering the Kallikaks among his ancestors. He spoke fierily of down-trodden minorities, wrote incendiary articles for the group's organ, *Earth,* and deftly maneuvered himself out of entering his father's law office as a clerk. He had, he said, a mission. Unfortunately, he got little sympathy from either the workers or their oppressors.

A psychologist could have analyzed Crockett easily enough. He was a tall, thin, intense-looking young man, with rather beady little eyes, and a nice taste in neckties. All he needed was a vigorous kick in the pants.

But definitely not administered by a gnome!

He was junketing through the country, on his father's money, investigating labor conditions, to the profound annoyance of such laborers as he encountered. It was with this idea in mind that he surreptitiously got into the Ajax coal mine—or, at least, one shaft of it—after disguising himself as a miner and rubbing his face well with black dust. Going down in the lift, he looked singularly untidy in the midst of a group of well-scrubbed faces. Miners look dirty only after a day's work.

Dornsef Mountain is honeycombed, but not with the shafts of the Ajax Company. The gnomes have ways of blocking their tunnels when humans dig too close. The whole place was a complete confusion to Crockett. He let himself drift along with the others, till they began to work. A filled car rumbled past on its tracks. Crockett hesitated, and then sidled over to a husky specimen who seemed to have the marks of a great sorrow stamped on his face.

"Look," he said, "I want to talk to you."

"Inglis?" asked the other inquiringly. "Viskey. Chin. Vine. Hell."

Having thus demonstrated his somewhat incomplete command of English, he bellowed hoarsely with laughter and returned to work, ignoring the baffled Crockett, who turned away to find another victim. But this section of the mine seemed deserted. Another loaded car rumbled past, and Crockett decided to see where it came from. He found out, after banging his head painfully and falling flat at least five times.

It came from a hole in the wall. Crockett entered it, and simultaneously heard a hoarse cry from behind him. The unknown requested Crockett to come back.

"So I can break your slab-sided neck," he promised, adding a stream of sizzling profanity. "Come outa there!"

Crockett cast one glance back, saw a gorillalike shadow lurching after him, and instantly decided that his stratagem had been discovered. The owners of the Ajax mine had sent a strong-arm man to murder him—or, at least, to beat him to a senseless pulp. Terror lent wings to Crockett's flying feet. He rushed on, frantically searching for a side tunnel in which he might lose himself. The bellowing from behind re-echoed against the walls. Abruptly Crockett caught a significant sentence clearly.

"—before that dynamite goes off!"

It was at that exact moment that the dynamite went off.

Crockett, however, did not know it. He discovered, quite briefly, that he was flying. Then he was halted, with painful suddenness, by the roof. After that he knew nothing at all, till he recovered to find a head regarding him steadfastly.

It was not a comforting sort of head—not one at which you would instinctively clutch for companionship. It was, in fact, a singularly odd, if not actually revolting, head. Crockett was too much engrossed with staring at it to realize that he was actually seeing in the dark.

How long had he been unconscious? For some obscure reason Crockett felt that it had been quite a while. The explosion had—what?

Buried him here behind a fallen roof of rock? Crockett would have felt little better had he known that he was in a used-up shaft, valueless now, which had been abandoned long since. The miners, blasting to open a new shaft, had realized that the old one would be collapsed, but that didn't matter.

Except to Tim Crockett.

He blinked, and when he reopened his eyes, the head had vanished. This was a relief. Crockett immediately decided the unpleasant thing had been a delusion. Indeed, it was difficult to remember what it had looked like. There was only a vague impression of a turnip-shaped outline, large, luminous eyes, and an incredibly broad slit of a mouth.

Crockett sat up, groaning. Where was this curious silvery radiance coming from? It was like daylight on a foggy afternoon, coming from nowhere in particular, and throwing no shadows. "Radium," thought Crockett, who knew very little of mineralogy.

He was in a shaft that stretched ahead into dimness till it made a sharp turn perhaps fifty feet away. Behind him—behind him the roof had fallen. Instantly Crockett began to experience difficulty in breathing. He flung himself upon the rubbly mound, tossing rocks frantically here and there, gasping and making hoarse inarticulate noises.

He became aware, presently, of his hands. His movements slowed till he remained perfectly motionless in a half-crouching posture, glaring at the large, knobbly, and surprising objects that grew from his wrists. Could he, during his period of unconsciousness, have acquired mittens? Even as the thought came to him, Crockett realized that no mittens ever knitted resembled in the slightest degree what he had a right to believe to be his hands. They twitched slightly.

Possibly they were caked with mud—no. It wasn't that. His hands had—altered. They were huge, gnarled, brown objects, like knotted oak roots. Sparse black hairs sprouted on their backs. The nails were definitely in need of a mani-cure—preferably with a chisel.

Crockett looked down at himself. He made soft cheeping noises, indicative of disbelief. He had squat bow legs, thick and strong, and no more than two feet long—less, if any-thing. Uncertain with disbelief, Crockett explored his body. It had changed—certainly not for the better.

He was slightly more than four feet high, and about three feet wide, with a barrel chest, enormous splay feet, stubby thick legs, and no neck whatsoever. He was wearing red sandals, blue shorts, and a red tunic which left his lean but sinewy arms bare. His head—

Turnip-shaped. The mouth—*Yipe*! Crockett had inad-vertently put his fist clear into it. He withdrew the offend-ing hand instantly, stared around in a dazed fashion, and collapsed on the ground. It couldn't be happening. It was quite impossible. Hallucinations. He was dying of asphyx-iation, and delusions were preceding his death.

Crockett shut his eyes, again convinced that his lungs were laboring for breath. "I'm dying," he said. "I c-can't breathe."

A contemptuous voice said, "I hope you don't think you're breathing *air*!"

"I'm n-not—" Crockett didn't finish the sentence. His eyes popped again. He was hearing things.

He heard it again. "You're a singularly lousy specimen of gnome," the voice said. "But under Nid's law we can't pick and choose. Still, you won't be put to digging hard metals, I can see that. Anthracite's about your speed. What're you staring at? You're *very* much uglier than I am."

Crockett, endeavoring to lick his dry lips, was horrified to discover the end of his moist tongue dragging limply over his eyes. He whipped it back, with a loud smacking noise, and managed to sit up. Then he remained perfectly motion-less, staring.

The head had reappeared. This time there was a body under it.

"I'm Gru Magru," said the head chattily. "You'll be given a gnomic name, of course, unless your own is guttural enough. What is it?"

"Crockett," the man responded, in a stunned, automatic manner.

"Hey?"

"Crockett."

"Stop making noises like a frog and—oh, I see. Crockett. Fair enough. Now get up and follow me or I'll kick the pants off you."

But Crockett did not immediately rise. He was watching Gru Magru—obviously a gnome. Short, squat and stunted, the being's figure resembled a bulging little barrel, topped by an inverted turnip. The hair grew up thickly to a peak —the root, as it were. In the turnip face was a loose, immense slit of a mouth, a button of a nose, and two very large eyes.

"Get *up*!" Gru Magru said.

This time Crockett obeyed, but the effort exhausted him completely. If he moved again, he thought, he would go mad. It would be just as well. Gnomes—

Gru Magru planted a large splay foot where it would do the most good, and Crockett described an arc which ended at a jagged boulder fallen from the roof. "Get up," the gnome said, with gratuitous bad temper, "or I'll kick you again. It's bad enough to have an outlying prospect patrol, where I might run into a man any time, with—*Up*! Or—"

Crockett got up. Gru Magru took his arm and impelled him into the depths of the tunnel.

"Well, you're a gnome now," he said. "It's the Nid law. Sometimes I wonder if it's worth the trouble. But I suppose it is—since gnomes can't propagate, and the average population has to be kept up somehow."

"I want to die," Crockett said wildly.

Gru Magru laughed. "Gnomes *can't* die. They're immortal, till the Day. Judgment Day, I mean."

"You're not logical," Crockett pointed out, as though by disproving one factor he could automatically disprove the whole fantastic business. "You're either flesh and blood and have to die eventually, or you're not, and then you're not real."

"Oh, we're flesh and blood, right enough," Gru Magru said. "But we're not mortal. There's a distinction. Not that I've anything against some mortals," he hastened to explain. "Bats, now—and owls—they're fine. But men!" He shuddered. "No gnome can stand the sight of a man."

Crockett clutched at a straw. "I'm a man."

"You were, you mean," Gru said. "Not a very good specimen, either, for my ore. But you're a gnome now. It's the Nid law."

"You keep talking about the Nid law," Crockett complained.

"Of course you don't understand," said Gru Magru, in a patronizing fashion. "It's this way. Back in ancient times, it was decreed that if any humans got lost in underearth, a tithe of them would be transformed into gnomes. The first gnome emperor, Podrang the Third, arranged that. He saw that fairies could kidnap human children and keep them, and spoke to the authorities about it. Said it was unfair. So when miners and such-like are lost underneath, a tithe of them are transformed into gnomes and join us. That's what happened to you. See?"

"No," Crockett said weakly. "Look. You said Podrang was the first gnome emperor. Why was he called Podrang the Third?"

"No time for questions," Gru Magru snapped. "Hurry!"

He was almost running now, dragging the wretched Crockett after him. The new gnome had not yet mastered his rather unusual limbs, and, due to the extreme wideness of his sandals, he trod heavily on his right hand, but after that learned to keep his arms bent and close to his sides. The walls, illuminated with that queer silvery radiance, spun past dizzily.

"W-what's that light?" Crockett managed to gasp. "Where's it coming from?"

"Light?" Gru Magru inquired. "It isn't light."

"Well, it isn't dark—"

"Of course it's dark," the gnome snapped. "How could we see if it wasn't dark?"

There was no possible answer to this, except, Crockett

thought wildly, a frantic shriek. And he needed all his breath for running. They were in a labyrinth now, turning and twisting and doubling through innumerable tunnels, and Crockett knew he could never retrace his steps. He regretted having left the scene of the cave-in. But how could he have helped doing so?

"Hurry!" Gru Magru urged. "Hurry!"

"Why?" Crockett got out breathlessly.

"There's a fight going on!" the gnome said.

Just then they rounded a corner and almost blundered into the fight. A seething mass of gnomes filled the tunnel, battling with frantic fury. Red and blue pants and tunics moved in swift patchwork frenzy; turnip heads popped up and down vigorously. It was apparently a free-for-all.

"See!" Gru gloated. "A fight! I could smell it six tunnels away. Oh, a beauty!" He ducked as a malicious-looking little gnome sprang out of the huddle to seize a rock and hurl it with vicious accuracy. The missile missed its mark, and Gru, neglecting his captive, immediately hurled himself upon the little gnome, bore him down on the cave floor, and began to beat his head against it. Both parties shrieked at the tops of their voices, which were lost in the deafening din that resounded through the tunnel.

"Oh—my," Crockett said weakly. He stood staring, which was a mistake. A very large gnome emerged from the pile, seized Crockett by the feet, and threw him away. The terrified inadvertent projectile sailed through the tunnel to crash heavily into something which said, *"Whoodoof!"* There was a tangle of malformed arms and legs.

Crockett arose to find that he had downed a vicious-looking gnome with flaming red hair and four large diamond buttons on his tunic. This repulsive creature lay motionless, out for the count. Crockett took stock of his injuries—there were none. His new body was hardy, anyway.

"You saved me!" said a new voice. It belonged to a—lady gnome. Crockett decided that if there was anything uglier than a gnome, it was the female of the species. The creature stood crouching just behind him, clutching a large rock in one capable hand.

Crockett ducked.

"I won't hurt you," the other howled above the din that

filled the passage. "You saved me! Mugza was trying to pull my ears off—oh! He's waking up!"

The red-haired gnome was indeed recovering consciousness. His first act was to draw up his feet and, without rising, kick Crockett clear across the tunnel. The feminine gnome immediately sat on Mugza's chest and pounded his head with the rock till he subsided.

Then she arose. "You're not hurt? Good! I'm Brockle Buhn . . . Oh, look! He'll have his head off in a minute!"

Crockett turned to see that his erstwhile guide, Gru Magru, was gnomefully tugging at the head of an unidentified opponent, attempting, apparently, to twist it clear off. "What's it all about?" Crockett howled. "Uh—Brockle Buhn! *Brockle Buhn!*"

She turned unwillingly. "What?"

"The fight! What started it?"

"I did," she explained. "I said, 'Let's have a fight.'"

"Oh, that was all?"

"Then we started." Brockle Buhn nodded. "What's your name?"

"Crockett."

"You're new here, aren't you? Oh—I know. You were a human being!" Suddenly a new light appeared in her bulging eyes. "Crockett, maybe you can tell me something. What's a kiss?"

"A—kiss?" Crockett repeated, in a baffled manner.

"Yes. I was listening inside a knoll once, and heard two human beings talking—male and female, by their voices. I didn't dare look at them, of course, but the man asked the woman for a kiss."

"Oh," Crockett said, rather blankly. "He asked for a kiss, eh?"

"And then there was a smacking noise and the woman said it was wonderful. I've wondered ever since. Because if any gnome asked me for a kiss, I wouldn't know what he meant."

"Gnomes don't kiss?" Crockett asked in a perfunctory way.

"Gnomes dig," said Brockle Buhn. "And we eat. I like to eat. Is a kiss like mud soup?"

"Well, not exactly." Somehow Crockett managed to explain the mechanics of osculation.

The gnome remained silent, pondering deeply. At last she said, with the air of one bestowing mud soup upon a hungry applicant, "I'll give you a kiss."

Crockett had a nightmare picture of his whole head being engulfed in that enormous maw. He backed away. "No-no," he got out. "I—I'd rather not."

"Then let's fight," said Brockle Buhn, without rancor, and swung a knotted fist which smacked painfully athwart Crockett's ear. "Oh, no," she said regretfully, turning away. "The fight's over. It wasn't very long, was it?"

Crockett, rubbing his mangled ear, saw that in every direction gnomes were picking themselves up and hurrying off about their business. They seemed to have forgotten all about the recent conflict. The tunnel was once more silent, save for the padpadding of gnomes' feet on the rock. Gru Magru came over, grinning happily.

"Hello, Brockle Buhn," he greeted. "A good fight. Who's this?" He looked down at the prostrate body of Mugza, the red-haired gnome.

"Mugza," said Brockle Buhn. "He's still out. Let's kick him."

They proceeded to do it with vast enthusiasm, while Crockett watched and decided never to allow himself to be knocked unconscious. It definitely wasn't safe. At last, however, Gru Magru tired of the sport and took Crockett by the arm again. "Come along," he said, and they sauntered along the tunnel, leaving Brockle Buhn jumping up and down on the senseless Mugza's stomach.

"You don't seem to mind hitting people when they're knocked out," Crockett hazarded.

"It's *much* more fun," Gru said happily. "That way you can tell just where you want to hit 'em. Come along. You'll have to be inducted. Another day, another gnome. Keeps the population stable," he explained, and fell to humming a little song.

"Look," Crockett said. "I just thought of something. You say human beings are turned into gnomes to keep the population stable. But if gnomes don't die, doesn't that mean that there are more gnomes now than ever? The population keeps rising, doesn't it?"

"Be still," Gru Magru commanded. "I'm singing."

It was a singularly tuneless song. Crockett, his thoughts veering madly, wondered if the gnomes had a national anthem. Probably "Rock Me to Sleep." Oh, well.

"We're going to see the Emperor," Gru said at last. "He always sees the new gnomes. You'd better make a good impression, or he'll put you to placer-mining lava."

"Uh—" Crockett glanced down at his grimy tunic. "Hadn't I better clean up a bit? That fight made me a mess."

"It wasn't the fight," Gru said insultingly. "What's wrong with you, anyway? I don't see anything amiss."

"My clothes—they're dirty."

"Don't worry about that," said the other. "It's good filthy dirt, isn't it? Here!" He halted, and, stooping, seized a handful of dust, which he rubbed into Crockett's face and hair. "That'll fix you up."

"I—*pffht!* . . . Thanks . . . *pffh!*" said the newest gnome. "I hope I'm dreaming. Because if I'm not—" He didn't finish. Crockett was feeling unwell.

They went through a labyrinth, far under Dornsef Mountain, and emerged at last in a bare, huge chamber with a throne of rock at one end of it. A small gnome was sitting on the throne paring his toenails. "Bottom of the day to you," Gru said. "Where's the Emperor?"

"Taking a bath," said the other. "I hope he drowns. Mud, mud, mud—morning, noon and night. First it's too hot. Then it's too cold. Then it's too thick. I work my fingers to the bone mixing his mud baths, and all I get is a kick," the small gnome continued plaintively. "There's such a thing as being *too* dirty. Three mud baths a day—that's carrying it too far. And never a thought for me! Oh, no. I'm a mud puppy, that's what I am. He called me that today. Said there were lumps in the mud. Well, why not? That damned loam we've been getting is enough to turn a worm's stomach. You'll find His Majesty in there," the little gnome finished, jerking his foot toward an archway in the wall.

Crockett was dragged into the next room, where, in a sunken bath filled with steaming, brown mud, a very fat gnome sat, only his eyes discernible through the oozy coating that covered him. He was filling his hands with mud and letting it drip over his head, chuckling in a senile sort of way as he did so.

"Mud," he remarked pleasantly to Gru Magru, in a voice like a lion's bellow. "Nothing like it. Good rich mud. *Ah!*"

Gru was bumping his head on the floor, his large, capable hand around Crockett's neck forcing the other to follow suit.

"Oh, get up," said the Emperor. "What's this? What's this gnome been up to? Out with it."

"He's new," Gru explained. "I found him topside. The Nid law, you know."

"Yes, of course. Let's have a look at you. Ugh! I'm Podrang the Second, Emperor of the Gnomes. What have you to say to that?"

All Crockett could think of was: "How—how can you be Podrang the Second? I thought Podrang the Third was the first emperor."

"A chatterbox," said Podrang II, disappearing beneath the surface of the mud and spouting as he rose again. "Take care of him, Gru. Easy work at first. Digging anthracite. Mind you don't eat any while you're on the job," he cautioned the dazed Crockett. "After you've been here a century, you're allowed one mud bath a day. Nothing like 'em," he added, bringing up a gluey handful to smear over his face.

Abruptly he stiffened. His lion's bellow rang out.

"Drook! *Drook!*"

The little gnome Crockett had seen in the throne room scurried in, ringing his hands. "Your Majesty! Isn't the mud warm enough?"

"You crawling blob!" roared Podrang II. "You slobbering, offspring of six thousand individual offensive stenches! You mica-eyed, incompetent, draggle-eared, writhing blot on the good name of gnomes! You geological mistake! You—You—"

Drook took advantage of his master's temporary inarticulacy. "It's the best mud, Your Majesty! I refined it myself. Oh, Your Majesty, what's wrong?"

"There's a worm in it!" His Majesty bellowed, and launched into a stream of profanity so horrendous that it practically made the mud boil. Clutching his singed ears, Crockett allowed Gru Magru to drag him away.

"I'd like to get the old boy in a fight," Gru remarked, when they were safely in the depths of a tunnel, "but he'd use magic, of course. That's the way he is. Best emperor we've ever had. Not a scrap of fair play in his bloated body."

"Oh," Crockett said blankly. "Well, what next?"

"You heard Podrang, didn't you? You dig anthracite. And if you eat any, I'll kick your teeth in."

Brooding over the apparent bad tempers of gnomes, Crockett allowed himself to be conducted to a gallery where dozens of gnomes, both male and female, were using picks and mattocks with furious vigor. "This is it," Gru said. "Now! You dig anthracite. You work twenty hours, and then sleep six."

"Then what?"

"Then you start digging again," Gru explained. "You have a brief rest once every ten hours. You mustn't stop digging in between, unless it's for a fight. Now, here's the way you locate coal. Just think of it."

"Eh?"

"How do you think I found you?" Gru asked impatiently. "Gnomes have—certain senses. There's a legend that fairy folk can locate water by using a forked stick. Well, we're attracted to metals. Think of anthracite," he finished, and Crockett obeyed. Instantly he found himself turning to the wall of the tunnel nearest him.

"See how it works?" Gru grinned. "It's a natural evolution, I suppose. Functional. We have to know where the underneath deposits are, so the authorities gave us this sense when we were created. Think of ore—or any deposit in the ground—and you'll be attracted to it. Just as there's a repulsion in all gnomes against daylight."

"Eh?" Crockett started slightly. "What was that?"

"Negative and positive. We need ores, so we're attracted

to them. Daylight is harmful to us, so if we think we're getting too close to the surface, we think of light, and it repels us. Try it!"

Crockett obeyed. Something seemed to be pressing down the top of his head.

"Straight up," Gru nodded. "But it's a long way. I saw daylight once. And—a man, too." He stared at the other. "I forgot to explain. Gnomes can't stand the sight of human beings. They—well, there's a limit to how much ugliness a gnome can look at. Now you're one of us, you'll feel the same way. Keep away from daylight, and never look at a man. It's as much as your sanity is worth."

There was a thought stirring in Crockett's mind. He could, then, find his way out of this maze of tunnels, simply by employing his new sense to lead him to daylight. After that—well, at least he would be aboveground.

Gru Magru shoved Crockett into a place between two busy gnomes and thrust a pick into his hands. "There. Get to work."

"Thanks for—" Crockett began, when Gru suddenly kicked him and then took his departure, humming happily to himself. Another gnome came up, saw Crockett standing motionless, and told him to get busy, accompanying the command with a blow on his already tender ear. Perforce Crockett seized the pick and began to chop anthracite out of the wall.

"Crockett!" said a familiar voice. "It's you! I thought they'd send you here."

It was Brockle Buhn, the feminine gnome Crockett had already encountered. She was swinging a pick with the others, but dropped it now to grin at her companion.

"You won't be here long," she consoled. "Ten years or so. Unless you run into trouble, and then you'll be put at really hard work."

Crockett's arms were already aching. "*Hard* work! My arms are going to fall off in a minute."

He leaned on his pick. "Is this your regular job?"

"Yes—but I'm seldom here. Usually I'm being punished. I'm a troublemaker, I am. I eat anthracite."

She demonstrated, and Crockett shuddered at the audible crunching sound. Just then the overseer came up. Brockle Buhn swallowed hastily.

"What's this?" he snarled. "Why aren't you at work?"

"We were just going to fight," Brockle Buhn explained.

"Oh—just the two of you? Or can I join in?"

"Free for all," the unladylike gnome offered, and struck the unsuspecting Crockett over the head with her pick. He went out like a light.

Awakening some time later, he investigated bruised ribs and decided Brockle Buhn must have kicked him after he'd lost consciousness. What a gnome! Crockett sat up, finding himself in the same tunnel, dozens of gnomes busily digging anthracite.

The overseer came toward him. "Awake, eh? Get to work!"

Dazedly Crockett obeyed. Brockle Buhn flashed him a delighted grin. "You missed it. I got an ear—see?" She exhibited it. Crockett hastily lifted an exploring hand. It wasn't his.

Dig . . . dig . . . dig . . . the hours dragged past. Crockett had never worked so hard in his life. But he noticed, not a gnome complained. Twenty hours of toil, with one brief rest period—he'd slept through that. Dig . . . dig . . . dig . . .

Without ceasing her work, Brockle Buhn said, "I think you'll make a good gnome, Crockett. You're toughening up already. Nobody'd ever believe you were once a man."

"Oh—no?"

"No. What were you, a miner?"

"I was—" Crockett paused suddenly. A curious light came into his eyes.

"I was a labor organizer," he finished.

"What's that?"

"Ever heard of a union?" Crockett asked, his gaze intent.

"Is it an ore?" Brockle Buhn shook her head. "No, I've never heard of it. What's a union?"

Crockett explained. No genuine labor organizer would have accepted that explanation. It was, to say the least, biased.

Brockle Buhn seemed puzzled. "I don't see what you mean, exactly, but I suppose it's all right."

"Try another tack," Crockett said. "Don't you ever get tired of working twenty hours a day?"

"Sure. Who wouldn't?"

"Then why do it?"

"We always have," Brockle Buhn said indulgently. "We can't stop."

"Suppose you all did," Crockett insisted. "Every damn gnome. Suppose you had a sit-down strike."

"I'd be punished—beaten with stalactites, or something."

"Suppose you all had a sit-down strike."

"You're crazy," Brockle Buhn said. "Such a thing's never happened. It—it's *human*."

"Kisses never happened underground, either," said Crockett. "No, I don't want one! And I don't want to fight, either. Good heavens, let me get the setup here. Most of the gnomes work to support the privileged classes."

"No. We just work."

"But why?"

"We always have. And the Emperor wants us to."

"Has the Emperor ever worked?" Crockett demanded, with an air of triumph. "No! He just takes mud baths! Why shouldn't every gnome have the same privilege? Why—"

He talked on, at great length, as he worked. Brockle Buhn listened with increasing interest. And eventually she swallowed the bait—hook, line and sinker.

An hour later she was nodding agreeably. "I'll pass the word along. Tonight. In the Roaring Cave. Right after work."

"Wait a minute," Crockett objected. "How many gnomes can we get?"

"Well—not very many. Thirty?"

"We'll have to organize first. We'll need a definite plan." Brockle Buhn went off at a tangent. "Let's fight."

"No! Will you listen? We need a—a council. Who's the worst troublemaker here?"

"Mugza, I think," she said. "The red-haired gnome you knocked out when he hit me."

Crockett frowned slightly. Would Mugza hold a grudge? Probably not, he decided. Or, rather, he'd be no more ill tempered than other gnomes. Mugza might attempt to throttle Crockett on sight, but he'd no doubt do the same to any other gnome. Besides, as Brockle Buhn went on to explain, Mugza was the gnomic equivalent of a duke. His support would be valuable.

"And Gru Magru," she suggested. "He loves new things, especially if they make trouble."

"Yeah." These were not the two Crockett would have chosen, but at least he could think of no other candidates. "If we could get somebody who's close to the Emperor . . . What about Drook—the guy who gives Podrang his mud baths?"

"Why not? I'll fix it." Brockle Buhn lost interest and surreptitiously began to eat anthracite. Since the overseer was watching, this resulted in a violent quarrel, from which Crockett emerged with a black eye. Whispering profanity under his breath, he went back to digging.

But he had time for a few more words with Brockle Buhn. She'd arrange it. That night there would be a secret meeting of the conspirators.

Crockett had been looking forward to exhausted slumber, but this chance was too good to miss. He had no wish to continue his unpleasant job digging anthracite. His body ached fearfully. Besides, if he could induce the gnomes to strike, he might be able to put the squeeze on Podrang II. Gru Magru had said the Emperor was a magician. Couldn't he, then, transform Crockett back into a man?

"He's never done that," Brockle Buhn said, and Crockett realized he had spoken his thought aloud.

"Couldn't he, though—if he wanted?"

Brockle Buhn merely shuddered, but Crockett had a little gleam of hope. To be human again!

Dig . . . dig . . . dig . . . dig . . . with monotonous, deadening regularity Crockett sank into a stupor. Unless he got the gnomes to strike, he was faced with an eternity of arduous toil. He was scarcely conscious of knocking off, of feeling Brockle Buhn's gnarled hand under his arm, of being led through passages to a tiny cubicle, which was his new home. The gnome left him there, and he crawled into a stony bunk and went to sleep.

Presently a casual kick aroused him. Blinking, Crockett sat up, instinctively dodging the blow Gru Magru was aiming at his head. He had four guests—Gru, Brockle Buhn, Drook and the red-haired Mugza.

"Sorry I woke up too soon," Crockett said bitterly. "If I hadn't, you could have got in another kick."

"There's lots of time," Gru said. "Now, what's this all about? I wanted to sleep, but Brockle Buhn here said there was going to be a fight. A *big* one, huh?"

"Eat first," Brockle Buhn said firmly. "I'll fix mud soup for everybody." She bustled away, and presently was busy in a corner, preparing refreshments. The other gnomes squatted on their haunches, and Crockett sat on the edge of his bunk, still dazed with sleep.

But he managed to explain his idea of the union. It was received with interest—chiefly, he felt, because it involved the possibility of a tremendous scrap.

"You mean every Dornsef gnome jumps the Emperor?" Gru asked.

"No, no! Peaceful arbitration. We just refuse to work. All of us."

"*I* can't," Drook said. "Podrang's got to have his mud baths, the bloated old slug. He'd send me to the fumaroles till I was roasted."

"Who'd take you there?" Crockett asked.

"Oh—the guards, I suppose."

"But they'd be on strike, too. *Nobody'd* obey Podrang, till he gave in"

"Then he'd enchant me," Drook said.

"He can't enchant us all," Crockett countered.

"But he could enchant *me,*" Drook said with great firmness. "Besides, he *could* put a spell on every gnome in Dornsef. Turn us into stalactites or something."

"Then what? He wouldn't have any gnomes at all. Half a loaf is better than none. We'll just use logic on him. Wouldn't he rather have a little less work done than none at all?"

"Not him," Gru put in. "He'd rather enchant us. Oh, he's a bad one, he is," the gnome finished approvingly.

But Crockett couldn't quite believe this. It was too alien to his understanding of psychology—human psychology, of course. He turned to Mugza, who was glowering furiously.

"What do you think about it?"

"I want to fight," the other said rancorously. "I want to kick somebody."

"Wouldn't you rather have mud baths three times a day?"

Mugza grunted. "Sure. But the Emperor won't let me."

"Why not?"

"Because I want 'em."

"You can't be contented," Crockett said desperately. "There's more to life than—than digging."

"Sure. There's fighting. Podrang lets us fight whenever we want."

Crockett had a sudden inspiration. "But that's just it. He's going to stop all fighting! He's going to pass a new law forbidding fighting except to himself."

It was an effective shot in the dark. Every gnome jumped.

"Stop—*fighting!*" That was Gru, angry and disbelieving. "Why, we've always fought."

"Well, you'll have to stop," Crockett insisted.

"Won't!"

"Exactly! Why should you? Every gnome's entitled to life, liberty and the pursuit of—of pugilism."

"Let's go and beat up Podrang," Mugza offered, accepting a steaming bowl of mud soup from Brockle Buhn.

"No, that's not the way—no, thanks, Brockle Buhn—not the way at all. A strike's the thing. We'll peaceably force Podrang to give us what we want."

He turned to Drook. "Just what can Podrang do about it if we all sit down and refuse to work?"

The little gnome considered. "He'd swear. And kick me."

"Yeah—and then what?"

"Then he'd go off and enchant everybody, tunnel by tunnel."

"Uh-huh." Crockett nodded. "A good point. Solidarity is what we need. If Podrang finds a few gnomes together, he can scare the hell out of them. But if we're all together—that's it! When the strike's called, we'll all meet in the biggest cave in the joint."

"That's the Council Chamber," Gru said. "Next to Podrang's throne room."

"O.K. We'll meet there. How many gnomes will join us?"

"All of 'em," Mugza grunted, throwing his soup bowl at Drook's head. "The Emperor can't stop us fighting."

"And what weapons can Podrang use, Drook?"

"He might use the Cockatrice Eggs," the other said doubtfully.

"What are those?"

"They're not really eggs," Gru broke in. "They're magic jewels for wholesale enchantments. Different spells in each one. The green ones, I think, are for turning people into earthworms. Podrang just breaks one, and the spell spreads out for twenty feet or so. The red ones are—let's see. Transforming gnomes into human beings—though that's a bit *too* tough. No . . . yes. The blue ones—"

"Into *human beings!*" Crockett's eyes widened. "Where are the eggs kept?"

"Let's fight," Mugza offered, and hurled himself bodily on Drook, who squeaked frantically and beat his attacker over the head with his soup bowl, which broke. Brockle Buhn added to the excitement by kicking both battlers impartially, till felled by Gru Magru. Within a few moments the room resounded with the excited screams of gnomic battle. Inevitably Crockett was sucked in . . .

Of all the perverted, incredible forms of life that had ever existed, gnomes were about the oddest. It was impossible to understand their philosophy. Their minds worked along different paths from human intelligences. Self-preservation and survival of the race—these two vital human instincts were lacking in gnomes. They neither died nor propagated. They just worked and fought. Bad-tempered little monsters, Crockett thought irritably. Yet they had existed for—ages. Since the beginning, maybe. Their social organism was the result of evolution far older than man's. It might be well suited to gnomes. Crockett might be throwing the unnecessary monkey wrench in the machinery.

So what? He wasn't going to spend eternity digging anthracite, even though, in retrospect, he remembered feeling a curious thrill of obscure pleasure as he worked. Digging might be fun for gnomes. Certainly it was their *raison d'être*. In time Crockett himself might lose his human affil-

iations, and be metamorphosed completely into a gnome.
What had happened to other humans who had undergone
such an—alteration as he had done? All gnomes look alike.
But maybe Gru Magru had once been human—or Drook
—or Brockle Buhn.

They were gnomes now, at any rate, thinking and existing completely as gnomes. And in time he himself would be
exactly like them. Already he had acquired the strange
tropism that attracted him to metals and repelled him from
daylight. But he didn't *like* to dig!

He tried to recall the little he knew about gnomes—miners, metalsmiths, living underground. There was something
about the Picts—dwarfish men who hid underground
when invaders came to England, centuries ago. That
seemed to tie in vaguely with the gnomes' dread of human
beings. But the gnomes themselves were certainly not descended from Picts. Very likely the two separate races and
species had become identified through occupying the same
habitat.

Well, that was no help. What about the Emperor? He
wasn't, apparently, a gnome with a high I.Q., but he *was* a
magician. Those jewels—Cockatrice Eggs—were significant. If he could get hold of the ones that transformed
gnomes into men . . .

But obviously he couldn't, at present. Better wait. Till
the strike had been called. The strike . . .

Crockett went to sleep.

He was roused, painfully, by Brockle Buhn, who seemed
to have adopted him. Very likely it was her curiosity about
the matter of a kiss. From time to time she offered to give
Crockett one, but he steadfastly refused. In lieu of it, she
supplied him with breakfast. At least, he thought grimly,
he'd get plenty of iron in his system, even though the rusty
chips rather resembled corn flakes. As a special induce-
ment Brockle Buhn sprinkled coal dust over the mess.

Well, no doubt his digestive system had also altered.
Crockett wished he could get an X-ray picture of his insides. Then he decided it would be much too disturbing.
Better not to know. But he could not help wondering.
Gears in his stomach? Small millstones? What would happen if he inadvertently swallowed some emery dust? Maybe
he could sabotage the Emperor that way.

Perceiving that his thoughts were beginning to veer wildly, Crockett gulped the last of his meal and followed Brockle Buhn to the anthracite tunnel.

"How about the strike? How's it coming?"

"Fine, Crockett." She smiled, and Crockett winced at the sight. "Tonight all the gnomes will meet in the Roaring Cave. Just after work."

There was no time for more conversation. The overseer appeared, and the gnomes snatched up their picks. Dig . . . dig . . . dig . . . It kept up at the same pace. Crockett sweated and toiled. It wouldn't be for long. His mind slipped a cog, so that he relapsed into a waking slumber, his muscles responding automatically to the need. Dig, dig, dig. Sometimes a fight. Once a rest period. Then dig again.

Five centuries later the day ended. It was time to sleep.

But there was something much more important. The union meeting in the Roaring Cave. Brockle Buhn conducted Crockett there, a huge cavern hung with glittering green stalactites. Gnomes came pouring into it. Gnomes and more gnomes. The turnip heads were everywhere. A dozen fights started. Gru Magru, Mugza and Drook found places near Crockett. During a lull Brockle Buhn urged him to a platform of rock jutting from the floor.

"Now," she whispered. "They all know about it. Tell them what you want."

Crockett was looking out over the bobbing heads, the red and blue garments, all lit by that eerie silver glow. "Fellow gnomes," he began weakly.

"*Fellow gnomes!*" The words roared out, magnified by the acoustics of the cavern. That bull bellow gave Crockett courage. He plunged on.

"Why should you work twenty hours a day? Why should you be forbidden to eat the anthracite you dig, while Podrang squats in his bath and laughs at you? Fellow gnomes, the Emperor is only one; you are many! He can't make you work. How would you like mud soup three times a day? The Emperor can't fight you all. If you refuse to work —all of you—he'll have to give in! He'll have to!"

"Tell 'em about the nonfighting edict," Gru Magru called.

Crockett obeyed. That got 'em. Fighting was dear to every gnomic heart. And Crockett kept on talking.

"Podrang will try to back down, you know. He'll pretend he never intended to forbid fighting. That'll show he's afraid of you! We hold the whip hand! We'll strike—and the Emperor can't do a damn thing about it. When he runs out of mud for his baths, he'll capitulate soon enough."

"He'll enchant us all," Drook muttered sadly.

"He won't dare! What good would that do? He knows which side his—ugh—which side his mud is buttered on. Podrang is unfair to gnomes! That's our watchword!"

It ended, of course, in a brawl. But Crockett was satisfied. The gnomes would not go to work tomorrow. They would, instead, meet in the Council Chamber, adjoining Podrang's throne room—and sit down.

That night he slept well.

In the morning Crockett went, with Brockle Buhn, to the Council Chamber, a cavern gigantic enough to hold the thousands of gnomes who thronged it. In the silver light their red and blue garments had a curiously elfin quality. Or, perhaps, naturally enough, Crockett thought. Were gnomes, strictly speaking, elves?

Drook came up. "I didn't draw Podrang's mud bath," he confided hoarsely. "Oh, but he'll be furious. Listen to him."

And, indeed, a distant crackling of profanity was coming through an archway in one wall of the cavern.

Mugza and Gru Magru joined them. "He'll be along directly," the latter said. "What a fight there'll be!"

"Let's fight now," Mugza suggested. "I want to kick somebody. Hard."

"There's a gnome who's asleep," Crockett said. "If you sneak up on him, you can land a good one right in his face."

Mugza, drooling slightly, departed on his errand, and simultaneously Podrang II, Emperor of the Dornsef Gnomes, stumped into the cavern. It was the first time Crockett had seen the ruler without a coating of mud, and he could not help gulping at the sight. Podrang was *very* ugly. He combined in himself the most repulsive qualities of every gnome Crockett had previously seen. The result was perfectly indescribable.

"Ah," said Podrang, halting and swaying on his short bow legs. "I have guests. Drook! Where in the name of the nine steaming hells is my bath?" But Drook had ducked from sight.

The Emperor nodded. "I see. Well, I won't lose my temper, *I won't lose my temper!* I WON'T—"

He paused as a stalactite was dislodged from the roof and crashed down. In the momentary silence, Crockett stepped forward, cringing slightly.

"W-we're on strike," he announced. "It's a sit-down strike. We won't work till—"

"Yaah!" screamed the infuriated Emperor. "You won't work, eh? Why, you boggle-eyed, flap-tongued, drag-bellied offspring of unmentionable algae! You seething little leprous blotch of bat-nibbled fungus! You cringing parasite on the underside of a dwarfish and ignoble worm! Yaah!"

"Fight!" the irrepressible Mugza yelled, and flung himself on Podrang, only to be felled by a well-placed foul blow.

Crockett's throat felt dry. He raised his voice, trying to keep it steady.

"Your Majesty! If you'll just wait a minute—"

"You mushroom-nosed spawn of degenerate black bats," the enraged Emperor shrieked at the top of his voice. "I'll enchant you all! I'll turn you into naiads! Strike, will you! Stop me from having my mud bath, will you? By Kronos, Nid, Ymir and Loki, you'll have cause to regret this! *Yah!*" he finished, inarticulate with fury.

"Quick!" Crockett whispered to Gru and Brockle Buhn. "Get between him and the door, so he can't get hold of the Cockatrice Eggs."

"They're not in the throne room," Gru Magru explained unhelpfully. "Podrang just grabs them out of the air."

"Oh!" the harassed Crockett groaned. At that strategic moment Brockle Buhn's worst instincts overcame her. With a loud shriek of delight she knocked Crockett down, kicked him twice and sprang for the Emperor.

She got in one good blow before Podrang hammered her atop the head with one gnarled fist, and instantly her turnip-shaped skull seemed to prolapse into her torso. The

Emperor, bright purple with fury, reached out—and a yellow crystal appeared in his hand.

It was one of the Cockatrice Eggs.

Bellowing like a *musth* elephant, Podrang hurled it. A circle of twenty feet was instantly cleared among the massed gnomes. But it wasn't vacant. Dozens of bats rose and fluttered about, adding to the confusion.

Confusion became chaos. With yells of delighted fury, the gnomes rolled forward toward their ruler. "Fight!" the cry thundered out, reverberating from the roof. *"Fight!"*

Podrang snatched another crystal from nothingness—a green one, this time. Thirty-seven gnomes were instantly transformed into earthworms, and were trampled. The Emperor went down under an avalanche of attackers, who abruptly disappeared, turned into mice by another of the Cockatrice Eggs.

Crockett saw one of the crystals sailing toward him, and ran like hell. He found a hiding place behind a stalagmite, and from there watched the carnage. It was definitely a sight worth seeing, though it could not be recommended to a nervous man.

The Cockatrice Eggs exploded in an incessant stream. Whenever that happened, the spell spread out for twenty feet or more before losing its efficacy. Those caught on the fringes of the circle were only partially transformed. Crockett saw one gnome with a mole's head. Another was a worm from the waist down. Another was—*ulp!* Some of the spell patterns were not, apparently, drawn even from known mythology.

The fury of noise that filled the cavern brought stalactites crashing down incessantly from the roof. Every so often Podrang's battered head would reappear, only to go down again as more gnomes sprang to the attack—to be enchanted. Mice, moles, bats and other things filled the Council Chamber. Crockett shut his eyes and prayed.

He opened them in time to see Podrang snatch a red crystal out of the air, pause and then deposit it gently behind him. A purple Cockatrice Egg came next. This crashed against the floor, and thirty gnomes turned into tree toads.

Apparently only Podrang was immune to his own magic.

The thousands who had filled the cavern were rapidly thinning, for the Cockatrice Eggs seemed to come from an inexhaustible source of supply. How long would it be before Crockett's own turn came? He couldn't hide here forever.

His gaze riveted to the red crystal Podrang had so carefully put down. He was remembering something—the Cockatrice Egg that would transform gnomes into human beings. Of course! Podrang wouldn't use *that*, since the very sight of men was so distressing to gnomes. If Crockett could get his hands on that red crystal . . .

He tried it, sneaking through the confusion, sticking close to the wall of the cavern, till he neared Podrang. The Emperor was swept away by another onrush of gnomes, who abruptly changed into dormice, and Crockett got the red jewel. It felt abnormally cold.

He almost broke it at his feet before a thought stopped and chilled him. He was far under Dornsef Mountain, in a labyrinth of caverns. No human being could find his way out. But a gnome could, with the aid of his strange tropism to daylight.

A bat flew against Crockett's face. He was almost certain it squeaked, "What a fight!" in a parody of Brockle Buhn's voice, but he couldn't be sure. He cast one glance over the cavern before turning to flee.

It was a complete and utter chaos. Bats, moles, worms, ducks, eels and a dozen other species crawled, flew, ran, bit, shrieked, snarled, grunted, whooped and croaked all over the place. From all directions the remaining gnomes— only about a thousand now—were converging on a surging mound of gnomes that marked where the Emperor was. As Crockett stared the mound dissolved, and a number of gecko lizards ran to safety.

"Strike, will you!" Podrang bellowed. *"I'll show you!"*

Crockett turned and fled. The throne room was deserted, and he ducked into the first tunnel. There, he concentrated on thinking of daylight. His left ear felt compressed. He sped on till he saw a side passage on the left, slanting up, and turned into it at top speed. The muffled noise of combat died behind him.

He clutched the red Cockatrice Egg tightly. What had gone wrong? Podrang should have stopped to parley. Only

—only he hadn't. A singularly bad-tempered and short-sighted gnome. He probably wouldn't stop till he'd depopulated his entire kingdom. At the thought Crockett hurried along faster.

The tropism guided him. Sometimes he took the wrong tunnel, but always, whenever he thought of daylight, he would *feel* the nearest daylight pressing against him. His short, bowed legs were surprisingly hardy.

Then he heard someone running after him.

He didn't turn. The sizzling blast of profanity that curled his ears told him the identity of the pursuer. Podrang had no doubt cleared the Council Chamber, to the last gnome, and was now intending to tear Crockett apart pinch by pinch. That was only one of the things he promised.

Crockett ran. He shot along the tunnel like a bullet. The tropism guided him, but he was terrified lest he reach a dead end. The clamor from behind grew louder. If Crockett hadn't known better, he would have imagined that an army of gnomes pursued him.

Faster! Faster! But now Podrang was in sight. His roars shook the very walls. Crockett sprinted, rounded a corner, and saw a wall of flaming light—a circle of it, in the distance. It was daylight, as it appeared to gnomic eyes.

He could not reach it in time. Podrang was too close. A few more seconds, and those gnarled, terrible hands would close on Crockett's throat.

Then Crockett remembered the Cockatrice Egg. If he transformed himself into a man now, Podrang would not dare touch him. And he was almost at the tunnel's mouth.

He stopped, whirling and lifted the jewel. Simultaneously the Emperor, seeing his intention, reached out with both hands, and snatched six or seven of the crystals out of the air. He threw them directly at Crockett, a fusillade of rainbow colors.

But Crockett had already slammed the red gem down on the rock at his feet. There was an ear-splitting crash. Jewels seemed to burst all around Crockett—but the red one had been broken first.

The roof fell in.

A short while later, Crockett dragged himself painfully from the debris. A glance showed him that the way to the outer world was still open. And—thank heaven!—daylight looked normal again, not that flaming blaze of eye-searing white.

He looked toward the depths of the tunnel, and froze. Podrang was emerging, with some difficulty, from a mound of rubble. His low curses had lost none of their fire.

Crockett turned to run, stumbled over a rock, and fell flat. As he sprang up, he saw that Podrang had seen him.

The gnome stood transfixed for a moment. Then he yelled, spun on his heel, and fled into the darkness. He was gone. The sound of his rapid footfalls died.

Crockett swallowed with difficulty. *Gnomes are afraid of men—whew!* That had been a close squeak. But now . . .

He was more relieved than he had thought. Subconsciously he must have been wondering whether the spell would work, since Podrang had flung six or seven Cockatrice Eggs at him. But he had smashed the red one first. Even the strange, silvery gnome-light was gone. The depths of the cave were utterly black—and silent.

Crockett headed for the entrance. He pulled himself out, luxuriating in the warmth of the afternoon sun. He was near the foot of Dornsef Mountain, in a patch of brambles. A hundred feet away a farmer was plowing one terrace of a field.

Crockett stumbled toward him. As he approached, the man turned.

He stood transfixed for a moment. Then he yelled, spun on his heel, and fled.

His shrieks drifted back up the mountain as Crockett, remembering the Cockatrice Eggs, forced himself to look down at his own body.

Then he screamed too. But the sound was not one that could ever have emerged from a human throat.

Still, that was natural enough—under the circumstances.

The Big Night

Chapter 1. Last of the Hyper Ships

SHE CAME LUMBERING up out of the ecliptic plane of the planets like a wallowing space beast, her jet tubes scarred and stained, a molten streak across her middle where Venus's turgid atmosphere had scarred her, and every ancient spot weld in her fat body threatened to rip apart the moment she hit stress again.

The skipper was drunk in his cabin, his maudlin voice echoing through the compartments as he bewailed the unsympathetic harshness of the Interplanetary Trade Commission.

There was a mongrel crew from a dozen worlds, half of them shanghaied. Logger Hilton, the mate, was trying to make sense out of the tattered charts, and *La Cucaracha,* her engines quaking at the suicidal thought, was plunging ahead through space into the Big Night.

In the control room a signal light flared. Hilton grabbed a mike.

"Repair crew!" he yelled. "Get out on the skin and check jet A-six. Move!"

He turned back to his charts, chewing his lip and glancing at the pilot, a tiny, inhuman Selenite, with his arachnoid multiple limbs and fragile-seeming body. Ts'ss—that was his name, or approximated it—was wearing the awkward audio-converter mask that could make his subsonic voice audible to human ears, but, unlike Hilton, he wasn't wearing space armor. No Lunarian ever needed protection against deep space. In their million years on the Moon, they had got used to airlessness. Nor did the ship's atmosphere bother Ts'ss. He simply didn't trouble to breathe it.

"Blast you, take it easy!" Hilton said. "Want to tear off our hide?"

Through the mask the Selenite's faceted eyes glittered at the mate.

"No, sir. I'm going as slowly as I can on jet fuel. As soon as I know the warp formulae, things'll ease up a bit."

"Ride it! Ride it—without jets!"

"We need the acceleration to switch over to warp, sir."

"Never mind," Hilton said. "I've got it now. Somebody must have been breeding fruit-flies all over these charts. Here's the dope." He dictated a few equations that Ts'ss' photographic memory assimilated at once.

A distant howling came from far off.

"That's the skipper, I suppose," Hilton said. "I'll be back in a minute. Get into hyper as soon as you can, or we're apt to fold up like an accordion."

"Yes, sir. Ah—Mr. Hilton?"

"Well?"

"You might look at the fire extinguisher in the Cap'n's room."

"What for?" Hilton asked.

Several of the Selenite's multiple limbs pantomimed the action of drinking. Hilton grimaced, rose and fought the acceleration down the companionway. He shot a glance at the visio-screens and saw they were past Jupiter already, which was a relief. Going through the giant planet's gravity-pull wouldn't have helped La Cucaracha's aching bones. But they were safely past now. Safely! He grinned wryly as he opened the captain's door and went in.

Captain Sam Danvers was standing on his bunk, making a speech to an imaginary Interplanetary Trade Commission. He was a big man, or rather he had been once, but now the flesh had shrunk and he was beginning to stoop a little. The skin of his wrinkled face was nearly black with space-tan. A stubble of gray hair stood up angrily.

Somehow, though, he looked like Logger Hilton. Both were deep-space men. Hilton was thirty years younger, but he, too, had the same dark tan and the same look in his blue eyes. There's an old saying that when you go out into the Big Night, beyond Pluto's orbit, that enormous emptiness gets into you and looks out through your eyes. Hilton had that. So did Captain Danvers.

Otherwise—Hilton was huge and heavy where Danvers was a little frail now, and the mate's broad chest bulged his white tunic. He hadn't had time yet to change from dress uniform, though he knew that even this cellulose fabric couldn't take the dirt of a space-run without showing it. Not on *La Cucaracha,* anyway.

But this would be his last trip on the old tub.

Captain Danvers interrupted his speech to ask Hilton what the devil he wanted. The mate saluted.

"Routine inspection, sir," he observed, and took down a fire extinguisher from the wall. Danvers sprang from the bunk, but Hilton moved too fast. Before the captain reached him, Hilton had emptied the tank down the nearest disposal vent.

"Old juice," he explained. "I'll refill her."

"Listen, Mr. Hilton," Danvers said, swaying slightly and stabbing a long forefinger at the mate's nose. "If you think I had whiskey in there, you're crazy."

"Sure," Hilton said. "I'm crazy as a loon, skipper. How about some caffeine?"

Danvers weaved to the disposal port and peered down it vaguely.

"Caffeine. Huh? Look, if you haven't got sense enough to take *La Cucaracha* into hyper, you ought to resign."

"Sure, sure. But in hyper it won't take long to get to Fria. You'll have to handle the agent there."

"Christie? I—I guess so." Danvers sank down on the bunk and held his head. "I guess I just got mad, Logger. ITC—what do they know about it? Why, we opened that trading post on Sirius Thirty."

"Look, skipper, when you came aboard you were so high you forgot to tell me about it," Hilton said. "You just said we'd changed our course and to head for Fria. How come?"

"Interplanetary Trade Commission," Danvers growled. "They had their crew checking over *La Cucaracha.*"

"I know. Routine inspection."

"Well, those fat slobs have the brassbound nerve to tell

me my ship's unsafe! That the gravity-drag from Sirius is too strong—and that we couldn't go to Sirius Thirty!"

"Could be they're right," Hilton said thoughtfully. "We had trouble landing on Venus."

"She's old." Danvers' voice was defensive. "But what of it? I've taken *La Cucaracha* around Betelgeuse and plenty closer to Sirius than Sirius Thirty. The old lady's got what it takes. They built atomic engines in those days."

"They're not building them now," Hilton said, and the skipper turned purple.

"Transmission of matter!" he snarled. "What kind of a crazy set-up is that? You get in a little machine on Earth, pull a switch and there you are on Venus or Bar Canopus or—or Purgatory, if you like! I shipped on a hyper ship when I was thirteen, Logger. I grew up on hyper ships. They're solid. They're dependable. They'll take you where you want to go. Hang it, it isn't safe to space travel without an atmosphere around you, even if it's only in a suit."

"That reminds me," Hilton said. "Where's yours?"

"Ah, I was too hot. The refrigerating unit's haywire."

The mate found the lightweight armor in a closet and deftly began to repair the broken switch.

"You don't need to keep the helmet closed, but you'd better wear the suit," he said absently. "I've issued orders to the crew. All but Ts'ss, and he doesn't need any protection."

Danvers looked up. "How's she running?" he asked quickly.

"Well, she could use an overhaul," Hilton said. "I want to get into hyperspace fast. This straight running is a strain. I'm afraid of landing, too."

"Uh. Okay, there'll be an overhaul when we get back— *if* we make a profit. You know how much we made this last trip. Tell you what—you supervise the job and take a bigger cut for it."

Hilton's fingers slowed on the switch. He didn't look around.

"I'll be looking for a new berth," he said. "Sorry, skipper. But I won't be aboard after this voyage."

There was silence behind him. Hilton grimaced and began to work again on the spacesuit. He heard Danvers say:

"You won't find many hyper ships needing mates these days."

"I know. But I've got engineering training. Maybe they would use me on the matter transmitters. Or as an outpost-er—a trader."

"Oh, for the love of Pete! Logger, what are you talking about? A—*trader?* A filthy outposter? You're a hyper ship man!"

"In twenty years there won't be a hyper ship running," Hilton said.

"You're a liar. There'll be one."

"She'll fall apart in a couple of months!" Hilton said angrily. "I'm not going to argue. What are we after on Fria, the fungus?"

After a pause Danvers answered.

"What else is there on Fria? Sure, the fungus. It's pushing the season a little. We're not due there for three weeks Earth-time, but Christie always keeps a supply on hand. And that big hotel chain will pay us the regular cut. Blamed if I know why people eat that garbage, but they pay twenty bucks a plate for it."

"It could mean a profit, then," Hilton said. "Provided we land on Fria without falling apart." He tossed the repaired suit on the bunk beside Danvers. "There you are, skipper. I'd better get back to controls. We'll be hitting hyper pretty soon."

Danvers leaned over and touched a button that opened the deadlight. He stared at the star screen.

"You won't get this on a matter transmitter," he said slowly. "Look at it, Logger."

Hilton leaned forward and looked across the captain's shoulder. The void blazed. To one side a great arc of Jupiter's titan bulk blared coldly bright. Several of the moons were riding in the screen's field, and an asteroid or two caught Jupiter's light in their tenuous atmospheres and hung like shining veiled miniature worlds against that blazing backdrop. And through and beyond the shining stars and moons and planets showed the Big Night, the black emptiness that beats like an ocean on the rim of the Solar System.

"So it's pretty," Hilton said. "But it's cold, too."

"Maybe. Maybe it is. But I like it. Well, get a job as a

trader, you jackass. I'll stick to *La Cucaracha*. I know I can trust the old lady."

For answer the old lady jumped violently and gave a wallowing lurch.

Chapter 2. Bad News

HILTON INSTANTLY EXPLODED out of the cabin. The ship was bucking hard. Behind him the mate heard Danvers shouting something about incompetent pilots, but he knew it probably wasn't the Selenite's fault. He was in the control cabin while *La Cucaracha* was still shuddering on the downswing of the last jump. Ts'ss was a tornado of motion, his multiple legs scrabbling frantically at a dozen instruments.

"I'll call the shot!" Hilton snapped, and Ts'ss instantly concentrated on the incredibly complicated controls that were guiding the ship into hyper.

The mate was at the auxiliary board. He jerked down levers.

"Hyper stations!" he shouted. "Close helmets! Grab the braces, you sun-jumpers! Here we go!"

A needle swung wildly across a gauge, hovering at the mark. Hilton dropped into a seat, sliding his arms under the curved braces and hooking his elbows around them. His ankles found similar supports beneath him. The visioscreens blurred and shimmered with crawling colors, flicking back and forth, on and off, as *La Cucaracha* fought the see-saw between hyper and normal space.

Hilton tried another mike. "Captain Danvers. Hyper stations. All right?"

"Yeah, I'm in my suit," Danvers' voice said. "Can you take it? Need me? What's wrong with Ts'ss?"

"The vocor at my board blew out, Cap'n," Ts'ss said. "I couldn't reach the auxiliary."

"We must need an overhaul bad," Danvers said, and cut off.

Hilton grinned. "We need a rebuilding job," he muttered, and let his fingers hang over the control buttons, ready in case Ts'ss slipped.

But the Selenite was like a precision machine; he never

slipped. The old *Cucaracha* shook in every brace. The atomic engines channeled fantastic amounts of energy into the dimensional gap. Then, suddenly, the see-saw balanced for an instant, and in that split second the ship slid across its powerbridge and was no longer matter. It no longer existed, in the three-dimensional plane. To an observer, it would have vanished. But to an observer in hyperspace, it would have sprung into existence from white nothingness.

Except that there *were* no hyperspatial observers. In fact, there wasn't anything in hyper—it was, as some scientist had once observed, just stuff, and nobody knew what the stuff was. It was possible to find out some of hyper's properties, but you couldn't go much further than that. It was white, and it must have been energy, of a sort, for it flowed like an inconceivably powerful tide, carrying ships with it at speeds that would have destroyed the crew in normal space. Now, in the grip of the hyper current, *La Cucaracha* was racing toward the Big Night at a velocity that would take it past Pluto's orbit in a matter of seconds.

But you couldn't see Pluto. You had to work blind here, with instruments. And if you got on the wrong level, it was just too bad—for you!

Hastily Hilton checked the readings. This was Hyper C-758-R. That was right. On different dimensional levels of hyper, the flow ran in various directions. Coming back, they'd alter their atomic structure to ride Hyper M-75-L, which rushed from Fria toward Earth and beyond it.

"That's that," Hilton said, relaxing and reaching for a cigarette. "No meteors, no stress-strain problems—just drift till we get close to Fria. Then we drop out of hyper, and probably fall apart."

An annunciator clicked. Somebody said:

"Mr. Hilton, there's some trouble."

"There is. Okay, Wiggins. What now?"

"One of the new men. He was out skinside making repairs."

"You had plenty of time to get back inside," snapped Hilton, who didn't feel quite as sure of that as he sounded. "I called hyper stations."

"Yes, sir. But this fella's new. Looks like he never rode a hyper ship before. Anyhow, his leg's broken. He's in sick bay."

Hilton thought for a moment. *La Cucaracha* was understaffed anyway. Few good men would willingly ship on such an antique.

"I'll come down," he said, and nodded at Ts'ss. Then he went along the companionway, glancing in at the skipper, who had gone to sleep. He used the handholds to pull himself along, for there was no accelerative gravity in hyper. In sick bay he found the surgeon, who doubled in brass as cook, finishing a traction splint on a pale, sweating youngster who was alternately swearing feebly and groaning.

"What's the matter with him?" Hilton asked.

Bruno, the sawbones, gave a casual soft salute. "Simple fracture. I'm giving him a walker splint, so he'll be able to get around. And he shot his cookies, so he can't be used to hyper."

"Looks like it," Hilton said, studying the patient. The boy opened his eyes, glared at Hilton.

"I was shanghaied!" he yelped. "I'll sue you for all you're worth!"

The first officer was unperturbed.

"I'm not the skipper, I'm mate," Hilton said. "And I can tell you right now that we're not worth much. Ever hear about discipline?"

"I was shanghaied!"

"I know it. That's the only way we can get a full crew to sign articles on *La Cucaracha*. I mentioned discipline. We don't bother much with it here. Just the same, you'd better call me Mister when people are around. Now shut up and relax. Give him a sedative, Bruno."

"No! I want to send a spacegram!"

"We're in hyper. You can't. What's your name?"

"Saxon. Luther Saxon. I'm one of the consulting engineers on Transmat."

"The matter-transmission gang? What were you doing around the space docks?"

Saxon gulped. "Well—uh—I go out with the technical crews to supervise new installations. We'd just finished a Venusian transmission station. I went out for a few drinks —that was all! A few drinks, and—"

"You went to the wrong place," Hilton said, amused. "Some crimp gave you a Mickey. Your name's on the articles, anyhow, so you're stuck, unless you jump ship. You can send a message from Fria, but it'd take a thousand years to reach Venus or Earth. Better stick around, and you can ride back with us."

"On this crate? It isn't safe. She's so old I've got the jitters every time I take a deep breath."

"Well, stop breathing," Hilton said curtly. *La Cucaracha* was an old tramp, of course, but he had shipped on her for a good many years. It was all right for this Transmat man to talk; the Transmat crews never ran any risks.

"Ever been on a hyper ship before?" he asked.

"Naturally," Saxon said. "As a passenger! We have to get to a planet before we can install a transmission station, don't we?"

"Uh-huh." Hilton studied the scowling face on the pillow. "You're not a passenger now, though."

"My leg's broken."

"You got an engineering degree?"

Saxon hesitated and finally nodded.

"All right, you'll be assistant pilot. You won't have to walk much to do that. The pilot'll tell you what to do. You can earn your mess that way."

Saxon spluttered protests.

"One thing," Hilton said. "Better not tell the skipper you're a Transmat man. He'd hang you over one of the jets. Send him for'rd when he's fixed up, Bruno."

"Yessir," Bruno said, grinning faintly. An old deep-space man, he didn't like Transmat either.

Hilton pulled himself back to the control room. He sat down and watched the white visio-screens. Most of Ts'ss' many arms were idle. This was routine now.

"You're getting an assistant," Hilton said after a while. "Train him fast. That'll give us all a break. If that fat-headed Callistan pilot hadn't jumped on Venus, we'd be set."

"This is a short voyage," Ts'ss said. "It's a fast hyper flow on this level."

"Yeah. This new guy. Don't tell the skipper, but he's a Transmat man."

Ts'ss laughed a little.

"That will pass, too," he said. "We're an old race, Mr. Hilton. Earthmen are babies compared to the Selenites.

Hyper ships are fading out, and eventually Transmat will fade out too, when something else comes."

"We won't fade," Hilton said, rather surprised to find himself defending the skipper's philosophy. "*Your* people haven't—you Selenites."

"Some of us are left, that's true," Ts'ss said softly. "Not many. The great days of the Selenite Empire passed very long ago. But there are still a few Selenites left, like me."

"You keep going, don't you? You can't kill off a—a race."

"Not easily. Not at once. But you can, eventually. And you can kill a tradition, too, though it may take a long time. But you know what the end will be."

"Oh, shut up," Hilton said. "You talk too much."

Ts'ss bent again above the controls. *La Cucaracha* fled on through the white hyper flow, riding as smoothly as the day she had been launched.

But when they reached Fria, it would be rough space and high gravity. Hilton grimaced.

He thought: So what? This is just another voyage. The fate of the universe doesn't depend on it. Nothing depends on it, except, maybe, whether we make enough profit to have the old lady overhauled. And that won't matter to me for it's my last voyage into the Big Night.

He watched the screens. He could not see it, but he knew that it hung beyond the universal whiteness, in a plane invisible to his eyes. The little sparks of worlds and suns glowed in its immensity, but never brightened it. It was too vast, too implacable. And even the giant suns would be quenched in its ocean, in the end. As everything else would be quenched, as everything moved on the tides of time into that huge darkness.

That was progress. A wave was born and gathered itself and grew—and broke. A newer wave was behind it. And the old one slipped back and was lost forever. A few foam-flecks and bubbles remained, like Ts'ss, remnant of the giant wave of the ancient Selenite Empire.

The Empire was gone. It had fought and ruled a hundred worlds, in its day. But, in the end, the Big Night had conquered and swallowed it.

As it would swallow the last hyper ship eventually . . .

They hit Fria six days later, Earth time. And *hit* was the word. One of Ts'ss' chitin-covered arms was snapped off by the impact, but he didn't seem to mind. He couldn't feel pain, and he could grow another limb in a few weeks. The crew, strapped to their landing braces, survived with minor bruises.

Luther Saxon, the Transmat man, was in the auxiliary pilot's seat—he had enough specialized engineering training so that he learned the ropes fast—and he acquired a blue bump on his forehead, but that was all. *La Cucaracha* had come out of hyper with a jolt that strained her fat old carcass to the limit, and the atmosphere and gravity of Fria was the penultimate straw. Seams ripped, a jet went out, and new molten streaks appeared on the white-hot hull.

The crew had been expecting liberty. There was no time for that. Hilton told off working gangs to relieve each other at six-hour intervals, and he said, rather casually, that Twilight was out of bounds. He knew the crew would ignore that order. There was no way to keep the men aboard, while Twilight sold liquor and even more effective escape mechanisms. Still, there were few women on Fria, and Hilton hoped that enough working stiffs would keep on the job to get *La Cucaracha* repaired and spaceworthy before the fungus cargo was loaded.

He knew that Wiggins, the second mate, would do his best. For himself he went with the skipper in search of Christie, the Fria trader. The way led through Twilight, the roofed settlement that was shielded from the hot, diamond-bright glare of the primary. It wasn't big. But then Fria was an outpost, with a floating population of· a few hundred. They came in and out with the ships and the harvest seasons. If necessary, Hilton thought, some of the bums could be shanghaied. Still, it wasn't too likely that any of the crew would desert. None of them would be paid off till they went back in the Solar System.

They found Christie in his plasticoid cabin, a fat, bald, sweating man puffing at a huge meerschaum pipe. He looked up, startled, and then resignedly leaned back in his chair and waved them to seats.

"Hello, Chris," Danvers said. "What's new?"

"Hello, Skipper. Hi, Logger. Have a good trip?"

"The landing wasn't so good," Hilton said.

"Yeah, I heard about it. Drinks?"

"Afterward," Danvers said, though his eyes gleamed. "Let's clean up the business first. Got a good shipment ready?"

Christie smoothed one of his fat, glistening cheeks. "Well—you're a couple of weeks early."

"You keep a stockpile."

The trader grunted. "Fact is—look, didn't you get my message? No, I guess there wasn't time. I sent a spacemail on the *Blue Sky* last week for you, Skipper."

Hilton exchanged glances with Danvers.

"You sound like bad news, Chris," he said. "What is it?"

Christie said uncomfortably, "I can't help it. You can't meet competition like Transmat. You can't afford to pay their prices. You got running expenses on *La Cucaracha*. Jet fuel costs dough, and—well, Transmat sets up a transmitting station, pays for it, and the job's done, except for the power outlay. With atomic, what does that amount to?"

Danvers was growing red.

"Is Transmat setting up a station here?" Hilton said hastily.

"Yeah. I can't stop 'em. It'll be ready in a couple of months."

"But why? The fungus isn't worth it. There isn't enough market. You're pulling a bluff, Chris. What do you want? A bigger cut?"

Christie regarded his meerschaum. "Nope. Remember the ore tests twelve years ago? There's valuable ores on Fria, Logger. Only it's got to be refined plenty. Otherwise it's too bulky for shipment. And the equipment would cost too much to freight by spaceship. It's big stuff—I mean big."

Hilton glanced at Danvers. The skipper was purple now, but his mouth was clamped tightly.

"But—hold on, Chris. How can Transmat get around that? By sending the crude ores to Earth in their gadgets?"

"The way I heard it," Christie said, "is that they're going to send the refining machines here and set 'em up right on Fria. All they need for that is one of their transmitters. The field can be expanded to take almost anything, you know. Shucks you could move a planet that way if you had the power! They'll do the refining here and transmit the re-fined ores back Earthside."

"So they want ores," Danvers said softly. "They don't want the fungus, do they?"

Christie nodded. "It looks like they do. I had an offer. A big one. I can't afford to turn it down, and you can't afford to meet it, Skipper. You know that as well as I do. Thirteen bucks a pound."

Danvers snorted. Hilton whistled.

"No, we can't meet that," he said. "But how can they afford to pay it?"

"Quantity. They channel everything through their trans-mitters. They set one up on a world, and there's a door right to Earth—or any planet they name. One job won't net them much of a profit, but a million jobs—and they take everything! So what can I do, Logger?"

Hilton shrugged. The captain stood up abruptly.

Christie stared at his pipe.

"Look, Skipper. Why not try the Orion Secondaries? I heard there was a bumper crop of bluewood gum there."

"I heard that a month ago." Danvers said. "So did every-body else. It's cleaned out by now. Besides, the old lady won't stand a trip like that. I've got to get an overhaul fast, and a good one, back in the System."

There was a silence. Christie was sweating harder than ever. "What about that drink?" he suggested. "We can maybe figure a way."

"I can still pay for my own drinks," Danvers lashed out. He swung around and was gone.

"Jehoshaphat, Logger!" Christie said. "What could I do?"

"It's not your fault, Chris," Hilton said. "I'll see you later, unless—anyhow, I'd better get after the skipper. Looks like he's heading for Twilight."

He followed Danvers, but already he had lost hope.

Chapter 3. Danvers Lays the Course

Two days later the skipper was still drunk.

In the half-dusk of Twilight, Hilton went into a huge, cool barn where immense fans kept the hot air in circulation, and found Danvers, as usual, at a back table, a glass in his hand. He was talking to a tiny-headed Canopian, one of that retrovolved race that is only a few degrees above the moron level. The Canopian looked as though he was covered with black plush, and his red eyes glowed startlingly through the fur. He, too, had a glass.

Hilton walked over to the two. "Skipper," he said.

"Blow," Danvers said. "I'm talking to this guy."

Hilton looked hard at the Canopian and jerked his thumb. The red-eyed shadow picked up his glass and moved away quickly. Hilton sat down.

"We're ready to jet off," he said.

Danvers blinked at him blearily. "You interrupted me, mister. I'm busy."

"Buy a case and finish your binge aboard," Hilton said. "If we don't jet soon, the crew will jump."

"Let 'em."

"Okay. Then who'll work *La Cucaracha* back to Earth?"

"If we go back to Earth, the old lady will land on the junkpile," Danvers said furiously. "The ITG won't authorize another voyage without a rebuilding job."

"You can borrow dough."

"Ha!"

Hilton let out his breath with a sharp, angry sound. "Are you sober enough to understand me? Then listen. I've talked Saxon around."

"Who's Saxon?"

"He was shanghaied on Venus. Well—he's a Transmat engineer." Hilton went on quickly before the skipper could speak. "That was a mistake. The crimp's mistake and ours. Transmat stands behind its men. Saxon looked up the Transmat crew on Fria, and their superintendent paid me a visit. We're in for trouble. A damage suit. But there's one way out. No hyper ship's due to hit Fria for months and the matter transmitter won't be finished within two months. And it seems Transmat has a shortage of engineers. If we can get Saxon back to Venus or Earth fast, he'll cover. There'll be no suit."

"Maybe he'll cover. But what about Transmat?"

"If Saxon won't sign a complaint, what can they do?" Hilton shrugged. "It's our only out now."

Danvers' brown-splotched fingers played with his glass.

"A Transmat man," he muttered. "Ah-h. So we go back Earthside. What then? We're stuck." He looked under his drooping lids at Hilton. "I mean *I'm* stuck. I forgot you're jumping after this voyage."

"I'm not jumping. I sign for one voyage at a time. What do you want me to do, anyhow?"

"Do what you like. Run out on the old lady. You're no deep-space man." Danvers spat.

"I know when I'm licked," Hilton said. "The smart thing then is to fight in your own weight, when you're outclassed on points, not wait for the knockout. You've had engineering training. You could get on with Transmat, too."

For a second Hilton thought the skipper was going to throw the glass at him. Then Danvers dropped back in his chair, trying to force a smile.

"I shouldn't blow my top over that," he said, with effort. "It's the truth."

"Yeah. Well—are you coming?"

"The old lady's ready to jet off?" Danvers said. "I'll come, then. Have a drink with me first."

"We haven't time."

With drunken dignity Danvers stood up. "Don't get too big for your boots, mister. The voyage isn't over yet. I said have a drink! That's an order."

"Okay, okay!" Hilton said. "One drink. Then we go?"

"Sure."

Hilton gulped the liquor without tasting it. Rather too late, he felt the stinging ache on his tongue. But before he could spring to his feet, the great dim room folded down upon him like a collapsing umbrella, and he lost consciousness with the bitter realization that he had been Mickeyed like the rawest greenhorn. But the skipper had poured that drink . . .

The dreams were confusing. He was fighting something, but he didn't know what. Sometimes it changed its shape, and sometimes it wasn't there at all, but it was always enormous and terribly powerful.

He wasn't always the same, either. Sometimes he was the wide-eyed kid who had shipped on *Starhopper*, twenty-five years ago, to take his first jump into the Big Night. Then he was a little older, in a bos'n's berth, his eye on a master's ticket, studying, through the white, unchangeable days and nights of hyperspace, the intricate logarithms a skilled pilot must know.

He seemed to walk on a treadmill toward a goal that slid away, never quite within reach. But he didn't know what that goal was. It shone like success. Maybe it was success. But the treadmill had started moving before he'd really got started. In the Big Night a disembodied voice was crying thinly:

"You're in the wrong game, Logger. Thirty years ago you'd have a future in hyper ships. Not any more. There's a new wave coming up. Get out, or drown."

A red-eyed shadow leaned over him. Hilton fought out of his dream. Awkwardly he jerked up his arm and knocked away the glass at his lips. The Canopian let out a shrill, harsh cry. The liquid that had been in the glass was coalescing in midair into a shining sphere.

The glass floated—and the Canopian floated too. They were in hyper. A few lightweight straps held Hilton to his bunk, but this was his own cabin, he saw. Dizzy, drugged weakness swept into his brain.

The Canopian struck a wall, pushed strongly, and the recoil shot him toward Hilton. The mate ripped free from the restraining straps. He reached out and gathered in a handful of furry black plush. The Canopian clawed at his eyes.

"Captain!" he screamed. "Captain Danvers!"

Pain gouged Hilton's cheek as his opponent's talons drew blood. Hilton roared with fury. He shot a blow at the Canopian's jaw, but now they were floating free, and the punch did no harm. In midair they grappled, the Canopian incessantly screaming in that thin, insane shrilling.

The door handle clicked twice. There was a voice outside—Wiggins, the second. A deep thudding came. Hilton, still weak, tried to keep the Canopian away with jolting blows. Then the door crashed open, and Wiggins pulled himself in.

"Dzann!" he said. "Stop it!" He drew a jet-pistol and leveled it at the Canopian.

On the threshold was a little group. Hilton saw Saxon, the Transmat man, gaping there, and other crew members, hesitating, unsure. Then, suddenly, Captain Danvers' face appeared behind the others, twisted, strained with tension.

The Canopian had retreated to a corner and was making mewing, frightened noises.

"What happened, Mr. Hilton?" Wiggins said. "Did this tomcat jump you?"

Hilton was so used to wearing deep-space armor that till now he had scarcely realized its presence. His helmet was hooded back, like that of Wiggins and the rest. He pulled a weight from his belt and threw it aside; the reaction pushed him toward a wall where he gripped a brace.

"Does he go in the brig?" Wiggins asked.

"All right, men," Danvers said quietly. "Let me through." He propelled himself into Hilton's cabin. Glances of discomfort and vague distrust were leveled at him. The skipper ignored them.

"Dzann!" he said. "Why aren't you wearing your armor? Put it on. The rest of you—get to your stations. You too, Mr. Wiggins. I'll handle this."

Still Wiggins hesitated. He started to say something.

"What are you waiting for?" Hilton said. "Tell Bruno to bring some coffee. Now beat it." He maneuvered himself into a sitting position on his bunk. From the tail of his eye he saw Wiggins and the others go out. Dzann, the Canopian, had picked up a suit from the corner and was awkwardly getting into it.

Danvers carefully closed the door, testing the broken lock.

"Got to have that fixed," he murmured. "It isn't ship-shape this way." He found a brace and stood opposite the mate, his eyes cool and watchful, the strain still showing on his tired face. Hilton reached for a cigarette.

"Next time your tomcat jumps me, I'll burn a hole through him," he promised.

"I stationed him here to guard you, in case there was trouble," Danvers said. "To take care of you if we cracked up or ran into danger. I showed him how to close your helmet and start the oxygen."

"Expect a half-witted Canopian to remember that?" Hilton said. "You also told him to keep drugging me." He reached toward the shining liquid sphere floating nearby and pushed a forefinger into it. He tasted the stuff. "Sure.

Vakheesh. That's what you slipped in my drink on Fria. Suppose you start talking, skipper. What's this Canopian doing aboard?"

"I signed him," Danvers said.

"For what? Supercargo?"

Danvers answered that emotionlessly, watching Hilton. "Cabin boy."

"Yeah. What did you tell Wiggins? About me, I mean?"

"I said you'd got doped up," Danvers said, grinning. "You were doped, too."

"I'm not now." Hilton's tone rang hard. "Suppose you tell me where we are? I can find out. I can get the equations from Ts'ss and run chart-lines. Are we on M-75-L?"

"No, we're not. We're riding another level."

"Where to?"

The Canopian shrilled, "I don't know name. Has no name. Double sun it has."

"You crazy!" Hilton glared at the skipper. "Are you heading us for a double primary?"

Danvers still grinned. "Yeah. Not only that, but we're going to land on a planet thirty thousand miles from the suns—roughly."

Hilton flicked on his deadlight and looked at white emptiness.

"Closer than Mercury is to Sol. You can't do it. How big are the primaries?"

Danvers told him.

"All right. It's suicide. You know that. *La Cucaracha* won't take it."

"The old lady will take anything the Big Night can hand out."

"Not this. Don't kid yourself. She might have made it back to Earth—with a Lunar landing—but you're riding into a meat grinder."

"I haven't forgotten my astrogation," Danvers said. "We're coming out of hyper with the planet between us and the primaries. The pull will land us."

"In small pieces," Hilton agreed. "Too bad you didn't keep me doped. If you keep your mouth shut, we'll replot our course to Earth and nobody'll get hurt. If you want to start something, it'll be mutiny, and I'll take my chances at Admiralty."

The captain made a noise that sounded like laughter.

"All right," he said, "suit yourself. Go look at the equations. I'll be in my cabin when you want me. Come on, Dzann."

He pulled himself into the companionway, the Canopian gliding behind him as silently as a shadow.

Hilton met Bruno with coffee as he followed Danvers. The mate grunted, seized the covered cup, and sucked in the liquid with the deftness of long practice under antigravity conditions. Bruno watched him.

"All right, sir?" the cook-surgeon said.

"Yeah. Why not?"

"Well—the men are wondering."

"What about?"

"I dunno, sir. You've never—you've always commanded the launchings, sir. And that Canopian—the men don't like him. They think something's wrong."

"Oh, they do, do they?" Hilton said grimly. "I'll come and hold their hands when they turn in for night watch. They talk too much."

He scowled at Bruno and went on toward the control room. Though he had mentioned mutiny to the skipper, he was too old a hand to condone it, except in extremity. And discipline had to be maintained, even though Danvers had apparently gone crazy.

Ts'ss and Saxon were at the panels. The Selenite slanted a glittering stare at him, but the impassive mask under the audio filter showed no expression. Saxon, however, swung around and began talking excitedly.

"What's happened, Mr. Hilton? Something's haywire. We should be ready for an Earth landing by now. But we're not. I don't know enough about these equations to chart back, and Ts'ss won't tell me a blamed thing."

"There's nothing to tell," Ts'ss said. Hilton reached past the Selenite and picked up a folder of ciphered figures. He said absently to Saxon:

"Pipe down. I want to concentrate on this."

He studied the equations.

He read death in them.

Chapter 4. Gamble with Death

LOGGER HILTON WENT into the skipper's cabin, put his back against the wall, and started cursing fluently and softly. When he had finished, Danvers grinned at him.

"Through?" he asked.

Hilton switched his stare to the Canopian, who was crouched in a corner, furtively loosening the locks of his spacesuit.

"That applies to you, too, tomcat," he said.

"Dzann won't mind that," Danvers said. "He isn't bright enough to resent cussing. And I don't care, as long as I get what we want. Still going to mutiny and head for Earth?"

"No, I'm not," Hilton said. With angry patience he ticked off his points on his fingers. "You can't switch from one hyperplane to another without dropping into ordinary space first, for the springboard. If we went back into normal space, the impact might tear *La Cucaracha* into tiny pieces. We'd be in suits, floating free, a hundred million miles from the nearest planet. Right now we're in a fast hyper flow heading for the edge of the universe, apparently."

"There's one planet within reach," Danvers said.

"Sure. The one that's thirty thousand miles from a double primary. And nothing else."

"Well? Suppose we do crack up? We can make repairs once we land on a planet. We can get the materials we need. You can't do that in deep space. I know landing on this world will be a job. But it's that or nothing—now."

"What are you after?"

Danvers began to explain:

"This Canopian—Dzann—he made a voyage once, six years ago. A tramp hyper ship. The controls froze, and the tub was heading for outside. They made an emergency landing just in time—picked out a planet that had been detected and charted, but never visited. They repaired there, and came back into the trade routes. But there was a guy aboard, an Earthman who was chummy with Dzann. This guy was smart, and he'd been in the drug racket, I think. Not many people know what raw, growing *paraine* looks like, but this fellow knew. He didn't tell anybody. He took samples, intending to raise money, charter a ship and pick up a cargo later. But he was knifed in some dive on Callisto. He didn't die right away, though, and he liked Dzann. So he gave Dzann the information."

"That halfwit?" Hilton said. "How could he remember a course?"

"That's one thing the Canopians can remember. They may be morons, but they're fine mathematicians. It's their one talent."

"It was a good way for him to bum a drink and get a free berth," Hilton said.

"No. He showed me the samples. I can talk his lingo, a little, and that's why he was willing to let me in on his secret, back on Fria. Okay. Now. We land on this planet—it hasn't been named—and load a cargo of *paraine*. We repair the old lady, if she needs it—"

"She will!"

"And then head back."

"To Earth?"

"I think Silenus. It's an easier landing."

"Now you're worrying about landings," Hilton said bitterly. "Well, there's nothing I can do about it, I suppose. I'm stepping out after this voyage. What's the current market quotation on *paraine?*"

"Fifty a pound. At Medical Center, if that's what you mean."

"Big money," the mate said. "You can buy a new ship with the profits and still have a pile left for happy days."

"You'll get your cut."

"I'm still quitting."

"Not till this voyage is over," Danvers said. "You're mate on *La Cucaracha*." He chuckled. "A deep-space man has plenty of tricks up his sleeve—and I've been at it longer than you."

"Sure," Hilton said. "You're smart. But you forgot Saxon. He'll throw that damage suit against you now, with Transmat behind him."

Danvers merely shrugged. "I'll think of something. It's your watch. We have about two hundred hours before we come out of hyper. Take it, mister."

He was laughing as Hilton went out . . .

In two hundred hours a good deal can happen. It was Hilton's job to see that it didn't. Luckily, his reappearance had reassured the crew, for when masters fight, the crew will hunt for trouble. But with Hilton moving about *La Cucaracha,* apparently as casual and assured as ever, even the second mate, Wiggins, felt better. Still, it was evident that they weren't heading for Earth. It was taking too long.

The only real trouble came from Saxon, and Hilton was able to handle that. Not easily, however. It had almost come to a showdown, but Hilton was used to commanding men, and finally managed to bluff the Transmat engineer. Dissatisfied but somewhat cowed, Saxon grumblingly subsided.

Hilton called him back.

"I'll do my best for you, Saxon. But we're in the Big Night now. You're not in civilized space. Don't forget that the skipper knows you're a Transmat man, and he hates your insides. On a hyper ship, the Old Man's word is law. So—for your own sake—watch your step!"

Saxon caught the implication. He paled slightly, and after that managed to avoid the captain.

Hilton kept busy checking and rechecking *La Cucaracha.* No outside repairs could be done in hyper, for there was no gravity, and ordinary physical laws were inoperative—magnetic shoes, for example, wouldn't work. Only in the ship itself was there safety. And that safety was illusory for the racking jars of the spatial see-saw might disintegrate *La Cucaracha* in seconds.

Hilton called on Saxon. Not only did he want technical aid, but he wanted to keep the man busy. So the pair worked frantically over jury-rigged systems that would provide the strongest possible auxiliary bracing for the ship. Torsion, stress and strain were studied, the design of the craft analyzed, and structural alloys X-ray tested.

Some flaws were found—*La Cucaracha* was a very old lady—but fewer than Hilton expected. In the end, it became chiefly a matter of ripping out partitions and bulkheads and using the material for extra bracing.

But Hilton knew, and Saxon agreed with him, that it would not be enough to cushion the ship's inevitable crash.

There was one possible answer. They sacrificed the after section of the craft. It could be done, though they were racing against time. The working crews mercilessly cut away beams from aft and carried them forward and welded them into position, so that, eventually, the forward half of the ship was tremendously strong and cut off, by tough airtight partitions, from a skeleton after half. And that half Hilton flooded with manufactured water, to aid in the cushioning effect.

Danvers, of course, didn't like it. But he had to give in. After all, Hilton was keeping the ship on the skipper's course, insanely reckless as that was. If *La Cucaracha* survived, it would be because of Hilton. But Captain Danvers shut himself in his cabin and was sullenly silent.

Towards the end, Hilton and Ts'ss were alone in the control room, while Saxon, who had got interested in the work for its own sake, superintended the last-minute jobs of spot bracing. Hilton, trying to find the right hyper space level that would take them back to Earth after they had loaded the *paraine* cargo, misplaced a decimal point and began to curse in a low, furious undertone.

He heard Ts'ss laugh softly and whirled on the Selenite.

"What's so funny?" he demanded.

"It's not really funny, sir," Ts'ss said. "There have to be people like Captain Danvers, in any big thing."

"What are you babbling about now?" he asked curiously.

Ts'ss shrugged. "The reason *I* keep shipping on *La Cucaracha* is because I can be busy and efficient aboard, and planets aren't for Selenites any more. We've lost our own world. It died long ago. But I still remember the old traditions of our Empire. If a tradition ever becomes great, it's because of the men who dedicate themselves to it. That's why anything ever became great. And it's why hyper ships came to mean something, Mr. Hilton. There were men who lived and breathed hyper ships. Men who worshipped hyper ships, as a man worships a god. Gods fall, but a few men will still worship at the old altars. They can't change. If they were capable of changing, they wouldn't have been the type of men to make their gods great."

"Been burning *paraine*?" Hilton demanded unpleasantly. His head ached, and he didn't want to find excuses for the skipper.

"It's no drug dream," Ts'ss said. "What about the chivalric traditions? We had our Chyra Emperor, who fought for—"

"I've read about Chyra," Hilton said. "He was a Selenite King Arthur."

Slowly Ts'ss nodded his head, keeping his great eyes on Hilton.

"Exactly. A tool who was useful in his time, because he served his cause with a single devotion. But when that cause died, there was nothing for Chyra—or Arthur—to do except die too. But until he did die, he continued to serve his broken god, not believing that it had fallen. Captain Danvers will never believe the hyper ships are passing. He will be a hyper ship man until he dies. Such men make causes great—but when they outlive their cause, they are tragic figures."

"Well, I'm not that crazy," Hilton growled. "I'm going into some other game. Transmat or something. You're a technician. Why don't you come with me after this voyage?"

"I like the Big Night," Ts'ss said. "And I have no world of my own—no living world. There is nothing to—to make me want success, Mr. Hilton. In *La Cucaracha* I can do as I want. But away from the ship, I find that people don't like Selenites. We are too few to command respect or friendship any more. And I'm quite old, you know."

Startled, Hilton stared at the Selenite. There was no way to detect signs of age on the arachnoid beings. But they always knew, infallibly, how long they had to live, and could predict the exact moment of their death.

Well, *he* wasn't old. And he wasn't a deep-space man as Danvers was. He followed no lost causes. There was nothing to keep him with the hyper ships, after this voyage, if he survived.

A signal rang. Hilton's stomach jumped up and turned into ice, though he had been anticipating this for hours. He reached for a mike.

"Hyper stations! Close helmets! Saxon, report!"

"All work completed, Mr. Hilton," said Saxon's voice, strained but steady.

"Come up here. May need you. General call: stand by! Grab the braces. We're coming in."

Then they hit the see-saw!

Chapter 5. Hilton's Choice

No DOUBT ABOUT it, she was tough—that old lady. She'd knocked around a thousand worlds and ridden hyper for more miles than a man could count. Something had got into her from the Big Night, something stronger than metal bracing and hard alloys. Call it soul, though there never was a machine that had a soul. But since the first log-craft was launched on steaming seas, men have known that a ship gets a soul—from somewhere.

She hopped like a flea. She bucked like a mad horse. Struts and column snapped and buckled, and the echoing companionways were filled with an erratic crackling and groaning as metal, strained beyond its strength, gave way. Far too much energy rushed through the engines. But the battered old lady took it and staggered on, lurching, grunting, holding together somehow.

The see-saw bridged the gap between two types of space, and *La Cucaracha* yawned wildly down it, an indignity for an old lady who, at her age, should ride sedately through free void—but she was a hyper ship first and a lady second. She leaped into normal space. The skipper had got his figures right. The double sun wasn't visible, for it was eclipsed by the single planet, but the pull of that monstrous twin star clamped down like a giant's titanic fist closing on *La Cucaracha* and yanking her forward irresistibly.

There was no time to do anything except stab a few buttons. The powerful rocket jets blazed from *La Cucaracha*'s hull. The impact stunned every man aboard. No watcher saw, but the automatic recording charts mapped what happened then.

La Cucaracha struck what was, in effect, a stone wall. Not even that could stop her. But it slowed her enough for the minimum of safety, and she flipped her stern down and crashed on the unnamed planet with all her after jets firing gallantly, the flooded compartments cushioning the shock, and a part of her never made of plastic or metal holding her together against even that hammer blow struck at her by a world.

Air hissed out into a thinner atmosphere and dissipated. The hull was half molten. Jet tubes were fused at a dozen spots. The stern was hash.

But she was still—a ship.

The loading of cargo was routine. The men had seen too many alien planets to pay much attention to this one. There was no breathable air, so the crew worked in their suits—except for three who had been injured in the crash, and were in sick-bay, in a replenished atmosphere within the sealed compartments of the ship. But only a few compartments were so sealed. *La Cucaracha* was a sick old lady, and only first aid could be administered here.

Danvers himself superintended that. *La Cucaracha* was his own, and he kept half the crew busy opening the heat-sealed jets, doing jury-rig repairs, and making the vessel comparatively spaceworthy. He let Saxon act as straw boss, using the engineer's technical knowledge, though his eyes chilled whenever he noticed the Transmat man.

As for Hilton, he went out with the other half of the crew to gather the *paraine* crop. They used strong-vacuum harvesters, running long, flexible carrier tubes back to *La Cucaracha*'s hold, and it took two weeks of hard, driving effort to load a full cargo. But by then the ship was bulging with *paraine,* the repairs were completed, and Danvers had charted the course to Silenus.

Hilton sat in the control room with Ts'ss and Saxon. He opened a wall compartment, glanced in, and closed it again. Then he nodded at Saxon.

"The skipper won't change his mind," he said. "Silenus is our next port. I've never been there."

"I have," Ts'ss said. "I'll tell you about it later."

Saxon drew an irritated breath. "You know what the gravity pull is, then, Ts'ss. I've never been there either, but I've looked it up in the books. Giant planets, mostly, and you can't come from hyper into normal space after you've reached the radius. There's no plane of the ecliptic in that system. It's crazy. You have to chart an erratic course toward Silenus, fighting varying gravities from a dozen planets all the way, and then you've still got the primary's pull to consider. You know *La Cucaracha* won't do it, Mr. Hilton."

"I know she won't," Hilton said. "We pushed our luck this far, but any more would be suicide. She simply won't hold together for another run. We're stranded here. But the skipper won't believe that."

"He's insane," Saxon said. "I know the endurance limits of a machine—that can be found mathematically—and this ship's only a machine. Or do you agree with Captain Danvers? Maybe you think she's alive!"

Saxon was forgetting discipline, but Hilton knew what strain they were all under.

"No, she's a machine all right," he merely said. "And we both know she's been pushed too far. If we go to Silenus, it's—" He made a gesture of finality.

"Captain Danvers says—Silenus," Ts'ss murmured. "We can't mutiny, Mr. Hilton."

"Here's the best we can do," Hilton said. "Get into hyper somehow, ride the flow, and get out again somehow. But then we're stuck. Any planet or sun with a gravity pull would smash us. The trouble is, the only worlds with facilities to overhaul *La Cucaracha* are the big ones. And if we don't get an overhaul fast we're through. Saxon, there's one answer, though. Land on an asteroid."

"But why?"

"We could manage that. No gravity to fight, worth mentioning. We certainly can't radio for help, as the signals would take years to reach anybody. Only hyper will take us. fast enough. Now—has Transmat set up any stations on asteroids?"

Saxon opened his mouth and closed it again.

"Yes. There's one that would do, in the Rigel system. Far out from the primary. But I don't get it. Captain Danvers wouldn't stand for that."

Hilton opened the wall compartment. Gray smoke seeped out.

"This is *paraine*," he said. "The fumes are being blown into the skipper's cabin through his ventilator. Captain Danvers will be para-happy till we land on that Rigel asteroid, Saxon."

There was a little silence. Hilton suddenly slammed the panel shut.

"Let's do some charting," he said. "The sooner we reach the Rigel port, the sooner we can get back to Earth—via Transmat."

Curiously, it was Saxon who hesitated.

"Mr. Hilton. Wait a minute. Transmat—I know I work

for the outfit, but they—they're sharp. Businessmen. You have to pay plenty to use their matter transmitters."

"They can transmit a hyper ship, can't they? Or is it too big a job?"

"No, they can expand the field enormously. I don't mean that. I mean they'll want payment, and they'll put on the squeeze. You'll have to give up at least half of the cargo."

"There'll still be enough left to pay for an overhaul job."

"Except they'll want to know where the *paraine* came from. You'll be over a barrel. You'll *have* to tell them, eventually. And that'll mean a Transmat station will be set up right here, on this world."

"I suppose so," Hilton said quietly. "But the old lady will be spaceworthy again. When the skipper sees her after the overhaul, he'll know it was the only thing to do. So let's get busy."

"Remind me to tell you about Silenus," Ts'ss said.

The Lunar Refitting Station is enormous. A crater has been roofed with a transparent dome, and under it the hyper ships rest in their cradles. They come in battered and broken, and leave clean and sleek and strong, ready for the Big Night again. *La Cucaracha* was down there, no longer the groaning wreck that had settled on the Rigel asteroid, but a lovely lady, shining and beautiful.

Far above, Danvers and Hilton leaned on the railing and watched.

"She's ready to jet," Hilton said idly. "And she looks good."

"No thanks to you, mister."

"Tush for that!" Hilton said. "If I hadn't doped you, we'd be dead and *La Cucaracha* floating in space in pieces. Now look at her."

"Yeah. Well, she does look good. But she won't carry another *paraine* cargo. That strike was mine. If you hadn't told Transmat the location, we'd be set." Danvers grimaced. "Now they're setting up a Transmat station there; a hyper ship can't compete with a matter transmitter."

"There's more than one world in the Galaxy."

"Sure. Sure." But Danvers' eyes brightened as he looked down.

"Where are you heading, Skipper?" Hilton said.

"What's it to you? You're taking that Transmat job, aren't you?"

"You bet. I'm meeting Saxon in five minutes. In fact, we're going down to sign the contracts. I'm through with deep space. But—where are you heading?"

"I don't know," Danvers said. "I thought I might run up around Arcturus and see what's stirring."

Hilton did not move for a long time. Then he spoke without looking at the captain.

"You wouldn't be thinking of a stopover at Canis after that, would you?"

"No."

"You're a liar."

"Go keep your appointment," Danvers said.

Hilton eyed the great hyper ship below. "The old lady's always been a nice, clean craft. She's never got out of line. She's always charted a straight course. It'd be too bad if she had to carry slaves from Arcturus to the Canis market. It's illegal, of course, but that isn't the point. It's a rotten, crooked racket."

"I didn't ask your advice, mister!" Danvers flared. "Nobody's talking about slave-running!"

"I suppose you weren't figuring on unloading the *paraine* at Silenus? You can get a good price for *paraine* from Medical Center, but you can get six times the price from the drug ring on Silenus. Yeah, Ts'ss told me. He's been on Silenus."

"Oh, shut up," Danvers said.

Hilton tilted back his head to stare through the dome at the vast darkness above. "Even if you're losing a fight, it's better to fight clean," he said. "Know where it'd end?"

Danvers looked up, too, and apparently saw something in the void that he didn't like.

"How can you buck Transmat?" he demanded. "You've got to make a profit somehow."

"There's an easy, dirty way, and there's a clean, hard way. The old lady had a fine record."

"You're not a deep-space man. You never were. Beat it! I've got to get a crew together!"

"Listen—" Hilton said. He paused. "Ah, the devil with you. I'm through."

He turned and walked away through the long steel corridor.

Ts'ss and Saxon were drinking highballs at the Quarter Moon. Through the windows they could see the covered way that led to the Refitting Station, and beyond it the crags of a crater-edge, with the star-shot darkness hanging like a backdrop. Saxon looked at his watch.

"He isn't coming," Ts'ss said.

The Transmat man moved his shoulders impatiently. "No. You're wrong. Of course, I can understand your wanting to stay with *La Cucaracha*."

"Yes, I'm old. That's one reason."

"But Hilton's young, and he's smart. He's got a big future ahead of him. That guff about sticking to an ideal—well, maybe Captain Danvers is that sort of man, but Hilton isn't. He isn't in love with hyper ships."

Ts'ss turned his goblet slowly in his curious fingers. "You are wrong about one thing, Saxon. I'm not shipping on *La Cucaracha*."

Saxon stared. "But I thought—why not?"

"I will die within a thousand Earth hours," Ts'ss said softly. "When that time comes, I shall go down into the Selenite caverns. Not many know they exist, and only a few of us know the secret caves, the holy places of our race. But I know. I shall go there to die, Saxon. Every man has one thing that is strongest—and so it is with me. I must die on my own world. As for Captain Danvers, he follows his cause, as our Chyra Emperor did, and as your King Arthur did. Men like Danvers made hyper ships great. Now the cause is dead, but the type of men who made it great once can't change their allegiance. If they could, they would never have spanned the Galaxy with their ships. So Danvers will stay with *La Cucaracha*. And Hilton—"

"He's not a fanatic! He won't stay. Why should he?"

"In our legends Chyra Emperor was ruined, and his Empire broken," Ts'ss said. "But he fought on. There was one who fought on with him, though he did not believe in Chyra's cause. A Selenite named Jailyra. Wasn't there—in your legends—a Sir Lancelot? He didn't believe in Arthur's cause either, but he was Arthur's friend. So he stayed. Yes, Saxon, there are the fanatics who fight for what they believe—but there are also the others, who do not believe, and who fight in the name of a lesser cause. Something called friendship."

Saxon laughed and pointed out the window. "You're wrong, Ts'ss," he said triumphantly. "Hilton's no fool. For here he comes."

Hilton's tall form was visible moving quickly along the way. He passed the window and vanished. Saxon turned to the door.

There was a pause.

"Or, perhaps, it isn't a lesser cause," Ts'ss said. "For the Selenite Empire passed, and Arthur's court passed, and the hyper ships are passing. Always the Big Night takes them, in the end. But this has gone on since the beginning—"

"What?"

This time Ts'ss pointed.

Saxon leaned forward to look. Through the angle of the window he could see Hilton, standing motionless on the ramp. Passersby streamed about him unnoticed. He was jostled, and he did not know it, Hilton was thinking.

They saw the look of deep uncertainty on his face. They saw his face suddenly clear. Hilton grinned wryly to himself. He had made up his mind. He turned and went rapidly back the way he had come.

Saxon stared after the broad, retreating back, going the way it had come, toward the Refitting Station where Danvers and *La Cucaracha* waited. Hilton—going back where he had come from, back to what he had never really left.

"The crazy fool!" Saxon said. "He can't be doing this! Nobody turns down jobs with Transmat!"

Ts'ss gave him a wise, impassive glance. "You believe that," he said. "Transmat means much to you. Transmat needs men like you, to make it great—to keep it growing. You're a lucky man, Saxon. You're riding with the tide. A hundred years from now—two hundred—and you might be standing in Hilton's shoes. Then you'd understand."

Saxon blinked at him. "What do you mean?"

"Transmat is growing now," Ts'ss said gently. "It will be very great—thanks to men like you. But for Transmat too, there will come an end."

He shrugged, looking out beyond the crater's rim with his inhuman, faceted eyes, at the glittering points of light which, for a little while, seemed to keep the Big Night at bay.

Nothing But Gingerbread Left

THE ONLY WAY to make people believe this story is to write it in German. And there's no point in doing that, for the German-speaking world is already starting to worry about gingerbread left.

I speak figuratively. It's safer. Very likely Rutherford, whose interests are equally divided between semantics and Basin Street, could create an English equivalent of gingerbread left, God forbid. As it is, the song, with its *reductio ad absurdum* of rhythm and sense, is meaningless in translation. Try translating Jabberwocky into German. So what?

The song, as Rutherford wrote it in German, had nothing to do with gingerbread, but, since the original is obviously unavailable, I'm substituting the closest thing to it that exists in English. It's lacking in that certain compelling perfection on which Rutherford worked for months, but it'll give you an idea.

We'll start, I suppose, with the night Rutherford threw a shoe at his son. He had reason. Phil Rutherford was in charge of semantics at the University, and he was battling a hangover and trying to correct papers at the same time. Physical disabilities had kept him out of the army, and he was brooding over that, wondering if he should gulp some more Sherman units of thiamin, and hating his students. The papers they had handed in were no good. For the most part, they smelled. Rutherford had an almost illicit love for words, and it distressed him to see them kicked around thus. As Humpty Dumpty had said, the question was which was to be the master.

Usually it wasn't the students. Jerry O'Brien had a good

paper, though, and Rutherford went over it carefully, pencil in hand. The radio in the living room didn't bother him; the door was closed, anyhow. But, abruptly, the radio stopped.

"Hi," said Rutherford's thirteen-year-old son, poking his untidy head across the threshold. There was an ink smudge on the end of the youth's nose. "Hi, pop. Finished my homework. Can I go to the show?"

"It's too late," Rutherford said, glancing at his wristwatch. "Sorry. But you've an early class tomorrow."

"*Nom d'un plume*," Bill murmured. He was discovering French.

"Out. I've got work to do. Go listen to the radio."

"They make with corn tonight. Oh, well—" Bill retreated, leaving the door ajar. From the other room came confused, muffled sounds. Rutherford returned to his work.

He became aware, presently, that Bill was repeating a monotonous, rhythmic string of phrases. Automatically Rutherford caught himself listening, straining to catch the words. When he did, they were meaningless—the familiar catch phrases of kids.

"Ibbety zibbety zibbety zam—"

It occurred to Rutherford that he had been hearing this for some time, the mystic doggerel formula for choosing sides—"and out goes *you!*" One of those things that stick in your mind rather irritatingly.

"Ibbety zibbety—" Bill kept chanting it in an absentminded monotone, and Rutherford got up to close the door.

It didn't quite stop. He could still hear just enough of the rhythmic noises to start his mind moving in a similar rhythm. Ibbety zibbety—the hell with it.

After a while Rutherford discovered that his lips were moving silently, and he shoved the papers back on his desk, muttering darkly. He was tired, that was it. And correcting exams required concentration. He was glad when the bell rang.

It was Jerry O'Brien, his honor student. Jerry was a tall, thin, dark boy with a passion for the same low-down music that attracted Rutherford. Now he came in grinning.

"Hi, prof," he greeted the older man. "I'm in. Just got my papers today."

"Swell. Sit down and tell me."

There wasn't much to tell, but it lasted quite a while. Bill hung around, listening avidly. Rutherford swung to glare at his son.

"Lay off that ibbety-zibbety stuff, will you?"

"Huh? Oh sure. I didn't know I was—"

"For days he's been at it," Rutherford said glumly. "I can hear it in my sleep."

"Shouldn't bother a semanticist."

"Papers. Suppose I'd been doing important precision work. I mean really important. A string of words like that gets inside your head and you can't get it out."

"Especially if you're under any strain, or if you're concentrating a lot. Distracts your attention, doesn't it?"

"It doesn't bother *me,*" Bill said.

Rutherford grunted. "Wait'll you're older and really have to concentrate, with a mind like a fine-edged tool. Precision's important. Look what the Nazis have done with it."

"Huh?"

"Integration," Rutherford said absently. "Training for complete concentration. The Germans spent years building a machine—well, they make a fetish out of a wire-edged alertness. Look at the stimulant drugs they give their raiding pilots. They've ruthlessly cut out all distractions that might interfere with *über alles.*"

Jerry O'Brien lit a pipe. "They are hard to distract. German morale's a funny thing. They're convinced they're supermen, and that there's no weakness in *them.* I suppose, psychologically speaking, it'd be a nice trick to convince them of personal weakness."

"Sure. How? Semantics?"

"I dunno how. Probably it can't be done, except by blitzes. Even then, bombs aren't really an argument. Blowing a man to bits won't necessarily convince his comrades that he's a weakling. Nope, it'd be necessary to make Achilles notice he had a heel."

"Ibbety zibbety," Bill muttered.

"Like that," O'Brien said. "Get some crazy tune going around a guy's skull, and he'll find it difficult to concentrate. I know I do, sometimes, whenever I go for a thing like the Hut-Sut song."

Rutherford said suddenly, "Remember the dancing manias of the middle ages?"

"Form of hysteria, wasn't it? People lined up in queues and jitterbugged till they dropped."

"Rhythmic nervous exaltation. It's never been satisfactorily explained. Life is based on rhythm—the whole universe is—but I won't go cosmic on you. Keep it low-down, to the Basin Street level. Why do people go nuts about some kinds of music? Why did the 'Marseillaise' start a revolution?"

"Well, why?"

"Lord knows." Rutherford shrugged. "But certain strings of phrases, not necessarily musical, which possess rhythm, rhyme, or alliteration, do stick with you. You simply can't get 'em out of your mind. And—" He stopped.

O'Brien looked at him. "What?"

"Imperfect semantics," Rutherford said slowly. "I wonder. Look, Jerry. Eventually we forget things like the Hut-Sut. We can thrust 'em out of our minds. But suppose you got a string of phrases you *couldn't* forget? The perverse factor would keep you from erasing it mentally—the very effort to do so would cancel itself. Hm-m-m. Suppose you're carefully warned not to mention Bill Fields' nose. You keep repeating that to yourself 'Don't mention the nose.' The words, eventually, fail to make sense. If you met Fields, you'd probably say, quite unconsciously, 'Hello, Mr. Nose.' See?"

"I think so. Like the story that if you meet a piebald horse, you'll fall heir to a fortune if you don't think about the horse's tail till you're past."

"Exactly." Rutherford looked pleased. "Get a perfect semantic formula and you can't forget it. And the perfect formula would have everything. It'd have rhythm, and just enough sense to start you wondering what it meant. It wouldn't necessarily mean anything, but—"

"Could such a formula be invented?"

"Yeah. Yeah. Combine language with mathematics and psychology, and something could be worked out. Could be, such a thing was accidentally written in the middle ages. What price the dance manias?"

"I don't think I'd like it." O'Brien grimaced. "Too much like hypnosis."

"If it is, it's self-hypnosis, and unconscious. That's the beauty of it. Just for the hell of it—draw up a chair." Rutherford reached for a pencil.

"Hey, pop," Bill said, "why not write it in German?"

Rutherford and O'Brien looked at each other, startled. Slowly a gleam of diabolic understanding grew in their eyes.

"German?" Rutherford murmured. "You majored in it, didn't you, Jerry?"

"Yeah. And you're no slouch at it, either. Yeah—we *could* write it in German, couldn't we? The Nazis must be getting plenty sick of the Horst Wessel song."

"Just for the . . . uh . . . fun of it," Rutherford said, "let's try. Rhythm first. Catchy rhythm, with a break to avoid monotony. We don't need a tune." He scribbled for a bit. "It's quite impossible, of course, and even if we did it, Washington probably wouldn't be interested."

"My uncle's a senator," O'Brien said blandly.

LEFT!
LEFT!
LEFT a wife and SEVenteen children
STARVing condition with NOTHing but gingerbread
LEFT
LEFT!
LEFT a wife and SEVenteen children—

"Well, I might know something about it," said Senator O'Brien.

The officer stared at the envelope he had just opened. "So? A few weeks ago you gave me this, not to be opened till you gave the word. Now what?"

"You've read it."

"I've read it. So you've been annoying the Nazi prisoners in that Adirondack hotel. You've got 'em dizzy repeating some German song I can't make head nor tail out of."

"Naturally. You don't know German. Neither do I. But it seems to have worked on the Nazis."

"My private report says they're dancing and singing a lot of the time."

"Not dancing, exactly. Unconscious rhythmic reflexes.

And they keep repeating the . . . er . . . semantic formula."

"Got a translation?"

"Sure, but it's meaningless in English. In German it has the necessary rhythm. I've already explained—"

"I know, senator, I know. But the War Department has no time for vague theories."

"I request simply that the formula be transmitted frequently on broadcasts to Germany. It may be hard on the announcers but they'll get over it. So will the Nazis, but by that time their morale will be shot. Get the Allied radios to cooperate—"

"Do you really believe in this?"

The senator gulped. "As a matter of fact, no. But my nephew almost convinced me. He helped Professor Rutherford work out the formula."

"Argued you into it?"

"Not exactly. But he keeps going around muttering in German. So does Rutherford. Anyway—this can do no harm. And I'm backing it to the limit."

"But—" The officer peered at the formula in German. "What possible harm can it do for people to repeat a song? How can it help us—"

LEFT!
LEFT!
LEFT a wife and SEVenteen children in
STARVing condition with NOTHing but gingerbread
LEFT
LEFT—

"Aber," said Harben, *"aber, aber, aber!"*

"But me no buts," retorted his superior officer, Eggerth. "The village must be searched completely. The High Command is quartering troops here tomorrow, on their way to the eastern front, and we must make sure there are no weapons hidden anywhere."

"Aber we search the village regularly."

"Then search it again," Eggerth ordered. "You know how those damned Poles are. Turn your back for a minute and they've snatched a gun out of thin air. We want no bad reports going back to the Führer. Now get out; I must finish *my* report, and it must be accurate." He thumbed through a sheaf of notes. "How many cows, how many sheep, the harvest possibilities—*ach*. Go away and let me concentrate. Search carefully."

"Heil," Harben said glumly, and turned. On the way out his feet found a familiar rhythm. He started to mutter something.

"Captain Harben!"

Harben stopped.

"What the devil are you saying?"

"Oh—the men have a new marching song. Nonsense, but it's catchy. It is excellent to march to."

"What is it?"

Harben made a deprecating gesture. "Meaningless. It goes 'Left, left, left a wife and seventeen children—' "

Eggerth stopped him. "That. I've heard it. *Unsinn. Heil.*"

Heiling, Harben went away, his lips moving. Eggerth bent over the report, squinting in the bad light. Ten head of cattle, scarcely worth slaughtering for their meat, but the cows giving little milk . . . Hm-m-m. Grain—the situation was bad there, too. How the Poles managed to eat at all—they'd be glad enough to have gingerbread, Eggerth thought. For that matter, gingerbread was nutritious, wasn't it? Why were they in starving condition if there was still gingerbread? Maybe there wasn't *much*—

Still, why nothing *but* gingerbread? Could it be, perhaps, that the family disliked it so much they ate up everything else first? A singularly shortsighted group. Possibly their ration cards allowed them nothing but gingerbread *LEFT*

LEFT

LEFT a wife and SEVenteen children in

STARVing condition—

Eggerth caught himself sharply, and his pencil began to move again. The grain—he figured rather more slowly than usual, because his mind kept skipping back to a ridiculous rhythm. *Verdammt!* He would not—

Inhabitants of the village, thirty families, or was it forty? Forty, yes. Men, women, children—small families mostly. Still, one could seldom expect to find seventeen children. With that many, a *frau* could be wealthy through bounties alone. Seventeen children. In starving condition. Why didn't *they* eat the gingerbread? Ridiculous. What, in the name of *Gott,* did it matter whether seventeen nonexistent, completely hypothetical children ate gingerbread, or, for that matter, whether they ate nothing but gingerbread LEFT

LEFT a wife and SEVenteen children—

"Hell fire and damnation!" exploded Eggerth, looking furiously at his watch. "I might have finished the report by the time. Seventeen children, *pfui!*"

Once more he bent to his work, determined not to think of . . . of—

But it nibbled at the corners of his mind, like an intrusive mouse. Each time he recognized its presence, he could thrust it away. Unfortunately, Eggerth was repeating to his subconscious, "Don't think of it. Forget it."

"Forget what?" asked the subconscious automatically.

"Nothing but gingerbread LEFT—"

"Oh, yeah?" said the subconscious.

The search party wasn't working with its accustomed zeal and accuracy. The men's minds didn't seem entirely on their business. Harben barked orders, conscious of certain distractions—sweat trickling down inside his uniform, the harsh scratchiness of the cloth, the consciousness of the Poles silently watching and waiting. That was the worst of being in an army of occupation. You always felt that the conquered people were waiting. Well—

"Search," Harben commanded. "By pairs. Be thorough."

And they were thorough enough. They marched here and there through the village, to a familiar catchy rhythm, and their lips moved. Which, of course, was harmless. The only untoward incident occurred in an attic which two soldiers were searching. Harben wandered in to supervise. He was astonished to see one of his men open a cupboard, stare directly at a rusty rifle barrel, and then shut the door again. Briefly Harben was at a loss. The soldier moved on.

"Attention!" Harben said. Heels clicked. "Vogel, I saw that."

"Sir?" Vogel seemed honestly puzzled, his broad, youthful face blank.

"We are searching for guns. Or, perhaps, the Poles have bribed you to overlook certain matters—eh?"

Vogel's cheeks reddened. "No, sir."

Harben opened the cupboard and took out a rusty antique matchlock. It was obviously useless as a weapon now, but nevertheless it should have been confiscated. Vogel's jaw dropped.

"Well?"

"I . . . didn't see it, sir."

Harben blew out his breath angrily. "I'm not an idiot. I saw you, man! You looked right at that gun. Are you trying to tell me—"

There was a pause. Vogel said stolidly, "I did not see it, sir."

"Ah? You are growing absentminded. You would not take bribes, Vogel; I know you're a good party man. But when you do anything, you must keep your wits about you. Wool-gathering is dangerous business in an occupied village. Resume your search."

Harben went out, wondering. The men definitely seemed slightly distracted by something. What the devil could be preying on their minds so that Vogel, for example, could look right at a gun and not see it? Nerves? Ridiculous. Nordics were noted for self-control. Look at the way the men moved—their coordinated rhythm that bespoke perfect military training. Only through discipline could anything valuable be attained. The body and the mind were, in fact, machines, and should be controlled. There a squad went down the street, marching left, left, left a wife and—

That absurd song. Harben wondered where it had come from. It had grown like a rumor. Troops stationed in the village had passed it on, but where they had learned it Heaven knew. Harben grinned. When he got leave, he'd remember to tell the lads in Unter den Linden about that ridiculous song—it was just absurd enough to stick in your mind. Left. Left.

LEFT a wife and SEVenteen children in
STARVing condition—

After a while the men reported back; they hadn't found anything. The antique flintlock wasn't worth bothering about, though, as a matter of routine, it must be reported and the Polish owner questioned. Harben marched the men back to their quarters and went to Eggerth's billet. Eggerth, however, was still busy, which was unusual, for he was usually a fast worker. He glowered at Harben.

"Wait. I cannot be interrupted now." And he returned to his scribbling. The floor was already littered with crumpled papers.

Harben found an old copy of *Jugend* that he hadn't read, and settled himself in a corner. An article on youth training was interesting. Harben turned a page, and then realized that he'd lost the thread. He went back.

He read a paragraph, said, "Eh?" and skipped back again. The words were there; they entered his mind; they made sense—of course. He was concentrating. He wasn't allowing that damned marching song to interfere, with its gingerbread LEFT

LEFT

LEFT a wife and SEVenteen children—

Harben never did finish that article.

Witter of the Gestapo sipped cognac and looked across the table at Herr Doktor Schneidler. Outside the café, sunlight beat down strongly on the Königstrasse.

"The Russians—" Schneidler said.

"Never mind the Russians," Witter broke in hastily. "I am still puzzled by that Polish affair. Guns—machine guns —hidden in that village, after it had been searched time and again. It is ridiculous. There were no raids over that locality recently; there was no way for the Poles to have got those guns in the last few weeks."

"Then they must have had them hidden for more than a few weeks."

"Hidden? We search carefully, Herr Doktor. I am going to interview that man Eggerth again. And Harben. Their records are good, but—" Witter fingered his mustache nervously. "No. We can take nothing for granted. You are a clever man; what do you make of it?"

"That the village was *not* well searched."

"Yet it was. Eggerth and Harben maintain that, and their men support them. It's ridiculous to suppose that bulky machine guns could have been passed over like little automatics that can be hidden under a board. So. When the troops marched into that village, the Poles killed forty-seven

German soldiers by machine-gunning them from the roof-tops." Witter's fingers beat on the table top in a jerky rhythm.

Tap.

Yap.

Tap-ta-tap-ta—

"Eh?" Witter said. "I didn't catch—"

"Nothing. Merely that you will, of course, investigate carefully. You have a regular routine for such investigations, eh? Well, then—it is simply a matter of scientific logic, as in my own work."

"How is that progressing?" Witter asked, going off at a tangent.

"Soon. Soon."

"I have heard that before. For some weeks, in fact. Have you run into a snag? Do you need help?"

"*Ach,* no," Schneidler snapped, with sudden irritation. "I want no damn fool assistants. This is precision work, Witter. It calls for split-second accuracy. I have been specially trained in thermodynamics, and I know just when a button should be pressed, or an adjustment made. The heat-radiation of disintegrating bodies—" Presently Schneidler stopped, confused. "Perhaps, though, I need a rest. I'm fagged out. My mind's stale. I concentrate, and suddenly I find I have botched an important experiment. Yesterday I had to add exactly six drops of a . . . a fluid to a mixture I'd prepared, and before I knew it the hypo was empty, and I'd spoiled the whole thing."

Witter scowled. "Is something worrying you? Preying on your mind? We cannot afford to have that. If it is your nephew—"

"No, no. I am not worried about Franz. He's probably enjoying himself in Paris. I suppose I'm . . . *damn!*" Schneidler smashed his fist down on the table. "It is ridiculous. A crazy song!"

Witter raised an eyebrow and waited.

"I have always prided myself on my mind. It is a beautifully coherent and logical machine. I could understand its failing through a sensible cause—worry, or even madness. But when I can't get an absurd nonsense rhyme out of my head—I broke some valuable apparatus today," Schneidler confessed, compressing his lips. "Another spoiled experiment. When I realized what I'd done, I swept the whole mess off the table. I do not want a vacation; it is important that I finish my work quickly."

"It is important that you finish," Witter said. "I advise you to take that vacation. The Bavarian Alps are pleasant. Fish, hunt, relax completely. Do not think about your work. I would not mind going with you, but—" He shrugged.

Storm troopers passed along the Königstrasse. They were repeating words that made Schneidler jerk nervously. Witter's hands resumed their rhythm on the table top.

"I shall take that vacation," Schneidler said.

"Good. It will fix you up. Now I must get on with my investigation of that Polish affair, and then a check-up on some Luftwaffe pilots—"

The Herr Doktor Schneidler, four hours later, sat alone in a train compartment, already miles out of Berlin. The countryside was green and pleasant outside the windows. Yet, for some reason, Schneidler was not happy.

He lay back on the cushions, relaxing. Think about nothing. That was it. Let the precision tool of his mind rest for a while. Let his mind wander free. Listen to the somnolent rhythm of the wheels, *clickety-clickety*—

CLICK!

CLICK!

CLICK a wife and CLICKenteen children in STARVing condition with NOTHing but gingerbread *LEFT*—

Schneidler cursed thickly, jumped up, and yanked the cord. He was going back to Berlin. But not by train. Not in any conveyance that had wheels. *Gott,* no!

The Herr Doktor walked back to Berlin. At first he walked briskly. Then his face whitened, and he lagged. But the compelling rhythm continued. He went faster, trying to break step. For a while that worked. Not for long. His mind kept slipping his gears, and each time he'd find himself going LEFT—

He started to run. His beard streaming, his eyes aglare, the Herr Doktor Schneidler, great brain and all, went rushing madly back to Berlin, but he couldn't outpace the silent voice that said, faster and faster, LEFT

LEFT
LeftawifeandSEVenteenchildrenin
STARVingcondition—

"Why did that raid fail?" Witter asked.

The Luftwaffe pilot didn't know. Everything had been planned, as usual, well in advance. Every possible contingency had been allowed for, and the raid certainly shouldn't have failed. The R. A. F. planes should have been taken by surprise. The Luftwaffe should have dropped their bombs on the targets and retreated across the channel without difficulty.

"You had your shots before going up?"

"Yes, sir."

"Kurtman, your bombardier, was killed?"

"Yes, sir."

"Inexcusably?"

There was a pause. Then—"Yes, sir."

"He could have shot down that Hurricane that attacked you?"

"I . . . yes, sir."

"Why did he fail?"

"He was . . . singing, sir."

Witter leaned back in his chair. "He was singing. And I suppose he got so interested in the song that he forgot to fire."

"Yes, sir."

"Then, why in the name of . . . of—Why didn't you dodge that Hurricane?"

"I was singing, too, sir."

The R. A. F. were coming over. The man at the antiaircraft whistled between his teeth and waited. The moonlight would help. He settled himself in the padded seat and peered into the eyepiece. All was ready. Tonight there were at least some British ships that would go raiding no more.

It was a minor post in occupied France, and the man wasn't especially important, except that he was a good marksman. He looked up, watching a little cloud luminous in the sky. He was reminded of a photographic negative. The British planes would be dark, unlike the cloud, until the searchlights caught them. Then—

Ah, well. Left. Left a wife and seventeen—

They had sung that at the canteen last night, chanting it in chorus. A catchy piece. When he got back to Berlin—if ever—he must remember the words. How did they go?

In starving condition—

His thoughts ran on independently of the automatic rhythm in his brain. Was he dozing? Startled, he shook himself, and then realized that he was still alert. There was no danger. The song kept him awake, rather than inducing slumber. It had a violent, exciting swing that got into a man's blood with its LEFT

LEFT

LEFT a wife—

However, he must remain alert. When the R. A. F. bombers came over, he must do what he had to do. And they were coming now. Distantly he could hear the faint drone of their motors, pulsing monotonously like the song, bombers for Germany, starving condition, with nothing but gingerbread

LEFT!

LEFT

LEFT a wife and SEVenteen children in

STARVing condition with—

Remember the bombers, your hand on the trigger, your eye to the eyepiece, with nothing but gingerbread

LEFT!

LEFT

LEFT a wife and—

Bombers are coming, the British are coming, but don't fire too quickly, just wait till they're closer, and LEFT

LEFT

LEFT a wife and there are their motors, and there go the searchlights, and there they come over, in starving condition with nothing but gingerbread

LEFT!

LEFT!

LEFT a wife and *SEV*enteen children in—

They were gone. The bombers had passed over. He hadn't fired at all. He'd *forgotten!*

They'd passed over. Not one was left. Nothing was left. Nothing but gingerbread

LEFT!

The Minister of Propaganda looked at the report as though it might suddenly turn into Stalin and bite him. "No," he said firmly. "No, Witter. If this is false, it is false. If it is true, we dare not admit it."

"I don't see why," Witter argued. "It's that song. I've been checking up for a long time, and it's the only logical answer. The thing has swept the German-speaking world. Or it soon will."

"And what harm can a song do?"

Witter tapped the report. "You read this. The troops breaking ranks and doing . . . what is it? . . . snake dances! And singing that piece all the while."

"Forbid them to sing it." But the minister's voice was dubious.

"*Ja*, but can they be forbidden to think it? They *always* think of what is *verboten*. They can't help it. It's a basic human instinct."

"That is what I mean when I said we couldn't admit the menace of this—song, Witter. It mustn't be made important to Germans. If they consider it merely as an absurd string of words, they'll forget it. Eventually," the minister added.

"The Führer—"

"He must not know. He must not hear about this. He is a nervous type, Witter; you realize that. I hope he will not hear the song. But, even if he does, he *must not* realize that it is potentially dangerous."

"Potentially?"

The minister gestured significantly. "Men have killed themselves because of that song. The scientist Schneidler was one. A nervous type. A manic-depressive type, in fact. He brooded over the fact that the ginger—that the phrases stuck in his mind. In a depressive mood, he swallowed poison. There have been others. Witter, between ourselves, this is extremely dangerous. Do you know why?"

"Because it's—absurd?"

"Yes. There is a poem, perhaps you know it—life is real, life is earnest. Germany believes that. We are a logical race. We conquer through logic, because Nordics are the super race. And if supermen discover that they cannot control their minds—"

Witter sighed. "It seems strange that a song should be so important."

"There is no weapon against it. If we admit that it is dangerous, we double or triple its menace. At present, many people find it hard to concentrate. Some find rhythmic movements necessary—uncontrollable. Imagine what would happen if we forbade the people to think of the song."

"Can't we use psychology? Make it ridiculous—explain it away?"

"It is ridiculous already. It makes no pretense at being anything more than an absurd string of nearly meaningless words. And we can't admit it *has* to be explained away. Also, I hear that some are finding treasonable meanings in it, which is the height of nonsense."

"Oh? How?"

"Famine. The necessity for large families. Even desertion of the Nazi ideal. Er . . . even the ridiculous idea that gingerbread refers to—" The minister glanced up at the picture on the wall.

Witter looked startled, and, after a hesitant pause, laughed. "I never thought of that. Silly. What I always wondered was why they were starving when there was still plenty of gingerbread. Is it possible to be allergic to gingerbread?"

"I do not think so. The gingerbread may have been poisoned—a man who would desert his family might have cause to hate them, also. Perhaps hate them enough to— *Captain Witter!*"

There was a blank silence. Presently Witter got up, heiled, and departed, carefully breaking step. The minister looked again at the picture on the wall, tapped the bulky report before him, and shoved it away to examine a typewritten sheaf which was carefully labeled IMPORTANT. It was important. In half an hour the Führer would broadcast a speech, one for which the world had been waiting. It would explain certain things about dubious matters, such as the Russian campaign. And it was a good speech—excellent propaganda. There were to be two broadcasts, the first to Germany, the second to the rest of the world.

The minister rose and walked back and forth on the rich carpet. His lip lifted in a sneer. The way to conquer any enemy was to crush him—face him and smash him. If the rest of Germany had his own mentality, his own self-confidence, that ridiculous song would lose all its force.

"So," the minister said. "It goes so. Left. Left. Left a wife and seventeen children—so. It cannot harm me. It can get no hold on my mind. I repeat it, but only when I wish to do so; and I wish to do so to prove that the doggerel is futile—on me, anyway. So. Left. Left. Left a wife—"

Back and forth strode the Minister of Propaganda, his hard, clipped voice snappily intoning the phrases. This wasn't the first time. He often repeated the song aloud—but, of course, merely to prove to himself that he was stronger than it.

Adolf Hitler was thinking about gingerbread and Russia. There were other problems, too. It was difficult being Leader. Eventually, when a better man came along, he would step out, his work done. The well-worn record slipped from its groove, and Hitler pondered the speech he held. Yes, it was good. It explained much—why things had gone wrong in Russia, why the English invasion had failed, why the English were doing the impossible by way of raiding the continent. He had worried about those problems. They were not really problems, but the people might not understand, and might lose confidence in their Führer. However, the speech would explain everything—even Hess. Goebbels had worked for days on the psychological effects of the speech, and it was, therefore, doubly important that it go through without a hitch. Hitler reached for an atomizer and sprayed his throat, though that was really unnecessary. His voice was in top shape.

It would be distressing if—

Pfui! There would be no hitch. The speech was too important. He had made speeches before, swayed people with the weapon of his oratory. The crucial point, of course, was the reference to Russia and the ill-fated spring campaign. Yet Goebbels had a beautiful explanation; it was true, too.

"It is true," Hitler said aloud.

Well, it was. And sufficiently convincing. From the Russian discussion he would go on to Hess, and then—

But the Russian question—that was vital. He must throw all his power into the microphones at that moment.

He rehearsed mentally. A pause. Then, in a conversational voice, he would say, "At last I may tell you the truth about our Russian campaign, and why it was a triumph of strategy for German arms——"

He'd prove it, too.

But he must not forget for a moment how vitally important this speech was, and especially the crucial point in it. Remember. Remember. Do it exactly as rehearsed. Why, if he failed——

There was no such word.

But *if* he failed——

No. Even if he did——

But he wouldn't. He mustn't. He never had. And this was a crisis. Not an important one, after all, he supposed, though the people were no longer wholeheartedly behind him. Well, what was the worst that could happen? He might be unable to make the speech. It would be postponed. There could be explanations. Goebbels could take care of that. It *wasn't* important.

Don't think about it.

On the contrary, think about it. Rehearse again. The pause. "At last I may tell you——"

It was time.

All over Germany people were waiting for the speech. Adolf Hitler stood before the microphones, and he was no longer worried. At the back of his mind, he created a tiny phonograph record that said, over and over, "Russia. Russia. Russia." It would remind him what to do, at the right moment. Meanwhile, he launched into his speech.

It was good. It was a Hitler speech.

"Now!" said the record.

Hitler paused, taking a deep breath, throwing his head arrogantly back. He looked out at the thousands of faces beneath his balcony. But he wasn't thinking about them. He was thinking of the pause, and the next line; and the pause lengthened.

Important! Remember! Don't fail!

Adolf Hitler opened his mouth. Words came out. Not quite the right words.

Ten seconds later Adolf Hitler was cut off the air.

It wasn't Hitler personally who spoke to the world a few hours later. Goebbels had had a record made, and the transcription, oddly enough, didn't mention Russia. Or any of the vital questions that had been settled so neatly. The Führer simply couldn't talk about those questions. It wasn't mike fright, exactly. Whenever Hitler reached the crucial point in his speech, he turned green, gritted his teeth, and said—the wrong thing. He couldn't get over that semantic bloc. The more he tried, the less he succeeded. Finally Goebbels saw what was happening and called it off.

The world broadcast was emasculated. At the time there was considerable discussion as to why Hitler hadn't stuck to his announced program. He'd intended to mention Russia. Why, then—

Not many people knew. But more people will know now. In fact, a lot of people in Germany are going to know. Things get around there. Planes go over and drop leaflets, and people whisper, and they'll remember a certain catchy German stanza that's going the rounds.

Yeah. Maybe this particular copy of *Astounding* will find its way to England, and maybe an R. A. F. pilot will drop it near Berlin, or Paris, for that matter. Word will get around. There are lots of men on the continent who can read English.

And they'll talk.

They won't believe, at first. But they'll keep their eyes open. And there's a catchy little rhythm they'll remember. Some day the story will reach Berlin or Berchtesgarten. Some day it'll reach the guy with the little mustache and the big voice.

And, a little while later—days or weeks, it doesn't matter—Goebbels is going to walk into a big room, and there he's going to see Adolf Hitler goose-stepping around and yelling:

LEFT

LEFT

LEFT a wife and SEVenteen children in

STARVing condition with NOTHing but gingerbread *LEFT*—

The Iron Standard

Alien races didn't have to be either friendly or unfriendly; they could be stubbornly indifferent—with serious effect.

"SO THE GHOST won't walk for a year—Venusian time," Thirkell said, spooning up cold beans with a disgusted air.

Rufus Munn, the captain, looked up briefly from his task of de-cockroaching the soup. "Dunno why we had to import these. A year plus four weeks, Steve. There'll be a month at space before we hit Earth again."

Thirkell's round, pudgy face grew solemn. "What happens in the meantime? Do we starve on cold beans?"

Munn sighed, glancing through the open, screened port of the spaceship *Goodwill* to where dim figures moved in the mists outside. But he didn't answer. Barton Underhill, supercargo and handy man, who had wangled his passage by virtue of his father's wealth, grinned tightly and said, "What d'you expect? We don't dare use fuel. There's just enough to get us home. So it's cold beans or nothing."

"Soon it will be nothing," Thirkell said solemnly. "We have been spendthrifts. Wasting our substance in riotous living."

"Riotous living!" Munn growled. "We gave most of our grub to the Venusians."

"Well," Underhill murmured, "they fed us—for a month."

"Not now. There's an embargo. What do they have against us, anyhow?"

Munn thrust back his stool with sudden decision.

268

"That's something we'll have to figure out. Things can't go on like this. We simply haven't enough food to last us a year. And we can't live off the land—" He stopped as someone unzipped the valve screen and entered, a squat man with high cheekbones and a beak of a nose in a red-bronze face.

"Find anything, Redskin?" Underhill asked.

Mike Soaring Eagle tossed a plastisac on the table. "Six mushrooms. No wonder the Venusians use hydroponics. They have to. Only fungi will grow in this sponge of a world, and most of that's poisonous. No use, skipper."

Munn's mouth tightened. "Yeah. Where's Bronson?"

"Panhandling. But he won't get a *fal*." The Navaho nodded towards the port. "Here he comes now."

After a moment the others heard Bronson's slow footsteps. The engineer came in, his face red as his hair. "Don't ask me," he murmured. "Don't say a word, anybody. Me, a Kerry man, trying to bum a lousy *fal* from a shagreen-skinned so-and-so with an iron ring in his nose like a Ubangi savage. Think of it! The shame will stay with me forever."

"My sympathy," Thirkell said. "But did you get any *fals?*"

Bronson glared at him. "Would I have taken his dirty coins if he'd offered them?" the engineer yelled, his eyes bloodshot. "I'd have flung them in his slimy face, and you can take my word for it. *I* touch their rotten money? Give me some beans." He seized a plate and morosely began to eat.

Thirkell exchanged glances with Underhill. "He didn't get any money," the latter said.

Bronson started back with a snort. "He asked me if I belonged to the Beggars' Guild! Even tramps have to join a union on this planet!"

Captain Munn scowled thoughtfully. "No, it isn't a union, Bronson, or even much like the medieval guilds. The *tarkomars* are a lot more powerful and a lot less principled. Unions grew out of a definite social and economic background, and they fill a purpose—a check-and-balance system that keeps building. I'm not talking about unions; on Earth some of 'em are good—like the Air Transport—and some are graft-ridden, like Undersea Dredgers. The *tarko-*

mars are different. They don't fulfill any productive purpose. They just keep the Venusian system in its backwater."

"Yes," Thirkell said, "and unless we're members, we
aren't allowed to work—at anything. And we can't be
members till we pay the initiation fee—a thousand *sofals.*"

"Easy on those beans," Underhill cautioned. "We've
only ten more cans."

There was silence. Presently Munn passed cigarettes.
"We've got to do something, that's certain," he said.
"We can't get food except from the Venusians, and they
won't give it to us. One thing in our favor: the laws are so
arbitrary that they can't refuse to *sell* us grub—it's illegal
to refuse legal tender."

Mike Soaring Eagle glumly sorted his six mushrooms.
"Yeah. *If* we can get our hands on legal tender. We're
broke—broke on Venus—and we'll soon be starving to
death. If anybody can figure out an answer to that one—"

This was in 1964, three years after the first successful
flight to Mars, five years since Dooley and Hastings had
brought their ship down in Mare Imbrium. The Moon, of
course, was uninhabited, save by active but unintelligent algae. The big-chested, alert Martians, with their high me-
tabolism and their brilliant, erratic minds, had been friendly, and it was certain that the cultures of Mars and Earth
would not clash. As for Venus, till now, no ship had landed
there.

The *Goodwill* was the ambassador. It was an experiment, like the earlier Martian voyage, for no one knew
whether or not there was intelligent life on Venus. Supplies
for more than a year were stowed aboard, dehydrates, plastibulbs, concentrates and vitamin foods, but every man of
the crew had a sneaking hunch that food would be found in
plenty on Venus.

There was food—yes. The Venusians grew it, in their
hydroponic tanks under the cities. But on the surface of the
planet grew nothing edible at all. There was little animal or
bird life, so hunting was impossible, even had the Earthmen been allowed to retain their weapons. And in the beginning it had seemed like a gala holiday after the arduous

space trip—a year-long fete and carnival in an alien, fascinating civilization.

It was alien, all right. The Venusians were conservative. What was good enough for their remote ancestors was quite good enough for them. They didn't *want* changes, it seemed. The current setup had worked O.K. for centuries; why alter it now?

The Earthmen meant change—that was obvious.

Result: a boycott of the Earthmen.

It was all quite passive. The first month had brought no trouble; Captain Munn had been presented with the keys of the capital city, Vyring, on the outskirts of which the *Goodwill* now rested, and the Venusians brought food in plenty—odd but tasty dishes from the hydroponic gardens. In return, the Earthmen were lavish with their own stores, depleting them dangerously.

And the Venusian food spoiled quickly. There was no need to preserve it, for the hydroponic tanks turned out a steady, unfailing supply. In the end the Earthmen were left with a few weeks' stock of the food they had brought with them, and a vast pile of garbage that had been lusciously appetizing a few days before.

Then the Venusians stopped bringing their quick-spoiling fruits, vegetables and meat-mushrooms and clamped down. The party was over. They had no intention of harming the Earthmen; they remained carefully friendly. But from now on it was Pay as You're Served—and no checks cashed. A big meat-mushroom, enough for four hungry men, cost ten *fals*.

Since the Earthmen had no *fals,* they got no meat-mushrooms—nor anything else.

In the beginning it hadn't seemed important. Not until they got down to cases and began to wonder exactly how they could get food.

There was no way.

So they sat in the *Goodwill* eating cold beans and looking like five of the Seven Dwarfs, a quintet of stocky, short, husky men, big-boned and muscular, especially chosen for their physiques to stand the rigors of space flight—and their brains, also specially chosen, couldn't help them now.

It was a simple problem—simple and primitive. They,

the representatives of Earth's mightiest culture, were hungry. They would soon be hungrier.

And they didn't have a *fal*—nothing but worthless gold, silver and paper currency. There was metal in the ship, but none of the pure metal they needed, except in alloys that couldn't be broken down.

Venus was on the iron standard.

"—there's got to be an answer," Munn said stubbornly, his hard-bitten, harsh face somber. He pushed back his plate with an angry gesture. "I'm going to see the Council again."

"What good will that do?" Thirkell wanted to know. "We're on the spot, there's no getting around it. Money talks."

"Just the same, I'm going to talk to Jorust," the captain growled. "She's no fool."

"Exactly," Thirkell said cryptically.

Munn stared at him, beckoned to Mike Soaring Eagle and turned towards the valve. Underhill jumped up eagerly.

"May I go?"

Bronson gloomily toyed with his beans. "Why do *you* want to go? You couldn't even play a slot machine in Vyring's skid row—if they had slot machines. Maybe you think if you tell 'em your old man's a Tycoon of Amalgamated Ores, they'll break down and hand out meal tickets—eh?"

But his tone was friendly enough, and Underhill merely grinned. Captain Munn said, "Come along, if you want, but hurry up." The three men went out into the steaming mists, their feet sloshing through sticky mud.

It wasn't uncomfortably hot; the high winds of Venus provided for quick evaporation, a natural air conditioning that kept the men from feeling the humidity. Munn referred to his compass. The outskirts of Vyring were half a mile away, but the fog was, as usual, like pea soup. On Venus it is always bird-walking weather. Silently the trio slogged on.

"I thought Indians knew how to live off the land," Underhill presently remarked to the Navaho. Mike Soaring Eagle looked at him quizzically.

"I'm not a Venusian Indian," he explained. "Maybe I could make a bow and arrow and bring down a Venusian —but that wouldn't help, unless he had a lot of *sofals* in his purse."

"We might eat him," Underhill murmured. "Wonder what roast Venusian would taste like?"

"Find out and you can write a best seller when you get back home," Munn remarked. *"If* you get back home. Vyring's got a police force, chum."

"Oh, well," Underhill said, and left it at that. "Here's the Water Gate. Lord—I smell somebody's dinner!"

"So do I," the Navaho grunted, "but I hoped nobody would mention it. Shut up and keep walking."

The wall around Vyring was in the nature of a dike, not a fortification. Venus was both civilized and unified; there were, apparently, no wars and no tariffs—a natural development for a world state. Air transports made sizzling noises as they shot past, out of sight in the fog overhead. Mist shrouded the streets, torn into tatters by occasional huge fans. Vyring, shielded from the winds, was unpleasantly hot, except indoors where artificial air conditioning could be brought into use.

Underhill was reminded of Venice: the streets were canals. Watercraft of various shapes and sizes drifted, glided or raced past. Even the beggars traveled by water. There were rutted, muddy footpaths beside the canals, but no one with a *fal* to his name ever walked.

The Earthmen walked, cursing fervently as they splashed through the muck. They were, for the most part, ignored.

A water taxi scooted towards the bank, its pilot, wearing the blue badge of his *tarkomar,* hailing them. "May I escort you?" he wanted to know.

Underhill exhibited a silver dollar. "If you'll take this— sure." All the Earthmen had learned Venusian quickly; they were good linguists, having been chosen for this as well as other transplanetary virtues. The phonetic Venusian tongue was far from difficult.

It was no trouble at all to understand the taxi pilot when he said no.

"Toss you for it," Underhill said hopefully. "Double or nothing."

But the Venusians weren't gamblers. "Double what?" the pilot inquired. "That coin? It's silver." He indicated the silver, rococo filigree on the prow of his craft. "Junk!"

"This would be a swell place for Benjamin Franklin," Mike Soaring Eagle remarked. "His false teeth were made of iron, weren't they?"

"If they were, he had a Venusian fortune in his mouth," Underhill said.

"Not quite."

"If it could buy a full-course dinner, it's a fortune," Underhill insisted.

The pilot, eyeing the Earthmen scornfully, drifted off in search of wealthier fares. Munn, doggedly plodding on, wiped sweat from his forehead. Swell place, Vyring, he thought. Swell place to starve to death.

Half an hour of difficult hiking roused Munn to a slow, dull anger. If Jorust refused to see him, he thought, there was going to be trouble, even though they'd taken away his guns. He felt capable of tearing down Vyring with his teeth. And eating the more edible portions.

Luckily, Jorust was available. The Earthmen were ushered into her office, a big, luxurious room high above the city, with windows open to the cooling breezes. Jorust was skittering around the room on a high chair, equipped with wheels and some sort of motor. Along the walls ran a slanting shelf, like a desk and presumably serving the same function. It was shoulder-high, but Jorust's chair raised her to its level. She probably started in one corner in the morning, Munn thought, and worked her way around the room during the day.

Jorust was a slim, gray-haired Venusian woman with a skin the texture of fine shagreen, and alert black eyes that were wary now. She climbed down from her chair, gestured the men to seats, and took one herself. She lit a pipe that looked like an oversized cigarette holder, stuffing it with a cylinder of pressed yellow herbs. Aromatic smoke drifted up. Underhill sniffed wistfully.

"May you be worthy of your fathers," Jorust said politely, extending her six-fingered hand in greeting. "What brings you?"

"Hunger," Munn said bluntly. "I think it's about time for a showdown."

Jorust watched him inscrutably. "Well?"

"We don't like being pushed around."

"Have we harmed you?" the Council head asked.

Munn looked at her. "Let's put our cards on the table. We're getting the squeeze play. You're a big shot here, and you're either responsible or you know why. How about it?"

"No," Jorust said after a pause, "no, I'm not as powerful as you seem to think, I am one of the administrators. I do not make the laws. I merely see that they are carried out. We are not enemies."

"That might happen," Munn said grimly. "If another expedition comes from Earth and finds us dead—"

"We would not kill you. It is untraditional."

"You could starve us to death, though."

Jorust narrowed her eyes. "Buy food. Any man can do that, no matter what his race."

"And what do we use for money?" Munn asked. "You won't take our currency. We haven't any of yours."

"Your currency is worthless," Jorust explained. "We have gold and silver for the mining—it is common here. A *difal*—twelve *fals*—will buy a good deal of food. A *sofal* will buy even more than that."

She was right, of course, Munn knew. A *sofal* was one thousand seven hundred twenty-eight *fals*. Yeah!

"And how do you expect us to get any of your iron money?" he snapped.

"Work for it, as our own people do. The fact that you are from another world does not dispose of your obligatory duty to create through labor."

"All right," Munn pursued, "we're willing. Get us a job."

"What kind?"

"Dredging canals! Anything!"

"Are you a member of the canal dredgers' *tarkomar*?"

"No," Munn said. "How could I have forgotten to join?"

Jorust ignored the sarcasm. "You must join. All trades here have their *tarkomars*."

"Lend me a thousand *sofals* and I'll join one."

"You have tried that before," Jorust told him. "Our moneylenders reported that your collateral was worthless."

"Worthless! D'you mean to say we've nothing in our ship worth a thousand *sofals* to your race? It's a squeeze play and you know it. Our water purifier alone is worth six times that to you."

Jorust seemed affronted. "For a thousand years we have cleansed our water with charcoal. If we changed now, we would be naming our ancestors fools. They were not fools; they were great and wise."

"What about progress?"

"I see no need for it," Jorust said. "Our civilization is a perfect unit as it stands. Even the beggars are well fed. There is no unhappiness on Venus. The ways of our ancestors have been tested and found good. So why change?"

"But—"

"We would merely upset the *status quo* if we altered the balance," Jorust said decisively, rising. "May you be worthy of your fathers' names."

"Listen—" Munn began.

But Jorust was back on her chair, no longer listening.

The three Earthmen looked at one another, shrugged and went out. The answer was definitely no.

"And that," Munn said, as they descended in the elevator, "is emphatically that. Jorust plans to have us starve to death. The word's out."

Underhill was inclined to disagree. "She's all right. As she said, she's just an administrator. It's the *tarkomars* who are the pressure group here. They're a powerful bloc."

"They run Venus. I know." Munn grimaced. "It's difficult to understand the psychology of these people. They seem unalterably opposed to change. We represent change. So they figure they'll simply ignore us."

"It won't work," Underhill said. "Even if we starve to death, there'll be more Earth ships later."

"The same gag could work on them, too."

"Starvation? But—"

"Passive resistance. There's no law compelling Venusians to treat with Earthmen. They can simply adopt a closed-door policy, and there's not a thing we can do about it. There's no welcome mat on Venus."

Mike Soaring Eagle broke a long silence as they

emerged to the canal bank. "It's a variation of ancestor worship, their psychology. Transferred egotism, perhaps—a racial inferiority complex."

Munn shook his head. "You're drawing it a bit fine."

"All right, maybe I am. But it boils down to worship of the past. And fear. Their present social culture has worked for centuries. They want no intrusions. It's logical. If you had a machine that worked perfectly at the job for which it had been designed, would you want improvements?"

"Why not?" Munn said. "Certainly I would."

"Why?"

"Well—to save time. If a new attachment would make the machine double its production, I'd want that."

The Navaho looked thoughtful. "Suppose it turned out —say—refrigerators. There'd be repercussions. You'd need less labor, which would upset the economic structure."

"Microscopically."

"In that case. But there'd also be a change in the consumer's angle. More people would have refrigerators. More people would make homemade ice cream. Sales on ice cream would drop—retail sales. The wholesalers would buy less milk. The farmers would—"

"I know," Munn said. "For want of a nail the kingdom was lost. You're speaking of microcosms. Even if you weren't, there are automatic adjustments—there always are."

"An experimental, growing civilization is willing to stand for such adjustments," Mike Soaring Eagle pointed out. "The Venusians are ultraconservative. They figure they don't need to grow or change any more. Their system has worked for centuries. It's perfectly integrated. Intrusion of anything might upset the apple cart. The *tarkomars* have the power, and they intend to keep it."

"So we starve," Underhill put in.

The Indian grinned at him. "Looks like it. Unless we can dope out some way of making money."

"We ought to," Munn said. "We were chosen for our I.Q., among other things."

"Our talents aren't too suitable," Mike Soaring Eagle remarked, kicking a stone into the canal. "You're a physicist.

I'm a naturalist. Bronson's an engineer and Steve Thirkell's a sawbones. You, my useless young friend, are a rich man's son."

Underhill smiled in an embarrassed fashion. "Well, dad came up the hard way. He knew how to make money. That's what we need now, isn't it?"

"How did he clean up?"

"Stock market."

"That helps a lot," Munn said. "I think our best plan is to find some process the Venusians really *need*, and then sell it to them."

"If we could wireless back to Earth for help—" Underhill began.

"—then we'd have nothing to worry about," the Navaho ended. "Unfortunately Venus has a Heaviside layer, so we can't wireless. You'd better try your hand at inventing something, Skipper. But whether or not the Venusians will want it afterwards, *I* don't know."

Munn brooded. "The *status quo* can't remain permanently that way. It ain't sensible, as my grandfather used to say about practically everything. There are always inventors. New processes—they've got to be assimilated into the social setup. I should be able to dope out a gadget. Even a good preservative for foods might do it."

"Not with the hydroponic gardens producing as they do."

"Um-m. A better mousetrap—something useless but intriguing. A one-armed bandit—"

"They'd pass a law against it."

"Well, you suggest something."

"The Venusians don't seem to know much about genetics. If I could produce some unusual foods by crossbreeding . . . eh?"

"Maybe," Munn said. "Maybe."

Steve Thirkell's pudgy face looked into the port. The rest of the party were seated at the table, scribbling on stylopads and drinking weak coffee.

"I have an idea," Thirkell said.

Munn grunted. "I know your ideas. What is it now?"

"Very simple. A plague strikes the Venusians and I find an antivirus that will save them. They will be grateful—"

"—and you'll marry Jorust and rule the planet," Munn finished. "Ha!"

"Not exactly," Thirkell went on imperturbably. "If they're not grateful, we'll simply hold out on the antitoxin till they pay up."

"The only thing wrong with that brainstorm is that the Venusians don't seem to be suffering from a plague," Mike Soaring Eagle pointed out. "Otherwise it's perfect."

Thirkell sighed. "I was afraid you'd mention that. Maybe we could be unethical—just a little, you know—and start a plague. Typhoid or something."

"What a man!" The Navaho said admiringly. "You'd make a grand murderer, Steve."

"I have often thought so. But I didn't intend to go as far as murder. A painful, incapacitating disease—"

"Such as?" Munn asked.

"Diphtheria?" the murderous physician suggested hopefully.

"A cheerful prospect," Mike Soaring Eagle muttered. "You sound like an Apache."

"Diphtheria, beriberi, leprosy, bubonic plague," Pat Bronson said violently. "I vote for all of 'em. Give the nasty little frogs a taste of their own medicine. Wallop 'em good."

"Suppose we let you start a mild plague," Munn said. "Something that couldn't conceivably be fatal—how would you go about it?"

"Pollute the water supply or something . . . eh?"

"What with?"

Thirkell suddenly looked heartbroken. "Oh! *Oh!*"

Munn nodded. "The *Goodwill* isn't stocked for that sort of thing. We're germless. Antiseptic inside and out. Have you forgotten the physical treatment they gave us before we left?"

Bronson cursed. "Never will I forget that—a hypo every hour! Antitoxins, shots, ultraviolet X-rays, till my bones turned green."

"Exactly," Munn said. "We're practically germless. It's a precaution they had to take, to prevent our starting a plague on Venus."

"But we *want* to start a plague," Thirkell said plaintively.

"You couldn't even give a Venusian a head cold," Munn told him. "So that's out. What about Venusian anaesthetics? Are they as good as ours?"

"Better," the physician admitted. "Not that they need them, except for the children. Their synapses are funny. They've mastered self-hypnosis so they can block pain when it's necessary."

"Sulfa drugs?"

"I've thought of that. They've got those, too."

"My idea," Bronson broke in, "is water power. Or dams. Whenever it rains, there's a flood."

"There's good drainage, though," Munn said. "The canals take care of that."

"Now let me finish! Those fish-skinned so-and-sos have hydropower, but it isn't efficient. There's so much fast water all over the place that they build plants wherever it seems best—thousands of them—and half the time they're useless, when the rains concentrate on another district. Half of the plants are inoperable all the time. Which costs money. If they'd build dams, they'd have a steady source of power without the terrific overhead."

"It's a thought," Munn acknowledged.

Mike Soaring Eagle said, "I'll stick to my crossbreeds in the hydroponic gardens. I can raise beefsteak-mushrooms to taste of Worcestershire sauce or something. An appeal to the palate, you know—"

"Fair enough. Steve?"

Thirkell rumpled his hair. "I'll think of an angle. Don't rush me."

Munn looked at Underhill. "Any flashes of intellect, chum?"

The youngster grimaced. "Not just now. All I can think of is manipulating the stock market."

"Without money?"

"That's the trouble."

Munn nodded. "Well, my own idea is advertising. As a physicist, it's in my line."

"How?" Bronson wanted to know. "Demonstrating atom-smashing? A strong-man act?"

"Pipe down. Advertising isn't known on Venus, though commerce is. That's funny. I should think the retailers would jump at the chance."

"They've got radio commercials."

"Stylized and ritualistic. Their televisors are ready-made for splash advertising. A visual blurb . . . yeah. Trick gadgets I could make to demonstrate the products. Why not?"

"I think I'll build an X-ray machine," Thirkell said suddenly, "if you'll help me, skipper."

Munn said sure. "We've got the equipment—and the blueprints. Tomorrow we'll start. It must be pretty late."

It was, though there was no sunset on Venus. The quintet retired, to dream of full-course dinners—all but Thirkell, who dreamed he was eating a roast chicken that abruptly turned into a Venusian and began to devour him, starting at the feet. He woke up sweating and cursing, took some nembutal, and finally slept again.

The next morning they scattered. Mike Soaring Eagle took a microscope and other gadgets to the nearest hydroponic center and went to work. He wasn't allowed to carry spores back to the *Goodwill,* but there was no objection to his experimenting in Vyring itself. He made cultures and used forced growth vitamin complexes and hoped for the best.

Pat Bronson went to see Skottery, head of Water Power. Skottery was a tall, saturnine Venusian who knew a lot about engineering and insisted on showing Bronson the models in his office before they settled down to a talk.

"How many power stations do you have?" Bronson asked.

"Third power twelve times four dozens. Forty-two dozen in this district."

Nearly a million altogether, Bronson made it. "How many in actual operation now?" he carried on.

"About seventeen dozen."

"That means three hundred idle—twenty-five dozen, that is. Isn't the upkeep a factor?"

"Quite a factor," Skottery acknowledged. "Aside from the fact that some of those stations are now permanently inoperable. The terrain changes rapidly. Erosion, you know. We'll build one station on a gorge one year, and the next the water will be taking a different route. We build about a dozen a day. But we salvage something from the old ones, of course."

Bronson had a brainstorm. "No watershed?"

"Eh?"

The Earthman explained. Skottery shook his shoulders in negation.

"We have a different type of vegetation here. There's so much water that roots don't have to strike deeply."

"But they need soil?"

"No. The elements they need are in suspension in the water."

Bronson described how watersheds worked. "Suppose you imported Earth plants and trees and forested the mountains. And built dams to retain your water. You'd have power all the time, and you'd need only a few big stations. And they'd be permanent."

Skottery thought that over. "We have all the power we need."

"But look at the expense!"

"Our rates cover that."

"You could make more money—*difals* and *sofals*—"

"We have made exactly the same profits for three hundred years," Skottery explained. "Our net remains constant. It works perfectly. You fail to understand our economic system, I see. Since we have everything we need, there's no use making more money—not even a *fal* more."

"Your competitors—"

"We have only three, and they are satisfied with their profits."

"Suppose I interest them in my plan?"

"But you couldn't," Skottery said patiently. "They wouldn't be interested any more than I am. I'm glad you dropped in. May you be worthy of your father's name."

"Ye soulless fish!" Bronson yelled, losing his temper. "Is there no red blood in your green-skinned carcass? Does no one on this world know what fight means?" He hammered a fist into his palm. "I wouldn't be worthy of the old Seumas Bronson's name unless I took a poke at that ugly phiz of yours right now—"

Skottery had pressed a button. Two large Venusians appeared. The head of Water Power pointed to Bronson.

"Remove it," he said.

Captain Rufus Munn was in one of the telecasting studios with Bart Underhill. They were sitting beside Hakkapuy, owner of Veetsy—which might be freely translated as Wet Tingles. They were watching the telecast commercial plug for Hakkapuy's product, on the 'visor screen high on the wall.

A Venusian faded in, legs wide apart, arms akimbo. He raised one hand, six fingers spread wide.

"All men drink water. Water is good. Life needs water. Veetsy is good also. Four *fals* buys a globe of Veetsy. That is all."

He vanished. Colors rippled across the screen and music played in off-beat rhythm. Munn turned to Hakkapuy.

"That isn't advertising. You can't get customers that way."

"Well, it's traditional," Hakkapuy said weakly.

Munn opened the pack at his feet, brought out a tall glass beaker, and asked for a globe of Veetsy. It was given him, and he emptied the green fluid into his beaker. After that, he dropped in a half dozen colored balls and added a chunk of dry ice, which sank to the bottom. The balls went up and down rapidly.

"See?" Munn said. "Visual effect. The marbles are only slightly heavier than Veetsy. It's the visual equivalent of Wet Tingles. Show that on the televisor, with a good sales talk, and see how your sales curve jumps."

Hakkapuy looked interested. "I'm not sure—"

Munn dragged out a sheaf of papers and hammered at the breach in the wall. After a time a fat Venusian came in and said, "May you be worthy of your ancestors' names." Hakkapuy introduced him as Lorish.

"I thought Lorish had better see this. Would you mind going over it again?"

"Sure," Munn said. "Now the principle of display windows—"

When he had finished, Hakkapuy looked at Lorish, who shook his shoulders slowly.

"No," he said.

Hakkapuy blew out his lips. "It would sell more Veetsy."

"And upset the economy charts," Lorish said. "No."

Munn glared at him. "Why not? Hakkapuy owns Veetsy, doesn't he? Who are you, anyhow—a censor?"

"I represent the advertisers' *tarkomar*," Lorish explained. "You see, advertising on Venus is strongly ritual. It is never changed. Why should it be? If we let Hakkapuy use your ideas, it would be unfair to other makers of soft drinks."

"They could do the same thing," Munn pointed out.

"A pyramiding competition leading to ultimate collapse. Hakkapuy makes enough money. Don't you, Hakkapuy?"

"I suppose so."

"Are you questioning the motives of the *tarkomars*?"

Hakkapuy gulped. "No," he said hastily. "No. no, no! You're perfectly right."

Lorish looked at him. "Very well. As for you, Earthman, you had better not waste your time pursuing this—scheme—further."

Munn reddened. "Are you threatening me?"

"Of course not. I simply mean that no advertiser could use your idea without consulting my *tarkomar*, and we would veto it."

"Sure," Munn said. "O.K. Come on, Bart. Let's get out of here."

They departed, to stroll along a canal bank and confer. Underhill was thoughtful.

"The *tarkomars* have held the balance of power for a long time, it looks like. They want things to stay as they are. That's obvious."

Munn growled.

Underhill went on, "We'd have to upset the whole apple cart to get anywhere. There's one thing in our favor, though."

"What?"

"The laws."

"How do you figure that out?" Munn asked. "They're all against us."

"So far—yes. But they're traditionally rigid and unswerving. A decision made three hundred years ago can't be changed except by a long court process. If we can find a loophole in those laws, they can't touch us."

"All right, find the loophole," Munn said grumpily. "I'm going back to the ship and help Steve build an X-ray machine."

"I think I'll go down to the stock exchange and snoop," Underhill said. "It's just possible—"

After a week, the X-ray device was finished. Munn and Thirkell looked through the Vyring law records and found they were permitted to sell a self-created device without belonging to a *tarkomar,* provided they obeyed certain trivial restrictions. Leaflets were printed and strewed around the city, and the Venusians came to watch Munn and Thirkell demonstrating the merits of Roentgen rays.

Mike Soaring Eagle knocked off work for the day and recklessly smoked a dozen cigarettes from his scanty store, burning with dull fury as he puffed. He had run into trouble with his hydroponic cultures.

"Crazy!" he told Bronson. "Luther Burbank would have gone nuts—the way I'm going. How the devil can I guess-pollinate those ambiguous specimens of Venusian flora?"

"Well, it doesn't seem exactly fair," Bronson consoled. "Eighteen sexes, eh?"

"Eighteen so far. And four varieties that apparently haven't any sex at all. How can you crossbreed those perverted mushrooms? You'd have to exhibit the result in a side show."

"You're getting nowhere?"

"Oh, I'm getting places," Mike Soaring Eagle said bitterly. "I'm getting all sorts of results. The trouble is nothing stays constant. I get a rum-flavored fungus one day, and it doesn't breed true—its spores turn into something that tastes like turpentine. So you see."

Bronson looked sympathetic. "Can't you swipe some grub when they're not looking? That way the job wouldn't be a complete washout."

"They search me," the Navaho said.

"The dirty skunks," Bronson yelped. "What do they think we are? Crooks?"

"Mph. Something's going on outside. Let's take a look." They went out of the *Goodwill* to find Munn arguing passionately with Jorust, who had come in person to examine the X-ray machine. A crowd of Venusians watched avidly. Munn's face was crimson.

"I looked it up," he was saying. "You can't stop me this time, Jorust. It's perfectly legal to build a machine and sell it outside the city limits."

"Certainly," Jorust said. "I'm not complaining about that."

"Well? We're not breaking any law."

The woman beckoned, and a fat Venusian waddled forward. "Patent three gross squared fourteen two dozen, issued to Metzi-Stang of Mylosh year fourth power twelve, subject sensitized plates."

"What's that?" Munn asked.

"It's a patent," Jorust told him. "It was issued some time ago to a Venusian inventor named Metzi-Stang. A *tarkomar* bought and suppressed the process, but it's still illegal to infringe on it."

"You mean somebody's already invented an X-ray machine on Venus?"

"No. Merely sensitized film. But that's part of your device, so you can't sell it."

Thirkell pushed forward. "I don't need film—"

The fat Venusian said, "Vibrationary patent three gross two dozen and seven—"

"What now?" Munn broke in.

Jorust smiled. "Machines employing vibration must not infringe on the patent."

"This is an X-ray machine," Thirkell snapped.

"Light is vibration," Jorust told him. "You can't sell it without buying permission from the *tarkomar* now owning that patent. It should cost—let's see—five thousand *sofals* or so."

Thirkell turned abruptly and went into the ship, where he mixed a whiskey-and-soda and thought wistfully about diphtheria germs. After a time the others appeared, looking disconsolate.

"Can she do it?" Thirkell asked.

Munn nodded. "She can do it, Chum. She's done it."

"We're not infringing on their patents."

"We're not on Earth. The patent laws here are so wide

that if a man invents a gun, nobody else can make telescopic sights. We're rooked again."

Underhill said, "It's the *tarkomars* again. When they see a new process or invention that might mean change, they buy it up and suppress it. I can't think of any gadget we could make that wouldn't be an infringement on some Venusian patent or other."

"They stay within the law," Munn pointed out. *"Their* law. So we can't even challenge them. As long as we're on Venus, we're subject to their jurisprudence."

"The beans are getting low," Thirkell said morosely.

"Everything is," the captain told him. "Any ideas, somebody?"

There was silence. Presently Underhill took out a globe of Veetsy and put it on the table.

"Where'd you get that?" Bronson asked. "It costs four *fals*."

"It's empty," Underhill said. "I found it in an ash can. I've been investigating glassite—the stuff they use for things like this."

"What about it?"

"I found out how they make it. It's a difficult, expensive process. It's no better than our flexiglass, and a lot harder to make. If we had a flexiglass factory here—"

"Well?"

"The bottom would drop out of Amalgamated Glassite."

"I don't get it," Bronson said. "So what?"

"Ever heard of a whispering campaign?" Underhill asked. "My father wangled many an election that way, the old devil. Suppose we passed the word around that there was a new process for making a cheaper, better substitute for glassite? Wouldn't Amalgamated stock drop?"

"Possibly," Munn said.

"We could clean up."

"What with?"

"Oh." Underhill was silent. "It takes money to make money."

"Always."

"I wonder. Here's another idea. Venus is on the iron standard. Iron's cheap on Earth. Suppose we talked about bringing in iron here—strewing it broadcast. There'd be a panic, wouldn't there?"

"Not without some iron to strew around," Munn said. "Counterpropaganda would be telecast; we couldn't compete with it. Our whispering campaign would be squashed before we got it started. The Venusian government—the *tarkomars*—would simply deny that Earth had unlimited iron supplies. We wouldn't profit, anyway."

"There must be some angle," Underhill scowled. "There's got to be. Let's see. What's the basis of the Venusian system?"

"No competition," Mike Soaring Eagle said. "Everybody has all he wants."

"Maybe. At the top. But the competitive instinct is too strong to be suppressed like that. I'll bet plenty of Venusians would like to make a few extra *fals*."

"Where does that get us?" Munn wanted to know.

"The way my father did it . . . Hm-m-m. He manipulated, pulled the wires, made people come to him. What's the weak spot in Venusian economy?"

Munn hesitated. "Nothing we can strike at—we're too handicapped."

Underhill shut his eyes. "The basis of an economic and social system is—what?"

"Money," Bronson said.

"No. Earth's on the radium standard. Years ago it was gold or silver. Venus is on iron. And there's the barter system, too. Money's a variable."

"Money represents natural resources—" Thirkell began.

"Man-hours," Munn put in quietly.

Underhill jumped. "That's it! Of course—man-hours! That's the constant. The amount of production a man can turn out in an hour represents an arbitrary constant—two dollars, a dozen *difals* or whatever it is. That's the base for any economic setup. And it's the base we've got to hit. The ancestor worship, the power of the *tarkomars*—they're superficial really. Once the basic system is challenged, they'll go down."

"I don't see where it gets us," Thirkell said.

"Make the man-hours variable," Underhill explained. "Once we do that, anything can happen."

"Something had better happen," Bronson said, "and quick. We've little food left."

"Shut up," Munn said. "I think the kid's got the right angle. Alter the man-hour constant, eh? How can we do that? Specialized training? Train a Venusian to turn out twice as much stuff in the same period of time? Skilled labor?"

"They've got skilled labor," Underhill said. "If we could make 'em work faster, or increase their stamina—"

"Benzedrine plus," Thirkell interrupted. "With enough caffeine, vitamin complex and riboflavin—I could whip up a speeder-upper, all right."

Munn nodded slowly. "Pills, not shots. If this works out, we'll have to do it undercover after a while."

"What the devil will it get us to make the Venusians work faster?" Bronson asked.

Underhill snapped his fingers. "Don't you see? Venus is ultraconservative. The economic system is frozen static. It isn't adapted to change. There'll be hell popping!"

Munn said, "We'll need advertising to arouse public interest first of all. A practical demonstration." He looked around the table his gaze settling on Mike Soaring Eagle. "Looks like you're elected, Redskin. You've more stamina than any of us, according to the tests we took back on Earth."

"All right," the Navaho said. "What do I do?"

"Work!" Underhill told him. "Work till you drop!"

It began early the next morning in the main plaza of Vyring. Munn had checked up carefully, determined to make sure nothing would go wrong, and had learned that a recreation building was to be constructed on the site of the plaza. "Work won't start for several weeks," Jorust said. "Why?"

"We want to dig a hole there," Munn said. "Is it legal?"

The Venusian smiled. "Why, of course. That's public domain—until the contractors begin. But a demonstration of your muscular prowess won't help you, I'm afraid."

"Eh?"

"I'm not a fool. You're trying to land a job. You hope to do that by advertising your abilities. But why do it in just this way? Anybody can dig a hole. It isn't specialized."

Munn grunted. If Jorust wanted to jump at that conclusion, swell. He said, "It pays to advertise. Put a steam shovel to work, back on Earth, and a crowd will gather to watch it. We don't have a steam shovel, but—"

"Well, whatever you like. Legally you're within your rights. Nevertheless you can't hold a job without joining a *tarkomar*."

"Sometimes I think your planet would be a lot better off without the *tarkomars*," Munn said bluntly.

Jorust moved her shoulders. "Between ourselves, I have often thought so. I am merely an administrator, however. I have no real power. I do what I'm told to do. If I were permitted, I would be glad to lend you the money you need—"

"What?" Munn looked at her. "I thought—"

The woman froze. "It is not permitted. Tradition is not always wisdom, but I can do nothing about it. To defy the *tarkomars* is unthinkable and useless. I am sorry."

Munn felt a little better after that, somehow. The Venusians weren't all enemies. The all-powerful *tarkomars*, jealous of their power, fanatically desirous of preserving the *status quo*, were responsible for this mess.

When he got back to the plaza, the others were waiting. Bronson had rigged up a scoreboard, in phonetic Venusian, and had laid out mattock, pick, shovel, wheelbarrow and boards for the Navaho, who stood, a brawny, red-bronze figure, stripped to the waist in the cool wind. A few canal-boats had stopped to watch.

Munn looked at his watch. "O.K., Redskin. Let's go. Steve can start—"

Underhill began to beat a drum. Bronson put figures on the scoreboard: 4:03:00, Venusian Vyring Time. Thirkell went to a nearby camp table, littered with bottles and medical equipment, shook from a vial one of the stimulant pills he had concocted, and gave it to Mike Soaring Eagle. The Indian ate it, heaved up the mattock and went to work.

That was all.

A man digging a hole. Just why the spectacle should be so fascinating no one has ever figured out. The principle remains the same, whether it's a steam shovel scooping out half a ton of earth at a bite, or a sweating, stocky Navaho wielding shovel and pick. The boats grew thicker.

Mike Soaring Eagle kept working. An hour passed. Another. There were regular, brief rest periods, and Mike kept rotating his tools, to get all his muscles into play. After breaking earth for a while with the mattock, he would shovel it into the wheelbarrow, roll his burden up a plank and dump it on an ever growing pile some distance away. Three hours. Four. Mike knocked off for a brief lunch. Bronson kept track of the time on his scoreboard.

Thirkell gave the Navaho another pill. "How're you doing?"

"Fine. I'm tough enough."

"I know, but these stimulants—they'll help."

Underhill was at a typewriter. He had already ground out a tremendous lot of copy, for he had been working since Mike Soaring Eagle started. Bronson had discovered a long-forgotten talent and was juggling makeshift Indian clubs and colored balls. He'd been keeping that up for quite a while, too.

Captain Rufus Munn was working a sewing machine. He didn't especially like the task, but it was precision work, and therefore helpful to the plan. All the party except Thirkell was doing something, and the physician was busy administering pills and trying to look like an alchemist.

Occasionally he visited Munn and Underhill, collected stacks of paper and carefully sewn scraps of cloth, and deposited them in various boxes near the canal, labeled, "Take One." On the cloth a legend was machine-embroidered in Venusian: "A Souvenir from Earth." The crowds thickened.

The Earthmen worked on. Bronson kept juggling, with pauses for refreshment. Eventually he experimented with coin and card tricks. Mike Soaring Eagle kept digging. Munn sewed. Underhill continued to type—and the Venusians read what his flying fingers turned out.

"Free! Free! Free!" the leaflets said. "Souvenir pillowcase covers from Earth! A free show! Watch the Earthmen demonstrate stamina, dexterity and precision in four separate ways. How long can they keep it up? With the aid of POWER PILLS—indefinitely! Their output is doubled and their precision increased by POWER PILLS—they pep you up! A medical product on Earth that can make any man worth twice his weight in *sofals!*"

It went on like that. The old army game—with variations. The Venusians couldn't resist. Word got around. The mob thickened. How long could the Earthmen keep up the pace?

They kept it up. Thirkell's stimulant pills—as well as the complex shots he had given his companions that morning —seemed to be working. Mike Soaring Eagle dug like a beaver. Sweat poured from his shining red-bronze torso. He drank prodigiously and ate salt tablets.

Munn kept sewing, without missing a stitch. He knew that his products were being scanned closely for signs of sloppy workmanship. Bronson kept juggling and doing coin tricks, never missing. Underhill typed with aching fingers.

Five hours. Six hours. Even with the rest periods, it was gruelling. They had brought food from the *Goodwill*, but it wasn't too palatable. Still, Thirkell had selected it carefully for caloric.

Seven hours. Eight hours. The crowds made the canals impassable. A policeman came along and argued with Thirkell, who told him to see Jorust. Jorust must have put a flea in his ear, for he came back to watch, but not to interfere.

Nine hours. *Ten hours.* Ten hours of Herculean effort. The men were exhausted—but they kept going.

They had made their point by then, though, for a few Venusians approached Thirkell and inquired about the Power Pills. What were they? Did they really make you work faster? How could they buy the—

The policeman appeared to stand beside Thirkell. "I've a message from the medical *tarkomar*," he announced. "If you try to sell any of those things, you go to jail."

"Wouldn't think of it," Thirkell said. "We're giving away free samples. Here, buddy." He dug into a sack and tossed the nearest Venusian a Power Pill. "Two days' work in that instead of your usual one. Come back for more tomorrow. Want one, pal? Here. You, too. Catch."

"Wait a minute—" the policeman said.

"Go get a warrant," Thirkell told him. "There's no law against making presents."

Jorust appeared with a burly, intolerant-looking Venusian. She introduced the latter as head of the Vyring *tarkomars*.

"And I'm here to tell you to stop this," the Venusian said.

Thirkell knew what to say. His companions kept on with their work, but he felt them watching and listening.

"What rule do you invoke?"

"Why . . . why, peddling."

"I'm not selling anything. This is public domain; we're putting on a free show."

"Those . . . ah . . . Power Pills—"

"Free gifts," Thirkell said. "Listen, pal. When we gave all our food to you Venusian crooks, did you squawk? No, you took it. And then clamped down. When we asked for our grub back, you just told us that we had no legal recourse; possession is nine points of the law, and we had a perfect right to make free gifts. That's what we're doing now—giving presents. So what?"

Jorust's eyes were twinkling, but she hooded them swiftly. "I fear he speaks the truth. The law protects him. It is no great harm."

Thirkell, watching her, wondered. Had Jorust guessed the right answer? Was she on their side? The *tarkomar* leader turned dark green, hesitated, swung on his heel and went away. Jorust gave the Earthmen a long, enigmatic look, moved her shoulders and followed.

"I'm still stiff," Mike Soaring Eagle said a week later in the *Goodwill*. "Hungry, too. When do we get grub?"

Thirkell, at the valve, handed out a Power Pill to a Venusian and came back rubbing his hands and grinning. "Wait. Just wait. What's going on, skipper?"

Munn nodded towards Underhill. "Ask the kid. He got back from Vyring a few minutes ago."

Underhill chuckled. "There was hell popping. All in a week, too. We've certainly struck at the economic base. Every Venusian who labors on a piecework basis wants our pills, so he can speed up his production and make more *fals*. It's the competitive instinct—which is universal."

"Well?" Bronson asked. "How do the lizard-faced big shots like that?"

"They don't like it. It's hit the economic setup they've had for centuries. Till now, one Venusian would make exactly ten *sofals* a week—say—by turning out five thousand bottle caps. With the pills Steve made up, he's turning out eight or ten thousand and making correspondingly more dough. The guy at the next bench says what the hell, and comes to us for a Power Pill for himself. Thus it goes. And the lovely part is that not all the labor is on piecework basis. It can't be. You need tangibles for piecework. Running a weather machine has got to be measured by time—not by how many raindrops you make in a day."

Munn nodded. "Jealousy, you mean?"

Underhill said, "Well, look. A weather-machine operator has been making ten *sofals* a week, the same as a bottle capper on piecework. Now the bottle capper's making twenty *sofals*. The weather-machine man doesn't see the point. He's willing to take Power Pills, too, but that won't step up his production. He asks for a raise. If he gets it, the economy is upset even more. If he doesn't, other weather-machine operators get together with him and figure it's unfair discrimination. They get mad at the *tarkomars*. They strike!"

Mike Soaring Eagle said, "The *tarkomars* have forbidden work to any Venusian taking Power Pills."

"And still the Venusians ask us for Power Pills. So what? How can you prove a man's been swallowing them? His production steps up, sure, but the *tarkomars* can't clamp down on everybody with a good turnout. They tried that, and a lot of guys who never tried the Power Pills got mad. They were fast workers, that was all."

"The demonstration we put on was a good idea," Thirkell said. "It was convincing. I've had to cut down the strength of the pills—we're running low—but the power of suggestion helps us."

Underhill grinned. "So the base—the man-hour unit—had gone cockeyed. One little monkey wrench, thrown where it'll do the most good. It's spreading, too. Not only Vyring. The news is going all over Venus, and the workers in the other cities are asking why half of Vyring's laborers should get better pay. That's where the equal standard of exchange helps us—one monetary system all over Venus. Nothing has ever been off par here for centuries. Now—"

Munn said, "Now the system's toppling. It's a natural fault in a perfectly integrated, rigid setup. For want of a nail the *tarkomars* are losing their grip. They've forgotten how to adjust."

"It'll spread," Underhill said confidently. "It'll spread. Steve, here comes another customer."

Underhill was wrong. Jorust and the Vyring *tarkomar* leader came in. "May you be worthy of your ancestors' names," Munn said politely. "Drag up a chair and have a drink. We've still got a few bulbs of beer left."

Jorust obeyed, but the Venusian rocked on his feet and glowered. The woman said, "Malsi is distressed. These Power Pills are causing trouble."

"I don't know why," Munn said. "They increase production, don't they?"

Malsi grimaced. "This is a trick! A stratagem! You are abusing our hospitality!"

"What hospitality?" Bronson wanted to know.

"You threatened the system," Malsi plunged on doggedly. "On Venus there is no change. There must be none."

"Why not?" Underhill asked. "There's only one real reason, and you know it. Any advances might upset the *tarkomars*—threaten the power they hold. You racketeers have had the whip hand for centuries. You've suppressed inventions, kept Venus in a backwater, tried to drive initiative out of the race, just so you could stay on top. It can't be done. Changes happen; they always do. If we hadn't come, there'd have been an internal explosion eventually."

Malsi glared at him. "You will stop making these Power Pills."

"Point of law," Thirkell said softly. "Show precedent."

Jorust said, "The right of free gift is one of the oldest on Venus. That law could be changed, Malsi, but I don't think the people would like it."

Munn grinned. "No. They wouldn't. That would be the tipoff. Venusians have learned it's possible to make more money. Take that chance away from them, and the *tarkomars* won't be the benevolent rulers any more."

Malsi turned darker green. "We have power—"

"Jorust, you're an administrator. Are we protected by your laws?" Underhill asked.

She moved her shoulders. "Yes, you are. The laws are

sacrosanct. Perhaps because they have always been designed to protect the *tarkomars*."

Malsi swung towards her. "Are you siding with the Earthmen?"

"Why, of course not, Malsi. I'm merely upholding the law, according to my oath of office. Without prejudice—that's it, isn't it?"

Munn said, "We'll stop making the Power Pills if you like, but I warn you that it's only a respite. You can't halt progress." Malsi seemed unconvinced. "You'll stop?"

"Sure. If you pay us."

"We cannot pay you," Malsi said stubbornly. "You belong to no *tarkomar*. It would be illegal."

Jorust murmured, "You might give them a free gift of —say—ten thousand *sofals*."

"Ten thousand!" Malsi yelped. "Ridiculous!"

"So it is," Underhill said. "Fifty thousand is more like it. We can live well for a year on that."

"No."

A Venusian came to the valve, peeped in and said: "I made twice as many *difals* today. May I have another Power Pill?" He saw Malsi and vanished with a small shriek.

Munn shrugged. "Suit yourself. Pay up, or we go on handing out Power Pills—and you'll have to adjust a rigid social economy. I don't think you can do it."

Jorust touched Malsi's arm. "There is no other way."

"I—" The Venusian by now was almost black with impotent rage. "All right," he capitulated, spitting the words between his teeth. "I won't forget this, Jorust."

"But I must administer the laws," the woman said. "Why, Malsi! The rule of the *tarkomars* has always been unswerving honesty."

Malsi didn't answer. He scribbled a credit check for fifty thousand *sofals,* validated it and gave the tag to Munn. After that he sent a parting glare around the cabin and stamped out.

"Well!" Bronson said. "Fifty grand! Tonight we eat!"

"May you be worthy of your fathers' names," Jorust murmured. At the valve she turned. "I'm afraid you've upset Malsi."

"Too bad," Munn said hypocritically.

Jorust moved her shoulders slightly. "Yes. You've upset Malsi. And Malsi represents the *tarkomars*—"

"What can he do about it?" Underhill asked.

"Nothing. The laws won't let him. But—it's nice to know the *tarkomars* aren't infallible. I think the word will get around."

Jorust winked gravely at Munn and departed, looking as innocent as a cat, and as potentially dangerous.

"Well!" Munn said. "What does that mean? The end of the *tarkomar*'s rule, maybe?"

"Maybe," Bronson said. "I don't give a damn. I'm hungry and I want a beefsteak-mushroom. Where can we cash a check for fifty grand?"

Cold War

Chapter 1. Last of the Pughs

I'LL NEVER HAVE a cold in the haid again without I think of little Junior Pugh. Now there was a repulsive brat if ever I saw one. Built like a little gorilla, he was. Fat, pasty face, mean look, eyes so close together you could poke 'em both out at once with one finger. His paw thought the world of him though. Maybe that was natural, seeing as how little Junior was the image of his pappy.

"The last of the Pughs," the old man used to say stickin' his chest out and beamin' down at the little gorilla. "Finest little lad that ever stepped."

It made my blood run cold sometimes to look at the two of 'em together. Kinda sad, now, to think back to those happy days when I didn't know either of 'em. You may not believe it but them two Pughs, father and son, between 'em came within *that* much of conquerin' the world.

Us Hogbens is quiet folks. We like to keep our heads down and lead quiet lives in our own little valley, where nobody comes near withouten we say so. Our neighbors and the folks in the village are used to us by now. They know we try hard not to act conspicuous. They make allowances.

If Paw gets drunk, like last week, and flies down the middle of Main Street in his red underwear most people make out they don't notice, so's not to embarrass Maw. They know he'd walk like a decent Christian if he was sober.

The thing that druv Paw to drink that time was Little

Sam, which is our baby we keep in a tank down-cellar, startin' to teethe again. First time since the War Between the States. We'd figgered he was through teething, but with Little Sam you never can tell. He was mighty restless, too.

A perfesser we keep in a bottle told us once Little Sam e-mitted subsonic somethings when he yells but that's just his way of talking. Don't mean a thing. It makes your nerves twiddle, that's all. Paw can't stand it. This time it even woke up Grandpaw in the attic and he hadn't stirred since Christmas. First thing after he got his eyes open he burst out madder'n a wet hen at Paw.

"I see ye, wittold knave that ye are!" he howled. "Flying again, is it? Oh, sic a reowfule sigte! I'll ground ye, ywis!" There was a far-away thump.

"You made me fall a good ten feet!" Paw hollered from away down the valley. "It ain't fair. I could of busted something!"

"Ye'll bust us all, with your dronken carelessness," Grandpaw said. "Flying in full sight of the neighbors! People get burned at the stake for less. You want mankind to find out all about us? Now shut up and let me tend to Baby."

Grandpaw can always quiet the baby if nobody else can. This time he sung him a little song in Sanskrit and after a bit they was snoring a duet.

I was fixing up a dingus for Maw to sour up some cream for sour-cream biscuits. I didn't have much to work with but an old sled and some pieces of wire but I didn't need much. I was trying to point the top end of the wire north-northeast when I seen a pair of checked pants rush by in the woods.

It was Uncle Lem. I could hear him thinking. "It *ain't* me!" he was saying, real loud, inside his haid. "Git back to yer work, Saunk. I ain't within a mile of you. Yer Uncle Lem's a fine old feller and never tells lies. Think I'd fool ye, Saunkie boy?"

"You shore would," I thunk back. "If you could. What's up, Uncle Lem?"

At that he slowed down and started to saunter back in a wide circle.

"Oh, I just had an idy yer Maw might like a mess of

blackberries," he thunk, kicking a pebble very nonchalant. "If anybody asks you say you ain't seen me. It's no lie. You ain't."

"Uncle Lem," I thunk, real loud, "I gave Maw my bounden word I wouldn't let you out of range without me along, account of the last time you got away—"

"Now, now, my boy," Uncle Lem thunk fast. "Let bygones be bygones."

"You just can't say no to a friend, Uncle Lem," I reminded him, taking a last turn of the wire around the runner. "So you wait a shake till I get this cream soured and we'll both go together, wherever it is you have in mind."

I saw the checked pants among the bushes and he come out in the open and give me a guilty smile. Uncle Lem's a fat little feller. He means well, I guess, but he can be talked into most anything by most anybody, which is why we have to keep a close eye on him.

"How you gonna do it?" he asked me, looking at the creamjug. "Make the little critters work faster?"

"Uncle Lem!" I said. "You know better'n that. Cruelty to dumb animals is something I can't abide. Them there little critters work hard enough souring milk the way it is. They're such teensy-weensy fellers I kinda feel sorry for 'em. Why, you can't even see 'em without you go kinda crosseyed when you look. Paw says they're enzymes. But they can't be. They're too teeny."

"Teeny is as teeny does," Uncle Lem said. "How you gonna do it, then?"

"This here gadget," I told him, kinda proud, "will send Maw's creaming ahead into next week some time. This weather, don't take cream more'n a couple of days but I'm giving it plenty of time. When I bring it back—bingo, it's sour." I set the jug on the sled.

"I never seen such a do-lass brat," Uncle Lem said, stepping forward and bending a wire crosswise. "You better do it that away, on account of the thunderstorm next Tuesday. All right now, shoot her off."

So I shot her off. When she come back, sure enough, the cream was sour enough to walk a mouse. Crawling up the can there was a hornet from next week, which I squashed. Now that was a mistake. I knowed it the minute I touched the jug. Dang Uncle Lem, anyhow.

He jumped back into the underbrush, squealing real happy.

"Fooled you that time, you young stinker," he yelled back. "Let's see you get your thumb outa the middle of next week!"

It was the time-lag done it. I mighta knowed. When he crossed that wire he didn't have no thunderstorm in mind at all. Took me nigh onto ten minutes to work myself loose, account of some feller called Inertia, who mixes in if you ain't careful when you fiddle around with time. I don't understand much about it myself. I ain't got my growth yet. Uncle Lem says he's already forgot more'n I'll ever know.

With that head start I almost lost him. Didn't even have time to change into my store-bought clothes and I knowed by the way he was all dressed up fit to kill he was headed for somewheres fancy.

He was worried, too. I kept running into little stray worrisome thoughts he'd left behind him, hanging like teeny little mites of clouds on the bushes. Couldn't make out much on account of they was shredding away by the time I got there but he'd shore done something he shouldn't. That much *anybody* coulda told. They went something like this:

"Worry, worry—wish I hadn't done it—oh, heaven help me if Grandpaw ever finds out—oh, them nasty Pughs, how could I a-been such a fool? Worry, worry—pore ole feller, such a good soul, too, never done nobody no harm and look at me now.

"That Saunk, too big for his britches, teach him a thing or two, ha-ha. Oh, worry, worry—never mind, brace up, you good ole boy, everything's bound to turn out right in the end. You deserve the best, bless you, Lemuel. Grandpaw'll never find out."

Well, I seen his checkered britches high-tailing through the woods after a bit, but I didn't catch up to him until he was down the hill, across the picnic grounds at the edge of town and pounding on the sill of the ticket-window at the railroad station with a Spanish doubloon he snitched from Paw's seachest.

It didn't surprise me none to hear him asking for a ticket to State Center. I let him think I hadn't caught up. He argued something turrible with the man behind the window but finally he dug down in his britches and fetched up a silver dollar, and the man calmed down.

The train was already puffing up smoke behind the station when Uncle Lem darted around the corner. Didn't leave me much time but I made it too—just. I had to fly a little over the last half-dozen yards but I don't think anybody noticed.

Once when I was just a little shaver there was a Great Plague in London, where we were living at the time, and all us Hogbens had to clear out. I remember the hullabaloo in the city but looking back now it don't seem a patch on the hullabaloo in State Center station when the train pulled in. Times have changed, I guess.

Whistles blowing, horns honking, radios yelling bloody murder—seems like every invention in the last two hundred years had been noisier than the one before it. Made my head ache until I fixed up something Paw once called a raised decibel threshold, which was pure showing-off.

Uncle Lem didn't know I was anywhere around. I took care to think real quiet but he was so wrapped up in his worries he wasn't paying no mind to nothing. I followed him through the crowds in the station and out onto a wide street full of traffic. It was a relief to get away from the trains.

I always hate to think what's going on inside the boiler, with all the little bitty critters so small you can't hardly see 'em, pore things, flying around all hot and excited and bashing their heads together. It seems plumb pitiable.

Of course, it just don't do to think what's happening inside the automobiles that go by.

Uncle Lem knowed right where he was headed. He took off down the street so fast I had to keep reminding myself not to fly, trying to keep up. I kept thinking I ought to get in touch with the folks at home, in case this turned into something I couldn't handle, but I was plumb stopped everywhere I turned. Maw was at the church social that afternoon and she whopped me the last time I spoke to her outa thin air right in front of the Reverend Jones. He ain't used to us Hogbens yet.

Paw was daid drunk. No good trying to wake him up.

And I was scared to death I *would* wake the baby if I tried to call on Grandpaw.

Uncle Lem scuttled right along, his checkered legs a-twinkling. He was worrying at the top of his mind, too. He'd caught sight of a crowd in a side-street gathered around a big truck, looking up at a man standing on it and waving bottles in both hands.

He seemed to be making a speech about headaches. I could hear him all the way to the corner. There was big banners tacked along the sides of the truck that said, PUGH HEADACHE CURE.

"Oh, worry, worry!" Uncle Lem thunk. "Oh, bless my toes, what *am* I going to do? I never *dreamed* anybody'd marry Lily Lou Mutz. Oh, worry!"

Well, I reckon we'd all been surprised when Lily Lou Mutz up and got herself a husband awhile back—around ten years ago, I figgered. But what it had to do with Uncle Lem I couldn't think. Lily Lou was just about the ugliest female that ever walked. Ugly ain't no word for her, pore gal.

Grandpaw said once she put him in mind of a family name of Gorgon he used to know. Not that she wasn't a goodhearted critter. Being so ugly, she put up with a lot in the way of rough acting-up from the folks in the village—the riff-raff lot, I mean.

She lived by herself in a little shack up the mountain and she musta been close onto forty when some feller from the other side of the river come along one day and rocked the whole valley back on its heels by asking her to marry up with him. Never saw the feller myself but I heard tell he wasn't no beauty-prize winner neither.

Come to think of it, I told myself right then, looking at the truck—come to think of it, feller's name was Pugh.

Chapter 2. A Fine Old Feller

Next thing I knowed, Uncle Lem had spotted somebody under a lamp-post on the sidewalk, at the edge of the crowd. He trotted over. It seemed to be a big gorilla and a little gorilla, standing there watching the feller on the truck selling bottles with both hands.

"Come and get it," he was yelling. "Come and get your bottle of Pugh's Old Reliable Headache Cure while they last!"

"Well, Pugh, here I am," Uncle Lem said, looking up at the big gorilla. "Hello, Junior," he said right afterward, glancing down at the little gorilla. I seen him shudder a little.

You shore couldn't blame him for that. Two nastier specimens of the human race I never did see in all my born days. If they hadn't been *quite* so pasty-faced or just the least mite slimmer, maybe they wouldn't have put me so much in mind of two well-fed slugs, one growed-up and one baby-sized. The paw was all dressed up in a Sunday-meeting suit with a big gold watch-chain across his front and the way he strutted you'd a thought he'd never had a good look in a mirror.

"Howdy, Lem," he said, casual-like. "Right on time, I see. Junior, say howdy to Mister Lem Hogben. You owe Mister Hogben a lot, sonny." And he laughed a mighty nasty laugh.

Junior paid him no mind. He had his beady little eyes fixed on the crowd across the street. He looked about seven years old and mean as they come.

"Shall I do it now, paw?" he asked in a squeaky voice. "Can I let 'em have it now, paw? Huh, paw?" From the tone he used. I looked to see if he'd got a machine gun handy. I didn't see none but if looks was ever mean enough to kill Junior Pugh could of mowed the crowd right down.

"Manly little feller, ain't he, Lem?" Paw Pugh said, real smug. "I tell you, I'm mighty proud of this youngster. Wish his dear grandpaw coulda lived to see him. A fine old family line, the Pughs is. Nothing like it anywhere. Only trouble is, Junior's the last of his race. You see why I got in touch with you, Lem."

Uncle Lem shuddered again. "Yep," he said. "I see, all right. But you're wasting your breath, Pugh. I ain't a-gonna do it."

Young Pugh spun around in his tracks.

"Shall I let him have it, paw?" he squeaked, real eager. "Shall I, paw? Now, paw? Huh, paw?"

"Shaddup, sonny," the big feller said and he whammed

the little feller across the side of the haid. Pugh's hands was like hams. He shore was built like a gorilla.

The way his great big arms swung down from them big hunched shoulders, you'd of thought the kid would go flying across the street when his paw whopped him one. But he was a burly little feller. He just staggered a mite and then shook his haid and went red in the face.

He yelled out, loud and squeaky, "Paw, I warned you! The last time you whammed me I warned you! Now I'm gonna let you have it!"

He drew a deep breath and his two little teeny eyes got so bright I coulda sworn they was gonna touch each other across the middle of his nose. His pasty face got bright red.

"Okay, Junior," Paw Pugh said, real hasty. "The crowd's ready for you. Don't waste your strength on me, sonny. Let the crowd have it!"

Now all this time I was standing at the edge of the crowd, listening and watching Uncle Lem. But just then somebody jiggled my arm and a thin kinda voice said to me, real polite, "Excuse me, but may I ask a question?"

I looked down. It was a skinny man with a kind-hearted face. He had a notebook in his hand.

"It's all right with me," I told him, polite. "Ask away, mister."

"I just wondered how you feel, that's all," the skinny man said, holding his pencil over the notebook ready to write down something.

"Why, peart," I said. "Right kind of you to inquire. Hope you're feeling well too, mister."

He shook his head, kind of dazed. "That's the trouble," he said. "I just don't understand it. I feel fine."

"Why not?" I asked. "Fine day."

"Everybody here feels fine," he went right on, just like I hadn't spoke. "Barring normal odds, everybody's in average good health in this crowd. But in about five minutes or less, as I figure it—" He looked at his wristwatch.

Just then somebody hit me right on top of the haid with a red-hot sledgehammer.

Now you shore can't hurt a Hogben by hitting him on the haid. Anybody's a fool to try. I felt my knees buckle a little but I was all right in a couple of seconds and I looked around to see who'd whammed me.

Wasn't a soul there. But oh my, the moaning and groaning that was going up from that there crowd! People was a-clutching at their foreheads and a-staggering around the street, clawing at each other to get to that truck where the man was handing out the bottles of headache cure as fast as he could take in the dollar bills.

The skinny man with the kind face rolled up his eyes like a duck in thunder.

"Oh, my head!" he groaned. "What did I tell you? Oh, my head!" Then he sort of tottered away, fishing in his pocket for money.

Well, the family always did say I was slow-witted but you'd have to be downright feeble-minded if you didn't know there was something mighty peculiar going on around here. I'm no ninny, no matter what Maw says. I turned around and looked for Junior Pugh.

There he stood, the fat-faced little varmint, red as a turkey-gobbler, all swole up and his mean little eyes just a-flashing at the crowd.

"It's a hex," I thought to myself, perfectly calm. "I'd never have believed it but it's a real hex. Now how in the world—"

Then I remembered Lily Lou Mutz and what Uncle Lem had been thinking to himself. And I began to see the light.

The crowd had gone plumb crazy, fighting to get at the headache cure. I purty near had to bash my way over toward Uncle Lem. I figgered it was past time I took a hand, on account of him being so soft in the heart and likewise just about as soft in the haid.

"Nosirree," he was saying, firm-like. "I won't do it. Not by no manner of means I won't."

"Uncle Lem," I said.

I bet he jumped a yard into the air.

"Saunk!" he squeaked. He flushed up and grinned sheepish and then he looked mad, but I could tell he was kinda relieved, too. "I told you not to foller me," he said.

"Maw told me not to let you out of my sight," I said. "I promised Maw and us Hogbens never break a promise. What's going on here, Uncle Lem?"

"Oh, Saunk, everything's gone dead wrong!" Uncle Lem wailed out. "Here I am with a heart of gold and I'd just as soon be dead! Meet Mister Ed Pugh, Saunk. He's trying to get me kilt."

"Now, Lem," Ed Pugh said. "You know that ain't so. I just want my rights, that's all. Pleased to meet you, young fellow. Another Hogben, I take it. Maybe you can talk your uncle into—"

"Excuse me for interrupting, Mister Pugh," I said, real polite. "But maybe you'd better explain. All this is purely a mystery to me."

He cleared his throat and threw his chest out, important-like. I could tell this was something he liked to talk about. Made him feel pretty big, I could see.

"I don't know if you was acquainted with my dear departed wife, Lily Lou Mutz that was," he said. "This here's our little child, Junior. A fine little lad he is too. What a pity we didn't have eight or ten more just like him." He sighed real deep.

"Well, that's life. I'd hoped to marry young and be blessed with a whole passel of younguns, being as how I'm the last of a fine old line. I don't mean to let it die out, neither." Here he gave Uncle Lem a mean look. Uncle Lem sorta whimpered.

"I ain't a-gonna do it," he said. "You can't make me do it."

"We'll see about that," Ed Pugh said, threatening. "Maybe your young relative here will be more reasonable. I'll have you know I'm getting to be a power in this state and what I says goes."

"Paw," little Junior squeaked out just then, "Paw, they're kinda slowing down. Kin I give it to 'em double-strength this time, Paw? Betcha I could kill a few if I let myself go. Hey, Paw—"

Ed Pugh made as if he was gonna clonk the little varmint again, but I guess he thought better of it.

"Don't interrupt your elders, sonny," he said. "Paw's busy. Just tend to your job and shut up." He glanced out over the moaning crowd. "Give that bunch over beyond the truck a little more treatment," he said. "They ain't buying fast enough. But no double-strength, Junior. You gotta save your energy. You're a growing boy."

He turned back to me. "Junior's a talented child," he said, very proud. "As you can see. He inherited it from his

dear dead-and-gone mother, Lily Lou. I was telling you
about Lily Lou. It was my hope to marry young, like I
said, but the way things worked out, somehow I just didn't
get around to wifin' till I'd got well along into the prime of
life."

He blew out his chest like a toadfrog, looking down admiring. I never did see a man that thought better of himself. "Never found a woman who'd look at—I mean, never
found the right woman," he went on, "till the day I met
Lily Lou Mutz."

"I know what you mean," I said, polite. I did, too. He
musta searched a long, long ways before he found somebody ugly enough herself to look twice at him. Even Lily
Lou, pore soul, musta thunk a long time afore she said yes.

"And that," Ed Pugh went on, "is where your Uncle
Lem comes in. It seems like he'd give Lily Lou a bewitchment quite some while back."

"I never!" Uncle Lem squealed. "And anyway, how'd I
know she'd get married and pass it on to her child? Who'd
ever think Lily Lou would—"

"He gave her a bewitchment," Ed Pugh went right on
talking. "Only she never told me till she was a-layin' on her
death-bed a year ago. Lordy, I sure woulda whopped her
good if I'd knowed how she held out on me all them years!
It was the hex Lemuel gave her and she inherited it on to
her little child."

"I only done it to protect her," Uncle Lem said, right
quick. "You know I'm speaking the truth, Saunk boy. Pore
Lily Lou was so pizon ugly, people used to up and heave a
clod at her now and then afore they could help themselves.
Just automatic-like. Couldn't blame 'em. I often fought
down the impulse myself.

"But pore Lily Lou, I shore felt sorry for her. You'll
never know how long I fought down my good impulses,
Saunk. But my heart of gold does get me into messes. One
day I felt so sorry for the pore hideous critter I gave her
the hexpower. Anybody'd have done the same, Saunk."

"How'd you do it?" I asked, real interested, thinking it
might come in handy someday to know. I'm young yet, and
I got lots to learn.

Well, he started to tell me and it was kinda mixed up.
Right at first I got a notion some furrin feller named Gene

Chromosome had done it for him and after I got straight on that part he'd gone cantering off into a rigamarole about the alpha waves of the brain.

Shucks, I knowed that much my own self. Everybody musta noticed the way them little waves go a-sweeping over the tops of people's haids when they're thinking. I've watched Grandpaw sometimes when he had as many as six hundred different thoughts follering each other up and down them little paths where his brain is. Hurts my eyes to look too close when Grandpaw's thinking.

"So that's how it is, Saunk," Uncle Lem wound up. "And this here little rattlesnake's inherited the whole she-bang."

"Well, why don't you get this here Gene Chromosome feller to unscramble Junior and put him back the way other people are?" I asked. "I can see how easy you could do it. Look here, Uncle Lem." I focused down real sharp on Junior and made my eyes go funny the way you have to when you want to look inside a person.

Sure enough, I seen just what Uncle Lem meant. There was teensy-weensy little chains of fellers, all banging onto each other for dear life, and skinny little rods jiggling around inside them awful teensy cells everybody's made of —except maybe Little Sam, our baby.

"Look here, Uncle Lem," I said. "All you did when you gave Lily Lou the hex was to twitch these here little rods over *that-away* and patch 'em onto them little chains that wiggle so fast. Now why can't you switch 'em back again and make Junior behave himself? It oughta be easy."

"It would be easy," Uncle Lem kinda sighed at me. "Saunk, you're a scatterbrain. You wasn't listening to what I said. I can't switch 'em back without I kill Junior."

"The world would be a better place," I said.

"I know it would. But you know what we promised Grandpaw? No more killings."

"But Uncle Lem!" I bust out. "This is turrible! You mean this nasty little rattlesnake's gonna go on all his life hexing people?"

"Worse than that, Saunk," pore Uncle Lem said, almost crying. "He's gonna pass the power on to his descendants, just like Lily Lou passed it on to him."

For a minute it sure did look like a dark prospect for the human race. Then I laughed.

"Cheer up, Uncle Lem," I said. "Nothing to worry about. Look at the little toad. There ain't a female critter alive who'd come within a mile of him. Already he's as repulsive as his daddy. And remember, he's Lily Lou Mutz's child, too. Maybe he'll get even horribler as he grows up. One thing's sure—he ain't never gonna get married."

"Now there's where you're wrong," Ed Pugh busted in, talking real loud. He was red in the face and he looked mad. "Don't think I ain't been listening," he said. "And don't think I'm gonna forget what you said about my child. I told you I was a power in this town. Junior and me can go a long way, using his talent to help us.

"Already I've got on to the board of aldermen here and there's gonna be a vacancy in the state senate come next week—unless the old coot I have in mind's a lot tougher than he looks. So I'm warning you, young Hogben, you and your family's gonna pay for them insults."

"Nobody oughta get mad when he hears the gospel truth about himself," I said. "Junior *is* a repulsive specimen."

"He just takes getting used to," his paw said. "All us Pughs is hard to understand. Deep, I guess. But we got our pride. And I'm gonna make sure the family line never dies out. Never, do you hear that, Lemuel?"

Uncle Lem just shut his eyes up tight and shook his head fast. "Nosirree," he said. "I'll never do it. Never, never, never, never—"

"Lemuel," Ed Pugh said, real sinister. "Lemuel, do you want me to set Junior on you?"

"Oh, there ain't no use in that," I said. "You seen him try to hex me along with the crowd, didn't you? No manner of use, Mister Pugh. Can't hex a Hogben."

"Well—" He looked around, searching his mind. "Hm-m. I'll think of something. I'll—soft-hearted, aren't you? Promised your Grandpappy you wouldn't kill nobody, hey? Lemuel, open your eyes and look over there across the street. See that sweet old lady walking with the cane? How'd you like it if I had Junior drop her dead in her tracks?"

Uncle Lemuel just squeezed his eyes tighter shut.

"I won't look. I don't know the sweet old thing. If she's that old, she ain't got much longer anyhow. Maybe she'd be better off dead. Probably got rheumatiz something fierce."

"All right, then, how about that purty young girl with the baby in her arms? Look, Lemuel. Mighty sweet-looking little baby. Pink ribbon in its bonnet, see? Look at them dimples. Junior, get ready to blight them where they stand. Bubonic plague to start with maybe. And after that—"

"Uncle Lem," I said, feeling uneasy. "I dunno what Grandpaw would say to this. Maybe—"

Uncle Lem popped his eyes wide open for just a second. He glared at me, frantic.

"I can't help it if I've got a heart of gold," he said. "I'm a fine old feller and everybody picks on me. Well, I won't stand for it. You can push me just so far. Now I don't care if Ed Pugh kills off the whole human race. I don't care if Grandpaw *does* find out what I done. I don't care a hoot about nothing no more." He gave a kind of wild laugh.

"I'm gonna get out from under. I won't know nothing about nothing. I'm gonna snatch me a few winks, Saunk."

And with that he went rigid all over and fell flat on his face on the sidewalk, stiff as a poker.

Chapter 3. Over a Barrel

Well, worried as I was, I had to smile. Uncle Lem's kinda cute sometimes. I knowed he'd put hisself to sleep again, the way he always does when trouble catches up with him. Paw says it's catalepsy but cats sleep a lot lighter than that.

Uncle Lem hit the sidewalk flat and kinda bounced a little. Junior give a howl of joy. I guess maybe he figgered he'd had something to do with Uncle Lem falling over. Anyhow, seeing somebody down and helpless, Junior naturally rushed over and pulled his foot back and kicked Uncle Lem in the side of the haid.

Well, like I said, us Hogbens have got pretty tough haids. Junior let out a howl. He started dancing around nursing his foot in both hands.

"I'll hex you good!" he yelled at Uncle Lem. "I'll hex you good, you—you ole Hogben, you!" He drew a deep breath and turned purple in the face and—

And then it happened.

It was like a flash of lightning. I don't take no stock in hexes, and I had a fair idea of what was happening, but it took me by surprise. Paw tried to explain to me later how it worked and he said it just stimulated the latent toxins inherent in the organism. It made Junior into a catalytoxic agent on account of the way the rearrangement of the desoxyribonucleic acid his genes was made of worked on the kappa waves of his nasty little brain, stepping them up as much as thirty microvolts. But shucks, you know Paw. He's too lazy to figger the thing out in English. He just steals them fool words out of other folks' brains when he needs 'em.

What really happened was that all the pizon that little varmint had bottled up in him, ready to let go on the crowd, somehow seemed to r'ar back and smack Uncle Lem right in the face. I never seen such a hex. And the awful part was—it worked.

Because Uncle Lem wasn't resisting a mite now he was asleep. Red-hot pokers wouldn't have waked him up and I wouldn't put red-hot pokers past little Junior Pugh. But he didn't need 'em this time. The hex hit Uncle Lem like a thunderbolt.

He turned pale green right before our eyes.

Somehow it seemed to me a turrible silence fell as Uncle Lem went green. I looked up, surprised. Then I realized what was happening. All that pitiful moaning and groaning from the crowd had stopped.

People was swigging away at their bottles of headache cure, rubbing their foreheads and kinda laughing weak-like with relief. Junior's whole complete hex had gone into Uncle Lem and the crowd's headaches had naturally stopped right off.

"What's happened here?" somebody called out in a kinda familiar voice. "Has that man fainted? Why don't you help him? Here, let me by—I'm a doctor."

It was the skinny man with the kind-looking face. He was still drinking out of the headache bottle as he pushed his way through the crowd toward us but he'd put his notebook away. When he saw Ed Pugh he flushed up angry like.

"So it's you, is it, Alderman Pugh?" he said. "How is it you're always around when trouble starts? What did you do to this poor man, anyhow? Maybe this time you've gone too far."

"I didn't do a thing," Ed Pugh said. "Never touched him. You watch your tongue, Dr. Brown, or you'll regret it. I'm a powerful man in this here town."

"Look at that!" Dr. Brown yells, his voice going kinda squeaky as he stares down at Uncle Lem. "The man's dying! Call an ambulance, somebody, quick!"

Uncle Lem was changing color again. I had to laugh a little, inside my haid. I knowed what was happening and it was kinda funny. Everybody's got a whole herd of germs and viruses and suchlike critters swarming through them all the time, of course.

When Junior's hex hit Uncle Lem it stimulated the entire herd something turrible, and a flock of little bitty critters Paw calls antibodies had to get to work pronto. They ain't really as sick as they look, being white by nature.

Whenever a pizon starts chawing on you these pale little fellers grab up their shooting-irons and run like crazy to the battlefield in your insides. Such fighting and yelling and swearing you never seen. It's a regular Bull Run.

That was going on right then inside Uncle Lem. Only us Hogbens have got a special militia of our own inside us. And they got called up real fast.

They was swearing and kicking and whopping the enemy so hard Uncle Lem had gone from pale green to a sort of purplish color, and big yeller and blue spots was beginning to bug out all over him where it showed. He looked oncommon sick. Course it didn't do him no real harm. The Hogbens militia can lick any germ that breathes.

But he sure looked revolting.

The skinny doctor crouched down beside Uncle Lem and felt his pulse.

"Now you've done it," he said, looking up at Ed Pugh. "I don't know how you've worked this, but for once you've gone too far. This man seems to have bubonic plague. I'll see you're put under control this time and that young Kallikak of yours, too."

Ed Pugh just laughed a little. But I could see he was mad.

"Don't you worry about me, Dr. Brown," he said, mean. "When I get to be governor—and I got my plans all made —that there hospital you're so proud of ain't gonna operate on state funds no more. A fine thing!

"Folks laying around in hospitals eating their fool heads off! Make 'em get out and plough, that's what I say. Us Pughs never gets sick. I got lots of better uses for state money than paying folks to lay around in bed when I'm governor."

All the doctor said was, "Where's that ambulance?"

"If you mean that big long car making such a noise," I said, "it's about three miles off but coming fast. Uncle Lem don't need no help, though. He's just having an attack. We get 'em in the family all the time. It don't mean nothing."

"Good heavens!" the doc said, staring down at Uncle Lem. "You mean he's had this before and lived?" Then he looked up at me and smiled all of a sudden. "Oh, I see," he said. "Afraid of hospitals, are you? Well, don't worry. We won't hurt him."

That surprised me some. He was a smart man. I'd fibbed a little for just that reason. Hospitals is no place for Hogbens. People in hospitals are too danged nosy. So I called Uncle Lem real loud, inside my head.

"Uncle Lem," I hollered, only thinking it, not out loud. "Uncle Lem, wake up quick! Grandpaw'll nail your hide to the barn door if'n you let yourself get took to a hospital. You want 'em to find out about them two hearts you got in your chest? And the way your bones are fixed and the shape of your gizzard? Uncle Lem! Wake up!"

It wasn't no manner of use. He never even twitched.

Right then I began to get really scared. Uncle Lem had sure landed me in the soup. There I was with all that responsibility on my shoulders and I didn't have the least idea how to handle it. I'm just a young feller after all. I can hardly remember much farther back than the great fire of London, when Charles II was king, with all them long curls a-hanging on his shoulders. On him, though, they looked good.

"Mister Pugh," I said, "you've got to call off Junior. I

can't let Uncle Lem get took to the hospital. You know I can't."

"Junior, pour it on," Mister Pugh said, grinning real nasty. "I want a little talk with young Hogben here." The doctor looked up, puzzled, and Ed Pugh said, "Step over here a mite, Hogben. I want a private word with you. Junior, bear down!"

Uncle Lem's yellow and blue spots got green rings around their outside edges. The doctor sorta gasped and Ed Pugh took my arm and pulled me back. When we was out of earshot he said to me, confidential, fixing me with his tiny little eyes:

"I reckon you know what I want, Hogben. Lem never did say he *couldn't*, he only said he wouldn't, so I know you folks can do it for me."

"Just exactly what is it you want, Mister Pugh?" I asked him.

"You know. I want to make sure our fine old family line goes on. I want there should always be Pughs. I had so much trouble getting married off myself and I know Junior ain't going to be easy to wife. Women don't have no taste nowadays.

"Since Lily Lou went to glory there hasn't been a woman on earth ugly enough to marry a Pugh and I'm skeered Junior'll be the last of a great line. With his talent I can't bear the thought. You just fix it so our family won't never die out and I'll have Junior take the hex off Lemuel."

"If I fixed it so your line didn't die out," I said, "I'd be fixing it so everybody else's line *would* die out, just as soon as there was enough Pughs around."

"What's wrong with that?" Ed Pugh asked, grinning. "Way I see it we're good strong stock." He flexed his gorilla arms. He was taller than me, even. "No harm in populatin' the world with good stock, is there? I figger given time enough us Pughs could conquer the whole danged world. And you're gonna help us do it, young Hogben."

"Oh, no," I said. "Oh, no! Even if I knowed how—"

There was a turrible noise at the end of the street and the crowd scattered to make way for the ambulance, which drawed up at the curb beside Uncle Lem. A couple of fellers in white coats jumped out with a sort of pallet on sticks. Dr. Brown stood up, looking real relieved.

"Thought you'd never get here," he said. "This man's a quarantine case, I think. Heaven knows what kind of results we'll find when we start running tests on him. Hand me my bag out of the back there, will you? I want my stethoscope. There's something funny about this man's heart."

Well, *my* heart sunk right down into my boots. We was goners and I knowed it—the whole Hogben tribe. Once them doctors and scientists find out about us we'll never know a moment's peace again as long as we live. We won't have no more privacy than a corncob.

Ed Pugh was watching me with a nasty grin on his pasty face.

"Worried, huh?" he said. "You gotta right to be worried. I know about you Hogbens. All witches. Once they get Lem in the hospital, no telling what they'll find out. Against the law to be witches, probably. You've got about half a minute to make up your mind, young Hogben. What do you say?"

Well, what could I say? I couldn't give him a promise like he was asking, could I? Not and let the whole world be overrun by hexing Pughs. Us Hogbens live a long time. We've got some pretty important plans for the future when the rest of the world begins to catch up with us. But if by that time the rest of the world is all Pughs, it won't hardly seem worth while, somehow. I couldn't say yes.

But if I said no Uncle Lem was a goner. Us Hogbens was doomed either way, it seemed to me.

Looked like there was only one thing to do. I took a deep breath, shut my eyes, and let out a desperate yell inside my head.

"Grandpaw!" I hollered.

"Yes, my boy?" said a big deep voice in the middle of my brain. You'd athought he'd been right alongside me all the time, just waiting to be called. He was a hundred-odd miles off, and sound asleep. But when a Hogben calls in the tone of voice *I* called in he's got a right to expect an answer—quick. I got it.

Mostly Grandpaw woulda dithered around for fifteen minutes, asking cross questions and not listening to the answers, and talking in all kinds of queer old-fashioned dialects, like Sanskrit, he's picked up through the years. But this time he seen it was serious.

"Yes, my boy?" was all he said.

I flapped my mind wide open like a schoolbook in front of him. There wasn't no time for questions and answers. The doc was getting out his dingus to listen to Uncle Lem's two hearts beating out of tune and once he heard that the jig would be up for us Hogbens.

"Unless you let me kill 'em, Grandpaw," I added. Because by that time I knowed he'd read the whole situation from start to finish in one fast glance.

It seemed to me he was quiet an awful long time after that. The doc had got the dingus out and he was fitting its little black arms into his ears. Ed Pugh was watching me like a hawk. Junior stood there all swole up with pizon, blinking his mean little eyes around for somebody to shoot it at. I was half hoping he'd pick on me. I'd worked out a way to make it bounce back in his face and there was a chance it might even kill him.

I heard Grandpaw give a sorta sigh in my mind.

"They've got us over a barrel, Saunk," he said. I remember being a little surprised he could speak right plain English when he wanted to. "Tell Pugh we'll do it."

"But Grandpaw—" I said.

"*Do as I say!*" It gave me a headache, he spoke so firm. "Quick, Saunk! Tell Pugh we'll give him what he wants."

Well, I didn't dare disobey. But this once I really came close to defying Grandpaw.

It stands to reason even a Hogben has got to get senile someday, and I thought maybe old age had finally set in with Grandpaw at last.

What I thunk at him was, "All right, if you say so, but I sure hate to do it. Seems like if they've got us going and coming, the least we can do is take our medicine like Hogbens and keep all that pizon bottled up in Junior stead of spreading it around the world." But out loud I spoke to Mister Pugh.

"All right, Mister Pugh, I said, real humble. "You win. Only, call off your hex. Quick, before it's too late."

Chapter 4. Pughs A-Coming

Mister Pugh had a great big yellow automobile, low-slung, without no top. It went awful fast. And it was sure awful noisy. Once I'm pretty sure we run over a small boy in the road but Mister Pugh paid him no mind and I didn't dare say nothing. Like Grandpaw said, the Pughs had us over a barrel.

It took quite a lot of palaver before I convinced 'em they'd have to come back to the homestead with me. That was part of Grandpaw's orders.

"How do I know you won't murder us in cold blood once you get us out there in the wilderness?" Mister Pugh asked.

"I could kill you right here if I wanted," I told him. "I would too but Grandpaw says no. You're safe if Grandpaw says so, Mister Pugh. The word of a Hogben ain't never been broken yet."

So he agreed, mostly because I said we couldn't work the spells except on home territory. We loaded Uncle Lem into the back of the car and took off for the hills. Had quite an argument with the doc, of course. Uncle Lem sure was stubborn.

He wouldn't wake up nohow but once Junior took the hex off Uncle Lem faded out fast to a good healthy color again. The doc just didn't believe it coulda happened, even when he saw it. Mister Pugh had to threaten quite a lot before we got away. We left the doc sitting on the curb, muttering to himself and rubbing his haid dazed like.

I could feel Grandpaw a-studying the Pughs through my mind all the way home. He seemed to be sighing and kinda shaking his haid—such as it is—and working out problems that didn't make no manner of sense to me.

When we drawed up in front of the house there wasn't a soul in sight. I could hear Grandpaw stirring and muttering on his gunnysack in the attic but Paw seemed to have went invisible and he was too drunk to tell me where he was when I asked. The baby was asleep. Maw was still at the church sociable and Grandpaw said to leave her be.

"We can work this out together, Saunk," he said as soon as I got outa the car. "I've been thinking. You know that sled you fixed up to sour your Maw's cream this morning? Drag it out, son. Drag it out."

I seen in a flash what he had in mind. "Oh, no, Grandpaw!" I said, right out loud.

"Who you talking to?" Ed Pugh asked, lumbering down outa the car. "I don't see nobody. This your homestead? Ratty old dump, ain't it? Stay close to me, Junior. I don't trust these folks any farther'n I can see 'em."

"Get the sled, Saunk," Grandpaw said, very firm. "I got it all worked out. We're gonna send these two gorillas right back through time, to a place they'll really fit."

"But Grandpaw!" I hollered, only inside my head this time. "Let's talk this over. Lemme get Maw in on it anyhow. Paw's right smart when he's sober. Why not wait till he wakes up? I think we oughta get the Baby in on it too. I don't think sending 'em back through time's a good idea at all, Grandpaw."

"The Baby's asleep," Grandpaw said. "You leave him be. He read himself to sleep over his Einstein, bless his little soul."

I think the thing that worried me most was the way Grandpaw was talking plain English. He never does when he's feeling normal. I thought maybe his old age had all caught up with him at one bank, and knocked all the sense outa his—so to speak—haid.

"Grandpaw," I said, trying to keep calm. "Don't you see? If we send 'em back through time and give 'em what we promised it'll make everything a million times worse than before. You gonna strand 'em back there in the year one and break your promise to 'em?"

"Saunk!" Grandpaw said.

"I know. If we promised we'd make sure the Pugh line won't die out, then we gotta make sure. But if we send 'em back to the year one that'll mean all the time between then and now they'll spend spreading out and spreading out. More Pughs every generation.

"Grandpaw, five seconds after they hit the year one, I'm liable to feel my two eyes rush together in my haid and my face go all fat and pasty like Junior. Grandpaw, everybody in the world may be Pughs if we give 'em that much time to spread out in!"

"Cease thy chirming, thou chilce dolt," Grandpaw hollered. "Do my bidding, young fool!"

That made me feel a little better but not much. I went and dragged out the sled. Mister Pugh put up quite a argument about that.

"I ain't rid on a sled since I was so high," he said. "Why should I git on one now? This is some trick. I won't do it."

Junior tried to bite me.

"Now, Mister Pugh," I said, "you gotta cooperate or we won't get nowheres. I know what I'm doing. Just step up here and set down. Junior, there's room for you in front. That's fine."

If he hadn't seen how worried I was I don't think he'd a-done it. But I couldn't hide how I was feeling.

"Where's your Grandpaw?" he asked, uneasy. "You're not going to do this whole trick by yourself, are you? Young ignorant feller like you? I don't like it. Suppose you made a mistake?"

"We give our word." I reminded him. "Now just kindly shut up and let me concentrate. Or maybe you don't want the Pugh line to last forever?"

"That was the promise," he says, settling himself down. "You gotta do it. Lemme know when you commence."

"All right, Saunk," Grandpaw says from the attic, right brisk. "Now you watch. Maybe you'll learn a thing or two. Look sharp. Focus your eyes down and pick out a gene. Any gene."

Bad as I felt about the whole thing I couldn't help being interested. When Grandpaw does a thing he does it up brown. Genes are mighty slippery little critters, spindle-shaped and awful teensy. They're partners with some skinny guys called chromosomes, and the two of 'em show up everywhere you look, once you've got your eyes focused just right.

"A good dose of ultraviolet ought to do the trick," Grandpaw muttered. "Saunk, you're closer."

I said, "All right, Grandpaw," and sort of twiddled the light as it sifted down through the pines above the Pughs. Ultraviolet's the color at the *other* end of the line, where the colors stop having names for most people.

Grandpaw said, "Thanks, son. Hold it for a minute."

The genes began to twiddle right in time with the light waves. Junior said, "Paw, something's tickling me."

Ed Pugh said, "Shut up."

Grandpaw was muttering to himself. I'm pretty sure he stole the words from that perfesser we keep in the bottle, but you can't tell, with Grandpaw. Maybe he was the first person to make 'em up in the beginning.

"The euchromatin," he kept muttering. "That ought to fix it. Ultraviolet gives us hereditary mutation and the euchromatin contains the genes that transmit heredity. Now that other stuff's heterochromatin and *that* produces evolutionary change of the cataclysmic variety.

"Very good, very good. We can always use a new species. Hum-m-m. About six bursts of heterochromatinic activity ought to do it." He was quiet for a minute. Then he said, "Ich am eldre and ek magti! Okay, Saunk, take it away."

I let the ultraviolet go back where it came from.

"The year one, Grandpaw?" I asked, very doubtful.

"That's close enough," he said. "Wite thou the way?"

"Oh yes, Grandpaw," I said. And I bent over and give them the necessary push.

The last thing I heard was Mister Pugh's howl.

"What's that you're doin'?" he hollered at me. "What's the idea? Look out, there, young Hogben or—what's this? Where we goin'? Young Saunk, I warn you, if this is some trick I'll set Junior on you! I'll send you such a hex as even you-u . . ."

Then the howl got real thin and small and far away until it wasn't no more than the noise a mosquito makes. After that it was mighty quiet in the dooryard.

I stood there all braced, ready to stop myself from turning into a Pugh if I could. Them little genes is tricky fellers.

I knowed Grandpaw had made a turrible mistake.

The minute them Pughs hit the year one and started to bounce back through time toward now I knowed what would happen.

I ain't sure how long ago the year one was, but there was plenty of time for the Pughs to populate the whole planet. I put two fingers against my nose to keep my eyes from banging each other when they started to rush together in the middle like all us Pughs' eyes do—

"You ain't a Pugh yet, son," Grandpaw said, chuckling. "Kin ye see 'em?"

"No," I said. "What's happening?"

"The sled's starting to slow down," he said. "Now it's stopped. Yep, it's the year one, all right. Look at all them men and women flockin' outa the caves to greet their new company! My, my, what great big shoulders the men have got. Bigger even than Paw Pugh's.

"An' ugh—just look at the women! I declare, little Junior's positively handsome alongside them folks! He won't have no trouble finding a wife when the time comes."

"But, Grandpaw, that's turrible!" I said.

"Don't sass your elders, Saunk." Grandpaw chuckled. "Looka there now. Junior's just pulled a hex. Another little child fell over flat on his ugly face. Now the little child's mother is knocking Junior endwise. Now his pappy's sailing into Paw Pugh. Look at that fight! Just look at it! Oh, I guess the Pugh family's well took care of, Saunk."

"But what about our family?" I said, almost wailing.

"Don't you worry," Grandpaw said. "Time'll take care of that. Wait a minute, let me watch. Hm-m. A generation don't take long when you know how to look. My, my, what ugly little critters the ten baby Pughs was! They was just like their pappy and their grandpappy.

"I wish Lily Lou Mutz could see her grandbabies, I shorely do. Well, now, ain't that cute? Every one of them babies growed up in a flash, seems like, and each of 'em has got ten babies of their own. I like to see my promises working out, Saunk. I said I'd do this, and I done it."

I just moaned.

"All right," Grandpaw said. "Let's jump ahead a couple of centuries. Yep, still there and spreading like crazy. Family likeness is still strong too. Hum-m. Another thousand years and—well, I declare! If it ain't Ancient Greece! Hasn't changed a bit, neither. What do you know, Saunk!" He cackled right out, tickled pink.

"Remember what I said once about Lily Lou putting me in mind of an old friend of mine named Gorgon? No wonder! Perfectly natural. You ought to see Lily Lou's great-

great-great-grandbabies! No, on second thought, it's lucky you can't. Well, well, this is shore interesting."

He was still about three minutes. Then I heard him laugh.

"Bang," he said. "First heterochromatinic burst. Now the changes start."

"What changes, Grandpaw?" I asked, feeling pretty miserable.

"The changes," he said, "that show your old Grandpaw ain't such a fool as you thought. I know what I'm doing. They go fast, once they start. Look there now, that's the second change. Look at them little genes mutate!"

"You mean," I said, "I ain't gonna turn into a Pugh after all? But Grandpaw, I thought we'd promised the Pughs their line wouldn't die out."

"I'm keeping my promise," Grandpaw said, dignified. "The genes will carry the Pugh likeness right on to the toot of the judgment horn, just like I said. And the hex power goes right along with it."

Then he laughed.

"You better brace yourself, Saunk," he said. "When Paw Pugh went sailing off into the year one seems like he uttered a hex threat, didn't he? Well, he wasn't fooling. It's a-coming at you right now."

"Oh, Lordy!" I said. "There'll be a million of 'em by the time they get here! Grandpaw! What'll I do?"

"Just brace yourself," Grandpaw said, real unsympathetic. "A million, you think? Oh, no, lots more than a million."

"How many?" I asked him.

He started in to tell me. You may not believe it but he's *still* telling me. It takes that long. There's that many of 'em.

You see, it was like with that there Jukes family that lived down south of here. The bad ones was always a mite worse than their children and the same dang thing happened to Gene Chromosome and his kin, so to speak. The Pughs stayed Pughs and they kept the hex power—and I guess you might say the Pughs conquered the whole world, after all.

But it could of been worse. The Pughs could of stayed

the same size down through the generations. Instead they got smaller—a whole lot smaller. When I knowed 'em they was bigger than most folks—Paw Pugh, anyhow.

But by the time they'd done filtering the generations from the year one, they'd shrunk so much them little pale fellers in the blood was about their size. And many a knock-down drag-out fight they have with 'em, too.

Them Pugh genes took such a beating from the hetero-chromatinic bursts Grandpaw told me about that they got whopped all outa their proper form. You might call 'em a virus now—and of course a virus is exactly the same thing as a gene, except the virus is friskier. But heavens above, that's like saying the Jukes boys is exactly the same as George Washington!

The hex hit me—hard.

I sneezed something turrible. Then I heard Uncle Lem sneezing in his sleep, lying back there in the yaller car. Grandpaw was still droning on about how many Pughs was a-coming at me right that minute, so there wasn't no use asking questions. I fixed my eyes different and looked right down into the middle of that sneeze to see what had tickled me—

Well, you never seen so many Junior Pughs in all your born days! It was the hex, all right. Likewise, them Pughs is still busy, hexing everybody on earth, off and on. They'll do it for quite a time, too, since the Pugh line has got to go on forever, account of Grandpaw's promise.

They tell me even the microscopes ain't never yet got a good look at certain viruses. The scientists are sure in for a surprise someday when they focus down real close and see all them pasty-faced little devils, ugly as sin, with their eyes set real close together, wiggling around hexing everybody in sight.

It took a long time—since the year one, that is—but Gene Chromosome fixed it up, with Grandpaw's help. So Junior Pugh ain't a pain in the neck no more, so to speak.

But I got to admit he's an awful cold in the haid.

Or Else

MIGUEL AND FERNANDEZ were shooting inaccurately at each other across the valley when the flying saucer landed. They wasted a few bullets on the strange airship. The pilot appeared and began to walk across the valley and up the slope toward Miguel, who lay in the uncertain shade of a cholla, swearing and working the bolt of his rifle as rapidly as he could. His arm, never good, grew worse as the stranger approached. Finally, at the last minute, Miguel dropped his rifle, seized the machete beside him, and sprang to his feet.

"Die then," he said, and swung the blade. The steel blazed in the hot Mexican sun. The machete rebounded elastically from the stranger's neck and flew high in the air, while Miguel's arm tingled as though from an electric shock. A bullet came from across the valley, making the kind of sound a wasp's sting might make if you heard it instead of feeling it. Miguel dropped and rolled into the shelter of a large rock. Another bullet shrieked thinly, and a brief blue flash sparkled on the stranger's left shoulder.

"*Estoy perdido,*" Miguel said, giving himself up for lost. Flat on his stomach, he lifted his head and snarled at his enemy.

The stranger, however, made no inimical moves. Moreover, he seemed to be unarmed. Miguel's sharp eyes searched him. The man was unusually dressed. He wore a cap made of short, shiny blue feathers. Under it his face was hard, ascetic and intolerant. He was very thin, and nearly seven feet tall. But he did seem to be unarmed. That gave Miguel courage. He wondered where his machete had

325

fallen. He did not see it, but his rifle was only a few feet away.

The stranger came and stood above Miguel.

"Stand up," he said. "Let us talk."

He spoke excellent Spanish, except that his voice seemed to be coming from inside Miguel's head.

"I will not stand up," Miguel said. "If I stand up, Fernandez will shoot me. He is a very bad shot, but I would be a fool to take such a chance. Besides, this is very unfair. How much is Fernandez paying you?"

The stranger looked austerely at Miguel.

"Do you know where I came from?" he asked.

"I don't care a centavo where you came from," Miguel said, wiping sweat from his forehead. He glanced toward a nearby rock where he had cached a goatskin of wine. "From *los estados unidos,* no doubt, you and your machine of flight. The Mexican government will hear of this."

"Does the Mexican government approve of murder?"

"This is a private matter," Miguel said. "A matter of water rights, which are very important. Besides, it is self-defense. That *cabrón* across the valley is trying to kill me. And you are his hired assassin. God will punish you both." A new thought came to him. "How much will you take to kill Fernandez?" he inquired. "I will give you three pesos and a fine kid."

"There will be no more fighting at all," the stranger said. "Do you hear that?"

"Then go and tell Fenandez," Miguel said. "Inform him that the water rights are mine. I will gladly allow him to go in peace." His neck ached from staring up at the tall man. He moved a little, and a bullet shrieked through the still, hot air and dug with a vicious splash into a nearby cactus.

The stranger smoothed the blue feathers on his head.

"First I will finish talking with you. Listen to me, Miguel."

"How do you know my name?" Miguel demanded, rolling over and sitting up cautiously behind the rock. "It is as I thought. Fernandez has hired you to assassinate me."

"I know your name because I can read your mind a little. Not much, because it is so cloudy."

"Your mother was a dog," Miguel said.

The stranger's nostrils pinched together slightly, but he

ignored the remark. "I come from another world," he said. "My name is—" In Miguel's mind it sounded like Quetzal-coatl.

"Quetzalcoatl?" Miguel repeated, with fine irony. "Oh, I have no doubt of that. And mine is St. Peter, who has the keys to heaven."

Quetzalcoatl's thin, pale face flushed slightly, but his voice was determinedly calm. "Listen, Miguel. Look at my lips. They are not moving. I am speaking inside your head, by telepathy, and you translate my thoughts into words that have meaning to you. Evidently my name is too difficult for you. Your own mind has translated it as Quetzalcoatl. That is not my real name at all."

"*De veras,*" Miguel said. "It is not your name at all, and you do not come from another world. I would not believe a *norteamericano* if he swore on the bones of ten thousand highly placed saints."

Quetzalcoatl's long, austere face flushed again.

"I am here to give orders," he said. "Not to bandy words with—Look here, Miguel. Why do you suppose you couldn't kill me with your machete? Why can't bullets touch me?"

"Why does your machine of flight fly?" Miguel riposted. He took out a sack of tobacco and began to roll a cigarette. He squinted around the rock. "Fernandez is probably trying to creep up on me. I had better get my rifle."

"Leave it alone," Quetzalcoatl said. "Fernandez will not harm you."

Miguel laughed harshly.

"And you must not harm him," Quetzalcoatl added firm-ly.

"I will, then, turn the other cheek," Miguel said, "so that he can shoot me through the side of my head. I will believe Fernandez wishes peace, *Señor* Quetzalcoatl, when I see him walking across the valley with his hands over his head. Even then I will not let him come close, because of the knife he wears down his back."

Quetzalcoatl smoothed his blue steel feathers again. His bony face was frowning.

"You must stop fighting forever, both of you," he said. "My race polices the universe and our responsibility is to bring peace to every planet we visit."

"It is as I thought," Miguel said with satisfaction. "You come from *los estados unidos*. Why do you not bring peace to your own country? I have seen *los señores* Humphrey Bogart and Edward Robinson in *las películas*. Why, all over Nueva York gangsters shoot at each other from one skyscraper to another. And what do you do about it? You dance all over the place with *la señora* Betty Grable. Ah yes, I understand very well. First you will bring peace, and then you will take our oil and our precious minerals."

Quetzalcoatl kicked angrily at a pebble beside his shiny steel toe.

"I must make you understand," he said. He looked at the unlighted cigarette dangling from Miguel's lips. Suddenly he raised his hand, and a white-hot ray shot from a ring on his finger and kindled the end of the cigarette. Miguel jerked away, startled. Then he inhaled the smoke and nodded. The white-hot ray disappeared.

"Muchas gracias, señor," Miguel said.

Quetzalcoatl's colorless lips pressed together thinly. "Miguel," he said, "could a *norteamericano* do that?"

"Quién sabe?"

"No one living on your planet could do that, and you know it."

Miguel shrugged.

"Do you see that cactus over there?" Quetzalcoatl demanded. "I could destroy it in two seconds."

"I have no doubt of it, *señor*."

"I could, for that matter, destroy this whole planet."

"Yes, I have heard of the atomic bombs," Miguel said politely. "Why, then, do you trouble to interfere with a quiet private little argument between Fernandez and me, over a small water hole of no importance to anybody but—"

A bullet sang past.

Quetzalcoatl rubbed the ring on his finger with an angry gesture.

"Because the world is going to stop fighting," he said ominously. "If it doesn't we will destroy it. There is no reason at all why men should not live together in peace and brotherhood."

"There is one reason, *señor*."

"What is that?"

"Fernandez," Miguel said.

"I will destroy you both if you do not stop fighting."

"*El señor* is a great peacemaker," Miguel said courteously. "I will gladly stop fighting if you will tell me how

"Fernandez will stop fighting too."

Miguel removed his somewhat battered sombrero, reached for a stick, and carefully raised the hat above the rock. There was a nasty crack. The hat jumped away, and Miguel caught it as it fell.

"Very well," he said. "Since you insist, *señor,* I will stop fighting. But I will not come out from behind this rock. I am perfectly willing to stop fighting. But it seems to me that you demand I do something which you do not tell me how to do. You could as well require that I fly through the air like your machine of flight."

Quetzalcoatl frowned more deeply. Finally he said, "Miguel, tell me how this fight started."

"Fernandez wishes to kill me and enslave my family."

"Why should he want to do that?"

"Because he is evil," Miguel said.

"How do you know he is evil?"

"Because," Miguel pointed out logically, "he wishes to kill me and enslave my family."

There was a pause. A road runner darted past and paused to peck at the gleaming barrel of Miguel's rifle. Miguel sighed.

"There is a skin of good wine not twenty feet away—" he began, but Quetzalcoatl interrupted him.

"What was it you said about the water rights?"

"Oh, that," Miguel said. "This is a poor country, *señor.* Water is precious here. We have had a dry year and there is no longer water enough for two families. The water hole is mine. Fernandez wishes to kill me and enslave—"

"Are there no courts of law in your country?"

"For such as us?" Miguel demanded, and smiled politely.

"Has Fernandez a family too?" Quetzalcoatl asked.

"Yes, the poors," Miguel said. "He beats them when they do not work until they drop."

"Do you beat your family?"

"Only when they need it," Miguel said, surprised. "My wife is very fat and lazy. And my oldest, Chico, talks back. It is my duty to beat them when they need it, for their own good. It is also my duty to protect our water rights, since the evil Fernandez is determined to kill me and—"

Quetzalcoatl said impatiently. "This is a waste of time. Let me consider." He rubbed the ring on his finger again. He looked around. The road runner had found a more appetizing morsel than the rifle. He was now to be seen trotting away with the writhing tail of a lizard dangling from his beak.

Overhead the sun was hot in a clear blue sky. The dry air smelled of mesquite. Below, in the valley, the flying saucer's perfection of shape and texture looked incongruous and unreal.

"Wait here," Quetzalcoatl said at last. "I will talk to Fernandez. When I call, come to my machine of flight. Fernandez and I will meet you there presently."

"As you say, *señor*," Miguel agreed. His eyes strayed.

"And do not touch your rifle," Quetzalcoatl added with great firmness.

"Why, no, *señor*," Miguel said. He waited until the tall man had gone. Then he crawled cautiously across the dry ground until he had recaptured his rifle. After that, with a little searching, he found his machete. Only then did he turn to the skin of wine. He was very thirsty indeed. But he did not drink heavily. He put a full clip in the rifle, leaned against a rock, and sipped a little from time to time from the wineskin as he waited.

In the meantime the stranger, ignoring fresh bullets that occasionally splashed blue from his steely person, approached Fernandez' hiding place. The sound of shots stopped. A long time passed, and finally the tall form reappeared and waved to Miguel.

"Yo voy, Señor," Miguel shouted agreeably. He put his rifle conveniently on the rock and rose very cautiously, ready to duck at the first hostile move. There was no such move.

Fernandez appeared beside the stranger. Immediately Miguel bent down, seized his rifle and lifted it for a snap shot.

Something thin and hissing burned across the valley. The rifle turned red-hot in Miguel's grasp. He squealed and dropped it, and the next moment his mind went perfectly blank.

"I die with honor," he thought, and then thought no more.

. . . When he woke, he was standing under the shadow of the great flying saucer. Quetzalcoatl was lowering his hand from before Miguel's face. Sunlight sparkled on the tall man's ring. Miguel shook his head dizzily.

"I live?" he inquired.

But Quetzalcoatl paid no attention. He had turned to Fernandez, who was standing beside him, and was making gestures before Fernandez' masklike face. A light flashed from Quetzalcoatl's ring into Fernandez' glassy eyes. Fernandez shook his head and muttered thickly. Miguel looked for his rifle or machete, but they were gone. He slipped his hand into his shirt, but his good little knife had vanished too.

He met Fernandez' eyes.

"We are both doomed, Don Fernandez," he said. "This *señor* Quetzalcoatl will kill us both. In a way I am sorry that you will go to hell and I to heaven, for we shall not meet again."

"You are mistaken," Fernandez replied, vainly searching for his own knife. "You will never see heaven. Nor is this tall *norteamericano* named Quetzalcoatl. For his own lying purposes he has assumed the name of Cortés."

"You will tell lies to the devil himself," Miguel said.

"Be quiet, both of you," Quetzalcoatl (or Cortés) said sharply. "You have seen a little of my power. Now listen to me. My race has assumed the high duty of seeing that the entire solar system lives in peace. We are a very advanced race, with power such as you do not yet dream of. We have solved problems which your people have no answer for, and it is now our duty to apply our power for the good of all. If you wish to keep on living, you will stop fighting immediately and forever, and from now on live in peace and brotherhood. Do you understand me?"

"That is all I have ever wished," Fernandez said, shocked. "But this offspring of a goat wishes to kill me."

"There will be no more killing," Quetzalcoatl said. "You will live in brotherhood, or you will die."

Miguel and Fernandez looked at each other and then at Quetzalcoatl.

"The *señor* is a great peacemaker," Miguel murmured.

"I have said it before. The way you mention is surely the best way of all to insure peace. But to us it is not so simple. To live in peace is good. Very well, *señor*. Tell us how."

"Simply stop fighting," Quetzalcoatl said impatiently.

"Now that is easy to say," Fernandez pointed out. "But life here in Sonora is not a simple business. Perhaps it is where you come from—"

"Naturally," Miguel put in. "In *los estados unidos* everyone is rich."

"—but it is not simple with us. Perhaps in your country, *señor,* the snake does not eat the rat, and the bird eat the snake. Perhaps in your country there is food and water for all, and a man need not fight to keep his family alive. Here it is not so simple."

Miguel nodded. "We shall certainly all be brothers some day," he agreed. "We try to do as the good God commands us. It is not easy, but little by little we learn to be better. It would be very fine if we could all become brothers at a word of magic, such as you command us. Unfortunately—" he shrugged.

"You must not use force to solve your problems," Quetzalcoatl siad with great firmness. "Force is evil. *You will make peace now.*"

"Or else you will destroy us," Miguel said. He shrugged again and met Fernandez' eyes. "Very well, *señor*. You have an argument I do not care to resist. *Al fin,* I agree. What must we do?"

Quetzàlcoatl turned to Fernandez.

"I too, *señor,*" the latter said, with a sigh. "You are, no doubt, right. Let us have peace."

"You will take hands," Quetzalcoatl said, his eyes gleaming. "You will swear brotherhood."

Miguel held out his hand. Fernandez took it firmly and the two men grinned at each other.

"You see?" Quetzalcoatl said, giving them his austere smile. "It is not hard at all. Now you are friends. Stay friends."

He turned away and walked toward the flying saucer. A door opened smoothly in the sleek hull. On the threshold Quetzalcoatl turned.

"Remember," he said. "I shall be watching."

"Without a doubt," Fernandez said. *"Adiós, señor."*

"Vaya con Dios," Miguel added.

The smooth surface of the hull closed after Quetzalcoatl. A moment later the flying saucer lifted smoothly and rose until it was a hundred feet above the ground. Then it shot off to the north like a sudden flash of lightning and was gone.

"As I thought," Miguel said. "He was from *los estados unidos.*"

Fernandez shrugged.

"There was a moment when I thought he might tell us something sensible," he said. "No doubt he had great wisdom. Truly, life is not easy."

"Oh, it is easy enough for him," Miguel said. "But he does not live in Sonora. We, however, do. Fortunately, I and my family have a good water hole to rely on. For those without one, life is indeed hard."

"It is a very poor water hole," Fernandez said. "Such as it is, however, it is mine." He was rolling a cigarette as he spoke. He handed it to Miguel and rolled another for himself. The two men smoked for a while in silence. Then, still silent, they parted.

Miguel went back to the wineskin on the hill. He took a long drink, grunted with pleasure, and looked around him. His knife, machete and rifle were carelessly flung down not far away. He recovered them and made sure he had a full clip.

Then he peered cautiously around the rock barricade. A bullet splashed on the stone near his face. He returned the shot.

After that, there was silence for a while. Miguel sat back and took another drink. His eye was caught by a road runner scuttling past, with the tail of a lizard dangling from his beak. It was probably the same road runner as before, and perhaps the same lizard, slowly progressing toward digestion.

Miguel called softly, *"Señor* Bird! It is wrong to eat lizards. It is very wrong."

The road runner cocked a beady eye at him and ran on.

Miguel raised and aimed his rifle.

"Stop eating lizards, *Señor* Bird. Stop, or I must kill you."

The road runner ran on across the rifle sights.

"Don't you understand how to stop?" Miguel called gently. "Must I explain how?"

The road runner paused. The tail of the lizard disappeared completely.

"Oh, very well," Miguel said. "When I find out how a road runner can stop eating lizards and still live, then I will tell you, *amigo*. But until then, go with God."

He turned and aimed the rifle across the valley again.

Endowment Policy

WHEN DENNY HOLT checked in at the telephone box, there was a call for him. Denny wasn't enthusiastic. On a rainy night like this it was easy to pick up fares, and now he'd have to edge his cab uptown to Columbus Circle.

"Nuts," he said into the mouthpiece. "Why me? Send one of the other boys; the guy won't know the difference. I'm way down in the Village."

"He wants you, Holt. Asked for you by name and number. Probably a friend of yours. He'll be at the monument —black overcoat and a cane."

"Who is he?"

"How should I know? He didn't say. Now get going."

Holt disconsolately hung up and went back to his cab. Water trickled from the visor of his cap; rain streaked the windshield. Through the dimout he could see faintly lighted doorways and hear jukebox music. It was a good night to be indoors. Holt considered the advisability of dropping into the Cellar for a quick rye. Oh, well. He meshed the gears and headed up Greenwich Avenue, feeling low.

Pedestrians were difficult to avoid these days; New Yorkers never paid any attention to traffic signals, anyway, and the dimout made the streets dark, shadowy canyons. Holt drove uptown, ignoring cries of "Taxi." The street was wet and slippery. His tires weren't too good, either.

The damp cold seeped into Holt's bones. The rattling in the engine wasn't comforting. Some time soon the old bus would break down completely. After that—well, it was easy to get jobs, but Holt had an aversion to hard work. Defense factories—*hm-m-m-m*.

Brooding, he swung slowly around the traffic circle at Columbus, keeping an eye open for his fare. There he was —the only figure standing motionless in the rain. Other pedestrians were scuttling across the street in a hurry, dodging the trolleys and automobiles.

Holt pulled in and opened the door. The man came forward. He had a cane but no umbrella, and water glistened on his dark overcoat. A shapeless slouch hat shielded his head, and keen dark eyes peered sharply at Holt.

The man was old—rather surprisingly old. His features were obscured by wrinkles and folds of sagging, tallowy skin.

"Dennis Holt?" he asked harshly.

"That's me, buddy. Hop in and dry off."

The old man complied. Holt said, "Where to?"

"Eh? Go through the park."

"Up to Harlem?"

"Why—yes, yes."

Shrugging, Holt turned the taxicab into Central Park. A screwball. And nobody he'd ever seen before. In the rear mirror he stole a glance at his fare. The man was intently examining Holt's photograph and number on the card. Apparently satisfied, he leaned back and took a copy of the *Times* from his pocket.

"Want the light, mister?" Holt asked.

"The light? Yes, thank you." But he did not use it for long. A glance at the paper satisfied him, and the man settled back, switched off the panel lamp and studied his wristwatch.

"What time is it?" he inquired.

"Seven, about."

"Seven. And this is January 10, 1943."

Holt didn't answer. His fare turned and peered out of the rear window. He kept doing that. After a time he leaned forward and spoke to Holt again.

"Would you like to earn a thousand dollars?"

"Are you joking?"

"This is no joke," the man said, and Holt realized abruptly that his accent was odd—a soft slurring of consonants, as in Castilian Spanish. "I have the money—your current currency. There is some danger involved, so I will not be overpaying you."

Holt kept his eyes straight ahead. "Yeah?"

"I need a bodyguard, that is all. Some men are trying to abduct or even kill me."

"Count me out," Holt said. "I'll drive you to the police station. That's what you need, mister."

Something fell softly on the front seat. Looking down, Holt felt his back tighten. Driving with one hand, he picked up the bundle of banknotes and thumbed through them. A thousand bucks—one grand.

They smelled musty.

The old man said, "Believe me, Denny, it is your help I need. I can't tell you the story—you'd think me insane— but I'll pay you that amount for your services tonight."

"Including murder?" Holt hazarded. "Where do you get off calling me Denny? I never say you before in my life."

"I have investigated you—I know a great deal about you. That's why I chose you for this task. And nothing illegal is involved. If you have reason to think differently, you are free to withdraw at any time, keeping the money."

Holt thought that over. It sounded fishy but enticing. Anyhow, it gave him an out. And a thousand bucks—

"Well, spill it. What am I supposed to do?"

The old man said, "I am trying to evade certain enemies of mine. I need your help for that. You are young and strong."

"Somebody's trying to rub you out?"

"Rub me . . . oh. I don't think it will come to that. Murder is frowned upon, except as a last resort. But they have followed me here; I saw them. I believe I shook them off my trail. No cabs are following us—"

"Wrong," Holt said.

There was a silence. The old man looked out the rear window again.

Holt grinned crookedly. "If you're trying to duck, Central Park isn't the place. I can lose your friends in traffic easier. O.K., mister, I'm taking the job. But I got the privilege of stepping out if I don't like the smell."

"Very well, Denny."

Holt cut left at the level of Seventy-second. "You know me, but I don't know you. What's the angle, checking up on me? You a detective?"

"No. My name's Smith."

"Naturally."

"And you—Denny—are twenty years old, and unavailable for military duty in this war because of cardiac trouble."

Holt grunted. "What about it?"

"I do not want you to drop dead."

"I won't. My heart's O.K. for most things. The medical examiner just didn't think so."

Smith nodded. "I know that. Now, Denny—"

"Well?"

"We must be sure we aren't followed."

Holt said slowly, "Suppose I stopped at F.B.I. headquarters? They don't like spies."

"As you like. I can prove to them I am not an enemy agent. My business has nothing to do with this war, Denny. I merely wish to prevent a crime. Unless I can stop it, a house will be burned tonight and a valuable formula destroyed."

"That's a job for the fire department."

"You and I are the only ones who can perform this task. I can't tell you why. A thousand dollars, remember."

Holt was remembering. A thousand dollars meant a lot go him at the moment. He had never had that much money in his life. It meant a stake; capital on which to build. He hadn't had a real education. Until now, he'd figured he'd continue in a dull, plodding job forever. But with a stake —well, he had ideas. These were boom times. He could go in business for himself; that was the way to make dough. One grand. Yeah. It might mean a future.

He emerged from the park at Seventy-second Street and turned south on Central Park West. From the corner of his eye he saw another taxi swing toward him. It was trying to pocket his cab. Holt heard his passenger gasp and cry something. He jammed on the brakes, saw the other car go by and swung the steering wheel hard, pushing his foot down on the accelerator. He made a U-turn, fast, and was headed north.

"Take it easy," he said to Smith.

There had been four men in the other taxicab; he had got only a brief glimpse. They were clean-shaven and wore dark clothes. They might have been holding weapons; Holt couldn't be certain of that. They were swinging around, too, now, having difficulties with the traffic but intent on pursuit.

At the first convenient street Holt turned left, crossed Broadway, took the cloverleaf into the Henry Hudson Parkway, and then, instead of heading south on the drive, made a complete circle and returned his route as far as West End Avenue. He went south on West End, cutting across to Eighth Avenue presently. There was more traffic now. The following cab wasn't visible.

"What now?" he asked Smith.

"I . . . I don't know. We must be sure we're not followed."

"O.K.," Holt said. "They'll be cruising around looking for us. We'd better get off the street. I'll show you." He turned into a parking garage, got a ticket and hurried Smith out of the cab. "We kill time now, till it's safe to start again."

"Where—"

"What about a quiet bar? I could stand a drink. It's a lousy night."

Smith seemed to have put himself completely in Holt's hands. They turned into Forty-second Street, with its dimly lit honky tonks, burlesque shows, dark theater marquees and penny arcades. Holt shouldered his way through the crowd, dragging Smith with him. They went through swinging doors into a gin mill, but it wasn't especially quiet. A jukebox was going full blast in a corner.

An unoccupied booth near the back attracted Holt. Seated there, he signaled the waiter and demanded a rye. Smith, after hesitating, took the same.

"I know this place," Holt said. "There's a back door. If we're traced, we can go out fast."

Smith shivered.

"Forget it," Holt comforted. He exhibited a set of brass knuckles. "I carry these with me, just in case. So relax. Here's our liquor." He downed the rye at a gulp and asked for another. Since Smith made no attempt to pay, Holt did. He could afford it, with a thousand bucks in his pocket.

Now, shielding the bills with his body, he took them out for a closer examination. They looked all right. They weren't counterfeit; the serial numbers were O.K.; and they had the same odd musty smell Holt had noticed before.

"You must have been hoarding these," he hazarded.

Smith said absently, "They've been on exhibit for sixty years—" He caught himself and drank rye.

Holt scowled. These weren't the old-fashioned large-sized bills. Sixty years, nuts! Not but what Smith looked that old; his wrinkled, sexless face might have been that of a nonagenarian. Holt wondered what the guy had looked like when he was young. When would that have been? During the Civil War, most likely!

He stowed the money away again, conscious of a glow of pleasure that wasn't due entirely to the liquor. This was the beginning for Denny Holt. With a thousand dollars he'd buy in somewhere and go to town. No more cabbing, that was certain.

On the postage-stamp floor dancers swayed and jitterbugged. The din was constant, loud conversation from the bar vying with the jukebox music. Holt, with a paper napkin, idly swabbed a beer stain on the table before him.

"You wouldn't like to tell me what this is all about, would you?" he said finally.

Smith's incredibly old face might have held some expression; it was difficult to tell. "I can't, Denny. You wouldn't believe me. What time is it now?"

"Nearly eight."

"Eastern Standard Time, old reckoning—and January tenth. We must be at our destination before eleven."

"Where's that?"

Smith took out a map, unfolded it and gave an address in Brooklyn. Holt located it.

"Near the beach. Pretty lonely place, isn't it?"

"I don't know. I've never been there."

"What's going to happen at eleven?"

Smith shook his head but did not answer directly. He unfolded a paper napkin.

"Do you have a stylo?"

Holt hesitated and then extended a pack of cigarettes.

"No, a . . . a pencil. Thank you. I want you to study this plan, Denny. It's the ground floor of the house we're going to in Brooklyn. Keaton's laboratory is in the basement."

"Keaton?"

"Yes," Smith said, after a pause. "He's a physicist. He's

working on a rather important invention. It's supposed to be a secret."

"O.K. What now?"

Smith sketched hastily. "There should be spacious grounds around the house, which has three stories. Here's the library. You can get into it by these windows, and the safe should be beneath a curtain about—here." The pencil point stabbed down.

Holt's brows drew together. "I'm starting to smell fish."

"Eh?" Smith's hand clenched nervously. "Wait till I've finished. That safe will be unlocked. In it you will find a brown notebook. I want you to get that notebook—"

"—and send it airmail to Hitler," Holt finished, his mouth twisting in a sneer.

"—and turn it over to the War Department," Smith said imperturbably. "Does that satisfy you?"

"Well—that sounds more like it. But why don't you do the job yourself?"

"I can't," Smith said. "Don't ask me why; I simply can't. My hands are tied." The sharp eyes were glistening. "That notebook, Denny, contains a tremendously important secret."

"Military?"

"It isn't written in code; it's easy to read. And apply. That's the beauty of it. Any man could—"

"You said a guy named Keaton owned that place in Brooklyn. What's happened to him?"

"Nothing," Smith said, "yet." He covered up hastily. "The formula mustn't be lost, that's why we've got to get there just before eleven."

"If it's that important, why don't we go out there now and get the notebook?"

"The formula won't be completed until a few minutes before eleven. Keaton is working out the final stages now."

"It's screwy," Holt complained. He had another rye. "Is this Keaton a Nazi?"

"No."

"Well, isn't he the one who needs a bodyguard, not you?"

Smith shook his head. "It doesn't work out that way, Denny. Believe me, I know what I'm doing. It's vitally, intensely important that you get that formula."

"Hm-m-m."

"There's a danger. My—enemies—may be waiting for us there. But I'll draw them off and give you a chance to enter the house."

"You said they might kill you."

"They might, but I doubt it. Murder is the last recourse, though euthanasia is always available. But I'm not a candidate for that."

Holt didn't try to understand Smith's viewpoint on euthanasia; he decided it was a place name and implied taking a powder.

"For a thousand bucks," he said, "I'll risk my skin."

"How long will it take us to get to Brooklyn?"

"Say an hour, in the dimout." Holt got up quickly. "Come on. Your friends are here."

Panic showed in Smith's dark eyes. He seemed to shrink into the capacious overcoat. "What'll we do?"

"The back way. They haven't seen us yet. If we're separated, go to the garage where I left the cab."

"Y-yes. All right."

They pushed through the dancers and into the kitchen, past that into a bare corridor. Opening a door, Smith came out in an alley. A tall figure loomed before him, nebulous in the dark. Smith gave a shrill, frightened squeak.

"Beat it," Holt ordered. He pushed the old man away. The dark figure made some movement, and Holt struck swiftly at a half-seen jaw. His fist didn't connect. His opponent had shifted rapidly.

Smith was scuttling off, already lost in shadows. The sound of his racing footsteps died.

Holt, his heart pounding reasonlessly, took a step forward. "Get out of my way," he said, so deep in his throat that the words came out as a purring snarl.

"Sorry," his antagonist said. "You mustn't go to Brooklyn tonight."

"Why not?" Holt was listening for sounds that would mean more of the enemy. But as yet he heard nothing, only distant honking of automobile horns and the low mingled tumult from Times Square, a half block away.

"I'm afraid you wouldn't believe me if I told you."

There was the same accent, the same Castilian slurring of consonants that Holt had noticed when Smith spoke. He strained to make out the other man's face. But it was too dark.

Surreptitiously, Holt slipped his hand into his pocket and felt the comforting coldness of the brass knuckles. He said, "If you pull a gun on me—"

"We do not use guns. Listen, Dennis Holt. Keaton's formula must be destroyed with him."

"Why, you—" Holt struck without warning. This time he didn't miss. He felt the brass knuckles hit solidly and then slide, slippery on bloody, torn flesh. The half-seen figure went down, a shout muffled in his throat. Holt looked around, saw no one and went at a loping run along the alley. Good enough, so far.

Five minutes later he was at the parking garage. Smith was waiting for him, a withered crow in a huge overcoat. The old man's fingers were tapping nervously on the cane.

"Come on," Holt said. "We'd better move fast now."

"Did you—"

"I knocked him cold. He didn't have a gun—or else he didn't want to use it. Lucky for me."

Smith grimaced. Holt recovered his taxi and maneuvered down the ramp, handling the car gingerly and keeping on the alert. A cab was plenty easy to spot. The dimout helped.

He kept south and east to the Bowery, but at Essex Street, by the subway station, the pursuers caught up. Holt swung into a side street. His left elbow, resting on the window frame, went numb and icy cold.

He steered with his right hand until the feeling wore off. The Williamsburg Bridge took him into Kings, and he dodged and alternately speeded and backtracked until he'd lost the shadows again. That took time. And there was still a long distance to go, by this circuitous route.

Holt, turning right, worked his way south to Prospect Park and then east, towards the lonely beach section between Brighton Beach and Canarsie. Smith, huddled in back, had made no sound.

"So far, so good," Holt said over his shoulder. "My arm's in shape again, anyhow."

"What happened to it?"

"Must have hit my funny bone."

"No," Smith said, "that was a paralyzer. Like this." He exhibited the cane.

Holt didn't get it. He kept driving until they were nearly at their destination. He pulled up around the corner from a liquor store.

"I'm getting a bottle," he said. "It's too cold and rainy without a shot of something to pep me up."

"We haven't time."

"Sure we have."

Smith bit his lip but made no further objection. Holt bought a pint of rye and, back in the cab, took a swig, after offering his fare a drink and getting a shake of the head for answer.

The rye definitely helped. The night was intensely cold and miserable; squalls of rain swept across the street, sluicing down the windshield. The worn wipers didn't help much. The wind screamed like a banshee.

"We're close enough," Smith suggested. "Better stop here. Find a place to hide the taxicab."

"Where? These are all private houses."

"A driveway . . . eh?"

"O.K.," Holt said, and found one shielded by overhanging trees and rank bushes. He turned off lights and motor and got out, hunching his chin down and turning up the collar of his slicker. The rain instantly drenched him. It came down with a steady, torrential pour, pattering noisily, staccato in the puddles. Underfoot was sandy, slippery mud.

"Wait a sec," Holt said, and returned to the cab for his flashlight. "All set. Now what?"

"Keaton's house." Smith was shivering convulsively. "It isn't eleven yet. We'll have to wait."

They waited, concealed in the bushes on Keaton's grounds. The house was a looming shadow against the fluctuating curtain of drenched darkness. A lighted window on the ground floor showed part of what seemed to be a library. The sound of breakers, throbbing heavily, came from their left.

Water trickled down inside Holt's collar. He cursed quietly. He was earning his thousand bucks, all right. But Smith was going through the same discomfort and not complaining about it.

"Isn't it—"

"*Sh-h!*" Smith warned. "The—others—may be here."

Obediently, Holt lowered his voice. "Then they'll be drowned, too. Are they after the notebook? Why don't they go in and get it?"

Smith bit his nails. "They want it destroyed."

"That's what the guy in the alley said, come to think of it," Holt nodded, startled. "Who are they, anyhow?"

"Never mind. They don't belong here. Do you remember what I told you, Denny?"

"About getting the notebook? What'll I do if the safe isn't open?"

"It will be," Smith said confidently. "Soon, now. Keaton is in his cellar laboratory, finishing his experiment."

Through the lighted window a shadow flickered. Holt leaned forward; he felt Smith go tense as wire beside him. A tiny gasp ripped from the old man's throat.

A man had entered the library. He went to the wall, swung aside a curtain, and stood there, his back to Holt. Presently he stepped back, opening the door of a safe.

"Ready!" Smith said. "This is it! He's writing down the final step of the formula. The explosion will come in a minute now. When it does, Denny, give me a minute to get away and cause a disturbance, if the others are here."

"I don't think they are."

Smith shook his head. "Do as I say. Run for the house and get the notebook."

"Then what?"

"Then get out of here as fast as you can. Don't let them catch you, whatever you do."

"What about you?"

Smith's eyes blazed with intense, violent command, shining out of the windy dark. "Forget me, Denny! I'll be safe."

"You hired me as a bodyguard."

"I'm discharging you, then. This is vitally important, more important than my life. That notebook must be in your hands—"

"For the War Department?"

"For . . . oh yes. You'll do that, now, Denny?"

Holt hesitated. "If it's that important—"

"It is. It is!"

"O.K., then."

The man in the house was at a desk, writing. Suddenly the window blew out. The sound of the blast was muffled, as though its source was underground, but Holt felt the ground shake beneath him. He saw Keaton spring up, take a half step away and return, snatching up the notebook. The physicist ran to the wall safe, threw the book into it, swung the door shut and paused there briefly, his back to Holt. Then he darted out of Holt's range of vision and was gone.

Smith said, his voice coming out in excited spurts, "He didn't have time to lock it. Wiat till you hear me, Denny, and then *get that notebook!*"

Holt said "O.K.," but Smith was already gone, running through the bushes. A yell from the house heralded red flames sweeping out a distant, ground-floor window. Something fell crashingly—masonry, Holt thought.

He heard Smith's voice. He could not see the man in the rain, but there was the noise of a scuffle. Briefly Holt hesitated. Blue pencils of light streaked through the rain, wan and vague in the distance.

He ought to help Smith—

He'd promised, though, and there was the notebook. The pursuers had wanted it destroyed. And now, quite obviously, the house was going up in flames. Of Keaton there was no trace.

He ran for the lighted window. There was plenty of time to get the notebook before the fire became dangerous.

From the corner of his eye he saw a dark figure cutting in toward him. Holt slipped on his brass knuckles. If the guy had a gun it would be unfortunate; otherwise, fair enough.

The man—the same one Holt had encountered in the Forty-second Street alley—raised a cane and aimed it. A wan blue pencil of light streaked out. Holt felt his legs go dead and crashed down heavily.

The other man kept running. Holt, struggling to his feet, threw himself desperately forward. No use.

The flames were brightening the night now. The tall, dark figure loomed for an instant against the library window; then the man had clambered over the sill. Holt, his legs stiff, managed to keep his balance and lurch forward.

It was agony: like pins and needles a thousand times intensified.

He made it to the window, and, clinging to the sill, stared into the room. His opponent was busy at the safe. Holt swung himself through the window and hobbled toward the man.

His brass-knuckled fist was ready.

The unknown sprang lightly away, swinging his cane. Dried blood stained his chin.

"I've locked the safe," he said. "Better get out of here before the fire catches you, Denny."

Holt mouthed a curse. He tried to reach the man but could not. Before he had covered more than two halting steps, the tall figure was gone, springing lightly out through the window and racing away into the rain.

Holt turned to the safe. He could hear the crackling of flames. Smoke was pouring through a doorway on his left.

He tested the safe; it was locked. He didn't know the combination—so he couldn't open it.

But Holt tried. He searched the desk, hoping Keaton might have scribbled the key on a paper somewhere. He fought his way to the laboratory steps and stood looking down into the inferno of the cellar, where Keaton's burning, motionless body lay. Yes, Holt tried. And he failed.

Finally the heat drove him from the house. Fire trucks were screaming closer. There was no sign of Smith or anyone else.

Holt stayed, amid the crowds, to search, but Smith and his trackers had disappeared as though they had vanished into thin air.

"We caught him, Administrator," said the tall man with the dried blood on his chin. "I came here directly on our return to inform you."

The administrator blew out his breath in a sigh of deep relief.

"Any trouble, Jorus?"

"Not to speak of."

"Well, bring him in," the administrator said. "I suppose we'd better get this over with."

Smith entered the office. His heavy overcoat looked incongruous against the celoflex garments of the others.

He kept his eyes cast down.

The administrator picked up a memo roll and read: "Sol 21, in the year of our Lord 2016. Subject: interference with probability factors. The accused has been detected in the act of attempting to tamper with the current probability-present by altering the past, thus creating a variable alternative present. Use of time machines is forbidden except by authorized officials. Accused will answer."

Smith mumbled, "I wasn't trying to change things, Administrator—"

Jorus looked up and said, "Objection. Certain key time-place periods are forbidden. Brooklyn, especially the area about Keaton's house, in the time near 11 P.M., January 10, 1943, is absolutely forbidden to time travelers. The prisoner knows why."

"I knew nothing about it, Ser Jorus. You must believe me."

Jorus went on relentlessly, "Administrator, here are the facts. The accused, having stolen a time traveler, set the controls manually for a forbidden space-time sector. Such sectors are restricted, as you know, because they are keys to the future; interference with such key spots will automatically alter the future and create a different line of probability. Keaton, in 1943, in his cellar laboratory, succeeded in working out the formula for what we know now as M-Power. He hurried upstairs, opened his safe, and noted down the formula in his book, in such a form that it could very easily have been deciphered and applied even by a layman. At that time there was an explosion in Keaton's laboratory and he replaced the notebook in the safe and went downstairs, neglecting, however, to relock the safe. Keaton was killed; he had not known the necessity of keeping M-Power away from radium, and the atomic synthesis caused the explosion. The subsequent fire destroyed Keaton's notebook, even though it had been within the safe. It was charred into illegibility, nor was its value suspected. Not until the first year of the twenty-first century was M-Power rediscovered."

Smith said, "I didn't know all that, Ser Jorus."

"You are lying. Our organization does not make mistakes. You found a key spot in the past and decided to change it, thus altering our present. Had you succeeded,

Dennis Holt of 1943 would have taken Keaton's notebook out of the burning house and read it. His curiosity would have made him open the notebook. He would have found the key to M-Power. And, because of the very nature of M-Power, Dennis Holt would have become the most powerful man in his world time. According to the variant probability line you were aiming at, Dennis Holt, had he got that notebook, would have been dictator of the world now. This world, as we know it, would not exist, though its equivalent would—a brutal, ruthless civilization ruled by an autocratic Dennis Holt, the sole possessor of M-Power. In striving for that end, the prisoner has committed a serious crime."

Smith lifted his head. "I demand euthanasia," he said. "If you want to blame me for trying to get out of this damned routine life of mine, very well. I never had a chance, that's all."

The administrator raised his eyebrows. "Your record shows you have had many chances. You are incapable of succeeding through your own abilities; you are in the only job you can do well. But your crime is, as Jorus says, serious. You have tried to create a new probability-present, destroying this one by tampering with a key spot in the past. And, had you succeeded, Dennis Holt would now be dictator of a race of slaves. Euthanasia is no longer your privilege; your crime is too serious. You must continue to live, at your appointed task, until the day of your natural death."

Smith choked. "It was *his* fault—if he'd got that notebook in time—"

Jorus looked quizzical. *"His?* Dennis Holt, at the age of twenty, in 1943 . . . his fault? No, it is yours, I think—for trying to change your past and your present."

The administrator said, "Sentence has been passed. It is ended."

And Dennis Holt, at the age of ninety-three, in the year of our Lord 2016, turned obediently and went slowly back to his job, the same one he would fill now until he died.

And Dennis Holt, at the age of twenty, in the year of our Lord 1943, drove his taxi home from Brooklyn, wondering what it had all been about. The veils of rain swept slanting across the windshield. Denny took another drink out of the bottle and felt the rye steal comfortingly through his body.

What had it all been about?

Banknotes rustled crisply in his pocket. Denny grinned. A thousand smackeroos! His stake. His capital. With that, now, he could do plenty—and he would, too. All a guy needed was a little ready money, and he could go places.

"You bet!" Dennis Holt said emphatically. "I'm not going to hold down the same dull job all my life. Not with a thousand bucks—not me!"

Housing Problem

JACQUELINE SAID IT was a canary, but I contended that there were a couple of lovebirds in the covered cage. One canary could never make that much fuss. Besides, I liked to think of crusty old Mr. Henchard keeping lovebirds; it was so completely inappropriate. But whatever our roomer kept in that cage by his window, he shielded it—or them —jealously from prying eyes. All we had to go by were the noises.

And they weren't too simple to figure out. From under the cretonne cloth came shufflings, rustlings, occasional faint and inexplicable pops, and once or twice a tiny thump that made the whole hidden cage shake on its redwood pedestal-stand. Mr. Henchard must have known that we were curious. But all he said when Jackie remarked that birds were nice to have around, was "Claptrap! Leave that cage alone, d'ya hear?"

That made us a little mad. We're not snoopers, and after that brushoff, we coldly refused to even look at the shrouded cretonne shape. We didn't want to lose Mr. Henchard, either. Roomers were surprisingly hard to get. Our little house was on the coast highway; the town was a couple of dozen homes, a grocery, a liquor store, the post office and Terry's restaurant. That was about all. Every morning Jackie and I hopped the bus and rode in to the factory, an hour away. By the time we got home, we were pretty tired. We couldn't get any household help—war jobs paid a lot better—so we both pitched in and cleaned. As for cooking, we were Terry's best customers.

The wages were good, but before the war we'd run up

too many debts, so we needed extra dough. And that's why we rented a room to Mr. Henchard. Off the beaten track with transportation difficult, and with the coast dimout every night, it wasn't too easy to get a roomer. Mr. Henchard looked like a natural. He was, we figured, too old to get into mischief.

One day he wandered in, paid a deposit; presently he showed up with a huge Gladstone and a square canvas grip with leather handles. He was a creaking little old man with a bristling tonsure of stiff hair and a face like Popeye's father, only more human. He wasn't sour; he was just crusty. I had a feeling he'd spent most of his life in furnished rooms, minding his own business and puffing innumerable cigarettes through a long black holder. But he wasn't one of those lonely old men you could safely feel sorry for—far from it! He wasn't poor and he was completely self-sufficient. We loved him. I called him grandpa once, in an outburst of affection, and my skin blistered at the resultant remarks.

Some people are born under lucky stars. Mr. Henchard was like that. He was always finding money in the street. The few times we shot craps or played poker, he made passes and held straights without even trying. No question of sharp dealing—he was just lucky.

I remember the time we were all going down the long wooden stairway that leads from the cliff-top to the beach. Mr. Henchard kicked at a pretty big rock that was on one of the steps. The stone bounced down a little way, and then went right through one of the treads. The wood was completely rotten. We felt fairly certain that if Mr. Henchard, who was leading, had stepped on that rotten section, the whole thing would have collapsed.

And then there was the time I was riding up with him in the bus. The motor stopped a few minutes after we'd boarded the bus; the driver pulled over. A car was coming toward us along the highway and, as we stopped, one of its front tires blew out. It skidded into the ditch. If we hadn't stopped when we did, there would have been a head-on collision. Not a soul was hurt.

Mr. Henchard wasn't lonely; he went out by day, I think, and at night he sat in his room near the window most of the time. We knocked, of course, before coming in to clean, and sometimes he'd say, "Wait a minute." There'd be a hasty rustling and the sound of that cretonne cover going on his birdcage. We wondered what sort of bird he had, and theorized on the possibility of a phoenix. The creature never sang. It made noises. Soft, odd, not-always-birdlike noises. By the time we got home from work, Mr. Henchard was always in his room. He stayed there while we cleaned. On week-ends, he never went out.

As for the cage . . .

One night Mr. Henchard came out, stuffing a cigarette into his holder, and looked us over.

"Mph," said Mr. Henchard. "Listen, I've got some property to 'tend to up north, and I'll be away for a week or so. I'll still pay the rent."

"Oh, well," Jackie said. "We can—"

"Claptrap," he growled. "It's my room. I'll keep it if I like. How about that, hey?"

We agreed, and he smoked half his cigarette in one gasp. "Mm-m. Well, look here, now. Always before I've had my own car. So I've taken my birdcage with me. This time I've got to travel on the bus, so I can't take it. You've been pretty nice—not peepers or pryers. You got sense. I'm going to leave my birdcage here, but *don't you touch that cover!*"

"The canary—" Jackie gulped. "It'll starve."

"Canary, hmm?" Mr. Henchard said, fixing her with a beady, wicked eye. "Never you mind. I left plenty o' food *and* water. You just keep your hands off. Clean my room when it needs it, if you want, but don't you dare touch the birdcage. What do you say?"

"Okay with us," I said.

"Well, you mind what I say," he snapped.

That next night, when we got home, Mr. Henchard was gone. We went into his room and there was a note pinned to the cretonne cover. It said, "Mind, now!" Inside the cage something went *rustle-whirr.* And then there was a faint pop.

"Hell with it," I said. "Want the shower first?"

"Yes," Jackie said.

Whirr-r went the cage. But it wasn't wings. *Thump!*

The next night I said, "Maybe he left enough food, but I bet the water's getting low."

"Eddie!" Jackie remarked.

"All right, I'm curious. But I don't like the idea of birds dying of thirst, either."

"Mr. Henchard said—"

"All right, again. Let's go down to Terry's and see what the lamb chop situation is."

The next night—Oh, well. We lifted the cretonne. I still think we were less curious than worried. Jackie said she once knew somebody who used to beat his canary.

"We'll find the poor beast cowering in chains," she remarked flicking her dust-cloth at the windowsill, behind the cage. I turned off the vacuum. *Whish—trot-trot-trot* went something under the cretonne.

"Yeah—" I said. "Listen, Jackie. Mr. Henchard's all right, but he's a crackpot. That bird or birds may be thirsty now. I'm going to take a look."

"No. Uh—yes. We both will, Eddie. We'll split the responsibility."

I reached for the cover, and Jackie ducked under my arm and put her hand over mine.

Then we lifted a corner of the cloth. Something had been rustling around inside, but the instant we touched the cretonne, the sound stopped. I meant to take only one swift glance. My hand continued to lift the cover, though. I could see my arm moving and I couldn't stop it. It was too busy looking.

Inside the cage was a—well, a little house. It seemed complete in every detail. A tiny house painted white, with green shutters—ornamental, not meant to close—for the cottage was strictly modern. It was the sort of comfortable, well-built house you see all the time in the suburbs. The tiny windows had chintz curtains; they were lighted up, on the ground floor. The moment we lifted the cloth, each window suddenly blacked out. The lights didn't go off, but shades snapped down with an irritated jerk. It happened fast. Neither of us saw who or what pulled down those shades.

I let go of the cover and stepped back, pulling Jackie with me.

"A d-doll house, Eddie!"

"With dolls in it?"

I stared past her at the hooded cage. "Could you, maybe, do you think, perhaps, train a canary to pull down shades?"

"Oh, my! Eddie, listen."

Faint sounds were coming from the cage. Rustles, and an almost inaudible pop. Then a scraping.

I went over and took the cretonne cloth clear off. This time I was ready; I watched the windows. But the shades flicked down as I blinked.

Jackie touched my arm and pointed. On the sloping roof was a miniature brick chimney; a wisp of pale smoke was rising from it. The smoke kept coming up, but it was so thin I couldn't smell it.

"The c-canaries are c-cooking," Jackie gurgled.

We stood there for a while, expecting almost anything. If a little green man had popped out of the front door and offered us three wishes, we shouldn't have been much surprised. Only nothing happened.

There wasn't a sound, now, from the wee house in the birdcage.

And the blinds were down. I could see that the whole affair was a masterpiece of detail. The little front porch had a tiny mat on it. There was a doorbell, too.

Most cages have removable bottoms. This one didn't. Resin stains and dull gray metal showed where soldering had been done. The door was soldered shut, too. I could put my forefinger between the bars, but my thumb was too thick.

"It's a nice little cottage, isn't it?" Jackie said, her voice quavering. "They must be such *little* guys—"

"Guys?"

"Birds. Eddie, who lives in that house?"

"Well," I said. I took out my automatic pencil, gently inserted it between the bars of the cage, and poked at an open window, where the shade snapped up. From within the house something like the needlebeam of a miniature flashlight shot into my eye, blinding me with its brilliance. As I grunted and jerked back, I heard a window slam and the shade come down again.

"Did you see what happened?"

"No, your head was in the way. But—"

As we looked, the lights went out. Only the thin smoke curling from the chimney indicated that anything was going on.

"Mr. Henchard's a mad scientist," Jackie muttered. "He shrinks people."

"Not without an atom-smasher," I said. "Every mad scientist's got to have an atom-smasher to make artificial lightning."

I put my pencil between the bars again. I aimed carefully, pressed the point against the doorbell, and rang. A thin shrilling was heard.

The shade at one of the windows by the door was twitched aside hastily, and something probably looked at me. I don't know. I wasn't quick enough to see it. The shade fell back in place, and there was no more movement. I rang the bell till I got tired of it. Then I stopped.

"I could take the cage apart," I said.

"Oh *no!* Mr. Henchard—"

"Well," I said, "when he comes back. I'm going to ask him what the hell. He can't keep pixies. It isn't in the lease."

"He doesn't have a lease," Jackie countered.

I examined the little house in the birdcage. No sound, no movement. Smoke coming from the chimney.

After all, we had no right to break into the cage. Housebreaking? I had visions of a little green man with wings flourishing a night stick, arresting me for burglary. Did pixies have cops? What sort of crimes . . .

I put the cover back on the cage. After a while, vague noises emerged. *Scrape. Thump. Rustle, rustle, rustle. Pop.* And an unbirdlike trilling that broke off short.

"Oh, my," Jackie said. "Let's go away quick."

We went right to bed. I dreamed of a horde of little green guys in Mack Sennett cop uniforms, dancing on a bilious rainbow and singing gaily.

The alarm clock woke me. I showered, shaved and dressed, thinking of the same thing Jackie was thinking of. As we put on our coats, I met her eyes and said, "Shall we?"

"Yes. Oh, golly, Eddie! D-do you suppose they'll be leaving for work, too?"

"What sort of work?" I inquired angrily. "Painting buttercups?"

There wasn't a sound from beneath the cretonne when we tiptoed into Mr. Henchard's room. Morning sunlight blazed through the window. I jerked the cover off. There was the house. One of the blinds was up; all the rest were tightly firm. I put my head close to the cage and stared through the bars into the open window, where scraps of chintz curtains were blowing in the breeze.

I saw a great big eye looking back at me.

This time Jackie was certain I'd got my mortal wound. The breath went out of her with a whoosh as I caromed back, yelling about a horrible bloodshot eye that wasn't human. We clutched each other for a while and then I looked again.

"Oh," I said, rather faintly. "It's a mirror."

"A *mirror?*" she gasped.

"Yeah, a big one, on the opposite wall. That's all I can see. I can't get close enough to the window."

"Look on the porch," Jackie said.

I looked. There was a milk bottle standing by the door —you can guess the size of it. It was purple. Beside it was a folded postage stamp.

"Purple milk?" I said.

"From a purple cow. Or else the bottle's colored. Eddie, is that a newspaper?"

It was. I strained my eyes to read the headlines. EXTRA was splashed redly across the sheet, in huge letters nearly a sixteenth of an inch high. EXTRA—FOTZPA MOVES ON TUR! That was all we could make out.

I put the cretonne gently back over the cage. We went down to Terry's for breakfast while we waited for the bus.

When we rode home that night, we knew what our first job would be. We let ourselves into the house, discovered that Mr. Henchard hadn't come back yet, switched on the light in his room, and listened to the noise from the birdcage.

"Music," Jackie said.

It was so faint I scarcely heard it, and, in any case, it wasn't real music. I can't begin to describe it. And it died away immediately. *Thump, scrape, pop, buzz.* Then silence, and I pulled off the cover.

The house was dark, the windows were shut, the blinds were down. Paper and milk bottle were gone from the porch. On the front door was a sign that said—after I used a magnifying glass: QUARANTINE! SCOPPY FEVER!

"Why, the little liars," I said. "I bet they haven't got scoppy fever at all."

Jackie giggled wildly. "You only get scoppy fever in April, don't you?"

"April and Christmas. That's when the bread-and-butter flies carry it. Where's my pencil?"

I rang the bell. A shade twitched aside, flipped back; neither of us had seen the—hand?—that moved it. Silence; no smoke coming out of the chimney.

"Scared?" I asked.

"No. It's funny, but I'm not. They're such standoffish little guys. The Cabots speak only to—"

"Where the pixies speak only to goblins, you mean," I said. "They can't snoot us this way. It's our house their house is in, if you follow me."

"What can we do?"

I manipulated the pencil, and, with considerable difficulty, wrote LET US IN on the white panel of the door. There wasn't room for more than that. Jackie tsked.

"Maybe you shouldn't have written that. We don't want to get *in*. We just want to see them."

"Too late now. Besides, they'll know what we mean."

We stood watching the house in the birdcage, and it watched us, in a sullen and faintly annoyed fashion. SCOPPY FEVER, indeed!

That was all that happened that night.

The next morning we found that the tiny front door had been scrubbed clean of my pencil marks, that the quarantine sign was still there, and that there was a bottle of green milk and another paper on the porch. This time the headline said. EXTRA—FOTZPA OVERSHOOTS TUR!

Smoke was idling from the chimney. I rang the bell again. No answer. I noticed a domino of a mailbox by the door, chiefly because I could see through the slot that there were letters inside. But the thing was locked.

"If we could see whom they were addressed to—" Jackie suggested.

"Or whom they're from. That's what interests me."

Finally, we went to work. I was preoccupied all day, and nearly welded my thumb onto a boogie-arm. When I met Jackie that night, I could see that she'd been bothered, too.

"Let's ignore them," she said as we bounced home on the bus. "We know when we're not wanted, don't we?"

"I'm not going to be high-hatted by a—by a critter. Besides, we'll both go quietly nuts if we don't find out what's inside that house. Do you suppose Mr. Henchard's a wizard?"

"He's a louse," Jackie said bitterly. "Going off and leaving ambiguous pixies on our hands!"

When we got home, the little house in the birdcage took alarm, as usual, and by the time we'd yanked off the cover, the distant, soft noises had faded into silence. Lights shone through the drawn blinds. The porch had only the mat on it. In the mailbox we could see the yellow envelope of a telegram.

Jackie turned pale. "It's the last straw," she insisted. "A telegram!"

"It may not be."

"It is, it is, I know it is. Aunt Tinker Bell's dead. Or Iolanthe's coming for a visit."

"The quarantine sign's off the door," I said. "There's a new one. It says 'wet paint.' "

"Well, you will scribble all over their nice clean door."

I put the cretonne back, turned off the light switch, and took Jackie's hand. We stood waiting. After a time something went *bump-bump-bump,* and then there was a singing, like a teakettle. I heard a tiny clatter.

Next morning there were twenty-six bottles of yellow milk—bright yellow—on the tiny porch, and the Lilliputian headline announced: EXTRA—TUR SLIDES TOWARD FOTZPA!

There was mail in the box, too, but the telegram was gone.

That night things continued much as before. When I pulled the cloth off there was a sudden, furious silence. We felt that we were being watched around the corners of the miniature shades. We finally went to bed, but in the middle of the night I got up and took another look at our mysterious tenants. Not that I saw *them*, of course. But they must have been throwing a party, for bizarre, small music and wild thumps and pops died into silence as I peeked.

In the morning there was a red bottle and a newspaper on the little porch. The headline said: EXTRA—FOTZPA GOES UP!

"My work's going to the dogs," I said. "I can't concentrate for thinking about this business—and wondering . . ."

"Me, too. We've *got* to find out somehow."

I peeked. A shade came down so sharply that it almost tore free from its roller.

"Do you think they're mad?" I asked.

"Yes," Jackie said, "I do. We must be bothering the very devil out of 'em. Look—I'll bet they're sitting inside by the windows, boiling mad, waiting for us to go away. Maybe we'd better go. It's time for the bus anyway."

I looked at the house, and the house, I felt, looked at me with an air of irritated and resentful fury. Oh, well. We went to work.

We were tired and hungry when we got back that night, but even before removing our coats we went into Mr. Henchard's room. Silence. I switched on the light while Jackie pulled off the cretonne cover from the cage.

I heard her gasp. Instantly I jumped forward, expecting to see a little green guy on that absurd porch—or anything, for that matter. I saw nothing unusual. There was no smoke coming from the chimney.

But Jackie was pointing to the front door. There was a neat, painted sign tacked to the panel. It said, very sedately simply, and finally: TO LET.

"Oh, oh, oh!" Jackie said.

I gulped. All the shades were up in the tiny windows and the chintz curtains were gone. We could see into the house for the first time. It was completely and awfully empty.

No furniture, anywhere. Nothing at all but a few scrapes and scratches on the polished hardwood floor. The wallpaper was scrupulously clean; the patterns, in the various rooms, were subdued and in good taste. The tenants had left their house in order.

"They moved," I said.

"Yes," Jackie murmured. "They moved out."

All of a sudden I felt lousy. The house—not the tiny one in the cage, but our own—was awfully empty. You know how it is when you've been on a visit, and come home into a place that's full of nothing and nobody?

I grabbed Jackie and held her tight. She felt pretty bad, too. You wouldn't think that a tiny to-let sign could make so much difference.

"What'll Mr. Henchard say?" Jackie asked, watching me with big eyes.

Mr. Henchard came home two nights later. We were sitting by the fire when he walked in, his Gladstone swinging, the black cigarette holder jutting from below his beak. "Mph," he greeted us.

"Hello," I said weakly. "Glad you're back."

"Claptrap!" said Mr. Henchard firmly as he headed for his room. Jackie and I looked at one another.

Mr. Henchard squalled in sheer fury. His twisted face appeared around the door.

"Busybodies!" he snarled. "I *told* you—"

"Wait a minute," I said.

"I'm moving out!" Mr. Henchard barked. "Now!" His head popped back out of sight; the door slammed and locked. Jackie and I waited, half expecting to be spanked.

Mr. Henchard bounced out of his room, Gladstone suspended from one hand. He whirled past us toward the door.

I tried to stop him. "Mr. Henchard—"

"Claptrap!"

Jackie pulled at one arm, I got a grip on the other. Between us, we managed to bring him to a stop.

"Wait," I said. "You've forgotten your—uh—birdcage."

"That's what you think," he snarled at me. "You can have it. Meddlers! It took me months to build that little house just right, and months more to coax 'em to live in it. Now you've spoiled it. They won't be back."

"Who?" Jackie gulped.

His beady eyes were fixed malignantly on us. "My tenants. I'll have to build a new house now—ha! But this time I won't leave it within reach of meddlers."

"Wait," I said. "Are—are you a m-magician?"

Mr. Henchard snorted. "I'm a good craftsman. That's all it takes. You treat them right, and they'll treat you right.

Still—" And he gleamed a bit with pride. "—it isn't everybody who knows how to build the right sort of house for *them!*"

He seemed to be softening, but my next question roused him again.

"What were they?" he snapped. "The Little Folk, of course. Call 'em what you like. Nixie, pixie, leprechaun, brownie—they've had lots of names. But they want a quiet, respectable neighborhood to live in, not a lot of peeping and prying. Gives the property a bad name. No wonder they moved out! And—mph!—they paid their rent on time, too. Still, the Little Folk always do," he added.

"Rent?" Jackie said faintly.

"Luck," Mr. Henchard said. "Good luck, What did you expect they'd pay in—money? Now I'll have to build another house to get my special luck back."

He gave us one parting glare, jerked open the door, and stamped out. We stood looking after him. The bus was pulling into the gas station down the slope, and Mr. Henchard broke into a run.

He caught the bus, all right, but only after he'd fallen flat on his face.

I put my arm around Jackie.

"Oh, gosh," she said. "His bad luck's working already."

"Not *bad,*" I pointed out. "Just normal. When you rent a little house to pixies, you get a lot of extra good luck."

We sat in silence, watching each other. Finally without saying a word, we went into Mr. Henchard's vacated room. The birdcage was still there. So was the house. So was the to-let sign.

"Let's go to Terry's," I said.

We stayed later than usual. Anybody would have thought we didn't want to go home because we lived in a haunted house. Except that in our case the exact opposite was true. Our house wasn't haunted any more. It was horribly, desolately, coldly vacant.

I didn't say anything till we'd crossed the highway, climbed the slope, and unlocked our front door. We went, I don't know why, for a final look at the empty house. The cover was back on the cage, where I'd replaced it, but—*thump, rustle, pop!* The house was tenanted again!

We backed out and closed the door before we breathed.

"No," Jackie said. "We mustn't look. We mustn't ever, *ever,* look under that cover."

"Never," I said. "Who do you suppose . . ."

We caught a very faint murmur of what seemed to be boisterous singing. That was fine. The happier they were, the longer they'd stay. When we went to bed, I dreamed that I was drinking beer with Rip Van Winkle and the dwarfs. I drank 'em all under the table.

It was unimportant that the next morning was rainy. We were convinced that bright yellow sunlight was blazing in through the windows. I sang under the shower. Jackie burbled inarticulately and joyously. We didn't open Mr. Henchard's door.

"Maybe they want to sleep late," I said.

It's always noisy in the machine-shop, and a hand-truckload of rough cylinder casings going past doesn't increase the din noticeably. At three o'clock that afternoon, one of the boys was rolling the stuff along toward the storeroom, and I didn't hear it or see it until I'd stepped back from my planer, cocking my eye at its adjustment.

Those big planers are minor juggernauts. They have to be bedded in concrete, in heavy thigh-high cradles on which a heavily weighted metal monster—the planer itself —slides back and forth.

I stepped back, saw the hand-truck coming, and made a neat waltz turn to get out of its way. The boy with the hand-truck swerved, the cylinders began to fall out, and I took an unbalanced waltz step that ended with my smacking my thighs against the edge of the cradle and doing a neat, suicidal half somersault. When I landed, I was jammed into the metal cradle, looking at the planer as it zoomed down on me. I've never in my life seen anything move so fast.

It was all over before I knew it. I was struggling to bounce myself out, men were yelling, the planer was bellowing with bloodthirsty triumph, and the cylinder heads were rolling around underfoot all over the place. Then there was the crackling, tortured crash of gears and cams going to pieces. The planer stopped. My heart started.

After I'd changed my clothes, I waited for Jackie to knock off. Rolling home on the bus, I told her about it. "Pure dumb luck. Or else a miracle. One of those cylinders bounced into the planer in just the right place. The planer's a mess, but I'm not. I think we ought to write a note of thanks to our—uh—tenants."

Jackie nodded with profound conviction. "It's the luck they pay their rent in, Eddie. I'm glad they paid in advance, too!"

"Except that I'm off the payroll till the planer's fixed," I said.

We went home through a storm. We could hear a banging in Mr. Henchard's room, louder than any noise that had ever come from the birdcage. We rushed upstairs and found the casement window had come open. I closed it. The cretonne cover had been half blown off the cage, and I started to pull it back in place. Jackie was beside me. We looked at the tiny house; my hand didn't complete its gesture.

The to-let sign had been removed from the door. The chimney was smoking greasily. The blinds were tightly down, as usual, but there were other changes.

There was a small smell of cooking—scorned beef and skunk cabbage, I thought wildly. Unmistakably it came from the pixie house. On the formerly immaculate porch was a sloping-over garbage can, and a minuscule orange crate with unwashed, atom-sized tin cans and what were indubitably empty liquor bottles. There was a milk bottle by the door, too, filled with a biliously lavender liquid. It hadn't been taken in yet, nor had the morning paper. It was certainly a different paper. The lurid size of the headlines indicated that it was a yellow tabloid.

A clothesline, without any clothes hanging on it at the moment, had been tacked up from one pillar of the porch to a corner of the house.

I jerked down the cover, and fled after Jackie into the kitchen. "My God!" I said.

"We should have asked for references," she gasped. "Those aren't *our* tenants!"

"Not the tenants we used to have," I agreed. "I mean the ones Mr. Henchard used to have. Did you see that garbage pail on the porch!"

"And the clothesline," Jackie added. "How—how sloppy."

"Jukes, Kallikaks and Jeeter Lesters. This isn't Tobacco Road."

Jackie gulped. "Mr. Henchard said they wouldn't be back, you know."

"Yeah, but, well—"

She nodded slowly, as though beginning to understand. I said, "Give."

"I don't know. Only Mr. Henchard said the Little Folk wanted a quiet, respectable neighborhood. And we drove them out. I'll bet we gave the birdcage—the location—a bad reputation. The better-class pixies won't live there. It's —oh, dear—maybe it's a slum."

"You're very nuts," I said.

"I'm not. It must be that. Mr. Henchard said as much. He told us he'd have to build a new house. Desirable tenants won't move into a bad neighborhood. We've got sloppy pixies, that's all."

My mouth opened. I stared at her.

"Uh-huh. The tenement type. I'll bet they keep a pixilated goat in the kitchen," Jackie babbled.

"Well," I said, "we're not going to stand for it. I'll evict 'em. I—I'll pour water down their chimney. Where's the teakettle?"

Jackie grabbed me. "No, you don't! We can't evict them, Eddie. We mustn't. They pay their rent," she said.

And then I remembered. "The planer—"

"Just that," Jackie emphasized, digging her fingers into my biceps. "You'd have been killed today if you hadn't had some extra good luck. Those pixies may be sloppy, but they pay their rent."

I got the angle. "Mr. Henchard's luck worked differently, though. Remember when he kicked that rock down the beach steps, and they started to cave in? Me, I do it the hard way. I fall in the planer, sure, and a cylinder bounces after me and stops the machine but I'll be out of a job till the planer's fixed. Nothing like that ever happened to Mr. Henchard."

"He had a better class of tenant," Jackie explained, with a wild gleam in her eye. "If Mr. Henchard had fallen in the planer, a fuse would have blown, I'll bet. Our tenants are sloppy pixies, so we get sloppy luck."

"They stay," I said. "We own a slum. Let's get out of here and go down to Terry's for a drink."

We buttoned our raincoats and departed, breathing the fresh, wet air. The storm was slashing down as furiously as ever. I'd forgotten my flashlight, but I didn't want to go back for it. We headed down the slope, toward Terry's faintly visible lights.

It was dark. We couldn't see much through the storm. Probably that was why we didn't notice the bus until it was bearing down on us, headlights almost invisible in the dim-out.

I started to pull Jackie aside, out of the way, but my foot slipped on the wet concrete, and we took a nosedive. I felt Jackie's body hurtle against me, and the next moment we were floundering in the muddy ditch beside the highway while the bus roared past us and was gone.

We crawled out and made for Terry's. The barman stared at us, said, "Whew!" and set up drinks without being asked.

"Unquestionably," I said, "our lives have just been saved."

"Yes," Jackie agreed, scraping mud from her ears. "But it wouldn't have happened this way to Mr. Henchard."

The barman shook his head. "Fall in the ditch, Eddie? And you too? Bad luck!"

"Not bad," Jackie told him feebly. "Good. But sloppy." She lifted her drink and eyed me with muddy misery. I clinked my glass against hers.

"Well," I said. "Here's luck."

What You Need

WE HAVE WHAT YOU NEED

THAT'S WHAT THE sign said. Tim Carmichael, who worked for a trade paper that specialized in economics, and eked out a meager salary by selling sensational and untrue articles to the tabloids, failed to sense a story in the reversed sign. He thought it was a cheap publicity gag, something one seldom encounters on Park Avenue, where the shop fronts are noted for their classic dignity. And he was irritated.

He growled silently, walked on, then suddenly turned and came back. He wasn't quite strong enough to resist the temptation to unscramble the sentence, though his annoyance grew. He stood before the window, staring up, and said to himself, " 'We have what you need.' Yeah?"

The sign was in prim, small letters on a black painted ribbon that stretched across a narrow glass pane. Below it was one of those curved, invisible-glass windows. Through the window Carmichael could see an expanse of white velvet, with a few objects carefully arranged there. A rusty nail, a snowshoe and a diamond tiara. It looked like a Dali décor for Cartier or Tiffany.

"Jewelers?" Carmichael asked silently. "But why *what you need?*" He pictured millionaires miserably despondent for lack of a matched pearl necklace, heiresses weeping inconsolably because they needed a few star sapphires. The principle of luxury merchandising was to deal with the whipped cream of supply and demand; few people needed diamonds. They merely wanted them and could afford them.

"Or the place might sell jinni flasks," Carmichael decided. "Or magic wands. Same principle as a Coney carny, though. A sucker trap. Bill the Whatzit outside and people will pay their dimes and flock in. For two cents—"

He was dyspeptic this morning, and generally disliked the world. Prospect of a scapegoat was attractive, and his press card gave him a certain advantage. He opened the door and walked into the shop.

It was Park Avenue, all right. There were no showcases or counters. It might be an art gallery, for a few good oils were displayed on the walls. An air of overpowering luxury, with the bleakness of an unlived-in place, struck Carmichael.

Through a curtain at the back came a very tall man with carefully combed white hair, a ruddy, healthy face and sharp blue eyes. He might have been sixty. He wore expensive but careless tweeds, which somehow jarred with the décor.

"Good morning," the man said, with a quick glance at Carmichael's clothes. He seemed slightly surprised. "May I help you?"

"Maybe." Carmichael introduced himself and showed his press card.

"Oh? My name is Talley. Peter Talley."

"I saw your sign."

"Oh?"

"Our paper is always on the lookout for possible write-ups. I've never noticed your shop before—"

"I've been here for years," Talley said.

"This is an art gallery?"

"Well—no."

The door opened. A florid man came in and greeted Talley cordially. Carmichael, recognizing the client, felt his opinion of the shop swing rapidly upward. The florid man was a Name—a big one.

"It's a bit early, Mr. Talley," he said, "but I didn't want to delay. Have you had time to get—what I needed?"

"Oh, yes. I have it. One moment." Talley hurried through the draperies and returned with a small, neatly wrapped parcel, which he gave to the florid man. The latter forked over a check—Carmichael caught a glimpse of the amount and gulped—and departed. His town car was at the curb outside.

Carmichael moved toward the door, where he could watch. The florid man seemed anxious. His chauffeur waited stolidly as the parcel was unwrapped with hurried fingers.

"I'm not sure I'd want publicity, Mr. Carmichael," Talley said. "I've a select clientele—carefully chosen."

"Perhaps our weekly economic bulletins might interest you."

Talley tried not to laugh. "Oh, I don't think so. It really isn't in my line."

The florid man had finally unwrapped the parcel and taken out an egg. As far as Carmichael could see from his post near the door, it was merely an ordinary egg. But its possessor regarded it almost with awe. Had Earth's last hen died ten years before, the man could have been no more pleased. Something like deep relief showed on the Florida-tanned face.

He said something to the chauffeur, and the car rolled smoothly forward and was gone.

"Are you in the dairy business?" Carmichael asked abruptly.

"No."

"Do you mind telling me what your business is?"

"I'm afraid I do, rather," Talley said.

Carmichael was beginning to scent a story. "Of course, I could find out through the Better Business Bureau—"

"You couldn't."

"No? They might be interested in knowing why an egg is worth five thousand dollars to one of your customers."

Talley said, "My clientele is so small I must charge high fees. You—ah—know that a Chinese mandarin has been known to pay thousands of taels for eggs of proved antiquity."

"That guy wasn't a Chinese mandarin," Carmichael said.

"Oh, well. As I say, I don't welcome publicity—"

"I think you do. I was in the advertising game for a while. Spelling your sign backwards is an obvious baited hook."

"Then you're no psychologist," Talley said. "It's just

that I can afford to indulge my whims. For five years I looked at that window every day and read the sign backwards—from inside my shop. It annoyed me. You know how a word will begin to look funny if you keep staring at it? Any word. It turns into something in no human tongue. Well, I discovered I was getting a neurosis about that sign. It makes no sense backwards, but I kept finding myself trying to read sense into it. When I started to say "Deen uoy tahw evah ew" to myself and looking for philological derivations, I called in a sign painter. People who are interested enough still drop in."

"Not many," Carmichael said shrewdly. "This is Park Avenue. And you've got the place fixed up too expensively. Nobody in the low-income brackets—or the middle brackets—would come in here. So you run an upper-bracket business."

"Well," Talley said, "yes, I do."

"And you won't tell me what it is?"

"I'd rather not."

"I can find out, you know. It might be dope, pornography, high-class fencing—"

"Very likely," Mr. Talley said smoothly. "I buy stolen jewels, conceal them in eggs and sell them to my customers. Or perhaps that egg was loaded with microscopic French postcards. Good morning, Mr. Carmichael."

"Good morning," Carmichael said, and went out. He was overdue at the office, but annoyance was the stronger motivation. He played sleuth for a while, keeping an eye on Talley's shop, and the results were thoroughly satisfactory —to a certain extent. He learned everything but why.

Late in the afternoon, he sought out Mr. Talley again.

"Wait a minute," he said, at sight of the proprietor's discouraging face. "For all you know, I may be a customer."

Talley laughed.

"Well, why not?" Carmichael compressed his lips. "How do you know the size of my bank account? Or maybe you've got a restricted clientele?"

"No. But—"

Carmichael said quickly, "I've been doing some investigating. I've been noticing your customers. In fact, following them. And finding out what they buy from you."

Talley's face changed. "Indeed?"

"In*deed*. They're all in a hurry to unwrap their little bundles. So that gave me my chance to find out. I missed a few, but—I saw enough to apply a couple of rules of logic, Mr. Talley. *Item:* your customers don't know what they're buying from you. It's a sort of grab bag. A couple of times they were plenty surprised. The man who opened his parcel and found an old newspaper clipping. What about the sunglasses? And the revolver? Probably illegal, by the way——no license. And the diamond—it must have been paste, it was so big."

"M-mmm," Mr. Talley said.

"I'm no smart apple, but I can smell a screwy setup. Most of your clients are big shots, in one way or another. And why didn't any of 'em pay you, like the first man—the guy who came in when I was here this morning?"

"It's chiefly a credit business," Talley said. "I've my ethics. I have to, for my own conscience. It's responsibility. You see, I sell—my goods—with a guarantee. Payment is made only if the product proves satisfactory."

"So. An egg. Sunglasses. A pair of asbestos gloves—I think they were. A newspaper clipping. A gun. And a diamond. How do you take inventory?"

Talley said nothing.

Carmichael grinned. "You've an errand boy. You send him out and he comes back with bundles. Maybe he goes to a grocery on Madison and buys an egg. Or a pawnshop on Sixth for a revolver. Or—well, anyhow, I told you I'd find out what your business is."

"And have you?" Talley asked.

"'We have what you need,'" Carmichael said. "But how do you *know?*"

"You're jumping to conclusions."

"I've got a headache—I didn't have sunglasses!—and I don't believe in magic. Listen, Mr. Talley, I'm fed up to the eyebrows and way beyond on queer little shops that sell peculiar things. I know too much about 'em—I've written about 'em. A guy walks along the street and sees a funny sort of store and the proprietor won't serve him—he sells only to pixies—or else he *does* sell him a magic charm with a double edge. Well—*pfui!*"

"Mph," Talley said.

"'Mph' as much as you like. But you can't get away

from logic. Either you've got a sound, sensible racket here, or else it's one of those funny, magic-shop setups—and I don't believe that. For it isn't logical."

"Why not?"

"Because of economics," Carmichael said flatly. "Grant the idea that you've got certain mysterious powers—let's say you can make telepathic gadgets. All right. Why the devil would you start a business so you could sell the gadgets so you could make money so you could live? You'd simply put on one of your gadgets, read a stockbroker's mind and buy the right stocks. That's the intrinsic fallacy in these crazy-shop things—if you've got enough stuff on the ball to be able to stock and run such a shop, you wouldn't need a business in the first place. Why go round Robin Hood's barn?"

Talley said nothing.

Carmichael smiled crookedly. " 'I often wonder what the vintners buy one half so precious as the stuff they sell,' " he quoted. "Well—what do *you* buy? I know what you sell —eggs and sunglasses."

"You're an inquisitive man, Mr. Carmichael," Talley murmured. "Has it ever occurred to you that this is none of your business?"

"I may be a customer," Carmichael repeated. "How about that?"

Talley's cool blue eyes were intent. A new light dawned in them; Talley pursed his lips and scowled. "I hadn't thought of that," he admitted. "You might be. Under the circumstances. Will you excuse me for a moment?"

"Sure," Carmichael said. Talley went through the curtains.

Outside, traffic drifted idly along Park. As the sun slid down beyond the Hudson, the street lay in a blue shadow that crept imperceptibly up the barricades of the buildings. Carmichael stared at the sign—WE HAVE WHAT YOU NEED —and smiled.

In a back room, Talley put his eye to a binocular plate and moved a calibrated dial. He did this several times. Then, biting his lip—for he was a gentle man—he called his errand boy and gave him directions. After that he returned to Carmichael.

"You're a customer," he said. "Under certain conditions."

"The condition of my bank account, you mean?"

"No," Talley said. "I'll give you reduced rates. Understand one thing. I really do have what you need. You don't *know* what you need, but I know. And as it happens—well, I'll sell you what you need for, let's say, five dollars."

Carmichael reached for his wallet. Talley held up a hand.

"Pay me after you're satisfied. And the money's the nominal part of the fee. There's another part. If you're satisfied, I want you to promise that you'll never come near this shop again and never mention it to anyone."

"I see," Carmichael said slowly. His theories had changed slightly.

"It won't be long before—ah, here he is now." A buzzing from the back indicated the return of the errand boy. Talley said, "Excuse me," and vanished. Soon he returned with a neatly wrapped parcel, which he thrust into Carmichael's hands.

"Keep this on your person," Talley said. "Good afternoon."

Carmichael nodded, pocketed the parcel and went out. Feeling affluent, he hailed a taxi and went to a cocktail bar he knew. There, in the dim light of a booth, he unwrapped the bundle.

Protection money, he decided. Talley was paying him off to keep his mouth shut about the racket, whatever it was. O.K., live and let live. How much would be—

Ten thousand? Fifty thousand? How big was the racket? He opened an oblong cardboard box. Within, nestling upon tissue paper, was a pair of shears, the blades protected by a sheath of folded, glued cardboard.

Carmichael said something softly. He drank his highball and ordered another, but left it untasted. Glancing at his wristwatch, he decided that the Park Avenue shop would be closed by now and Mr. Peter Talley gone.

" '. . . one half so precious as the stuff they sell,' " Carmichael said. "Maybe it's the scissors of Atropos. Blah." He unsheathed the blades and snipped experimentally at the air. Nothing happened. Slightly crimson around the cheekbones, Carmichael reholstered the shears and dropped them into the side pocket of his topcoat. Quite a gag!

He dicided to call on Peter Talley tomorrow.

Meanwhile, what? He remembered he had a dinner date with one of the girls at the office, and hastily paid his bill and left. The streets were darkening, and a cold wind blew southward from the Park. Carmichael wound his scarf tighter around his throat and made gestures toward passing taxis.

He was considerably annoyed.

Half an hour later a thin man with sad eyes—Jerry Worth, one of the copy writers from his office—greeted him at the bar where Carmichael was killing time. "Waiting for Betsy?" Worth said, nodding toward the restaurant annex. "She sent me to tell you she couldn't make it. A rush deadline. Apologies and stuff. Where were you today? Things got gummed up a bit. Have a drink with me."

They worked on a rye. Carmichael was already slightly stiff. The dull crimson around his cheekbones had deepened, and his frown had become set. "What you need," he remarked. "Double crossing little—"

"Huh?" Worth said.

"Nothing. Drink up. I've just decided to get a guy in trouble. If I can."

"You almost got in trouble yourself today. That trend analysis of ores—"

"Eggs. Sunglasses!"

"I got you out of a jam—"

"Shut up," Carmichael said, and ordered another round. Every time he felt the weight of the shears in his pocket he found his lips moving.

Five shots later Worth said plaintively, "I don't mind doing good deeds, but I do like to mention them. And you won't let me. All I want is a little gratitude."

"All right, mention them," Carmichael said. "Brag your head off. Who cares?"

Worth showed satisfaction. "That ore analysis—it was that. You weren't at the office today, but I caught it. I checked with our records and you had Trans-Steel all wrong. If I hadn't altered the figures, it would have gone down to the printer—"

"What?"

"The Trans-Steel. They—"

"Oh, you fool," Carmichael groaned. "I know it didn't check with the office figures. I meant to put in a notice to have them changed. I got my dope from the source. Why don't you mind your own business?"

Worth blinked. "I was trying to help."

"It would have been good for a five-buck raise," Carmichael said. "After all the research I did to uncover the real dope—Listen, has the stuff gone to bed yet?"

"I dunno. Maybe not. Croft was still checking the copy—"

"O.K.!" Carmichael said. "Next time—" He jerked at his scarf, jumped off the stool and headed for the door, trailed by the protesting Worth. Ten minutes later he was at the office, listening to Croft's bland explanation that the copy had already been dispatched to the printer.

"Does it matter? Was there—Incidentally, where were you today?"

"Dancing on the rainbow," Carmichael snapped, and departed. He had switched over from rye to whiskey sours, and the cold night air naturally did not sober him. Swaying slightly, watching the sidewalk move a little as he blinked at it, he stood on the curb and pondered.

"I'm sorry, Tim," Worth said. "It's too late now, though. There won't be any trouble. You've got a right to go by our office records."

"Stop me now," Carmichael said. "Lousy little—" He was angry and drunk. On impulse he got another taxi and sped to the printer's, still trailing a somewhat confused Jerry Worth.

There was rhythmic thunder in the building. The swift movement of the taxi had given Carmichael a slight nausea; his head ached, and alcohol was in solution in his blood. The hot, inky air was unpleasant. The great Linotypes thumped and growled. Men were moving about. It was all slightly nightmarish, and Carmichael doggedly hunched his shoulders and lurched on until something jerked him back and began to strangle him.

Worth started yelling. His face showed drunken terror. He made ineffectual gestures.

But this was all part of the nightmare. Carmichael saw what had happened. The ends of his scarf had caught in the moving gears somewhere and he was being drawn inexorably into meshing metal cogs. Men were running. The clanking, thumping, rolling sounds were deafening. He pulled at the scarf.

Worth screamed, " . . . knife! Cut it!"

The warping of relative values that intoxication gives saved Carmichael. Sober, he would have been helpless with panic. As it was, each thought was hard to capture, but clear and lucid when he finally got it. He remembered the shears, and he put his hand in his pocket. The blades slipped out of their cardboard sheath, and he snipped through the scarf with fumbling, hasty movements.

The white silk disappeared. Carmichael fingered the ragged edge at his throat and smiled stiffly.

Mr. Peter Talley had been hoping that Carmichael would not come back. The probability lines had shown two possible variants; in one, all was well; in the other . . .

Carmichael walked into the shop the next morning and held out a five-dollar bill. Talley took it.

"Thank you. But you could have mailed me a check."

"I could have. Only that wouldn't have told me what I wanted to know."

"No," Talley said, and sighed. "You've decided, haven't you?"

"Do you blame me?" Carmichael asked. "Last night—do you know what happened?"

"Yes."

"How?"

"I might as well tell you," Talley said. "You'd find out anyway. That's certain, anyhow."

Carmichael sat down, lit a cigarette and nodded. "Logic. You couldn't have arranged that little accident, by any manner of means. Betsy Hoag decided to break our date early yesterday morning. Before I saw you. That was the beginning of the chain of incidents that led up to the accident. *Ergo,* you must have known what was going to happen."

"I did know."

"Prescience?"

"Mechanical. I saw that you would be crushed in the machine—"

"Which implies an alterable future."

"Certainly," Talley said, his shoulders slumping. "There are innumerable possible variants to the future. Different lines of probability. All depending on the outcome of various crises as they arise. I happen to be skilled in certain branches of electronics. Some years ago, almost by accident, I stumbled on the principle of seeing the future."

"How?"

"Chiefly it involves a personal focus on the individual. The moment you enter this place"—he gestured—"you're in the beam of my scanner. In my back room I have the machine itself. By turning a calibrated dial, I check the possible futures. Sometimes there are many. Sometimes only a few. As though at times certain stations weren't broadcasting. I look into my scanner and see what you need—and supply it."

Carmichael let smoke drift from his nostrils. He watched the blue coils through narrowed eyes.

"You follow a man's whole life—in triplicate or quadruplicate or whatever?"

"No," Talley said. "I've got my device focused so it's sensitive to crisis curves. When those occur, I follow them farther and see what probability paths involve the man's safe and happy survival."

"The sunglasses, the egg and the gloves—"

Talley said, "Mr.—uh—Smith is one of my regular clients. Whenever he passes a crisis successfully, with my aid, he comes back for another checkup. I locate his next crisis and supply him with what he needs to meet it. I gave him the asbestos gloves. In about a month, a situation will arise where he must—under the circumstances—move a red-hot bar of metal. He's an artist. His hands—"

"I see. So it isn't always saving a man's life."

"Of course not," Talley said. "Life isn't the only vital factor. An apparently minor crisis may lead to—well, a divorce, a neurosis, a wrong decision and the loss of hundreds of lives indirectly. I insure life, health and happiness."

"You're an altruist. Only why doesn't the world storm your doors? Why limit your trade to a few?"

"I haven't got the time or the equipment."

"More machines could be built."

"Well," Talley said, "most of my customers are wealthy. I must live."

"You could read tomorrow's stock-market reports if you wanted dough," Carmichael said. "We get back to that old question. If a guy has miraculous powers, why is he satisfied to run a hole-in-the-wall store?"

"Economic reasons. I—ah—I'm averse to gambling."

"It wouldn't be gambling," Carmichael pointed out. " 'I often wonder what the vintners buy . . .' Just what *do* you get out of this?"

"Satisfaction," Talley said. "Call it that."

But Carmichael wasn't satisfied. His mind veered from the question and turned to the possibilities. Insurance, eh? Life, health and happiness.

"What about me? Won't there be another crisis in my life sometime?"

"Probably. Not necessarily one involving personal danger."

"Then I'm a permanent customer."

"I—don't—"

"Listen," Carmichael said, "I'm not trying to shake you down. I'll pay. I'll pay plenty. I'm not rich, but I know exactly what a service like this would be worth to me. No worries—"

"It couldn't be—"

"Oh, come off it. I'm not a blackmailer or anything. I'm not threatening you with publicity, if that's what you're afraid of. I'm an ordinary guy, not a melodramatic villain. Do I look dangerous? What are you afraid of?"

"You're an ordinary guy, yes," Talley admitted. "Only—"

"Why not?" Carmichael argued. "I won't bother you. I passed one crisis successfully, with your help. There'll be another one due sometime. Give me what I need for that. Charge me anything you like. I'll get the dough somehow. Borrow it, if necessary. I won't disturb you at all. All I ask is that you let me come in whenever I've passed a crisis and get ammunition for the next one. What's wrong with that?"

"Nothing," Talley said soberly.

"Well, then. I'm an ordinary guy. There's a girl—it's

Betsy Hoag. I want to marry her. Settle down somewhere in the country, raise kids and have security. There's nothing wrong with that either, is there?"

Talley said, "It was too late the moment you entered this shop today."

Carmichael looked up. "Why?" he asked sharply.

A buzzer rang in the back. Talley went through the curtains and came back almost immediately with a wrapped parcel. He gave it to Carmichael.

Carmichael smiled. "Thanks," he said. "Thanks a lot. Do you have any idea when my next crisis will come?"

"In a week."

"Mind if I—" Carmichael was unwrapping the package. He took out a pair of plastic-soled shoes and looked at Talley, bewildered.

"Like that, eh? I'll need—shoes?"

"Yes."

"I suppose—" Carmichael hesitated. "I guess you wouldn't tell me why?"

"No, I won't do that. But be sure to wear them whenever you go out."

"Don't worry about that. And—I'll mail you a check. It may take me a few days to scrape up the dough, but I'll do it. How much?"

"Five hundred dollars."

"I'll mail a check today."

"I prefer not to accept a fee until the client has been satisfied," Talley said. He had grown more reserved, his blue eyes cool and withdrawn.

"Suit yourself," Carmichael said. "I'm going out and celebrate. You—don't drink?"

"I can't leave the shop."

"Well, goodbye. And thanks again. I won't be any trouble to you, you know. I promise that!" He turned away.

Looking after him, Talley smiled a wry, unhappy smile. He did not answer Carmichael's goodbye. Not then.

When the door had closed behind him, Talley turned to the back of his shop and went through the door where the scanner was.

The lapse of ten years can cover a multitude of changes. A man with the possibility of tremendous power almost within his grasp can alter, in that time, from a man who will not reach for it to a man who will—and moral values be damned.

The change did not come quickly to Carmichael. It speaks well for his integrity that it took ten years to work such an alteration in all he had been taught. On the day he first went into Talley's shop there was little evil in him. But the temptation grew stronger week by week, visit by visit. Talley, for reasons of his own, was content to sit idly by, waiting for customers, smothering the inconceivable potentialities of his machine under a blanket of trivial functions. But Carmichael was not content.

It took him ten years to reach the day, but the day came at last.

Talley sat in the inner room, his back to the door. He was slumped low in an ancient rocker, facing the machine. It had changed little in the space of a decade. It still covered most of two walls, and the eyepiece of its scanner glittered under amber fluorescents.

Carmichael looked covetously at the eyepiece. It was window and doorway to a power beyond any man's dreams. Wealth beyond imagining lay just within that tiny opening. The rights over the life and death of every man alive. And nothing between that fabulous future and himself except the man who sat looking at the machine.

Talley did not seem to hear the careful footsteps or the creak of the door behind him. He did not stir as Carmichael lifted the gun slowly. One might think that he never guessed what was coming, or why, or from whom, as Carmichael shot him through the head.

Talley sighed and shivered a little, and twisted the scanner dial. It was not the first time that the eyepiece had shown him his own lifeless body, glimpsed down some vista of probability, but he never saw the slumping of that familiar figure without feeling a breath of indescribable coolness blow backwards upon him out of the future.

He straightened from the eyepiece and sat back in his chair, looking thoughtfully at a pair of rough-soled shoes lying beside him on a table. He sat quietly for a while, his eyes upon the shoes, his mind following Carmichael down the street and into the evening, and the morrow, and on towards that coming crisis which would depend on his secure footing on a subway platform as a train thundered by the place where Carmichael would be standing one day next week.

Talley had sent his messenger boy out this time for two pairs of shoes. He had hesitated long, an hour ago, between the rough-soled pair and the smooth. For Talley was a humane man, and there were many times when his job was distasteful to him. But in the end, this time, it had been the smooth-soled pair he had wrapped for Carmichael.

Now he sighed and bent to the scanner again, twisting the dial to bring into view a scene he had watched before.

Carmichael, standing on a crowded subway platform, glittering with oily wetness from some overflow. Carmichael, in the slick-soled shoes Talley had chosen for him. A commotion in the crowd, a surge towards the platform edge. Carmichael's feet slipping frantically as the train roared by.

"Goodbye, Mr. Carmichael," Talley murmured. It was the farewell he had not spoken when Carmichael left the shop. He spoke it regretfully, and the regret was for the Carmichael of today, who did not yet deserve that end. He was not now a melodramatic villain whose death one could watch unmoved. But the Tim Carmichael of today had atonement to make for the Carmichael of ten years ahead, and the payment must be exacted.

It is not a good thing to have the power of life and death over one's fellow humans. Peter Talley knew it was not a good thing—but the power had been put into his hands. He had not sought it. It seemed to him that the machine had grown almost by accident to its tremendous completion under his trained fingers and trained mind.

At first it had puzzled him. How ought such a device to be used? What dangers, what terrible potentialities, lay in that Eye that could see through the veil of tomorrow? His was the responsibility, and it had weighed heavily upon him until the answer came. And after he knew the answer —well, the weight was heavier still. For Talley was a mild man.

He could not have told anyone the real reason why he was a shopkeeper. Satisfaction, he had said to Carmichael.

And sometimes, indeed, there was deep satisfaction. But at other times—at times like this—there was only dismay and humility. Especially humility.

We have what you need. Only Talley knew that message was not for the individuals who came to his shop. The pronoun was plural, not singular. It was a message for the world—the world whose future was being carefully, lovingly reshaped under Peter Talley's guidance.

The main line of the future was not easy to alter. The future is a pyramid shaping slowly, brick by brick, and brick by brick Talley had to change it. There were some men who were necessary—men who could create and build —men who should be saved.

Talley gave them what they needed.

But inevitably there were others whose ends were evil. Talley gave them, too, what the world needed—death.

Peter Talley had not asked for this terrible power. But the key had been put in his hands, and he dared not delegate such authority as this to any other man alive. Sometimes he made mistakes.

He had felt a little surer since the simile of the key had occurred to him. The key to the future. A key that had been laid in his hands.

Remembering that, he leaned back in his chair and reached for an old and well-worn book. It fell open easily at a familiar passage. Peter Talley's lips moved as he read the passage once again, in his room behind the shop on Park Avenue.

"And I say also unto thee, that thou art Peter. . . . And I will give unto thee the keys of the Kingdom of Heaven. . . ."

Absalom

AT DUSK JOEL Locke came home from the university where he held the chair of psychonamics. He came quietly into the house, by a side door, and stood listening, a tall, tight-lipped man of forty with a faintly sardonic mouth and cool gray eyes. He could hear the precipitron humming. That meant that Abigail Schuler, the housekeeper, was busy with her duties. Locke smiled slightly and turned toward a panel in the wall that opened at his approach.

The small elevator took him noiselessly upstairs.

There, he moved with curious stealth. He went directly to a door at the end of the hall and paused before it, his head bent, his eyes unfocused. He heard nothing. Presently he opened the door and stepped into the room.

Instantly the feeling of unsureness jolted back, freezing him where he stood. He made no sign, though his mouth tightened. He forced himself to remain quiet as he glanced around.

It could have been the room of a normal twenty-year-old, not a boy of eight. Tennis rackets were heaped in a disorderly fashion against a pile of book records. The thiaminizer was turned on, and Locke automatically clicked the switch over. Abruptly he turned. The televisor screen was blank, yet he could have sworn that eyes had been watching him from it.

This wasn't the first time it had happened.

After a while Locke turned again and squatted to examine the book reels. He picked out one labeled BRIAFF ON ENTROPIC LOGIC and turned the cylinder over in his hands, scowling. Then he replaced it and went out of the room, with a last, considering look at the televisor.

Downstairs Abigail Schuler was fingering the Master-maid switchboard. Her prim mouth was as tight as the severe bun of gray-shot hair at the back of her neck.

"Good evening," Locke said. "Where's Absalom?"

"Out playing, Brother Locke," the housekeeper said formally. "You're home early. I haven't finished the living room yet."

"Well, turn on the ions and let 'em play," Locke said. "It won't take long. I've got some papers to correct, anyway."

He started out, but Abigail coughed significantly.

"Well?"

"He's looking peaked."

"Then outdoor exercise is what he needs," Locke said shortly. "I'm going to send him to a summer camp."

"Brother Locke," Abigail said, "I don't see why you don't let him go to Baja California. He's set his heart on it. You let him study all the hard subjects he wanted before. Now you put your foot down. It's none of my affair, but I can tell he's pining."

"He'd pine worse if I said yes. I've my reasons for not wanting him to study entropic logic. Do you know what it involves?"

"I don't—you know I don't. I'm not an educated woman Brother Locke. But Absalom is bright as a button."

Locke made an impatient gesture.

"You have a genius for understatement," he said. "Bright as a button!"

Then he shrugged and moved to the window, looking down at the play court below where his eight-year-old son played handball. Absalom did not look up. He seemed engrossed in his game. But Locke, watching, felt a cool, stealthy terror steal through his mind, and behind his back his hands clenched together.

A boy who looked ten, whose maturity level was twenty, and yet who was still a child of eight. Not easy to handle. There were many parents just now with the same problem —something was happening to the graph curve that charts the percentage of child geniuses born in recent times.

Something had begun to stir lazily far back in the brains of the coming generations and a new species, of a sort, was coming slowly into being. Locke knew that well. In his own time he, too, had been a child genius.

Other parents might meet the problem in other ways, he thought stubbornly. Not himself. He *knew* what was best for Absalom. Other parents might send their genius children to one of the crèches where they could develop among their own kind. Not Locke.

"Absalom's place is here," he said aloud. "With me, where I can—" He caught the housekeeper's eye and shrugged again, irritably, going back to the conversation that had broken off. "Of course he's bright. But not bright enough yet to go to Baja California and study entropic logic. Entropic logic! It's too advanced for the boy. Even you ought to realize that. It isn't like a lollypop you can hand the kid—first making sure there's castor oil in the bathroom closet. Absalom's immature. It would actually be dangerous to send him to the Baja California University now to study with men three times his age. It would involve mental strain he isn't fit for yet. I don't want him turned into a psychopath."

Abigail's prim mouth pursed up sourly.

"You let him take calculus."

"Oh, leave me alone." Locke glanced down again at the small boy on the play court. "I think," he said slowly, "that it's time for another rapport with Absalom."

The housekeeper looked at him sharply, opened her thin lips to speak, and then closed them with an almost audible snap of disapproval. She didn't understand entirely, of course, how a rapport worked or what it accomplished. She only knew that in these days there were ways in which it was possible to enforce hypnosis, to pry open a mind willy-nilly and search it for contraband thoughts. She shook her head, lips pressed tight.

"Don't try to interfere in things you don't understand," Locke said. "I tell you, I know what's best for Absalom. He's in the same place I was thirty-odd years ago. Who could know better? Call him in, will you? I'll be in my study."

Abigail watched his retreating back, a pucker between her brows. It was hard to know what was best. The mores of the day demanded rigid good conduct, but sometimes a person had trouble deciding in her own mind what was the right thing to do. In the old days, now, after the atomic wars, when license ran riot and anybody could do anything he pleased, life must have been easier. Nowadays, in the violent backswing to a Puritan culture, you were expected to think twice and search your soul before you did a doubtful thing.

Well, Abigail had no choice this time. She clicked over the wall microphone and spoke into it.

"Absalom?"

"Yes, Sister Schuler?"

"Come in. Your father wants you."

In his study Locke stood quiet for a moment, considering. Then he reached for the house microphone.

"Sister Schuler, I'm using the televisor. Ask Absalom to wait."

He sat down before his private visor. His hands moved deftly.

"Get me Dr. Ryan, the Wyoming Quizkid Crèche. Joel Locke calling."

Idly as he waited he reached out to take an old-fashioned cloth-bound book from a shelf of antique curiosa. He read:

But Absalom sent spies throughout all the tribes of Israel, saying, As soon as ye hear the sound of the trumpet, then ye shall say, Absalom reigneth in Hebron. . . .

"Brother Locke?" the televisor asked.

The face of a white-haired, pleasant-featured man showed on the screen. Locke replaced the book and raised his hand in greeting.

"Dr. Ryan. I'm sorry to keep bothering you."

"That's all right," Ryan said. "I've plenty of time. I'm supposed to be supervisor at the Crèche, but the kids are running it to suit themselves." He chuckled. "How's Absalom?"

"There's a limit," Locke said sourly. "I've given the kid his head, outlined a broad curriculum, and now he wants to study entropic logic. There are only two universities that handle the subject, and the nearest's in Baja California."

"He could commute by copter, couldn't he?" Ryan asked, but Locke grunted disapproval.

"Take too long. Besides, one of the requirements is in-boarding, under a strict regime. The discipline, mental and physical, is supposed to be necessary in order to master entropic logic. Which is spinach. I got the rudiments at home, though I had to use the tri-disney to visualize it."

Ryan laughed.

"The kids here are taking it up. Uh—are you sure you understood it?"

"Enough, yeah. Enough to realize it's nothing for a kid to study until his horizons have expanded."

"We're having no trouble with it," the doctor said. "Don't forget that Absalom's a genius, not an ordinary youngster."

"I know. I know my responsibility, too. A normal home environment has to be maintained to give Absalom some sense of security—which is one reason I don't want the boy to live in Baja California just now. I want to be able to protect him."

"We've disagreed on that point before. All the quizkids are pretty self-sufficient, Locke."

"Absalom's a genius, and a child. Therefore he's lacking in a sense of proportion. There are more dangers for him to avoid. I think it's a grave mistake to give the quizkids their heads and let them do what they like. I refused to send Absalom to a Crèche for an excellent reason. Putting all the boy geniuses in a batch and letting them fight it out. Completely artificial environment."

"I'm not arguing," Ryan said. "It's your business. Apparently you'll never admit that there's a sine curve of geniuses these days. A steady increase. In another generation—"

"I was a child genius myself, but I got over it," Locke said irritably. "I had enough trouble with my father. He was a tyrant, and if I hadn't been lucky, he'd have managed to warp me psychologically way out of line. I adjusted, but I had trouble. I don't want Absalom to have that trouble. That's why I'm using psychonamics."

"Narcosynthesis? Enforced hypnotism?"

"It's not enforced," Locke snapped. "It's a valuable

mental catharsis. Under hypnosis, he tells me everything that's on his mind, and I can help him."

"I didn't know you were doing that," Ryan said slowly. "I'm not at all sure it's a good idea."

"I don't tell you how to run your Crèche."

"No. But the kids do. A lot of them are smarter than I am."

"Immature intelligence is dangerous. A kid will skate on thin ice without making a test first. Don't think I'm holding Absalom back. I'm just running tests for him first. I make sure the ice will hold him. Entropic logic I can understand, but he can't, yet. So he'll have to wait on that."

"Well?"

Locke hesitated. "Uh—do you know if your boys have been communicating with Absalom?"

"I don't know," Ryan said. "I don't interfere with their lives."

"All right, I don't want them interfering with mine, or with Absalom's. I wish you'd find out if they're getting in touch with him."

There was a long pause. Then Ryan said slowly:

"I'll try. But if I were you, Brother Locke, I'd let Absalom go to Baja California if he wants to."

"I know what I'm doing," Locke said, and broke the beam. His gaze went toward the Bible again.

Entropic logic!

Once the boy reached maturity, his somatic and physiological symptoms would settle toward the norm, but meanwhile the pendulum still swung wildly. Absalom needed strict control, for his own good.

And, for some reason, the boy had been trying to evade the hypnotic rapports lately. There was something going on.

Thoughts moved chaotically through Locke's mind. He forgot that Absalom was waiting for him, and remembered only when Abigail's voice, on the wall transmitter, announced the evening meal.

At dinner Abigail Schuler sat like Atropos between father and son, ready to clip the conversation whenever it did not suit her. Locke felt the beginnings of a long-standing irritation at Abigail's attitude that she had to protect Absalom against his father. Perhaps conscious of that, Locke himself finally brought up the subject of Baja California.

"You've apparently been studying the entropic logic thesis." Absalom did not seem startled. "Are you convinced yet that it's too advanced for you?"

"No, Dad," Absalom said. "I'm not convinced of that."

"The rudiments of calculus might seem easy to a youngster. But when he got far enough into it . . . I went over that entropic logic, son, through the entire book, and it was difficult enough for me. And I've a mature mind."

"I know you have. And I know I haven't, yet. But I still don't think it would be beyond me."

"Here's the thing," Locke said. "You might develop psychotic symptoms if you studied that thing, and you might not be able to recognize them in time. If we could have a rapport every night, or every other night, while you were studying—"

"But it's in Baja California!"

"That's the trouble. If you want to wait for my Sabbatical, I can go there with you. Or one of the nearer universities may start the course. I don't want to be unreasonable. Logic should show you my motive."

"It does," Absalom said. "That part's all right. The only difficulty's an intangible, isn't it? I mean, you think my mind couldn't assimilate entropic logic safely, and I'm convinced that it could."

"Exactly," Locke said. "You've the advantage of knowing yourself better than I could know you. You're handicapped by immaturity, lack of a sense of proportion. And I've had the advantage of more experience."

"Your own, though, Dad. How much would such values apply to me?"

"You must let me be the judge of that, son."

"Maybe," Absalom said. "I wish I'd gone to a quizkid crèche, though."

"Aren't you happy here?" Abigail asked, hurt, and the boy gave her a quick, warm look of affection.

"Sure I am, Abbie. You know that."

"You'd be a lot less happy with dementia praecox," Locke said sardonically. "Entropic logic, for instance, presupposes a grasp of temporal variations being assumed for problems involving relativity."

"Oh, that gives me a headache," Abigail said. "And if you're so worried about Absalom's overtraining his mind, you shouldn't talk to him like that." She pressed buttons and slid the cloisonné metal dishes into the compartment. "Coffee Brother Locke . . . milk, Absalom . . . and I'll take tea."

Locke winked at his son, who merely looked solemn. Abigail rose with her teacup and headed toward the fireplace. Seizing the little hearth broom, she whisked away a few ashes, relaxed amid cushions, and warmed her skinny ankles by the wood fire. Locke patted back a yawn.

"Until we settle this argument, son, matters must stand. Don't tackle that book on entropic logic again. Or anything else on the subject. Right?"

There was no answer.

"Right?" Locke insisted.

"I'm not sure," Absalom said after a pause. "As a matter of fact, the book's already given me a few ideas."

Looking across the table, Locke was struck by the incongruity of that incredibly developed mind in the childish body.

"You're still young," he said. "A few days won't matter. Don't forget that legally I exercise control over you, though I'll never do that without your agreement that I'm acting justly."

"Justice for you may not be justice for me," Absalom said, drawing designs on the tablecloth with his fingernail.

Locke stood up and laid his hand on the boy's shoulder. "We'll discuss it again, until we've thrashed it out right. Now I've some papers to correct."

He went out.

"He's acting for the best, Absalom," Abigail said.

"Of course he is, Abbie," the boy agreed. But he remained thoughtful.

The next day Locke went through his classes in an absent-minded fashion and, at noon, he televised Dr. Ryan at the Wyoming Quizkid Crèche. Ryan seemed entirely too casual and noncommittal. He said he had asked the quizkids if they had been communicating with Absalom, and they had said no.

"But they'll lie at the drop of a hat, of course, if they

think it advisable," Ryan added, with inexplicable amusement.

"What's so funny?" Locke inquired.

"I don't know," Ryan said. "The way the kids tolerate me. I'm useful to them at times, but—originally I was supposed to be supervisor here. Now the boys supervise me."

"Are you serious?"

Ryan sobered.

"I've a tremendous respect for the quizkids. And I think you're making a very grave mistake in the way you're handling your son. I was in your house once, a year ago. It's *your* house. Only one room belongs to Absalom. He can't leave any of his possessions around anywhere else. You're dominating him tremendously."

"I'm trying to help him."

"Are you sure you know the right way?"

"Certainly," Locke snapped. "Even if I'm wrong, does that mean I'm committing fil—filio—"

"That's an interesting point," Ryan said casually. "You could have thought of the right words for matricide, parricide, or fratricide easily enough. But it's seldom one kills his son. The word doesn't come to the tongue quite as instantly."

Locke glared at the screen. "What the devil do you mean?"

"Just be careful," Ryan said. "I believe in the mutant theory, after running this Crèche for fifteen years."

"I was a child genius myself," Locke repeated.

"Uh-huh," Ryan said, his eyes intent. "I wonder if you know that the mutation's supposed to be cumulative? Three generations ago, two percent of the population were child geniuses. Two generations ago, five percent. One generation—a sine curve, Brother Locke. And the I.Q. mounts proportionally. Wasn't your father a genius too?"

"He was," Locke admitted. "But a maladjusted one."

"I thought so. Mutations take time. The theory is that the transition is taking place right now, from homo sapiens to homo superior."

"I know. It's logical enough. Each generation of mutations—this dominant mutation at least—taking another step forward till homo superior is reached. What that will be—"

"I don't think we'll ever know," Ryan said quietly. "I don't think we'd understand. How long will it take, I wonder? The next generation? I don't think so. Five more generations, or ten or twenty? And each one taking another step, realizing another buried potentiality of homo, until the summit is reached. Superman, Joel."

"Absalom isn't a superman," Locke said practically. "Or a superchild, for that matter."

"Are you sure?"

"Good Lord! Don't you suppose I know my own son?"

"I won't answer that," Ryan said. "I'm certain that I don't know all there is to know about the quizkids in my Crèche. Beltram, the Denver Crèche supervisor, tells me the same thing. These quizkids are the next step in the mutation. You and I are members of a dying species, Brother Locke."

Locke's face changed. Without a word he clicked off the televisor.

The bell was ringing for his next class. But Locke stayed motionless, his cheeks and forehead slightly damp.

Presently, his mouth twisted in a curiously unpleasant smile, he nodded and turned from the televisor . . .

He got home at five. He came in quietly, by the side entrance, and took the elevator upstairs. Absalom's door was closed, but voices were coming through it faintly. Locke listened for a time. Then he rapped sharply on the panel.

"Absalom. Come downstairs. I want to talk to you."

In the living room he told Abigail to stay out for a while. With his back to the fireplace, he waited until Absalom came.

> The enemies of my lord the king, and all that rise against thee to do thee hurt, be as that young man is. . . .

The boy entered without obvious embarrassment. He came forward and he faced his father, the boy-face calm and untroubled. He had poise, Locke saw, no doubt of that.

"I overheard some of your conversation, Absalom," Locke said.

"It's just as well," Absalom said coolly. "I'd have told you tonight anyway. I've got to go on with that entropic course."

Locke ignored that. "Who were you vising?"

"A boy I know. Malcolm Roberts, in the Denver quizkid Crèche."

"Discussing entropic logic with him, eh? After what I'd told you?"

"You'll remember that I didn't agree."

Locke put his hands behind him and interlaced his fingers.

"Then you'll also remember that I mentioned I had legal control over you."

"Legal," Absalom said, "yes. Moral, no."

"This has nothing to do with morals."

"It has, though. And with ethics. Many of the youngsters—younger than I—at the quizkid crèches are studying entropic logic. It hasn't harmed them. I must go to a crèche, or to Baja California. I must."

Locke bent his head thoughtfully.

"Wait a minute," he said. "Sorry, son. I got emotionally tangled for a moment. Let's go back on the plane of pure logic."

"All right," Absalom said, with a quiet, imperceptible withdrawal.

"I'm convinced that that particular study might be dangerous for you. I don't want you to be hurt. I want you to have every possible opportunity, especially the ones I never had."

"No," Absalom said, a curious note of maturity in his high voice. "It wasn't lack of opportunity. It was incapability."

"What?" Locke said.

"You could never allow yourself to be convinced I could safely study entropic logic. I've learned that. I've talked to other quizkids."

"Of private matters?"

"They're of my race," Absalom said. "You're not. And

please don't talk about filial love. You broke that law yourself long ago."

"Keep talking," Locke said quietly, his mouth tight. "But make sure it's logical."

"It is. I didn't think I'd ever have to do this for a long time, but I've got to now. You're holding me back from what I've got to do."

"The step mutation. Cumulative. I see."

The fire was too hot. Locke took a step forward from the hearth. Absalom made a slight movement of withdrawal. Locke looked at him intently.

"It *is* a mutation," the boy said. "Not the complete one, but Grandfather was one of the first steps. You, too—further along than he did. And I'm further than you. My children will be closer toward the ultimate mutation. The only psychonamic experts worth anything are the child geniuses of your generation."

"Thanks."

"You're afraid of me," Absalom said. "You're afraid of me and jealous of me."

Locke started to laugh. "What about logic now?"

The boy swallowed. "It *is* logic. Once you were convinced that the mutation was cumulative, you couldn't bear to think I'd displace you. It's a basic psychological warp in you. You had the same thing with Grandfather, in a different way. That's why you turned to psychonamics, where you were a small god, dragging out the secret minds of your students, molding their brains as Adam was molded. You're afraid that I'll outstrip you. And I will."

"That's why I let you study anything you wanted, I suppose?" Locke asked. "With this exception?"

"Yes, it is. A lot of child geniuses work so hard they burn themselves out and lose their mental capacities entirely. You wouldn't have talked so much about the danger if —under these circumstances—it hadn't been the one thing paramount in your mind. Sure you gave me my head. And, subconsciously, you were hoping I *would* burn myself out, so I wouldn't be a possible rival any more."

"I see."

"You let me study math, plane geometry, calculus, non-Euclidean, but you kept pace with me. If you didn't know the subject already, you were careful to bone up on it, to assure yourself that it was something you *could* grasp. You made sure I couldn't outstrip you, that I wouldn't get any knowledge you couldn't get. And that's why you wouldn't let me take entropic logic."

There was no expression on Locke's face.

"Why?" he asked coldly.

"You couldn't understand it yourself," Absalom said. "You tried it, and it was beyond you. You're not flexible. Your logic isn't flexible. It's founded on the fact that a second-hand registers sixty seconds. You've lost the sense of wonder. You've translated too much from abstract to concrete. I *can* understand entropic logic. I can understand it!"

"You've picked this up in the last week," Locke said.

"No. You mean the rapports. A long time ago I learned to keep part of my mind blanked off under your probing."

"That's impossible!" Locke said, startled.

"It is for you. I'm a further step in the mutation. I have a lot of talents you don't know anything about. And I know this—I'm not far enough advanced for my age. The boys in the crèches are ahead of me. Their parents followed natural laws—it's the role of any parent to protect its young. Only the immature parents are out of step—like you."

Locke was still quite impassive.

"I'm immature? And I hate you? I'm jealous of you? You've quite settled on that?"

"Is it true or not?"

Locke didn't answer. "You're still inferior to me mentally," he said, "and you will be for some years to come. Let's say, if you want it that way, that your superiority lies in your—flexibility—and your homo superior talents. Whatever they are. Against that, balance the fact that I'm a physically mature adult and you weigh less than half of what I do. I'm legally your guardian. And I'm stronger than you are."

Absalom swallowed again, but said nothing. Locke rose a little higher, looking down at the boy. His hand went to his middle, but found only a lightweight zipper.

He walked to the door. He turned.

"I'm going to prove to you that you're my inferior," he said coldly and quietly. "You're going to admit it to me."

Absalom said nothing.

Locke went upstairs. He touched the switch on his bureau, reached into the drawer, and withdrew an elastic lucite belt. He drew its cool, smooth length through his fingers once. Then he turned to the dropper again.

His lips were white and bloodless by now.

At the door of the living room he stopped, holding the belt. Absalom had not moved, but Abigail Schuler was standing beside the boy.

"Get out, Sister Schuler," Locke said.

"You're not going to whip him," Abigail said, her head held high, her lips purse-string tight.

"Get out."

"I won't. I heard every word. And it's true, all of it."

"Get out, I tell you!" Locke screamed.

He ran forward, the belt uncoiled in his hand. Absalom's nerve broke at last. He gasped with panic and dashed away, blindly seeking escape where there was none.

Locke plunged after him.

Abigail snatched up the little hearth broom and thrust it at Locke's legs. The man yelled something inarticulate as he lost his balance. He came down heavily, trying to brace himself against the fall with stiff arms.

His head struck the edge of a chair seat. He lay motionless.

Over his still body, Abigail and Absalom looked at each other. Suddenly the woman dropped to her knees and began sobbing.

"I've killed him," she forced out painfully. "I've killed him—but I couldn't let him whip you, Absalom! I couldn't!"

The boy caught his lower lip between his teeth. He came forward slowly to examine his father.

"He's not dead."

Abigail's breath came out in a long, shuddering sigh.

"Go on upstairs, Abbie," Absalom said, frowning a little. "I'll give him first aid. I know how."

"I can't let you—"

"Please, Abbie," he coaxed. "You'll faint or something. Lie down for a bit. It's all right, really."

At last she took the dropper upstairs. Absalom, with a thoughtful glance at his father, went to the televisor.

He called the Denver Crèche. Briefly he outlined the situation.

"What had I better do, Malcolm?"

"Wait a minute." There was a pause. Another young face showed on the screen. "Do this," an assured, high-pitched voice said, and there followed certain intricate instructions. "Got that straight, Absalom?"

"I have it. It won't hurt him?"

"He'll live. He's psychotically warped already. This will just give it a different twist, one that's safe for you. It's projection. He'll externalize all his wishes, feelings, and so forth. On you. He'll get his pleasure only out of what *you* do, but he won't be able to control you. You know the psychonamic key of his brain. Work with the frontal lobe chiefly. Be careful of Broca's area. We don't want aphasia. He must be made harmless to you, that's all. Any killing would be awkward to handle. Besides, I suppose you wouldn't want that."

"No," Absalom said. "H-he's my father."

"All right," the young voice said. "Leave the screen on. I'll watch and help."

Absalom turned toward the unconscious figure on the floor.

For a long time the world had been shadowy now. Locke was used to it. He could still fulfill his ordinary functions, so he was not insane, in any sense of the word.

Nor could he tell the truth to anyone. They had created a psychic bloc. Day after day he went to the university and taught psychonamics and came home and ate and waited in hopes that Absalom would call him on the televisor.

And when Absalom called, he might condescend to tell something of what he was doing in Baja California. What he had accomplished. What he had achieved. For those things mattered now. They were the only things that mattered. The projection was complete.

Absalom was seldom forgetful. He was a good son. He called daily, though sometimes, when work was pressing, he had to make the call short. But Joel Locke could always work at his immense scrapbooks, filled with clippings and photographs about Absalom. He was writing Absalom's biography, too.

He walked otherwise through a shadow world, existing in flesh and blood, in realized happiness, only when Absalom's face appeared on the televisor screen. But he had not forgotten anything. He hated Absalom, and hated the horrible, unbreakable bond that would forever chain him to his own flesh—the flesh that was not quite his own, but one step further up the ladder of the new mutation.

Sitting there in the twilight of unreality, his scrapbooks spread before him, the televisor set never used except when Absalom called, but standing ready before his chair, Joel Locke nursed his hatred and a quiet, secret satisfaction that had come to him.

Some day Absalom would have a son. Some day. Some day.

INCREDIBLE S-F
from
🅑🅑
BALLANTINE BOOKS